CONVICTION

Julia Dahl is a journalist specialising in crime and criminal justice. Her first novel, *Invisible City*, was named one of the *Boston Globe*'s Best Books of 2014, won the Macavity, Barry, and Shamus Awards, and was a finalist for an Edgar Award and a Mary Higgins Clark Award. Her acclaimed second novel, *Run You Down*, was published in 2016. She lives in Brooklyn, NY.

'An absolutely crackling, unputdownable mystery told by a narrator with one big, booming voice. I loved it.'
   Gillian Flynn, on *Invisible City*

'A strong sequel . . . Aviva emerges as a woman with the great strength to survive suffering on a biblical scale.'
   New York Times Book Review, on *Run You Down*

also by Julia Dahl

Run You Down
Invisible City

CONVICTION

Julia Dahl

FABER & FABER

First published in 2018
by Faber & Faber Limited
Bloomsbury House,
74–77 Great Russell Street,
London WC1B 3DA

First published in the United States in 2017
by Minotaur Books
an imprint of Macmillan
St Martin's Press
175 Fifth Avenue
New York NY 10010

Printed and bound by CPI Group (UK) Ltd, Croydon, CR0 4YY

A CIP record for this book
is available from the British Library

ISBN 978-0-571-34277-8

MIX
Paper from
responsible sources
FSC® C020471
FSC
www.fsc.org

10 9 8 7 6 5 4 3

For Mick

PART 1

CHAPTER ONE

Morning
July 5, 1992
Crown Heights, Brooklyn

The little boy walked to the storefront church alone, with blood on his hands and face.

Dorothy Norris arrived early, as usual, to lift the gate and set out the worship programs she'd photocopied the night before. She found him standing on the sidewalk, eyes unfocused, feet bare.

She bent down. "Ontario, where are your parents?"

He didn't answer. It was already eighty degrees, but his teeth were chattering.

Dorothy used her key and ushered him inside, flipped the lights, and walked straight to the phone in the pastor's tiny office. She dialed Ontario's foster parents, but no one answered, so she called Pastor Green, and then she called her husband and told him to stay home with the girls until she knew what was going on.

Dorothy asked and asked and asked, but Ontario wouldn't say a word.

Redmond Green's wife, Barbara, answered the phone

at his apartment. Red was in the bathroom scribbling last-minute sermon notes in a rare moment of solitude. Barbara sent fourteen-year-old Red Jr. to bang on the door and summon his father. Barbara hadn't asked for details—*Just go,* she told her husband—and as he walked the eleven blocks between their apartment and the church, he worked himself up, convinced the metal gate had been defaced again. Since opening Glorious Gospel on Easter morning 1982, Pastor Green had been losing a battle with vandals. He called the police often, but they rarely came to take a report. He knew that most of the officers in the precinct thought his crusade silly, given the many miseries plaguing the neighborhood, but he wasn't about to stop calling. In 1992, one year after the riots, Crown Heights was still a disaster. A battlefield and a garbage dump. It was getting hot again, and everyone seemed to hold their breath, waiting for the neighborhood to explode.

Pastor Green found the gate up when he arrived at Glorious Gospel. Dorothy Norris was inside with Malcolm and Sabrina Davises' foster son, Ontario. The pastor's first thought was that the boy had been attacked on his way to church. But Ontario was wearing sleep clothes, not church clothes.

"Something's happened at the Davises'," said Dorothy.

"What?"

"He won't say."

"Ontario? Are you hurt?"

4

Ontario stared at the pastor. Past him, really. Through him. Pastor Green kneeled down and touched his arm.

"He's freezing cold," he said, looking up.

"I think he's in shock," said Dorothy.

Ontario's face was smeared with red. If the pastor had to guess, he would say that the boy had rubbed his eyes with his bloody hands.

"Is this his blood?"

Dorothy lowered her voice. "I don't think so. But I don't know."

"Have you called the precinct?" asked Pastor Green.

"Yes," said Dorothy.

The pastor turned back to the boy.

"Ontario. Can I make sure you're not hurt?" He took the boy's right hand, turned it over, looked up and down his arm. He repeated the inspection on the boy's left arm. "Is it all right if I lift your shirt?" Ontario was still. "I just want to see if there are any scratches or cuts. . . . Good. Looks good. Ontario? Will you turn around for me? Just to check your back." As he turned, Pastor Green put his fingers on the boy's neck, and then his skull. "Good. Looks like you're okay."

He put his hand on his knee to straighten up, and as he did, Ontario vomited. Right on the pastor's Sunday wingtips. The boy's eyes widened and filled with tears.

"Oh, honey," said Dorothy, leaning down. "It's okay."

"It's all right, son," said Pastor Green. "Nothing a little water won't fix up."

5

Dorothy walked Ontario to the bathroom to wash out his mouth.

A voice came from the front door.

"NYPD."

CHAPTER TWO

Summer 2014
New York City

I know I didn't get the job when Gary, the *Trib*'s Sunday editor, calls and asks me to come in and chat.

"We decided to give the position to Jack," he says the next day. Jack, a Columbia Journalism School graduate, has been at the *Trib* six months to my two years. He is tall and blond and dresses like he grew up in Greenwich, Connecticut, even though he's from Queens. Tucked-in oxford, leather belt, blazer. He's one of those guys who walks on his toes; he bounces everywhere and so always seems as if he's excited to get where he's going, even if it's to the bathroom. Jack plays shortstop on the *Trib* softball team and is apparently a "big hitter." I've never been to a game.

"Honestly," says Gary, "we felt like he was a little more committed."

"Committed?"

Gary leans back in the creaky old chair, his arms folded over his stomach. I have no idea who this office belongs to. There are framed front pages of yore hanging crooked on the wall. Headlines from when the city was bankrupt, from the Son of Sam murders, from the first World Trade Center bombing.

"The whole Roseville thing," he says. "Those interviews you got were a real scoop. Nobody from the town has talked to a single reporter since the shooting. And you gave it to that magazine."

Of course. A couple months ago, a magazine called *American Voice* published a long article I wrote about the aftermath of a mass shooting in the ultra-Orthodox Jewish community of Roseville, New York, last year. It's not *The New Yorker,* but it's respected, and they paid me two thousand dollars, on top of the three-thousand-dollar fellowship I won from an organization called the Center on Culture, Crime and the Media to report the story. A Pulitzer Prize-winning reporter at *The Washington Post* tweeted that it was an "important" read, and I got invited to be a guest on a podcast out of Baltimore that focuses on healing after violence. I had fantasies that the article might lead to, say, a job offer from *The New York Times.*

So far, however, no go. I'm still working shifts at the *Trib.* I'm freelance, even though I work full-time, so I don't have any obligation to alert them if I've gotten work elsewhere—unless it's a competitor, like the *Ledger* or even *The Times.* When I finally told Gary and Mike, the city desk editor, about the fellowship, I said the Center had already set up publication with *American Voice.* But that wasn't completely true. The woman who approved my fellowship gave me the *American Voice* editor's e-mail address, but I spent weeks crafting a pitch, then had to write the entire draft on spec to convince the executive editor that a reporter from the *Trib* with "no feature experience" could produce something to meet "the standards of *American Voice*." I didn't tell Mike and Gary any of this, but they aren't stupid and they probably guessed the truth, which was that the *Trib* was my last choice for publication. I am prouder of what was printed in *American Voice* than anything else I've written—by far. It had context, depth, and even a little art in it. If I'd given the piece to the *Trib* it would have been a quarter as long and they would have played it like an exposé ("EXCLUSIVE! INSIDE THE ROSEVILLE MASSACRE") instead of an essay ("After Roseville"). So I suppose I shouldn't be surprised they're passing me over for a staff position. I don't bother protesting to Gary that I didn't have control over the execution of the fellowship. Like I said, he's not stupid.

"We might not be *American Voice,* but we break news here. Evan Morris beat *The Times* on the name of the officer in the Kendra Yaris shooting, *and* his history of excessive force complaints."

"I know."

Kendra Yaris was shot and killed by police in the East Village last week. Kendra was a line cook at the Dallas BBQ on Second Avenue and was on her way to the 6 train at Bleecker Street when the two plainclothes officers mistook the twenty-two-year-old gay woman in a Brooklyn Nets hat and baggy shorts for the "young black man, slim build, ball cap" who had just held up a bodega on St. Mark's. Kendra, who had been attacked by three drunken frat boys two weeks earlier, was carrying a knife. She noticed the men following her and began to run. When the officers caught up, she whirled around with her knife—and took four bullets to the chest. The shooting occurred five days after two cops on Staten Island tried to arrest an asthmatic man named Eric Garner for selling loose cigarettes, and ended up killing him in the process; and a month after a cop shot and killed eighteen-year-old Michael Brown in the middle of a Ferguson, Missouri, street. Within twenty-four hours, #Justice4Kendra joined #ICantBreathe and #HandsUpDontShoot as an internationally trending hashtag. The NYPD withheld the name of the officer who killed her, but Evan Morris, who used to cover Manhattan courts for the *Trib* and recently moved to writing features for the Sunday section, got a tip that he recently cost the city $150,000 after the family of a man whose arm he broke during an arrest on Avenue D in 2013 sued. Morris did a little digging and discovered that Detective James Womack had a long history of civilian complaints of excessive force. That, plus the fact that Womack and his partner chased and shot not just the wrong person, but a person of the wrong *gender*, made the story national news, and up until yesterday—when the

NYPD finally confirmed Womack's name and the exact sum of the recent settlement—every news outlet in the country credited the *Trib* when they reported the story.

"So," says Gary, getting up, "we'd still like you to write for the section. Pitch me ideas anytime."

We walk out of the office, and before I head to Mike's desk to get my assignment for the day, I duck into the bathroom to call Iris. She picks up on the first ring.

"So?"

"Nope," I say.

"I'm sorry," she says. "You kind of expected it, right? And did you even really want that job?"

"It would have been better than what I'm doing now."

"Maybe. Or it would have kept you from looking for something at a better publication. Maybe you'll meet somebody tonight who's hiring."

Tonight I am attending a cocktail party hosted by the organization that gave me the fellowship. It'll be the first time I've met any of the other journalists who've gotten support from the Center, and, yes, I've been fantasizing that I'll make a connection that might provide a path out of the *Trib*.

"We'll see," I say.

"Don't get all down about this, okay? It's not like you lost out on your dream job."

In the past two years, Iris has been promoted twice at the fashion magazine where she works. She's humble about it; she says it was just lucky that she happened to be there when people left, but I know she's also proud of herself. And she should be. Iris wants to be the editor-in-chief of a magazine by the time she's forty. Her dream is *Vogue*, of course, but I doubt they could get Anna Wintour out of that job with a shovel.

"I know," I say.

"Good. Hey, did you call that guy yet? Is his friend having people out again?"

That guy is Wyatt Singer, a twenty-six-year-old assistant director—or director's assistant, I don't remember—that I made out with at a pool party in the Hamptons two weeks ago. Iris dragged me to the land of the Kardashians when one of her colleagues had to bail on a prepaid weekend "share." The house was a poorly maintained seven-bedroom monstrosity. There were more than twenty people sleeping there, and by the end of the weekend two of the bathrooms were unusable. All the female occupants were related to fashion in some way, and the males were mostly in TV or movies.

"I'm not calling the random guy I hooked up with in the Hamptons."

"Why not!"

"Because I hate people who go to the Hamptons."

"So does he!"

"He only said that because he knew that's what I wanted him to say."

"*How* is that not a good thing? He was being intuitive."

"Oh, please."

"How long has it been since you slept with anybody?"

Creeping up on a year. Van Keller, a ridiculously good-looking sheriff's deputy from Orange County, New York, came to the city for a friend's birthday last fall, and we ended up spending the night together. We met last spring when I was investigating the death of Pessie Goldin, a Hasidic women found dead in her bathtub in Roseville, and were together when we heard about the shooting. The sex was great—urgent but unhurried, lots of kissing and locking eyes—but when he called a couple days later he said he didn't think we should do it again. *I think I'm too old for you,* he said. What he meant, though, was *I think you're too young.* I think you're too immature. He's on Facebook, and in June someone tagged a photo of him with his arm around a beautiful black-haired woman with freckles. She has a kid, I think.

"A while," I say to Iris. "Too long."

"Exactly, so let's fix that. His friend has a share and I literally cannot spend another weekend in this city. I basically had to bathe in the bathroom sink when I got into work this morning."

"When did you become such a pussy? The humidity was worse in Florida."

"Yeah, but I didn't have to dress up in Florida. My thighs stick together under this skirt. And the subway is *so bad.* I one-hundred-percent had my face in this dude's armpit all the way over the Manhattan Bridge this morning. There wasn't even enough room to turn my head. I could see the white chunks of deodorant in his armpit hair."

"Gross."

"Oh, it was horrible."

I hang up and go into one of the stalls. I don't want to spend my entire career at the *Trib,* but alienating the editors at a paper with a million readers—the only place that offered me a job when I moved here two years ago—is a bad move. I probably could have found a way to turn at least one of the stories I found in the past year interviewing the people of Roseville into a piece for the *Trib.* It just wasn't a priority. I started thinking of the fellowship as a way out the minute I got it. Does that make me a snob? The anxiety buzzing in my stomach, making me sweat in the air conditioning, tells me I've made a mistake. I've been in talk therapy, and taking daily antidepressants and the occasional antianxiety pill for a year now. The regimen controls the worst of it. I'm not running to the bathroom with the frequency I was last year, but my body still screams at me sometimes. Interacting with my mother sets it off, as does, apparently, the kind of self-doubt (or, as Iris would probably call it, self-flagellation) that losing a job I disdained ignites.

I pass Jack on my way toward the city desk and congratulate him.

"Thanks!" he says, chipper as always. "I read your piece in *American Voice.* Wow! That's, like, the byline of the century!"

I smile. "Thanks. On to the next, I guess."

Mike, as usual, is bent over his computer at the city desk.

"Hey," I say.

He lifts his head before his eyes. "Oh, good, you're in a dress."

"Excuse me?"

"That's not . . . I mean, I can send you someplace *professional*," he stammers. Unlike some of the red-faced, thrice-divorced men in the newsroom, Mike is not a flirt, and he's so clearly flustered by my insinuation that I forgive him immediately. Plus, it *is* somewhat remarkable that I am wearing a dress. I borrowed it from Iris this morning for the party.

"Someplace professional?"

"Sandra Michaels is speaking at an event at the Plaza. We can get you in." Sandra Michaels is a Brooklyn prosecutor and, according to a fawning cover story in last week's *New York* magazine, the presumed next district attorney of Kings County. Her boss, seventy-nine-year-old DA Stan Morrissey III, was diagnosed with stage two melanoma last month and Michaels is the one running the office—which means she is the one deciding whether to indict James Womack for killing Kendra Yaris. But my guess is that neither of these things are what the *Trib* wants me to ask her about. "Did you see the story about her ex this morning?" Mike asks.

I did. I picked up a copy of the *Trib* at the bodega

above my subway stop and went through it on the way to the office. On page five there was a story headlined "Exclusive: Next DA Is a 'Deadbeat' Mom." That article featured Michaels' ex-husband telling a *Trib* reporter that after their divorce in 2000, she missed three months of child support payments.

"I don't think she's qualified to be the DA if she didn't follow the law herself," said Tom McGinty.

"It's doing really well on the Web site," says Mike. "We want to get a response from Michaels for a follow."

It's the cheapest kind of tabloid story. If I'd gotten the Sunday job I might be able to spend a day or two working on a story about how much the city paid out each year to people who accused cops of misconduct, but as a runner on the city desk, I just have to go where they tell me.

At just before noon, I climb the red-carpeted steps to the Plaza Hotel where the New York Women's Law Coalition is holding its annual awards luncheon. I've never been here before, and it's less grand than I imagined. Wallpaper a little faded, lights a little too bright. But worst of all, the air conditioning seems to be on the fritz. It's easily eighty-five degrees in the lobby.

An easel displays a poster with the future DA's face on it: THE NEW YORK WOMEN'S LAW COALITION HONORS SANDRA MICHAELS. I approach the check-in table and say I am from the *Trib*. Both women manning the table look up from their clipboards aghast. Clearly, they've seen the article about her ex.

"ID please," says the one wearing a "J" necklace around her neck.

I show her my *Trib* badge. She looks at it longer than she needs to, hands it back, and says, "Table fourteen."

The room fills up quickly. Everyone is fanning themselves with their paper programs and motioning to the waiters for more ice water. My tablemates are three third-year law students on scholarships from the NYWLC, a reporter from the *East Coast Law Review,* and an intern in Michaels' office. Of the four, only the girl from the office had read the article about Michaels' ex.

"I didn't write it," I say.

"What a fucking asshole," says the intern. "Guy should be *embarrassed* his ex-wife had to give him money."

Well said.

While we wait for the program to begin, I grab the breadbasket and take two rolls and a pat of butter. Assignments involving free food are rare. Every once in a while I cover a press event with snacks, and last year I got sent to the annual chocolate show at the Javits Center; that was a highlight. But this is my first sit-down meal. After the waiters serve the entrée, the president of the NYWLC makes a speech and solicits donations for the organization's scholarships, gesturing to the girls at my table, who stand and smile to applause.

"And now," says the president, "it is my great pleasure

to present this year's NYWLC Woman of the Year, soon to be the first female district attorney of Kings County, Sandra Michaels."

Everyone claps, and Sandra Michaels stands up from her seat at the table by the little stage. Sandra is wearing a stylish sky-blue and cream suit and low beige heels. She's had her well-cut blond hair blown out this morning. I'd guess she's in her late fifties. She was in black-and-white on the cover of *New York* magazine. A Hillary-style headshot and the coverline "The Next DA of Brooklyn." They ran the statement without a question mark, which caused a fuss. When I saw it I wondered if she knew they were going to do that, or if they pulled a reverse *Sex and the City* and surprised her. According to the article, Sandra grew up in Brooklyn Heights, one of two daughters of a history professor and a piano teacher. She went to Fordham, then Columbia Law, and spent two years at the Children's Defense Fund before taking a job in Morrissey's office in the late 1980s. She started with drug cases, then got a chance at homicide in 1992 and rose quickly, "prosecuting some of the most complex cases of the crack era." Now, she teaches a course at NYU, and when Morrissey retires next year, will likely run for—and win—his position, making her just the second female district attorney in New York City history. The *New York* magazine profile did not mention her personal life at all. Not even a line about marriage or children, but I know from the *Trib* that she's been married at least once and has an adult son.

"I had a speech prepared, but honestly, it's too hot to listen to me talk for long."

Everyone chuckles.

"This award is especially meaningful to me because when I made the choice to leave advocacy law and begin prosecuting cases, I worried that many of the women I admired in law school and early in my career would think that I had abandoned those who were most needy in order to become part of the big, ugly machine. Don't get me wrong, the machine *can* be big and ugly. But I believed then and I believe even more strongly now that we cannot surrender the functioning of our justice system to men. We need women of substance, women with *backbone,* women with righteous anger. We need them to go after the child killers and the rapists and the stalkers and the abusers. As women, we *must* be present at the prosecutor's table, on the bench, and on the ballot."

She fans her face with her hand, and someone sitting at her table passes her a glass of ice water.

"God, it's bad in here. I'm going to cut it short so we can all escape. Thank you so much for recognizing the work prosecutors do. Thank you."

Everyone claps, and the president comes back, gives Sandra a hug, and reminds the audience to check the organization's Web site for upcoming events, job opportunities, and the mentorship program. People gather around Sandra at her table. I better just get this over with.

I wait in a not-insignificant line of well-wishers, and a couple other reporters, who either congratulate, question, or take a photo with the honoree. Close-up, Sandra Michaels is wearing a little too much makeup. Her nails are French manicured and a tasteful emerald band encircles the ring finger of her right hand.

"My name is Rebekah Roberts," I say, when it is my turn. "I'm a reporter with the *Trib,* and I wondered if you have any response to what your ex-husband is saying about child support."

I speak quickly, assuming she read the article I'm referring to. The way you articulate a question as a reporter is very important. You often only have one chance before whomever you're talking to moves on to another reporter, hangs up, shouts you off the lawn, or, in this case, potentially chases you out of the room.

Sandra Michaels flinches, and the president of the NYWLC, who is standing beside her, gasps.

"Who let you in? You should be ashamed of yourself." Sandra lifts her chin and shakes her head slowly: *tsk tsk.*

"It's hard to believe this is the best use of your time," she says, almost cordial in her condescension.

"I know . . . I'm just . . ."

"Oh, *please* don't even say you're just doing your job," says the young woman in line behind me.

I look at my notebook. All around me, women murmur their assent.

"Sandra *paved the way* for female prosecutors in the

city. And *this* is what you want to write a story about? It's *so* anti-feminist!"

"As you would have known had you talked to a single source other than my former husband for your story," says Michaels, "the period of time during which I did not send child support checks to Tom was a period of time when my son was living with me, and Tom was hospitalized for depression. Feel free to call the Marymount Psychiatric Center in Roslyn for confirmation. And feel free to request the *rest* of the public documents on the situation, which tell the story quite clearly."

I don't bother protesting that I had nothing to do with the original story. All I want is out of there.

"Got it," I say, stepping back. "Thanks. Sorry."

I beeline out of the hotel, half expecting to be pelted with scones, and jog across Fifty-ninth Street to the sidewalk at the top of Central Park. The horseshit smell is practically visible, hovering at nose level as the carriages wait for tourists to spend thirty-five dollars for a fifteen-minute memory. I call the city desk and am routed to Marisa, who used to run with me but switched to rewrite after she got pregnant.

"This story is so gross," she says.

"Oh, it's worse than that," I say. "It's not even true."

I fill her in, she tells me to hold, and after about four minutes she comes back on to tell me I'm done for the day.

"Aren't you glad you majored in journalism?" asks Marisa. "We're really doing God's work."

Most of the people I know that work at the *Trib* have a love-hate relationship with the paper. They complain and talk shit and make jokes about the managing editor, Albert Morgan, "going for a Pulitzer" when there's a spread or a series on something borderline ridiculous—like a map of the venues where Shia LeBeouf has been arrested. But they also talk shit about *The New York Times,* and the ridiculous stories they do about rich people decorating their TriBeCa lofts with driftwood from Hurricane Sandy, or the home fermentation "craze" in Williamsburg. *Trib* reporters take pride in the fact that we cover the murders and trials and corruption and union disputes that *The Times* ignores. Still, we'd all jump if *The Times*—or just about any other news organization—came calling.

I kill the rest of the afternoon in the air conditioning of the Barnes & Noble at Union Square, then head to the Village for the Center's cocktail party. The bronze plaque on the door of the brick townhouse just off Washington Square Park reads: THE UNDERHILL CLUB, est. 1913. In the foyer there is an easel holding a poster that bears the Center's name and the phrase WELCOME FELLOWS! Two easels in one day. Printed around the greeting are the names of news organizations that, presumably, my fellow fellows work for: NPR, the *Guardian, ProPublica, Frontline, Mother Jones, The Marshall Project.* A piece of paper with an arrow printed on it directs me upstairs. There are probably twenty-five people in the room—that perfectly awkward size between intimate and anonymous.

Iris's borrowed heels knock against the old wooden floor as I make my way to the bar: a card table set with bottles of wine, plastic glasses, and bowls of mixed nuts. I pour myself a glass of the chardonnay—it's too hot to even consider red wine—and scan the room for a familiar face. Valerie, the woman who gave me the fellowship and helped me place it with *American Voice,* appears deep in conversation with two women and a man. It's funny: I can walk up to a cranky stranger and bug them about why they're waiting in line for a pastry, or whether they'd be willing to share a memory of their just-murdered next-door neighbor, but the idea of starting a conversation with one of the people in this room terrifies me. If Iris were here, she'd drag me to Valerie. *Don't be lame,* she'd say. *Just because they have fancier jobs than you doesn't mean they're better than you.* I take a wide swallow of the lukewarm chardonnay and head over.

"The problem isn't space," says the older of the two women talking to Valerie. "It's not even will. Young editors have visions of Pulitzers, too. If they can get somebody else—somebody like the Center—to pay for the reporting, they'll run a big investigation. The problem is the readership. They don't fucking care! We exposed what agribusiness was doing to the California water supply five years ago! There were literally thousands of people who had *no water* all over the Central Valley—even back then. We're talking people—*working* people, people who own their homes—who ate exclusively microwave dinners so they didn't have to do dishes. But no one gave a shit. They held one hearing—one—in Sacramento. A couple CEOs got questioned, said they'd do better. It was utter bullshit. The only people who made the effort to come to the capitol and show support were four families who had been showering at a gym five miles from their home for literally *two years*. No one else cared enough to even, like, hold a fucking *sign* outside the hearing."

"That was at *The Chronicle*, right?" says the man. He's a little older than I am, possibly Filipino. He's wearing khakis and a seafoam polo shirt. "Didn't you guys win an IRE medal for that?"

"Sure. But do you know how many clicks the story got? Like, fifty. Seriously, the science page did better that week." She hikes up the soft briefcase she is carrying on one shoulder. "I mean, if people don't care, what the fuck are we doing? My sister says I should go into PR. I've got two kids about to take on huge student loan debt because I've been banging my head against a wall for fifty grand a year."

Valerie and the younger woman look mildly uncomfortable. Each nods and sneaks a look around them, which is good for me.

"Rebekah! So glad you could make it," says Valerie. "Kate, Domanick, Amanda, this is Rebekah Roberts. She wrote the piece for *American Voice* about the aftermath of the Roseville massacre."

"Great piece!" says Domanick. "I remember thinking

24

when it happened that we were never really going to know what was going on. I learned *a lot*. And the writing was really beautiful."

"Thanks," I say, unable to suppress a smile. "You just made my day."

"Domanick was a fellow, what? Two years ago?"

"Four."

"*Four!* John Jay College had collected a ton of great data on people who confessed to a crime but were exonerated by DNA. Really groundbreaking stuff, but they needed personal stories to drive it home. We hooked them up with Domanick."

"And I am forever grateful," says Domanick. "I was freelancing doctor profiles for a medical newsletter out of Pennsylvania to make rent. All of a sudden I got the cover story in *The Atlantic*."

"Not all of a sudden," says Valerie. "It took you, what, nine months of reporting?"

"At least."

"I remember it," I say. "We read it in school, in my investigative reporting class."

"Yeah? Well, that makes me feel good—and old." Everyone laughs. "It got a good response. I don't know about the clicks. I try not to pay attention, honestly."

"I learned a lot," I say. "I mean, it's hard to imagine why somebody would say they committed a crime—especially something like murder—when they didn't. But you made it come alive. How it felt to be in that room. You know, scared and tired and just wanting to go home. I remember one guy you profiled said he actually *knew* the kid who had done the shooting. He said a bunch of people saw it, right? And he was like, they'll figure it out eventually so, yeah, sure, I did it."

"Marco King," says Domanick, nodding. "He was seventeen. Did twenty-six years inside."

"That's what you get for trusting the system," says the younger woman.

"Amanda, I've been meaning to introduce you and Rebekah," says Valerie. "You're both in Brooklyn. Amanda does the Homicide Blog."

"That's you?" I say.

"That's me," she says.

I've heard of the Homicide Blog—the *Trib* did a short piece on it last year. Basically, they track every single homicide in New York City. I think there were around 350 murders last year, but they don't all make the paper. And a lot of the ones that do only make the blotter, often without a name. Just: victim. Amanda's blog makes a new page for every person killed. She maps the deaths, too. And updates the pages if there's an arrest.

Amanda does not look like a gritty homicide reporter. She's wearing what is essentially a muumuu, and, if I had to guess, I'd say she is pregnant.

"I'm a big fan," I say.

"Thanks." She smiles and I see she's got something stuck in between her two front teeth. Part of a nut shell, probably.

"Where are you now?" asks Kate.

"I'm at the *Tribune*," I say.

"Oh, yeah? Chicago's a great news town. I was at the *Sun-Times* in the nineties. Couldn't take the fucking cold, though. Damn."

"Not Chicago. The *New York Tribune*."

"The *Trib*?" Kate doesn't even attempt to hide her disdain. "Really? *Tell* me you didn't work on that bullshit from Sandra Michaels' ex."

I shake my head.

"Fucking *bullshit*," she continues, raising her voice. "Did you guys see it?"

Head shakes all around. Now all three of them are looking to get out of this conversation.

"You read the profile in *New York*, right?" Kate doesn't wait for a response. "Sandra Michaels has the best record of convicting violent domestic offenders in the city. She's going to be the next Brooklyn DA. Anyway, the fucking *Trib* digs up her ex-husband—who she divorced fifteen years ago and who I happen to know hasn't been *employed* since—to talk shit on her."

I decide not to mention the Palm Court luncheon.

"Sounds awful," says Valerie. She puts her hand on my shoulder. "I think we need to get this started. Are you all coming to the panels tomorrow?" The Center is hosting a conference on criminal justice reporting.

"Of course," says Kate. "I'm moderating the environmental crime panel."

"I have to work," I say. "I'm really sorry."

"We'll miss you," she says. "Keep in touch. I'd love to fund something else from you. We've gotten really great feedback on the *American Voice* article. That peek behind the curtain of the Hasidic world was really powerful."

"Thank you," I say. "I'll definitely be in touch."

"I was telling these guys that we just got funding to dig into wrongful convictions. Thanks, in part, to Domanick. So let me know if you've got anything there."

"Definitely."

Valerie walks away. Kate follows her without saying good-bye.

"Great meeting you ladies," says Domanick. "I'll see you tomorrow, Amanda?"

Amanda nods.

"Good luck, Rebekah," he says, handing me his card. "Let me know if I can ever help you with anything."

"I will," I say. "Thanks."

Domanick heads to the bar, where he immediately starts chatting with another group of people.

"Kate's an asshole," says Amanda. "She's the perfect example of people stuck in the old media model. I mean, come on. What did you think when you got into public service reporting, that you were gonna be able to pay for your kids to go to Yale? Please."

I smile, then lean in and whisper, "You've got a little something in your teeth."

Her hand goes up to cover her mouth.

"Oh, Christ," she says. "Thanks for telling me."

"I'd want to know."

"Exactly." She pulls out her phone and grins at the screen, picks the nut shell out with her fingernail. "All good?"

"Gone."

"I hate these things. I wouldn't have come except that Valerie's been really supportive of the blog. She recommended us to a couple other organizations that give grants, and without those we would be under."

"How many people work for you?"

"It's just me," she says.

"You do all that yourself?"

"Well, my husband helps with the back end. But basically, I never leave the house. And when this one comes I will officially never leave." She puts her hand on her belly.

"When are you due?"

"September."

"Is it your first?"

"Ha! I wish. No, I'm kidding. This'll be my third."

"Whoa."

"I know. I'm insane. But I was an only child. My husband's from a big family and I always really wanted that."

"How old are the other two?"

"Two and four. The oldest one starts preschool next month, *thank God*. Having three at home at the same time might actually kill me." She laughs. "That would be hilarious. You could take over the blog and write about me! Amanda Button, insane person, was found dead in her home. Police suspect her children are at fault, but can't find the murder weapon."

I laugh, too, partly because Amanda's laugh is so funny. It's this grumbling cackle that sounds like a cross between Dr. Evil and Bette Davis. I like this girl.

"How do you take care of two kids and do the blog? There's, like, almost a murder every day, right?"

"Just about. I do a lot when they're asleep. I'm kind of an insomniac. My husband works from home, too, so we trade off. He does freelance web design and software stuff."

"You do everything from home?"

She nods. "I've got a police scanner so I get alerted when there's a body. Then I start trolling social media for keywords in that neighborhood. Now that people know about the blog they tweet at me and send me Facebook messages. But what about you? What are you working on?"

"Nothing, really," I say. Amanda doesn't seem like the judgmental type. "I'm kind of looking for something."

"Well, if you're interested in pitching Valerie's wrongful conviction project, I get letters all the time from prisoners who say they're innocent. I don't have time to go through them, but there might be something there."

CHAPTER THREE

Two days after the cocktail party, I take the F train to a neighborhood called Ditmas Park, which is south of where I live in Gowanus and north of Borough Park. Amanda and her brood live on the second floor of an enormous old house that was probably once elegant, but is now covered entirely in roofing shingles. An exterior staircase indicates the home has been partitioned into apartments. It's the biggest house on the block—and all the houses are suburban-style big—but hands down the ugliest.

There are four buzzers by the front door. I press the button marked "BUTTON!" After about thirty seconds, Amanda opens the door, carrying a little boy on her hip.

"Welcome to the madhouse," she says.

"Who's this?" I ask. I'm not exactly a kid person, but it seems rude to ignore him.

"This is Liam," she says. "His brother is asleep and he's supposed to be asleep, too. Isn't he?"

Liam rests his head on his mommy's shoulder. Big eyes blink at me.

"Come on up. It's messy but we've got the AC cranking."

I follow her up the wide carpeted staircase to a landing with one door at either end.

"They split the house into apartments in the eighties, I think," says Amanda, pushing open one of the doors. The main room is enormous—someone must have knocked down a wall at some point. A bank of windows faces the backyard, and the space appears to function as a combination kitchen-office-playroom-living room-dining room. The floor is half-covered in foam tiles with a letter of the alphabet on each and strewn with toys. On one side is a playpen, a stationary tricycle, an easel, a plastic table and chairs set, and a tub full of more toys. On the other side is a flimsy IKEA desk with three computer monitors in a semicircle.

"This is mission control," says Amanda. "The bedrooms are tiny and there's only one bathroom, but this room makes it doable. I mean, it's insane. But doable. Do you want something to drink?" She opens the refrigerator. "I actually made lemonade last night. Do you want some?"

"I'd love some," I say. Liam has closed his eyes. "Looks like he's out."

Amanda looks down at him. "Sweet," she whispers. "Okay, give me a minute to see if I can put him down."

"I'm not in a hurry. Do what you gotta do."

Amanda smiles and disappears down the hall, waddling in bare feet, one baby in her belly, one on her hip. Before I got here, Iris and I had brunch. When I leave, I might take a nap. Tonight we're headed to Prospect Park for a free reggae concert. We'll take a blanket and a cooler and maybe stop at a bar on our way home. That's a Saturday in my life. But for a mom like Amanda, the work never ends. Even leisure life is work. I'm not going to lie: it doesn't look fun.

The dining room table is a circle with four chairs, two of which have booster seats strapped to them. I sweep a couple Cheerios off one that doesn't and drop them in a trash can near the stove, then sit down. As I do, one of the dark computer screens comes to life. Amanda is getting an alert. I get up to look and see her coming back from the bedrooms.

"Your computer just lit up."

"Oh, yeah? There was a stabbing in Brownsville last night. Female. She wasn't dead when the cops found her, but she might be now."

Amanda sits down at her station and moves the mouse around, presses a few keys. "Yeah, looks like. Getting RIP tweets from the neighborhood." She points at the middle screen, which shows a map of Brooklyn, and every few seconds a red flag pops up. "I can search for hashtags, like RIP, in the neighborhood where the cops find the body. Then whenever anybody who's got their locator on tweets with that hashtag it maps it. Look." She clicks on one flag and a window opens with a tweet from BayBeGurl89: *too young too soon. I'll always love you @Jasmeen190. #RIP #lovekills #prayersplease*

"Love kills," says Amanda. "I bet it turns out to be her boyfriend. Or an ex." Amanda clicks into the profile of Jasmeen190, aka Jaz. Her profile picture shows her as a young dark-skinned black woman with neon pink and black cornrows and a silver stud in the space above her lips where Cindy Crawford has a mole. Her personal description reads: *sing from the heart.*

"Sad," I say.

"Yup," says Amanda, clicking around. She opens a window on the computer screen to her left. "I entered a dummy post last night when I heard the scanner call. Female and Brownsville. I'm gonna message this baby girl eighty-nine and ask her if she has a photo of Jasmeen I can use. And see if she can hook me up with family for a full name and DOB. See if they're taking donations. I can post a link to that."

"Should I get out of your hair?"

"No, no. It's nice to have company. Jonathan's out of town all weekend doing an on-site with a client in North Carolina. Bastard!" She giggles. "I haven't left the city in *years*! That cocktail party was the first time I'd been in Manhattan since there was *snow*. Literally. Okay. Let me just send a couple quick messages. . . ." She types and clicks and then swivels around in her chair.

"Lemonade?"

"Sure," I say. "Thanks."

She pops up and goes to the refrigerator, which is covered with children's drawings, wedding announcements, and coupons from CVS. She grabs a Tupperware pitcher from the top shelf and rights two glasses that appear to be part of a set from McDonald's from their upside-down perch in the dish rack on the counter.

"Hope you don't mind the Hulk," she says.

"Not at all," I say. "I love the Hulk."

"So," she says. "The letters. I realized after I mentioned them to you that I really have no idea if they're even worth looking at. I started getting them a couple months after the blog went live. At first I was going through them, but then they just piled up. Everybody says they're innocent, obviously. But a lot of the cases are from the eighties and nineties, which was ground zero for murders in the city. There were more than two thousand murders in 1991. That's what, six times as many as last year? And it's not like there were six times as many cops or prosecutors. It makes sense that they might have botched some of the cases. DNA technology didn't really exist. And all that stuff Domanick wrote about with false confessions. Not to mention how unreliable eyewitness testimony is. . . ."

"The Central Park Five case was around then, right?"

"Exactly! Those poor kids were totally railroaded. I was in elementary school in 1989. My mom used to run in Prospect Park and my dad made her stop after that. We lived in Park Slope, which was nicer than Harlem or Crown Heights, but there was still, like, broken glass from crack pipes all over the sidewalks. I remember I wasn't allowed to wear open-toed shoes at all until high school when things started getting a little better. My dad was convinced I'd step on glass or a needle and get AIDS.

"The tabloids had everybody scared, too. They made it seem even worse than it was. Now, everybody's all over the killer cops, but back then it was all about the scary black men terrorizing the city. Men and boys. Teen super-predators, shit like that. Did you know Donald Trump actually took out a full-page ad to declare that the Central Park Five should get the death penalty? I'm serious! And they were more than happy to take his money." She pauses. "Sorry, I'm rambling."

"It's okay," I say. "I didn't grow up here, so there's a lot I don't know."

"Where are you from?"

"Florida."

"Oh, yeah? What part?"

"Orlando."

"Near Disney World?"

"Yeah," I say. "My grandpa worked there for years. In the corporate offices."

"Did you get discounts?"

I nod. "I worked in the park the summer right after high school. At one of the stores that sold Mickey hats

36

and stuff. It was hell. Hell. That's sort of when I decided I wouldn't have kids."

"I should have worked at Disney World!" shouts Amanda, laughing that enormous laugh. Then she covers her mouth. "Shit. I really hope I didn't wake them." She shakes her head, smiling.

"Are you sure this isn't something you want to work on?" I ask.

"Oh my God, no. The whole fucking 'justice' process makes me crazy." She uses her fingers to put air quotes around the word *justice*. "I'm about the victims. I mean, if somebody got wrongfully convicted, they're a victim, too, obviously. But mostly I try to give the people who *literally* can't speak—the dead people—a voice. Make sure they aren't completely forgotten. And the people left behind. Have you ever known anybody who was murdered?"

"No one I was close to," I say.

"Good," she says. "I don't wish it on anyone. When I was fourteen, my aunt's husband came home and shot her and then himself. They lived a couple blocks from us. She was a lot younger than my dad, and he'd practically raised her after his mom died from cancer. It destroyed him. My parents got divorced a couple years later. He just gave up on everything. He started drinking too much, lost his job. I was really pissed at him for a long time. I mean, I loved her, too. So did my mom. But you can't predict how a violent death like that is going to affect someone. Some people can take it. But, I mean, some people can take *war,* too. When somebody you love is murdered, it's like a bomb goes off in your life. If you survive intact you're lucky. And the thing is, there are neighborhoods in this city where bombs like that are going off every night. The same families are getting hit over and over. The cops come in and *maybe* the reporters come in, and they ask questions so they can do their jobs, and then they're gone. Can you imagine if your brother, or your best friend, was shot to death and didn't even get his picture in the paper? For you, for everybody around you, it's front-page news. It's bigger than 9/11. But for the rest of the world, it's like nothing even happened. That disconnect fucks with people. What I do is mark the deaths. All of them. The rest of it, 'justice,' that's somebody else's job."

Amanda puts eight packets from various prisoners across New York State into a paper shopping bag from Trader Joe's and tells me she'd love to help if I find anything interesting. I walk a few blocks south to Cortelyou Road, order an iced coffee at a café with a sidewalk patio, and start opening the envelopes. Some are more than an inch thick, with photocopies of motions and statements and judgments, sentencing reports, witness lists, disciplinary records, medical histories. Some even include crime-scene photos. Each begins with a letter, addressed to Amanda. *Dear Ms. Button.* The handwriting breaks my heart: careful, neat and even as a grade school cursive test. I almost feel embarrassed for the men writing, imagining them hunched over in a cell with a pen, trying to imbue each letter with the sincerity of their plea. Thinking, if this *f* is upright, she will believe me and I will go free.

Michael Malone, writing from Otisville Correctional Facility, was convicted of rape and burglary in 1997: *The victim had bite marks on her and a doctor said they matched my teeth.* He includes an article from *Mother Jones* with the headline: "Everything You Think You Know About Forensics Is Wrong: How Prosecutors Sold Bite Mark, Bullet Casing and Fingerprint Analysis as Real Science." Timothy Whiting, an inmate at Attica, says he has been serving time since 1989 for a bank robbery in Queens where a guard was shot and killed: *Two of my friends testified I was in Manhattan that day, but the prosecutor said they were lying because we grew up together.* Timothy's packet has statements from his friends, a photograph of his daughter (she was eighteen months old when he went upstate) and grandson, and a photocopy of a certificate that congratulates him for completing an associate's degree through Genesee Community College. Elmira inmate Kenneth Deeds, convicted of hit-and-run homicide in 1990, says that his lawyer was incompetent: *The witness who swore it was me told the cops she saw a tall man running away. I'm 5' 6" and my lawyer didn't ask her a single question at trial.* Deeds includes the witness's original signed statement to police, as well as a photograph of him standing next to a wall height chart.

DeShawn Perkins, a prisoner at Coxsackie State Prison in Greene County has written in blue ink.

Dear Ms. Button,
My name is DeShawn Perkins. Every time I can get to a computer, I read your blog. I think you are doing a very good thing. My mama died by murder when I was little but nobody cared. I'm glad to see some things are different now.

I got in a lot of trouble when I was a teenager. I stole and I lied. But I didn't do the crime I was convicted of. I'm not a murderer. Malcolm and Sabrina Davis took me in when I was 6 years old and they were my family.

I was with my girlfriend, LaToya Marshall, that night of the murders, but the cops didn't believe her when she told them. And the detective tricked me into confessing.

Since I've been inside I've learned a lot. I got a high school diploma and I work in the kitchen. I know life isn't fair. But somebody else killed my family and I'm paying for his crime.

Thank you. God bless.
DeShawn

Along with the letter, DeShawn included the original incident report on the murders, his signed confession, and a statement from a woman named Henrietta Eubanks.

I don't see anything about physical evidence, but there are some administrative-looking documents identifying DeShawn's lawyers—for the trial and his appeal—and a sentencing report. Sandra Michaels was the original prosecutor. The confession and the witness statements are both just a few lines long. The confession was signed and witnessed by Detective Pete Olivetti on July 6, 1992, at 2:15 P.M. Henrietta Eubanks' statement was signed and witnessed on July 5, 1992, at 8:45 P.M., by Officer Saul Katz.

"Holy shit," I say, out loud.

The waitress and the couple she's seating all look at me.

"Sorry," I say.

I haven't even known Saul Katz for two years, and yet he has become one of the central figures in my life. I met him one freezing night last January outside the home of a murdered Hasidic woman in Borough Park. He said I looked like my mother—the mother who abandoned my father and me when I was an infant—and ushered me into the ultra-Orthodox world she had been born into. It was a circuitous route, but Saul led me to Aviva. Now I know my mother. Or rather, I have met her and learned some things about her. I know, for example, that she didn't leave us because she wanted to go back to Brooklyn and live the strict Hasidic life she'd been raised in. Quite the opposite: getting knocked up was an accident, and she fled because becoming a mother at nineteen years old was the fate she thought she had escaped by running off to Florida with my dad. I know other, more human things, too. I know that when I hug her she feels fragile, but that she has endured shunning and homelessness and divorce and despair. I know that she cleans homes for a living, and I suspect it is partly because she never considered the idea that she could make money doing something she actually enjoyed. She didn't grow up being encouraged to strive for anything but motherhood, and she fucked that up early. I know that her sense of humor is limited. I know that, like me, she takes antidepressants. And I know that, until last year, she was mostly alone in the world. Now, she and Saul are together, which makes him almost like a stepdad. Saul owns a one-bedroom in Brighton Beach, but Aviva still lives up in New Paltz. They take turns driving to see each other every week.

I don't know much about Saul's life as a cop except that it ended badly. His son committed suicide a few years ago. As a boy, Binyamin had been sexually abused, and after he died Saul beat the man who helped cover it up into a coma, which got him suspended. When he pretended he was still on the job and convinced a rookie reporter (me) to use him as a source in the story of a murdered Hasidic woman, the NYPD finally fired him.

In 1992, when Saul witnessed this statement by Henrietta Eubanks, he would have been new to the force. I wonder if he even remembers the case.

CHAPTER FOUR

Olivetti knocked on the window of the unmarked sedan to get Saul's attention.

"Call the precinct," he said when the younger officer opened the door. "Tell them we need to transport a child, then meet me inside."

Saul did as he was told. It wasn't even ten o'clock, but when he stepped out of the air-conditioned vehicle, the wet July heat pressed back at him. Parishioners were beginning to arrive at Glorious Gospel, and he had to "excuse me" his way to the glass door of the church. The men and boys were dressed in suits and the women in jewel-colored dresses, stockings, matching hats. Some wore short gloves on their hands. The little girls had ribbons on their socks and the little boys wore bow ties. If you looked at it a certain way, Saul thought, you could find similarities in the attire of the Hasidim he had grown up among and these black church folk. Everyone in a costume signifying fellowship. A man in a certain hat was haredi. A woman in a certain hat was church-going. His wife, he knew, would call these people vain. *Do they think Hashem is impressed by sparkles?* Frieda's spirit had turned mean since Saul shaved off his peyes and enrolled in the police academy. He moved out of their little apartment three years ago, but she refused to grant him a divorce. If he wanted to see his son—which he did, desperately—Saul had to remain cordial, walking a fine line between respecting Frieda as his child's mother, and taking care not to give her hope for a reconciliation. He endured her venomous words against the people of Brooklyn whom he had sworn to protect, and only occasionally attempted to explain why he did the work he did. After the riots last year, he stopped bothering.

August 19, 1991, had been an unseasonably cool day. Barely eighty degrees. Saul was working patrol then, walking the beat in his blue uniform and the yarmulke the brass insisted he wear. Saul protested that he was no longer observant, but his captain didn't care. An obviously Jewish officer helped with "community relations." And Saul was not in a position to argue. He was working a four-to-twelve shift and was just two blocks away from the intersection of Utica and President when the 22-year-old Lubavitcher lost control of the big car he was driving and pinned the two black children against an iron window grate. He heard the long scrape of the car against the building; he heard the screams. He saw the twisted bicycle that the little boy had been fixing thrown into the street. And he saw, as the mêlée began: black men pulling the driver from his car and beating him; Jews taking him away in a Hatzolah ambulance; city workers trying to extricate seven-year-old Gavin Cato and his cousin Angela.

When he thought about it a year later, Saul supposed that what happened next was inevitable. Here they were, two communities with years of grievances against each other now face-to-face over the body of a child. Add a man like Al Sharpton, looking for attention, exploiting the anger and the timing (it was just a few months after America watched Los Angeles police officers beat Rodney King, after all), and cognizant of, indeed counting on, the fact that the longer the fires burned the more the TV and tabloid audiences would see his face and say his name. Saul sometimes wondered if the men and boys chanting "Heil Hitler!" and hurling rocks and smashing windows appreciated the awful symbolism of the boy being struck by a car in Rebbe Menachem Schneerson's motorcade: the power structure of one group literally colliding with the weakest members of the other. Saul knew it was just a terrible accident, but he couldn't help thinking that the neighborhood was being punished.

When the riots were over, the little boy beneath the car was dead, as was a Jewish student from Australia, set upon and stabbed in the street; and a salesman, maybe mistaken for a Jew because of his beard, dragged from his car and killed. An elderly Holocaust survivor was dead, too, but by her own hands—so distraught by the chants of "kill the Jews" that she leapt from her window.

It would be inaccurate to say that any "good" came from the riots, but there were people who saw the near destruction of the neighborhood as an opportunity to reset and rebuild, and even to reach out. Pastor Redmond Green was one of those people. Pastor Green was one of the first residents Saul met when he was assigned to the 77th precinct back in 1988. He and his then-patrol partner, Officer Kevin O'Connor, were driving past the storefront when Pastor Green flagged them down. Saul expected he was going to report being robbed—they'd just come from a stick-up at a Chinese food restaurant— but instead the pastor pointed to human feces at the doorstep of the church and demanded they write it up as vandalism. O'Connor didn't even want to take the report, but Saul admired Pastor Green for his commitment to his neighborhood.

Since being sworn in to the NYPD, Saul had found that there were all kinds of cops. The kind of cop he was—or at least, the kind of cop he wanted to be—was the kind that worked hard for people who didn't break the law, people who wanted to live peacefully and with a little dignity in the middle of an ugly, dangerous place. His days were filled with people spun out by rage and shame, people with deep holes in their souls. Many of his fellow officers focused on those people. They called the residents animals and complained that they didn't sign up to be zookeepers.

Why should they go out of their way, risk their lives, make their wives widows and their children orphans, to protect people who would kill their own mother for crack? Or shoot a teenager for sneakers? They considered themselves exterminators in a rat-infested building. Most did not believe the neighborhood would ever get better, and there were days when Saul felt that way, too. But he tried to focus on the people who called in the crimes. Without them the neighborhood *was* doomed. Saul saw it as part of his job to support people like Pastor Green. The more support they had, the more likely they were to lift Crown Heights out of the sticky hell it had fallen into.

Inside the church, Saul found the pastor kneeling beside a small boy with what looked like blood on his face and shirt. Olivetti and a black woman were standing beside him.

"Pastor Green," said Saul.

"Officer Katz," said the pastor, standing up. "Thank you for coming."

"You know each other?" asked Olivetti.

"I've taken some vandalism reports," said Saul. "What's going on?"

"The kid won't say," said Olivetti. "We'll go check at his house."

"I didn't clean him off," said the woman. "I thought perhaps there might be evidence."

"We're going to have him taken to the precinct," said Olivetti.

"I'd like to accompany him," said the woman.

"Fine."

Outside, the sidewalk was crowded with churchgoers.

"There a problem?" asked a man smoking a cigarette.

"Step back, please," said Olivetti.

"I'm a member here," he said. His tan suit was worn thin and shiny. "I got a right to know."

"Step back, please."

A squad car pulled up behind Olivetti's sedan.

"You *arresting* that little boy?"

"I'm not going to ask you again," said Olivetti.

"Go inside, Walter," said Dorothy. "Talk to Red."

"Where's Malcolm?" asked the man. "He know Ontario being taken away by the po-lice?"

"Walter, *please,*" said Dorothy.

Walter flicked his cigarette toward the marked car. Saul saw it, but mercifully, Olivetti didn't. Saul was working with Olivetti as part of his training for Anti-Crime. They were grooming him for detective, and Olivetti was the precinct's prodigy. He worked Homicide, officially, but like everyone else, Olivetti caught what came in, because there was too much crime and not enough cops. If it turned out to be murder, Olivetti stayed on the case. If not, he usually kicked it down. He was just thirty-five then, not much older than Saul, who had come to policing late, but Olivetti was beloved—revered, even. He helped other cops work their cases. He had no children or wife—he told Saul he'd married once and wasn't the kind of man to make the same mistake twice—so his financial obligations were minimal, and he could always be counted on to buy a round or two. In the beginning of his time as a cop, Saul had been surprised how much the camaraderie among officers resembled the camaraderie among the men in shul. In the police academy classrooms and the precinct locker rooms and the bars and on the street, the men in blue uniforms—like the men in black hats—had a common language, a common purpose, a common set of rules and prejudices. They were misunderstood by outsiders, but outsiders were not important. What was important was the man beside you. Olivetti personified this ethic. At first, he rubbed Saul the wrong way. He was impatient; an adrenaline junkie. In the academy, Saul learned that police work required precision. Evidence must be collected and preserved. Witnesses listened to carefully, inconsistencies probed. It only took a few days with Olivetti to see that precision was not chief among the detective's talents. It was hard to argue with the solve rate, though. Since January, Olivetti had been lead on twenty-two homicides and made arrests in seventeen. So, by the time they pulled up at Glorious Gospel, Saul realized that there was a lot he could learn from the man. They were to ride together for one month, and for that month Saul would follow Olivetti's lead.

"Here we go," said Saul, opening the back door of the squad car for Ontario and Dorothy.

"Come on, honey," said Dorothy. She sat down in

the car first and slid over, her church dress hiking up above her knee. She held out her arms to Ontario and he stepped inside. Saul shut the door, then leaned into the front window and handed the officer in the passenger seat a five-dollar bill.

"Pick up some breakfast from McDonald's for him. I don't know how long we'll be."

CHAPTER FIVE

There was no sign of forced entry on the front door to the Davises' ground-floor apartment. Olivetti knocked. Knocked again.

"NYPD," he shouted. The street was quiet, the sidewalks littered with detritus from the night before: popped bottle rockets, torn red, white, and blue streamers, and family-sized bags of chips, in addition to the usual cigarette butts and broken crack pipes and beer cans and dog shit.

Olivetti tried the knob and the door opened.

"NYPD. Anybody home?" He drew his weapon and motioned to Saul to draw his. "What was the name again?"

"Davis," said Saul.

"Mr. and Mrs. Davis?"

The house was still. They stepped into the front living room. A worn leather sectional sofa and a glass coffee table faced an old television set inside a wooden cabinet. Children's toys were put away neatly in one corner.

Above the fireplace hung framed portraits of Malcolm X, Martin Luther King Jr., and Jesus. Olivetti called out again. Silence. They checked the kitchen—mismatched dishes stacked in the drying rack, a frying pan soaking in the sink—and then Saul followed Olivetti down the hallway. The first bedroom had bunk beds, both unmade. In the second, there was a toddler bed and a play kitchen. The bathroom was clear.

"Can you smell that?" asked Olivetti.

They found the bodies in the master bedroom. Saul saw the little girl first, twisted near the end of the bed. Her torso flopped sideways, face blown open to the ceiling. The man was facedown in the pillows, one bare foot hanging off the side of the bed. But for the back of his skull being gone he could have been fast asleep. The woman was slumped against the headboard, eyes wide open, a hole in her chest.

Olivetti spoke first. "I'll call it in."

Saul thought of the little boy at the church, and then of his own son. He would rather Binyamin blinded than see what Ontario saw this morning. "Do you think the boy saw what happened?"

"Could be," said Olivetti. "Though, if the perp killed the girl you'd think he'd kill the boy, too. Kid was probably hiding. Or maybe asleep. Stay here. I don't have to tell you not to touch anything, right?"

"No," said Saul. The iron scent from the blood and the bits of gunpowder in the air tickled the inside of his nose.

The only sound was an air-conditioning unit humming somewhere, upstairs perhaps. There was blood spray up the wall behind the headboard. Blood spray on the carpet on both sides of the bed. Blood spray on the mirror of the woman's bureau. Blood spray on the pile of clothing in the laundry basket on the man's side of the bed. The sheets were soaked in blood. Saul tried not to look at the little girl who had lost her face. He tried not to look at the woman's bare chest, one breast gone, one exposed by a fallen nightdress. He tried to focus on the details of the room. There were no explicit signs of a robbery: no drawers pulled out, no overturned jewelry boxes or lamps on the floor. He looked at the carpet beneath his feet. The evidence team might be able to find footprints or hair. He wondered about drugs. The Davises wouldn't be the first straight-looking family to have a connection to the trade. Theirs could be a holding house. Perhaps one of the Davises had a past: maybe the husband left a gang years ago, or testified against someone. Maybe one of them was having an affair. The child was what threw him. A girl this young would never remember, let alone be able to describe or testify to the killer's face. He could have left her alive.

Olivetti returned with his camera and began taking pictures.

"I'll wait here for the techs," he said. "You knock upstairs. See what they know. Fucker picked a great night to shoot people. Nobody's gonna remember gunshots on the Fourth of July."

Saul left the bedroom. He stepped into the bathroom and glanced around. There was a child's training toilet and smears of finger paint on the inside of the plastic bathtub-shower insert. A black Barbie doll in an evening gown lay inside the tub. A cup held three toothbrushes. Saul looked into the bedroom with the bunk beds. Both appeared to have been slept in recently. The room was spare: one poster of Spider-Man, one of Michael Jordan; a bin full of sports equipment, and a row of sneakers along the wall. Two pairs appeared likely to be Ontario's, but two others belonged to a bigger boy. An older boy.

Saul rang the bell for the upstairs apartment, and after about a minute, he saw legs on the stairs. An old woman making her way down. He held up his badge and she opened the door.

"Good morning, Officer," said the woman. He could smell liquor on her breath.

"Good morning, ma'am. My name is Saul Katz; I'm with the 77th precinct. Do you mind if I ask you a few questions?"

"Is everything all right?"

"Perhaps we can talk inside."

"Is it Monique? Oh, dear God, what's she done now? I have done *everything* I can for that girl."

"No, ma'am," said Saul. "I just have a few questions. It's about your neighbors. The Davises."

"Sabrina and Malcolm? Oh, they're probably at church. If you come back in an hour or two . . . Though

54

they might take the kids to the park. Sometimes they pack a picnic on Sunday."

"Do you mind if I come inside, ma'am? It shouldn't take too long."

"Well, I suppose that's all right." He followed her up the green-and-blue carpeted staircase. Her back was bent and her heels cracked to white in her slippers. She wore a pink housedress that zipped up the front.

"Can I offer you some coffee, Officer. . . ?"

"Katz. No, thank you, ma'am."

"Like I said, Sabrina and Malcolm should be home this afternoon. They usually cook out on Sunday evenings."

Saul took out his notebook. "May I ask your name?"

"Mrs. Treble," she said. "Virginia Treble."

"When was the last time you saw your neighbors, Mrs. Treble?" asked Saul.

Mrs. Treble set a mug of coffee on the oilcloth covering the table. Her hands trembled, and she plopped down, barely bending her knees.

"The last time? What do you mean?"

"Did you see them last night?"

"I don't understand. Has something happened?"

"If you could just stay with me a minute, ma'am."

"Well, I suppose I saw them yesterday afternoon sometime. I don't stay up for all the hoopla." Saul imagined Virginia Treble passing out in the La-Z-Boy chair with a folding dinner tray beside her, ice melting in a glass. He imagined the television turned up loud. He wondered what her drink of choice was. Saul had a brother, Ira, who drank. He kept little bottles of gin in coat pockets and poured them into coffee mugs and plastic cups and water bottles. Mrs. Treble didn't seem drunk, but with a long-time drinker you often couldn't tell. Drunks were difficult to interview and made terrible witnesses. Saul needed her to focus her mind into the past and recall small details. If the case ever got to trial, she would drink before she got on the stand, and even if she managed to testify coherently, all the defense attorney would have to do to discredit her entirely is ask, *Have you been drinking today, ma'am?*

"Did you hear anything unusual last night? Shouting? Or . . . anything?"

"No. Not that I can recall. I'm a pretty sound sleeper. My husband snored something awful. Woke the kids up down the hall. Never bothered me, though. What's this about?"

"I'm sorry to have to tell you this," said Saul, "but the Davises were victims of a crime last night." He told Mrs. Treble that her neighbors were dead. He told her that Ontario appeared to have discovered them this morning, and walked to church to report what he'd seen. She listened, her hand over her mouth. When he finished, she put her shaking hands on the table.

"Honey," she said. "I've got a bottle in the cabinet above the sink. Bring it to me, would you? I need a steady."

Saul got her the bottle: vodka. She pointed to the dish drying rack, and he brought her a glass. She poured herself two fingers-full and drank it. She poured again and lifted it to her mouth, then set it down.

"What about DeShawn?"

"DeShawn?"

"DeShawn been with Sabrina and Malcolm for years."

"He's their son?"

"Foster son. Been with them longer than any of the others. Is he dead, too?"

"No," said Saul. "Do you know where I might find him?"

She shook her head. "Sabrina and Malcolm have been having trouble with him."

"What kind of trouble?"

"Skipping school. Smoking dope."

"How old is he?"

"Sixteen, I think."

"What's his full name?"

Mrs. Treble thought a moment. "Perkins. DeShawn Perkins."

"Do you know if he has a criminal record?"

"I know he was arrested once. But I don't know the details. Sabrina was ashamed. She and Malcolm are good people. The best kind. When they couldn't have children of their own they started taking in strays. That's what I called them. Sabrina didn't like that." Mrs. Treble took another drink from her vodka. Saul got up and filled a glass with water, set it beside her vodka. She acknowledged this gesture with a nod, but didn't take a drink.

"So the Davises had three foster children? The little girl . . ."

"Kenya. They'd just taken her around Christmas. Poor bird was born addicted to crack. She's little for her age." She drained the rest of the vodka glass.

"Can you think of anyone who might want to hurt them? Anyone who might have a grudge against them?"

"No one," she said.

"What about the parents of the children? Was there any trouble there?"

"Not that they mentioned."

"What sort of work did they do?"

"Malcolm works at the YMCA in Bedford-Stuyvesant. He runs athletic programs and after-school. Sabrina works for the city. Secretarial. She's very organized. She helps me with my taxes every year."

"Do you know if they were involved in drugs?"

"Absolutely not."

Saul knew she wouldn't necessarily know, or say, but his first read of her response was that she was telling the truth as she understood it.

"What about their relationship? Did you know about any problems?"

Mrs. Treble shook her head. "No. They love each other. They were a team." Saul noticed that Mrs. Treble vacillated between referring to her neighbors in the past and present tense.

"Most marriages have some troubles," said Saul.

"Of course. Lord knows. But nothing out of the ordinary. I never heard them arguing, if that's what you mean. Only time I ever heard shouting was between Malcolm and DeShawn."

"They argued?"

"Yes."

"Did you ever see him act out? Or get violent?"

"DeShawn? Oh, no, no, nothing like that." She looked at Saul. "You don't think he could have done this? He's practically a child!"

"I'm just gathering information, ma'am," said Saul. "Just asking questions."

"Well, I can't imagine that. He was going through a difficult period, but so many are now. It's *hard* to be a young man today. So much violence. Drugs everywhere. It wasn't always like this. Well, you must know. Did you grow up in Crown Heights?"

"Borough Park," said Saul.

"You know, you are the first Jewish police officer I've ever met. I remember when our folks used to get along just fine. My husband worked for a Jew once and he was good to him. Always paid on time. It's too bad the way things are now."

Saul nodded. That was putting it mildly.

"Have you seen anyone strange hanging around lately?" he asked. "Any strange cars?"

Mrs. Treble shook her head. Saul didn't think she would notice either way. Downstairs, he heard bootsteps and voices. He pulled a business card out of his shirt pocket. Saul didn't have his own cards—even detectives routinely waited years for cards with their personal information on them; the card listed the phone number and address for the precinct. Saul wrote his name on the back.

"Please call me if you think of anything else, or if you have any trouble at all. Until we find out who did this, you should keep your doors locked. Be on the lookout."

Mrs. Treble almost smiled. She tipped the vodka bottle and poured another drink. She hadn't touched the water. "In this neighborhood, I'm always on the lookout."

Saul showed himself out. Two uniforms were unrolling yellow crime-scene tape across the front porch, and neighbors were starting to gawk. Olivetti was on the porch, instructing two more uniforms to check the perimeter of the house and start talking to neighbors.

"There's an older son," said Saul, once the officers were off. "DeShawn Perkins. Sixteen. Been in some trouble before, apparently. We should pull his sheet."

Olivetti nodded. "Looks like the back door was locked, but one of the bedroom windows was open. The one with the bunk beds. And the screen was popped out. Certain kind of people, living on the ground floor in this neighborhood without bars on the window."

Saul relayed what Mrs. Treble told him about the Davises.

"They had straight jobs," he said. "Probably worth checking those out. If the husband worked with troubled kids he might have pissed somebody off."

"We need to talk to the little boy," said Olivetti. "I doubt he's going to be much help, but he might know where the brother is. Why don't you head back to the station and do that. I'll watch the techs and call if the uniforms pick up anything on the canvas. You want one of them to drive you?"

"I'll walk," said Saul. The precinct was eleven blocks away, and Saul tried to walk fifty blocks each day. It wasn't scenic, by any means—past piles of garbage baking in the sun, past men and women nodding against buildings and sleeping half naked on benches, past empty storefronts with torn, faded canvas awnings advertising shops and restaurants gone for years. He walked over broken sidewalks, dodging gum and glass and all other manner of human and animal discharge. Saul didn't want to stop being appalled at the condition of the neighborhood he policed; if he wasn't angry he wouldn't work as hard to save it.

Dorothy Norris and the boy were sitting together in the lobby. When Saul entered, Dorothy stood up; her eyes searched Saul's face for a glint of good news. He squinted at her, drew a shallow breath.

"May I speak to you a minute, Mrs. Norris," asked Saul.

Dorothy tucked her purse beneath her arm. She put her hand on Ontario's shoulder and said, "I'll be right back, honey."

Saul motioned to the officer behind the reception desk. "Keep an eye on him." The officer looked up at Saul and nodded, looked at the boy, then looked back down, flipped a page on the *New York Tribune* in front of him.

Saul took Dorothy into a small hallway off the main lobby, and then into an interrogation room.

"Were you close with the Davises?"

Dorothy nodded.

"I'm sorry to have to tell you that they've been killed."

"Malcolm *and* Sabrina?"

"And the little girl."

"Sweet Jesus." Dorothy made a fist and clutched the neck of her dress. She shook her head no. "What happened?"

"They were all shot."

Dorothy kept shaking her head.

"Do you have any idea who could have done this? Anyone who didn't like the Davises?"

More shaking. Her eyes began to turn red.

"I'm told the Davises had an older son. DeShawn? Do you know where I might find him?"

"No," she said. "Oh, Jesus, those poor boys."

"Do you know if the Davises have family in Brooklyn?"

"Sabrina's parents are dead. I think Malcolm's mother is still in Harlem where he grew up, but I don't think she's capable of taking care of two boys. . . ."

"We need to find DeShawn," said Saul. "And I need to interview Ontario."

"I'm not sure Ontario is going to be able to help you much," said Dorothy. "He hasn't said a word since I found him."

"We're going to need to take his clothing as evidence. Do you think you might be able to find a change for him?"

"I have two girls. But if I can use your phone, I'll call Pastor Green and have him bring something."

"Thank you," said Saul. "The Davises were fostering Ontario, am I correct?" Dorothy nodded. "I'll contact CPS about another placement. If you, or someone from the church, is willing . . . it might keep him from having to go to a group home."

"My husband and I will take him. At least for now. I don't know about DeShawn, though. With my two girls . . ." She trailed off, realizing belatedly, perhaps, that she didn't want to actually speak what she was thinking.

"I understand. What can you tell me about DeShawn?"

"Well, he's been hard lately. Sabrina told me she caught him stealing from her purse near the end of the school year. Malcolm wanted to file a police report but she begged him not to. He had some trouble this spring, and she didn't want him to get in any more. DeShawn has been with them since he was younger than Ontario. He's never been easy, but none of them are."

"Do you think he could have killed them?"

Dorothy shook her head. "I don't *think* so. He's never been violent, that I know. Just . . . restless. Angry. I really can't imagine him . . ." She squeezed the fabric of her dress again, making a fist so tight Saul saw the muscles in her arm tense. "Shooting his parents. Shooting that baby girl."

"You don't think he's the type?"

"Lord, I don't know. I just don't know! I can't believe this is happening. I just don't know!"

"Do you have any idea where we might find him?"

Dorothy furrowed her brow. "Maybe St. John's Park," she said. "I think he plays basketball there sometimes."

CHAPTER SIX

I call in for my shift Monday, and while I'm waiting for an assignment, I e-mail the library and ask them to run checks on LaToya Marshall, the girl DeShawn claims was with him the night of the murders, and Henrietta Eubanks, the eyewitness who picked him out of a lineup. The library is one of the perks of working at the *Trib*. They'll run a backgrounder on anyone and the information they get is vast: phone numbers and street addresses going back decades, criminal records, liens, even contact information for relatives and "possible" relatives. I also ask them to pull articles mentioning DeShawn Perkins and anything on the murders.

At nine thirty, Mike calls and tells me to go to Kendra Yaris's house in Crown Heights.

"Al Sharpton's supposed to be meeting with the mom before the march against police violence in Union Square tonight. Ask him what he'll do if they don't indict Womack."

"What time?"

"Afternoon. But go there now. We can't miss it."

I take my time in the cool shower, and after drying off I apply baby powder over the skin on my thighs that rubbed together all yesterday beneath my sundress, trying to soothe the raw bumps of a heat rash. I don't complain about the heat because I like it a lot better than the cold, but damn, summer in the city ain't pretty. Before I moved here, I basically lived my entire life in air conditioning. School, car, home, work—I don't think I was ever without central air in Florida. Here, I work outside half the time, and although we got a unit at Lowe's in June, lugging it up three flights of stairs and installing it, precariously, in our living room window, was so harrowing we haven't been able to bring ourselves to repeat the endeavor for our bedrooms. So, we sweat.

I'm waiting for an iced coffee at the bodega above my subway station when I get an e-mail from Jim, the librarian on duty:

LaToya's address is in Crown Heights. Got some clips on her being All-American in track in the early 90s, too. Found a criminal record for Henrietta Eubanks going back to 1982—drugs, prostitution, theft—the last address is from 1999. The articles I pulled mentioned a survivor, kid named Ontario Amos. He's in his 20s now, address in Bed-Stuy.

Attached is a document with contact information for LaToya, Henrietta, and Ontario, as well as five *Trib* articles: DeShawn's arrest on July 6, 1992 ("Psycho Son: Cops Nab Foster Kid in Brutal Triple Murder"); the Davises' funeral three days later ("Slain Family Mourned"); a fund-raiser for Ontario Amos ("Crown Heights Supports Survivor of Family Massacre"); DeShawn's conviction on October 19, 1992 ("2 Hours to Guilty! Jury Convicts Teen Murderer in Record Time"); and, in early 1993, DeShawn is the anecdotal lede in a story about new protocols for screening violent youth in the city's foster care system ("CPS Tries to Spot Killer Kids"). Then twenty years of nothing.

I decide to door-knock at LaToya's before heading to wait for Al Sharpton at the Yaris family home. Her address is in the Albany Houses, a collection of six fourteen-story brick buildings on a plot of grassy park that's slightly elevated from the street. I'm often self-conscious walking into public housing. There must be white people who live there, but I never seem to encounter them, and as much as I try to walk with purpose, I feel like an intruder.

The entryway door is propped open and a handwritten paper sign taped to the elevator reads *Broke*. Others have scribbled beside it: . . . *ass nigga!* and *Fuck deBlasio*. Two pieces of gum are also stuck to the sign. LaToya lives on the twelfth floor. I start the climb and am immediately overwhelmed by the smell of urine. There are no windows in the stairwell, and the overhead bulbs are either burnt out or flickering a weak orange. I try not to look in the corners, but there are definitely puddles. The *Trib* has done articles about how dangerous the stairwells in public housing are, and by the fifth floor I'm thinking that I should have at least called LaToya's number to make sure someone was at home. I pause at the landing of the ninth floor and text Iris:

I'm door-knocking in the Albany Houses. If you don't hear from me in two hours, call the cops ☺

On the eleventh-floor landing, Iris calls.

"What the fuck?" she says.

"It just occurred to me I should leave a record of where I am."

"Dude, *why* doesn't the *Trib* send a photog with you to places like that?"

"I'm here for that wrongful conviction story I'm researching for the Center."

"You're killing me, Roberts. I'm going to text you every ten minutes. I'm calling the cops if you don't text back."

"Give me an hour. I will definitely text you in an hour."

"Sixty-one minutes and I call the cops."

"Fine."

"You're a fucking nutball."

I knock at the door of 12G and after about thirty seconds someone comes to the peephole.

"Who is it?" a woman asks.

"My name's Rebekah," I say. "I'm a reporter. I'm looking for LaToya Marshall."

The woman flips the dead bolt and opens the door. She is wearing a scarf around her hair and a baggy T-shirt and workout shorts. Paper towels are woven between her toes: she's giving herself a pedicure.

"A reporter? Who you work for?"

"Um, the *Trib*," I say. I could have said I was from the Center, but it seemed like a shortcut to legitimacy to name a publication she was certain to recognize. It's a decision that could backfire, though. New Yorkers have strong opinions about the *Trib*, and they aren't always good. In April, I got sent to cover the opening night red carpet of the TriBeCa Film Festival, and one marginally famous actor (the ex-husband of a legitimately famous actress) saw my badge and refused to speak with me. "I don't talk to the *Trib*," he sneered.

"What you looking for?" asks the woman at the door.

"I'm researching a story about DeShawn Perkins."

"DeShawn? He out now?"

"No. I'm looking into wrongful convictions. . . ."

She puts a hand on her hip, raises a skeptical eyebrow. "That's a long time ago."

"Right," I say. "He just wrote me a letter, actually."

"Toya's sleeping," she says. "She works nights. I could see if she wants to get up."

"Yeah? That would be great."

"Come on back."

69

The woman walks on her heels down a narrow linoleum hallway, and I follow her, pulling out my phone to
text Iris while her back is turned.

all good

We walk past two closed doors and a bathroom and into
a back room that serves as a living room-laundry room-
kitchen. Half-dry clothing is hanging over every chair and
two foldout drying racks. There is a three-foot stack of magazines and newspapers in one corner and a pile of shoes in
another. It is mercilessly hot inside. An elaborate series of
fans keeps the air moving, although the one near the window is black with whatever it's pulling from outside.

The woman points to a piece of wicker porch furniture.

"Move something if you want," she says. "I'll see if
Toya wants to get up."

I take a pair of black pants off the seat and set it gently
over the T-shirts, then sit down. As I wait, I try to identify
the smell coming from the kitchen. Cheap cleaning liquid
over very spicy food, if I had to guess. I can't imagine
turning on the stove in this heat. Every square inch of my
body is sweating. My skin is covered in a thick film, like
the layer of grease raw chicken leaves on your fingers.

"Sorry it's so hot," says the woman as she comes back
into the main room. "You know they charge you for
having AC?"

"You mean Con Edison?"

"No, NYCHA." The New York City Housing Authority. "You gotta buy the thing, pay the electric, *and* pay them a couple hundred bucks for the right to put it in. And they strict, too. I seen a woman down there with a clipboard counting up all the ACs. They'll fine your ass if you got one you didn't tell them about."

"Wow," I say, thinking, maybe that's a story.

"So, what'd DeShawn do?"

"Nothing. I mean, he says he didn't. He says he's innocent. So I'm kind of looking into the case."

"Why?"

Because I'm hoping to get a fellowship, seems crass. So I repeat: "He wrote me a letter."

"That shit messed Toya up bad," she says.

"Yeah? So, are you her . . ."

"She's my baby sister."

"You guys live together?"

"I been here my whole life. Toya been back, like, ten years at least."

"She wasn't here for a while?"

"After DeShawn got arrested my mama sent Toya down to Atlanta. She stayed there for a while. Then Mama died and she came back."

"I'm sorry," I say.

"Lung cancer."

"Ugh."

"Runs in the family," she says. I wait for her to explain, but she doesn't.

"So, LaToya was in Atlanta?"

"With cousins, yeah. My mama wouldn't have sent her there if it wasn't for Winston. That was mama's boyfriend back then. He was real strict with Toya. He tried to play like he was all watching out for her 'cause she was smart and she was good at running and wanted to go to college. But he wanted to fuck her. So there was no way she could have a boyfriend. Said she'd end up with a baby like Mama and me."

"Did you know DeShawn?"

"She kept him away from us. She was worried I'd snitch on her."

"You woulda," says a voice behind me. Toya. She's taller than her sister, and thinner. There are freckles across her cheeks and nose, and her hair is in a messy, slept-on ponytail. Beneath her eyes are the most intense circles I've ever seen. Four shades darker than the rest of her face and ashy, like powdered cocoa. She is otherwise quite beautiful. Strong jaw, sharp cheekbones, amber eyes.

I stand up. "Hi. I'm sorry I woke you up. If it's better for me to come back . . ." I trail off; Toya doesn't respond. She rubs her eyes and plops on the sofa next to her sister.

"You writing about DeShawn?" she says.

"Yeah. Are you guys in touch?"

She shakes her head.

"He says he was with you the night his family died. Is that true?"

LaToya nods.

72

"But he still got convicted."

She shrugs. It's a gesture of resignation, not indifference.

"Did the jury not believe you?"

"I didn't go to the trial."

"You didn't testify?"

She shakes her head.

"Why not?"

LaToya bends forward, looks at her sister.

"I just turned fifteen. I wasn't supposed to be with DeShawn. We spent the night together at this kid's apartment. His mama nannied for a family in Manhattan and on weekends they kept her overnight a lot. People went there to drink and mess around. It wasn't a big deal. Some weed, but nothing crazy. Anyway, when the cops first asked I said we weren't together. Then later they didn't believe me when I said we were. They had me all confused. The detective kept asking, are you *sure* he never left? How could you be sure, you were asleep? And he said DeShawn confessed. He said somebody saw him. That got me doubting. I mean, I *was* asleep part of the night. What if he did do it? What if he murdered three people and then crawled back in bed with me? How did I not know?

"I was really scared. And Mama and Winston were pissed. They sent me down to Atlanta for the next school year. Winston was on and on about how I had to concentrate and that I'd blow my scholarship chances if I was distracted and no college would want me if they knew I was mixed up with a murderer."

73

She rubs her eyes and pulls her legs up, tucks her long feet beneath her.

"I blew it anyway. There wasn't no Facebook or whatever but people found out why I'd moved down there and they looked at me funny. I was a good girl, okay? I mean, me and DeShawn had sex once. For real. One time. And then all of a sudden I'm this girl whose boyfriend is a killer. Anyway, I wanted to fit in and I got drunk one night and fell down some stairs at somebody's apartment. Broke my foot. I couldn't run that year and I just kinda gave up. Got into drugs. Ended up dropping out. It was all shit from there. I finally got locked up for bad checks and got clean inside, got my GED and a certificate in Exercise Science. But when I got out they told me I couldn't coach kids 'cause of my record."

"It's not like she's a fucking *child molester* or some shit," says her sister.

"That sucks," I say.

Toya raises her eyebrows, picks up a magazine and fans herself.

"And you never heard from any of DeShawn's lawyers or anything?" I ask.

Toya shakes her head.

"So, like I told your sister, DeShawn wrote me a letter. He says he's innocent."

I wait for a response, but don't get one.

"What do you think? Do you think he did it?"

Toya shakes her head. "I thought maybe for a while.

But he was with me all night. I'm sure of it. He just . . . he wasn't that kind of person. I mean he acted tough sometimes, but when you got him alone he was really sweet. He would have done anything for me. He didn't care if he looked cool or not. I know he fought with his foster parents, but he loved them. I remember once I was telling him how our bathroom sink was all backed up and we'd been waiting days for somebody to come fix it. He said his dad could probably do it. He was, like, Malcolm—that was his name, right?"

I nod.

"Yeah, I remember. He was, like, Malcolm can fix anything. He said he put in a whole new shower—or maybe it was something in the kitchen? Anyway, he admired him. They fought and shit, sure, but we was teenagers. And the mom. He was all proud that she taught him to cook. I remember he came over one night when we knew Mama and Winston was gonna be out. He made this fancy pasta thing with some special cheese. And bread and salad and everything. That was the night we had sex. I was all bragging to people, like, my boyfriend is so *sweet*. . . ." She almost smiles, then looks at the ceiling, and I can see she's trying to roll back tears. "Ain't no man every cooked for me since."

For a few moments, none of us speak. LaToya's sister stares at the floor, her hands folded between her legs. I wonder if she's thinking the same thing I am, which is that no man has ever cooked for me. Toya was just fifteen, but she had something lovely. Something special. Until it was gone.

"Is Toya gonna be in the paper?" asks her sister, finally.

"Maybe," I say, looking at Toya to gauge her reaction. I haven't been writing anything down. "I'm only starting to look into the case. I mean, would you be willing to be quoted saying he was with you?"

"Yeah," says Toya. "But they didn't believe me then. Why they gonna believe me now?"

Before she was shot on her way home from work, Kendra Yaris lived with her mom and two siblings on the second floor of a brick house just off the Nostrand stop in Crown Heights, about a twenty-minute walk from LaToya's. I can see the signs on the lawn and the crowd on the sidewalk from a block away. I spot a reporter from the *Ledger*, a guy named Sebastian, and wave.

"You here for Sharpton?" he asks me.

"Yeah. Did I miss him?" It's just after noon.

"I don't think he's coming. Somebody inside said he canceled last minute."

"How come you're still here?"

"My desk wants me to follow the family to the march."

"I guess I better go knock," I say.

The front door on the side of the house where the Yarises live is open, just a screen door separating inside from out. I press the buzzer marked #2 and after a moment a male voice calls out, "Who is it?"

76

"My name's Rebekah," I say into the empty hall. "I'm a reporter for the *Trib*."

The man appears at the top of the stairs.

"You looking for Sharpton?"

"We were told he was going to be visiting before the march."

"He ain't here."

"Did he cancel?"

"So what? Why everybody so worried about Sharpton? This ain't about him. This about Kendra. And the fucking NYPD."

I scribble what he's said into my notebook.

"Do you think they'll indict Womack?" I ask.

"They better or we gonna shut this city down! My niece ain't even got a *record*. Fucking killer cops got to be stopped."

"You're Kendra's uncle?"

"Her mama's my half sister."

I get his name and call Mike from outside.

"'We're gonna shut this city down.' Great shit," he says. "Stick around in case Sharpton shows."

I sit on a curb across the street and Google Ontario Amos, who, I discover, is the sous chef at a new restaurant in Clinton Hill. Eater described it as "an inventive mix of Afro-Caribbean flavors expertly curated for new Brooklyn's tastes." A *New York Times* profile of his boss, a Haitian native and James Beard Award nominee named Jean-Phillippe Dade, mentions Ontario by name, saying that Dade passed over applicants who'd soused for Marcus Samuelsson and Dan Barber for the unknown whose food he tasted at a *Village Voice* showcase.

"I have never met anyone with a palate as refined as Ontario's," Dade told the *Times*. "His ideas are reflected in every dish at Dade."

At three thirty, Mike calls to tell me Sharpton is doing a live spot on CNN and I can cut out for the day. I hop on the B43 bus up Kingston Avenue to Bed-Stuy and knock at the address the library gave me for Ontario. From the landing, I can hear children. After about a minute, a woman opens the door. She is barefoot, wearing a jersey sundress that looks like it accidentally got thrown in the wash with some bleach. There is food—possibly banana—in her hair.

"Hi," I say. "I'm looking for Ontario Amos."

"He's at work."

"Oh, okay," I say. "Do you know when might be a good time to find him?"

"What you want?"

"I'm a reporter," I say, "from the *Trib*."

"You gonna do another story about how great J. P. Dade is? How about you do a story about how he work his people so hard they don't see their families no more? How about that?"

"I'm actually working on a story about Ontario's foster brother."

"James?"

"No," I say. "DeShawn."

"*DeShawn?* Shit. What'd he do now?"

"Nothing," I say. "I'm just looking into a couple of old cases."

"Well, Ontario ain't gonna want to talk about DeShawn. *I* don't want him talking about DeShawn. You know he still won't take the girls to the fireworks. It's been twenty years. He won't go. Stays home with his headphones on all night so he can't hear nothing. Won't take 'em off till the next day."

"So, he hasn't been in touch with him all this time?"

"Hell no," she says.

A little girl with half a dozen pigtails in her hair comes to hang on the woman's leg. "Mommy, I want some ice cream."

"Not till you finish your fish sticks."

"I don't want fish sticks!"

"Then you don't get ice cream."

"Noooooooooo!"

"I'm not gonna say it again, Kenya," says the woman. "If they're not gone when I get back your sister gonna get ice cream and you're not. I ain't playing. Go!"

The girl looks at me, then back at her mom, lip stuck out dramatically, arms crossed, and stomps away.

"Mommy being *mean*," I hear her say.

The woman angles her voice back into the house. "You think I can't hear you? You have three minutes. Three minutes. I'm counting." She turns back to me.

"Kenya," I say. "Isn't that the name. . . ?"

"I shoulda said no when he wanted to name her that."

"I'm Rebekah," I say. But she doesn't offer her name in return.

"I gotta go," she says.

"I might try stopping by the restaurant."

"We really don't need this shit right now. He working like a dog and we never see him. You go asking him about DeShawn and . . ." She sighs. "What's he gonna help you with? He was just a little boy."

Dade is a tiny sliver of a restaurant on Lafayette Avenue. There are no diners inside. Two men in chef whites and caps do a controlled dance in an open kitchen at the back of the dining room while a woman in a short black jumper folds napkins at the bar.

I open the door and walk in. The woman turns, smiles, and slides off her barstool.

"Can I help you?"

"Hi," I say. "I'm looking for Ontario Amos."

She turns to the men in white.

"He must be out back. Can I ask your name?"

"My name's Rebekah. I'm a reporter from the *Trib*."

"Oh, cool! Are you guys gonna write about him?"

I decide not to elaborate on the nature of my visit.

"We might," I say.

"Hold on. I'll get him."

She scurries off and returns a few minutes later with

Ontario. He is six-foot-something and close to three hundred pounds.

"Hi," I say. "I'm sorry to bug you at work." I wait for him to say something like, it's okay, but he doesn't. His wife, I'm guessing, has texted.

"Do you have a minute? I promise not to take up too much time."

"Even Dade hasn't been in the *Trib*," says the woman. Her earrings are bronze knives hanging to her chin. "I think it's great. Maybe more of the neighborhood people will get to know the place. Did you know we do BYOB? That really helps cut the price. Plus they're working on a fifteen-dollar lunch special for the fall."

"She ain't here to talk about food," says Ontario.

The woman looks at him, then me. She shrugs, and makes a face, like, sorry he's so grumpy.

"I got five minutes," he says. "Then I gotta get back to prep."

I follow him outside and he lights up. He doesn't offer me a smoke and he doesn't look at me.

"I guess your wife said I was by."

He nods, pulls off his white cap and stuffs it in the back pocket of his black-and-white–checked pants.

"I'm looking into some old cases," I say. "For a . . . project on wrongful convictions." He doesn't respond, so I prattle on, trying to connect. "Things were really different back then. Cops were, you know, really rushed and under the gun. . . ." Fuck. Wrong cliché. "And the standards of evidence were different. No DNA, that sort of thing. Plus now we know a lot more about how teenagers, like, sometimes make false confessions."

"What you saying? You saying DeShawn didn't do it?"

"I don't know," I say. "He wrote me a letter saying he didn't."

"So? What else he got to do up in there?"

"Do you think it's possible?"

"That he's innocent? Not really. He was always mad at Malcolm and Sabrina. He stole from them. He used to sneak out of the house, smoke weed in the bathroom. It got worse when they brought Kenya home. We had our own rooms before but they thought since she was a girl—and none of us was really related—she should get one. That pissed him off. I know Malcolm and Sabrina talked about putting him back into the system. Maybe a group home."

"You remember that?"

Ontario nods. "They should have. But they was good people. They didn't think they had a psycho murderer in their house."

"Do you remember anything about that night?"

"I remember hearing Kenya scream. But she screamed a lot. She had nightmares and she'd go into bed with them."

"What about the gunshots? Did you hear those?"

He nods almost imperceptibly.

"Did you think they were fireworks?"

He shakes his head, flicks his cigarette into the street. Wipes his nose.

"Did you hear anything else? Anybody coming or going?"

"I don't remember."

He's already told me more than I expected he would. I've interviewed dozens, maybe even hundreds of people who've been victims—or survivors—of crime in the two years since starting as a stringer for the *Trib,* and it never fails to surprise me how bad I am at guessing who's going to bury me in details and who's going to slam the door in my face. It doesn't break down by age or race or neighborhood or gender or religion or class. I once knocked on the door of a giant Frank Lloyd Wright rip-off in Westchester to try and get a quote from the daughter of a seventy-five-year-old who'd been arrested at JFK after getting drunk on a flight from Miami and screaming that the passenger sitting behind her, who happened to be wearing a hijab, was a terrorist. I figured the woman wouldn't even come to the door, but she invited me in, gave me a photo of the old lady, and said she'd had enough and hoped this whole thing shamed her mom into finally going to AA.

"Had DeShawn been with you guys that night?" I ask.

"Nah. He wasn't around much. And he definitely wasn't doing family things like fireworks and picnics."

"He says he was with a girl all night."

Ontario shrugs. "What's she say?"

"She says she was with him. But that nobody believed her."

This surprises Ontario, I think. He looks me in the eye for the first time since we've met.

"Where did you go . . . after?" I ask.

"You mean where'd I go live? I stayed with a church family for a little bit, then a group home in Brownsville. Then some different fosters. When I aged out, I moved in with some guys I knew from work. Me and Tammy been in Bed-Stuy a while now."

"Where'd you learn to cook?"

"Sabrina. She didn't cook fancy but she was real good at making cheap food taste great. Spices and stuff. She got me comfortable in the kitchen, and it was a good way to, like, get in with my other foster moms. They was always happy to have help. I got my first job at a takeout taco place when I was fifteen."

"I met one of your daughters," I say. "Kenya."

"Yeah. I don't know. Maybe it was bad luck to name her that. I barely knew her. But she had no chance, you know? No life at all. I remember it felt cool to be a big brother. And I always thought about her after. I thought about her a lot. I thought about how if she'd come sleep with me when she got them nightmares she'd be alive. I'd wonder what she'd be doing now. Then when Tammy had a girl . . ." He rubs his eyes. "You really listening to DeShawn?"

"I don't know," I say. "I'm trying to track down the

witness who said she saw him leaving the house. Other than that—and the confession—it doesn't seem like the police had much." When I hear myself say it, I realize it sounds a little silly: *just* an eyewitness and a confession. Not exactly nothing. "These days, they'd need more to get a jury to convict, I think."

"That doesn't mean he didn't do it. It wasn't no robbery. Malcolm and Sabrina didn't have nothing to steal. Everybody loved them."

"What about Kenya's mom and dad? Or even yours? Might somebody have been mad they were raising their kids?"

"I doubt it. Not my mama anyway. She gave me up when I was three. I don't think she knew who my dad was."

"Oh," I say, thinking, I wonder if it would have been better or worse if my mom had stuck around long enough for me to have a couple memories. "I'm sorry."

"I better get back."

"Thanks for talking," I say. I give him my card, which is a generic New York *Tribune* card with my name and cell number hand-written on the back. "If you think of anything, call me."

That night, Iris and I order Indian food from the new place across the street. We eat and watch an episode of *The Real Housewives* of Somewhere. At 10:00 P.M. I go into my room and start drafting a letter to DeShawn.

CHAPTER SEVEN

Evening
July 5, 1992
Crown Heights, Brooklyn

Saul and Olivetti found DeShawn at St. John's Park at dusk. He'd been arrested that spring for shoplifting, so they had a recent photo, and as the park started to empty out—families home for bath-time and bed, good kids to do the homework they'd neglected over the holiday weekend—DeShawn and his buddies were still fooling around on the court. Saul and Olivetti approached, and Olivetti called out.

"DeShawn Perkins."

The boys turned. "Who's asking?" said one, but DeShawn was already running. He was fast, but Saul was faster. He'd taken up running when he got into the academy, afraid of how far behind his classmates he would be in physical conditioning. Yeshiva boys didn't take gym, and exercise—beyond a Shabbos walk—wasn't thought worth pursuing. The mind, not the body, was important to Hashem. The running helped as things fell apart with Frieda. Last year, Saul placed ninth in the department's

5K. He caught DeShawn by the collar less than two blocks away, on the street in front of the precinct. Dumb kid had practically run through the station's doors. They stumbled forward together, DeShawn crashing to his knees on the sidewalk. Olivetti came jogging behind, chuckling.

"Bad move, bro. Bad move."

"Why did you run, DeShawn?" asked Saul, bringing him to his feet.

DeShawn's knees were bleeding. Olivetti took out his handcuffs.

"What'd I do?" asked DeShawn.

"You ran."

"That ain't against the law."

"Fuck it ain't," said Olivetti. "Resisting arrest."

"You arresting me for that? Running?"

Olivetti closed the cuffs around DeShawn's wrists.

"You got needles in here?" he asked as he patted the teenager down. "Am I gonna poke myself?"

"Nah, man. I ain't no junkie."

"Oh, you ain't, ain't you?" said Olivetti, pulling a dime bag of weed out of DeShawn's front pocket.

"I want a lawyer," said the boy.

Olivetti laughed.

"Where were you last night, DeShawn?" asked Saul.

"What you care?"

"Answer his question, asshole."

"With some a' my peeps. Watching the fireworks. Hanging out."

"What time you get home?"

"Why?"

"Answer the question," said Olivetti.

"I don't know, man. Right around midnight."

"You sure?"

"Yeah, I'm fucking sure."

"Whoa, watch your mouth there, boy. Officer Katz is being real nice to you."

"Whatever."

Olivetti grabbed DeShawn's cuffed arms and shoved him through the front door of the 77th precinct, right past the witness.

She had come in alone two hours before. *Wait here,* they told her when she said she wanted to talk to whoever was in charge of the Troy Avenue murder case. She sat on the bench across from the desk sergeant, skinny arms and legs braided together, leaning forward and tearing at her cuticles with burnt fingertips. Her flip-flops were two sizes too big, and looking down she decided she'd buy some new shoes—sexy shoes—with the money he was paying. A hundred dollars when she agreed, and nine hundred more when it was done. It would take months to earn that tricking.

After an hour, she went outside and found a cigarette on the sidewalk, smoked what was left. She found another. An officer walking in tossed a copy of the *Trib* in the garbage can just outside the doors. She picked it up and brought it inside. Sure was a lot of shit going down. She read about a big fire at a warehouse in Williamsburg, and a shoot-out in McCarren Park. She read that the saxophone-playing man trying to be president was coming to town and planned to eat at a Harlem restaurant. She read about Rodney King getting out of the hospital. Poor bastard. A cop shot her daddy in 1979. He was stealing a car, and when they rolled up behind him with their lights he jumped out and ran. He died in the street, her mama said. Like the dog he was. She has only a handful of memories: the time he brought a red tin bucket of popcorn for Christmas—or maybe it was Valentine's Day—and her mama let him stay for supper. The time she saw him passed out in the alleyway off Myrtle Avenue and kept on walking. His big white socks and his long arms. The time he carried her on his shoulders all the way up the stairs and she brushed her hands along the hallway ceiling like she was a giant.

Her mama said it wasn't the cops that killed him, it was the heroin. But Henrietta blamed the cops. And now, here she was, waiting to help them out. But really she was helping herself. That was what she had to remember.

A cop with a little Jewish hat came to get her.

"My name is Officer Katz," he said. "Come on back."

In the interview room he asked if she wanted something to drink.

"You got Dr Pepper?"

He brought her a Dr Pepper. She opened it and drank, waited for him to ask a question.

"What can I do for you?" he said finally.

"You working that case then?"

"Which case?"

"Those people that got killed on Troy."

He nodded.

"I saw somebody running out a' they house last night. Running fast. And I saw a gun in his hand."

"You know the family?"

She shook her head.

"How did you know it was their house?"

"I didn't. But this morning I saw all them cops. I asked around."

"You live in the neighborhood?"

Again, she shook her head.

"But you just happened to be on Troy Avenue?"

She nodded.

"What time was this?"

"One or two." She wasn't supposed to be too specific.

"And what did this person you saw running out of the house look like?"

"He was a black guy."

"Tall? Short? Skinny? Fat?"

"He was going pretty fast. Not fat, though. Not too tall."

"What about the gun?"

"What about it?"

"What kind of gun was it?"

"I don't know guns. The kind you can carry in your hand."

"What hand was he holding it in?"

"Right. His right hand."

"You're sure it was a gun?"

She nodded.

"You remember what he was wearing?"

She squinted, looked at the ceiling like she was thinking. "Basketball shorts. And a T-shirt."

"What color?"

"Like I said, he was running."

"Which way did he run?"

"Away from me."

"Toward Atlantic or Eastern Parkway?"

She picked one. "Atlantic."

"Where do you live?"

Pause. Was this a trick? She decided to tell the truth. "Bushwick."

"But you stayed in Crown Heights all night?"

"I was with some friends."

"Names?"

"We ain't close. We just hang sometimes."

"And you hung all night?"

"Huh?"

"You said you saw the police this morning."

"Yeah. Right. Yeah."

"This person you saw. Do you think you could identify him?"

"Maybe."

"Anything else you want to tell me?"

"Like what?"

"I'm asking you."

"No."

He stood up. "Wait here." She waited, and when he returned he asked her to write down what she saw on a yellow notepad and sign it.

"I need your full name and address and phone number," he said. "When I run you, am I gonna find a record?"

"Yeah. So?"

Hunny couldn't remember the last time she'd had a pen in her hand. In school they made her write with her right hand and she was terrible at it. She leaned over the notepad and wrote: *I saw a black man run out of the house on Troy Avenue after the fireworks. He was carrying a gun. He ran toward Atlantic.*

She gave him the piece of paper, and he disappeared again. While she waited, she thought about that hit her roommate, Gina, had waiting. Soon she'd have enough money to buy rock for months and months and months. She imagined a backpack full of rock. Imagined pouring it onto the bed and rolling around in it.

The officer came back with the typed statement.

"Read it over. Make sure it's right. Make sure the address and phone number are right."

She looked at the paper, nodded.

"Sign here," he said. "We'll be in touch."

CHAPTER EIGHT

After three hours in the interview room, DeShawn started to get nervous. Maybe this wasn't about his curfew. The pot was bad, but they ran after him before they found it in his pocket. He rolled back through the last few days in his mind. Had he done anything else they could violate him for? LaToya. Was it statutory rape if they were both underage? Toya wouldn't tell her mom's boyfriend she was with him—she'd be in for worse than him if she did— but maybe Winston followed her or something. Maybe he saw them leaving Michael's apartment this morning together. They should have walked out separately. He was just so sleepy and happy that he didn't think of it. Neither did she. He'd never actually spoken to Winston Lawrence, but he saw him around the Albany Houses sometimes. Before they were a couple, DeShawn used to hang out in one of the courtyards, hoping to catch Toya coming or going; bump into her casual-like. Winston was the kind of man Malcolm was afraid DeShawn would turn into: entitled and mean; a hustler with kids by who knows how many different women. Living off his girlfriend's welfare checks and whatever cash he could make selling dope or loosies or stolen electronics. Toya told him once she thought Winston had been a pimp when he was younger. She said he commented about her body constantly, "joking" that if she didn't make it as a runner she could make good money stripping. DeShawn asked her why she didn't tell her mom about it, but Toya said she did. *She doesn't believe me,* she said. *She thinks I'm just trying to make trouble because Winston's strict.* DeShawn wanted to introduce Toya to Malcolm and Sabrina, but he hadn't found the right time. He knew they'd like her—everybody liked her. He hoped if they saw a girl like her wanted to be with him, maybe they'd see that he wasn't so bad after all. That he was worth keeping.

DeShawn leaned forward in the hard metal chair, shoulders bowed over and arms crossed at the elbows, pressed between his legs. Malcolm and Sabrina had talked to him about his rights and stuff, but he never really absorbed the details. He knew he was supposed to be polite, and he knew he wasn't supposed to run. He remembered the part about asking for a lawyer. But he'd have to call Malcolm to get a lawyer. And he was already in deep shit with Malcolm. He shouldn't have said those things about Sabrina. Being a mom was the most important thing in the world to her. But the way she looked at him when the school called and said he'd been suspended for stealing money from a teacher's desk drawer (Five dollars! So he could buy LaToya a fucking slice after school!) made him so mad he started spewing ugliness he knew would hurt her.

"Why are you so surprised?" he yelled that night at home. "God didn't want you to be a mom. But you go taking other people's kids anyway thinking you gonna save us? Fuck that. Look what you done."

Malcolm didn't hit him—he never hit him—but for a second DeShawn thought he might. That was more than a month ago but the words he said still sat in every seat in the apartment. It was as if they were stenciled on the walls. *God didn't want you to be a mom.* He heard Malcolm and Sabrina whispering about him at night. Heard them saying maybe taking Kenya in was a mistake. Maybe DeShawn was too volatile. Maybe she was unsafe around him. That pissed him off, too. They thought he was gonna hurt a little girl? What did they think he was? He might be a fuck-up but he wasn't a *monster*. Where were they even getting that from? He'd never hurt anybody in his life.

After he got booked for the petty theft at school there were a whole bunch of new rules. He had a curfew, and was subject to random drug tests. But it had been weeks and he hadn't heard a thing. Now all of a sudden they come chase him down? Had Malcolm and Sabrina called his juvenile probation officer because he didn't come home last night? Sabrina was always talking about how important it was for DeShawn to stay out of "the system";

would they really have dropped a dime like that? It had to be Toya's step-dad. Had to be.

After another hour, the cop who cuffed him entered the room.

"What's this all about?" asked DeShawn, trying to sound tough, like he knew his rights and was ready to assert them.

"My name is Detective Pete Olivetti, son. I'm gonna ask you a few simple questions and you're going to tell me the truth. Got it?"

DeShawn didn't answer.

"I didn't hear you."

"Yeah, whatever."

"Where were you last night, DeShawn?"

"Home."

"Home on Troy Avenue?"

"I only got one home."

The cop smirked.

"What? Somebody saying something different?" What was the worst that could happen for a curfew violation? It wasn't worth getting Toya in trouble.

"Nope," he said.

"Can I go now?"

The cop laughed. "Nah, son," he said, affecting a slight accent he probably thought was funny. "We just getting started."

CHAPTER NINE

"She's left three messages since six," said the desk sergeant, handing Saul three slips of paper with the words *Katz* and *wife* written on them.

"Thank you," said Saul.

It was almost 11:00 P.M. when he finished with the witness. The 4-to-12 was starting to trickle in with collars of their own, and Olivetti had his feet up on his desk, finishing a sandwich from the filthy bodega across the street. Saul wouldn't buy a coffee there, let alone allow the sweaty workers to touch his food. He didn't keep kosher anymore, but he wasn't stupid. Olivetti was fresh-eyed; as animate as if it was the first twenty minutes of his shift, not six hours after he should've gone home. He was keeping the kid in an interview room. With no parents to complain, Saul wouldn't be surprised if DeShawn was still there when he came back in the morning. Olivetti liked to let them sit and stew; get angry and scared and hungry and generally as uncomfortable as possible. Olivetti was popular with everyone in the precinct except the maintenance staff, who had to clean up the urine when the detective wouldn't let his suspects use the bathroom. One kid he picked up for stealing cars took a shit in the corner of Interview Two last year. Olivetti made him stay in the room with it for nine hours until he finally gave up two buddies.

"What'd the crackhead have to say?" asked Olivetti.

"She says she saw a black man with a gun run out of the Davis house last night around one."

"Really." Olivetti kicked his legs down to the floor, wiped the crumbs off his shirt.

"She a neighborhood girl?"

Saul shook his head. "Address in Bushwick. Said she was with friends but wouldn't give me names."

"She got a record?"

Saul nodded.

"Let's bring her in for a lineup. She still here?"

"I let her go."

The desk sergeant came back.

"It's your wife again," he said. "Line two. Can you pick up? She kinda scares me."

Olivetti chuckled. Most of the men in the precinct complained about their wives and ex-wives. But as miserable as Fraidy made him, Saul felt even more miserable when he spoke about their troubles. The failure of his marriage was a failure he was responsible for; he understood that. He had been a different man—barely a man at nineteen, but nonetheless—when she was sanctified to him before Hashem and the community. It was his loss of faith that had turned her desperate and petty. He could not fault her for wanting to keep her family together, but as the years went by and she made no concessions to reality, it was clear to him that her behavior was at least as damaging to Binyamin as his own. He was beginning to lose patience.

Saul picked up a phone as close to the far end of the room as possible and pressed the blinking white button.

"Fraidy," he said.

"Your son has something he wants to tell you."

"Has something happened?"

"What kind of question is that?"

"You left three messages," he said. "Is everything all right? Is he hurt?"

"He is suffering! He has no father!"

Saul closed his eyes.

"He wants you to come speak to him right now."

"He has school tomorrow, yes? He should be asleep by now."

"What do you know!"

"May I speak with him, please?"

"You may speak with him when you get here."

She hung up the phone. His ears felt hot and his breath was shallow. He would go to her. He always did.

"Don't sweat it," said Olivetti. He was up from his desk now, folding a strip of gum into his mouth. "Patrol just called in a body on Pacific. I'll be here all night. The lineup'll have to wait. I'll keep the kid till the morning. Maybe he'll wise up and tell us what we already know."

"You think he's the shooter?"

"He ran. That shows a guilty conscience. And something like this you always look close to home. Shit was personal. I'll run checks on the mom and dad—see if they have any past we need to know about, but my money's on the kid. Call it intuition. I'll tell him this witness is coming and send some uniforms for her in the morning. Give him some time to decide if he's gonna cooperate or not."

"Does he have a lawyer coming?" Saul asked.

"He hasn't asked for one."

He had, of course. They'd both heard it. But Saul was following Olivetti's lead. And his son was waiting.

The apartment Saul once shared with his wife and son was just off New Utrect Avenue in Borough Park. The building was relatively new and the construction astonishingly shoddy. The concrete balconies jutting from the living rooms of every other unit were declared unsafe within six months; they were poured improperly and had begun to crack. Kitchen cabinets and the Formica counters laid atop them didn't meet at right angles; the prominently advertised individual laundry hookups ended up being nonfunctional because of improper plumbing; and paper-thin walls made an already gossip-prone community increasingly wary of—and entertained by—their neighbors. Saul hated the place the moment they moved in. Fraidy used the fact that the families on either side of them could hear every argument to try to shame him back into observance. During their arguments she took to addressing their neighbors: "Batya Levine, do you hear this? My husband has brought a radio into our home! A radio! He does not care what sort of poison goes into my poor Binyamin's ears!" Saul brought the radio home to break the silence of the apartment. He tuned it to the public station after his wife and son had gone to bed. He closed his eyes and listened to the wordless music—jazz, he knew now—and imagined himself with other people, people so full of life that they could blow into an object and make it sing. People so in sync with one another that they could create something together out of nothing at all. Their hearts, he felt, must be connected by some powerful force. Was it the music? Or was it something else and music came from that? Saul had never been in sync with anyone. He had only recently even considered what lived inside his own heart, and he certainly never imagined that anyone else could know what he was discovering there.

He felt like a prowler each time he visited Fraidy. The men and women who had been his friends, had attended his wedding and his son's bris, hurried past as if they did not know him. He understood, to an extent: if they were seen talking to him they, too, might be the subject of rumors. It was simply the way of the community. But knowing it was the way did nothing to dull the resentment and despair he felt when someone he once shared hours of conversation with no longer acknowledged him on the street. At the mailboxes just inside the downstairs entrance, two men—Aron Finkel and Yossi Gold—stood chatting. They saw him approach the glass door. It was nearly midnight; if Binyamin had fallen asleep, the bell would wake him. (Another problem with the building: the buzzers were firehouse-loud, announcing a friendly visit with a heart-stopping blast.) Saul put his hand up and waved; he had known these men his entire life. But they turned their backs on him.

Fraidy buzzed him in. She did not greet him at the apartment door, just left it ajar. Binyamin was sitting at their kitchen table, dressed in his pajamas. The boy had never been particularly hearty; he was born six weeks premature, with a tiny hole in his kidney that kept him in the hospital for a month. But Saul could not deny the clear effect that the breakup of his family had on his ten-year-old son. Binyamin was underweight, with the posture of an old woman and the eyes of an old man. He barely looked up when his father entered the room. Fraidy, too, had changed physically since Saul left their home three years ago. She was uglier, her face pinched. She stood in front of the refrigerator, arms crossed over her chest, the heel of her slipper knocking against the linoleum floor. He imagined the fury inside her exploding. Resentments and disappointments and fears spewed across the room, turning to monsters in the oxygen. Growing large enough to devour them all.

"Binyamin has something he wants to tell you."

Saul looked at the boy.

"Binyamin?" said Saul. He pulled out a chair and sat, leaned toward his son, but the boy said nothing. "Would you like to talk in your bedroom?"

"Absolutely not."

"Fraidy . . ."

"Rabbi Zelman warned me not to let you alone with him."

"What. . . ?"

"I will give you your divorce."

"Fraidy, I don't think this is the right time. . . ."

She picked up a folder from the kitchen counter and tossed it in front of him.

"Everything is signed. Just like you wanted."

"Binyamin, would you please go to your bedroom."

"You cannot tell him what to do! You are not my husband and you are not his father. No more."

Saul put his hand on his son's back, and his son flinched. It had been months since Saul wept over his estrangement from Binyamin. He missed everything about the boy. The way he smelled, the dirt under his fingernails, the sound of his sneeze. When Binyamin was an infant, Saul held him constantly. For weeks after he came home from the hospital, he would only fall asleep when he was lying on his father's chest. Saul used to close his eyes and smile, enjoying the weight of the tiny body pressed against his heart. He kissed the top of his head, inhaled, and thanked Hashem for the opportunity to learn how to love. Now the mere touch of his hand frightened Binyamin. It didn't matter that the source of the fear was not Saul but Fraidy, and Rabbi Zelman, and all the neighbors. All that mattered was that his boy felt unsafe around him. Was it cruel to force him to endure that?

"Tell him, Binyamin," said Fraidy. "Tell him what you told me."

"I don't want to see you anymore," he whispered.

What was the good of asking him to explain? Or asking if he was certain? Saul's heart was already so broken that he barely felt the blow. For now, he decided, it was best to leave it alone. The boy did not need to be pressured; certainly not this late at night. There was time, he thought. Time enough to show his son he was a good man, even if he was no longer religious.

CHAPTER TEN

I spend most of Tuesday standing outside a fancy TriBeCa apartment building waiting for a woman TMZ claims is the mistress of a movie mogul whose wife is pregnant with their third child. She never comes outside (smart woman), and when my shift is over I hop on the L train to Bushwick and Henrietta Eubanks' last address. It's a three-story building with ugly blue vinyl siding and six buzzers. I press #1 and after a moment, the door buzzes open. I push into the tiny hallway and a mop-haired kid about my age peeks his head out.

"Hi," I say. "I'm looking for someone who used to live here a long time ago. In the nineties."

"Ask Ronald," says the kid. "He's been here forever. If he's not sitting out front he's at the bar on the corner. Maria's."

"Thanks," I say.

The door to Maria's is propped open. It is gratuitiously dark inside and the bartender sports the most impressive

Mohawk I have ever seen: easily eight inches high, dyed pink with snow-white tips. It looks more like concrete, or maybe papier-mâché, than hair. I can't imagine how she sleeps. At the bar are a black man and two Latino women, all of whom are roughly fifty—emphasis on the rough. The jukebox is low, and instead of conversation, the patrons appear deeply engaged in watching NY1—muted, but with closed captioning—on the TV above the bar.

I slide into a barstool and the bartender comes over.

"Just a Bud Light," I say.

She bends down and slides open a cooler, twists off the cap, and sets the bottle in front of me.

"I'm looking for someone named Ronald," I say. "Do you know him?"

"Who's asking?" says the man at the bar.

"Ronald?" I ask. He nods. "My name's Rebekah. I'm a reporter for the *Trib*. I'm looking for a woman who lived here back in the early nineties. Henrietta Eubanks. Any chance you remember her?"

"Hunny Eubanks? *Damn*. I ain't heard that name in forever. She long gone."

"Yeah?"

"Ten years at least. Actually, shit. More like fifteen. She was gone before 9/11. Yeah, I'm sure she was."

"Do you have any idea where she went?"

"Nope."

"You're not still in touch?"

He shakes his head. "We was neighbors but not really

friends. We came up together. Same year in school. She had it tough. I guess we all did. We was both on the streets by sixteen."

"On the streets?"

"Up to no good. I did stick-ups. She was trickin'. Rock was turning folks into zombies. We was all just living one hit to the next. And AIDS. Shit. I got clean in prison." He lifts up his glass. "Club soda. She'll tell you."

The bartender nods. There is a tattoo of a tiger on the left side of her shaved head.

"I just like her company so much." Ronald chuckles, then coughs. The cough doesn't sound healthy. "So what you want Hunny for?"

"She was a witness in a murder case back in 1992. In Crown Heights."

"Oh, yeah?"

"You didn't know?"

"Nah, but that don't mean nothing. Hunny had her life and I had mine. We was all keeping our secrets as best we could."

CHAPTER ELEVEN

He came to her at strange times. She wasn't sure how he made his living, only that it seemed like some kind of hustle. Definitely not a nine-to-five. Once he hinted that he was paid to hurt people. He said he ran with a gang, but it wasn't one she knew about.

Gina thought he was full of shit. But Gina didn't know him like Hunny did.

She probably should have guessed he'd be waiting for her when she arrived home from the precinct. Gina was on the street in front of their building, pacing.

"I don't like how he just comes up when you're not here," she said. The glue holding Gina's magenta hairpiece in place was losing its grip on her forehead, the adhesive melting in the heat.

"You smoke it?" asked Hunny.

"I said I'd wait! But I ain't waiting all night."

"Just give me a couple minutes," she said. "An hour most."

"Fuck, Hunny."

He was standing at the window upstairs, his hands behind his back. He turned when she entered but did not speak.

"I done what you said," she told him.

"Good."

He pulled two fifty-dollar bills out of his pocket and gave them to her. His hands were steady; his gaze direct.

"You said a thousand."

"After they make an arrest."

She didn't argue. He left and Gina came back up.

"You get the money?"

Hunny didn't want to talk about it.

Two uniforms came for her early the next morning, just as she was coming down, getting ready to take a cold shower and maybe find some breakfast. The bell rang and when she went to the window she saw the cruiser. She put on her wig and went downstairs.

"Ms. Eubanks?" asked the young officer. He was blond with a military haircut. Sunglasses like the California motorcycle cops on TV. "We need to bring you down to the precinct to look at some photos."

She nodded and the second officer opened the back door to the cruiser.

"Your chariot, my lady," said sunglasses.

His partner snickered.

When they arrived at the precinct, sunglasses pointed to

the same bench where she'd sat the evening before and told her to wait. There was a copy of the *Trib* at the far end, and she scooted down to pick it up. On page three there was a photo of a couple and the headline "Massacred! Mom, Dad, Toddler Murdered in Bed." The black letters swelled. She squinted her eyes and tried to focus. The first floor of a house on Troy Avenue. Neighbors thought the gunshots were firecrackers. The victims were church folk who took in foster kids. How was he mixed up in this?

"Henrietta Eubanks?"

She looked up. The newspaper slid off her lap. The cop standing over her bent to pick it up. It wasn't the Jewish cop who interviewed her last night. This one was Italian, maybe. Hair on his knuckles and a gold cross around his neck. He smiled at her. The Jewish cop didn't smile.

"Thanks for coming in," he said. "Come on back."

She followed him toward the interview rooms, but instead of talking inside one of the boxes, the cop motioned for her to sit in a chair next to a desk in the big open room.

"Can I get you something while you wait?"

"Dr Pepper?"

He disappeared for a minute, returned with a can of Dr Pepper. She opened it and sipped. The woman in the newspaper photo was beautiful. Like a movie star.

"We're gonna take you into a room, and you'll see a group of men. You tell us which one you saw running out of the house last night. That's it. Easy as pie."

She nodded.

"You know it was real brave of you to come in and say what you saw," he said. "I don't know if my colleague, Officer Katz, adequately related that to you. He's new. But I've been around a while. I get the sense you been around, too. Am I right?"

She sipped.

"I know it wasn't easy for you to walk in here. I know some cops make life real hard for girls like you. I want you to know I think that's bullshit. Everybody gotta make a living, am I right? No shame in that. I tell you what, the cops I know go hardest at working girls, they're the same ones cruising 'round the point after shift. Shit, I know I don't have to tell you. But listen, I want you to know, we take care of people here at the 77. You help us, we help you. That goes from here on. You're in a jam, you call me. You got information, we got money for that. People like you, people willing to come forward, you are going to keep this community from destroying itself. Not the politicians. Not the cops, even. People like you."

He was a real talker. And she didn't quite know what to make of his speech. He was trying to convince her of something, that much she could see. But what? Maybe he was working up to it. Maybe he was about to tell her he knew she wasn't anywhere near Troy Avenue the night before last. He leaned forward, looked at her hard. She waited, ready with a story about watching the fireworks from the roof of a friend of a friend's apartment building.

But he didn't ask anything. He just tapped his palm on the desk.

"You need anything else?"

She shook her head.

"All right, then. Just hang tight."

She finished her soda and watched the other cops move in and out of the room, helping themselves to coffee and donuts from a station in the corner, click-clicking on typewriters, ignoring her entirely.

The Italian cop came back and asked her to follow him into a little hallway with a window that looked into another room. After a minute, the men walked in, each carrying a number. She knew one by sight. Quentin Something. He used to hang in Williamsburg, but she hadn't seen him in a while. He didn't ever seem like a killer. She looked at them all. Number four was the kid she'd seen the detectives bring in in cuffs last night. Maybe he was involved in some way. Made sense.

"Number four," she said. "That's him."

CHAPTER TWELVE

After the lineup, DeShawn asked to use the bathroom, but the Italian cop told him to sit in the interview room again and wait. The clock on the wall said it was 10:00 A.M. He'd been in the precinct almost fifteen hours. His head ached. It felt as though the nerves behind his eyes were exploding. They shot pain into his neck, his ears, his jaw. If they didn't let him go soon he was gonna piss himself. The night before last, with Toya, felt like weeks ago. He had barely slept then, either, but that happy exhaustion was animating. When they'd emerged together from Michael's building into the late-morning sun and walked the three blocks to Lou's Diner for pancakes, DeShawn felt ready to run a marathon. Even hours later, he was playing great when the cops yelled for him. Now that energy was gone entirely. He wanted to put his head on his arms and fall asleep for a day—two days. They still hadn't said why he was even in this windowless hole.

Another hour went by. And then two. He hadn't eaten

in a whole day. Wild, empty waves of nausea rolled through him. He squeezed his eyes shut and crossed his arms over his stomach. When the feeling passed he opened his eyes, but the darkness was still there, in blotches popping against the air. He'd seen enough TV to know the mirror opposite him was a window. Was someone watching? And what was that lineup all about?

Finally the door opened and the Italian cop entered the room.

"I want to call my dad," said DeShawn.

The cop chuckled. "Your dad?"

"Yeah. I know my rights. I'm a minor."

"I think we both know your dad isn't gonna be able to help you, DeShawn."

"What are you talking about?"

"Did he hit you?"

"What?"

"If he hit you, or touched you. He's not your biological dad, right? Maybe he was coming into your room at night. Maybe you couldn't take it anymore. Maybe he started doing it to your brother."

"What are you talking about? Malcolm didn't touch me! I want to call him. I know I get a phone call."

"You get a phone call when you get to jail, son."

DeShawn blinked. He put the heel of his hand into his right eye and pressed hard.

"I gotta use the bathroom."

"Too bad," said the cop. "So what was it, then?"

"What was what?"

"What pissed you off so bad? Did they threaten to kick you out?"

"What are you talking about, man?"

"Why'd you shoot them, DeShawn!"

Suddenly the cop was screaming at him. Standing up, spitting. He slapped his hands on the table and DeShawn jumped in his chair. His bladder gave way. Warm then cold down his leg, soaking his shorts. He'd peed the bed until he was in junior high. Sabrina said it was normal for someone who had been through trauma, but it embarrassed him. Made him remember that they weren't blood and that she and Malcolm could let him go anytime they wanted. But they never did let him go, and Sabrina saw that it pained him to bother her at night. She put extra sheets in his closet so he could change them himself.

"What? Shoot? I didn't shoot . . . what are you *talking* about?"

"You fucking shot your mama and daddy and that baby girl dead. I know you did it. You know you did it. And the woman who just picked you out of that lineup knows you did it."

DeShawn doesn't remember a lot about the rest of the conversation with the cop. He knows he said he didn't shoot them. He knows he said it over and over and over again. He knows he said he wasn't at home. And he knows he said LaToya's name. He didn't want to but he did. None of it felt real. He has no idea how long he was in the little

119

room crying, screaming, pleading, explaining, but he does remember the way the cop looked at him. Like the words he was saying weren't even English. After a while, the cop, disgusted, apparently, with DeShawn's unwillingness to confess to the slaughter of his parents and little Kenya, rose and left the room. While he was gone, DeShawn, his lower body sticky and cold with urine, tried to focus his mind. Could Malcolm and Sabrina really be dead? Where was Ontario? The cop hadn't said a word about his little brother. Maybe it was all some sort of test. Like that *Scared Straight* program on TV. Maybe Malcolm thought the only way to get DeShawn's attention, to get him back to right, was to do something dramatic. That had to be it. His foster parents weren't gang members. They didn't sell drugs. They weren't the kind of people who got gunned down in their home. This cop was fucking with him. He'd open the door and Malcolm and Sabrina would be there to take him home. He had to hand it to them—it wasn't the worst plan in the world. He imagined his bedroom, how he'd been complaining that since Kenya came he had to share with Ontario. Shit. He'd sleep on the floor for a month after this. All he wanted was a pillow.

But when the cop came back, he was alone, carrying a tape recorder.

"We've got your brother in the next room, DeShawn."

"Ontario?"

"You got another brother?"

DeShawn shook his head.

"Both of you are starting to piss me off. The only fingerprints on your parents' doorknob are yours and Ontario's. That's just a fact. If you're saying you weren't there, that you didn't do this, we're looking at him."

"He's nine years old!"

The cop shrugged, put the tape recorder on the table. "You think a nine-year-old can't pull a trigger on three sleeping people? I've seen kids younger than that kill their abusers."

"He wasn't abused!"

"Then why did you do it?!" The cop's voice cracked. A high-pitched blast blowing at his face. DeShawn's chest felt like an empty tin drum. His heart a solid rock rattling around. He wanted to stand, to leave, to run, but he could barely feel his legs. Did they even work anymore?

"I . . ."

"You already told us you were there last night, DeShawn. We know you ran out of your house. Did you run out because you'd just shot your family? Or did you run out because your little brother did? Did you run out because you were afraid? Tell me now. If he did it, you can't protect him. We'll break him sooner or later. Probably sooner. He doesn't look too tough."

DeShawn squinted. He was dehydrated. His eyes burning, his stomach in turmoil. He farted loudly. The detective looked disgusted. This man couldn't possibly think Ontario had murdered Malcolm and Sabrina and Kenya. This *had* to be some sort of test. Maybe Malcolm wanted to see if he was loyal to the family before he decided to kick him out. Malcolm was always bothering him about spending more time with Ontario. He said DeShawn had a chance to be a role model, to stand up for Ontario, to make his life better.

"Ontario didn't do nothing."

"So it was you."

"I'm not saying . . ."

"Which was it?"

"Ontario is a good kid!"

The detective glared at DeShawn and for a moment the teenager readied himself for a smack across the face. But then the man's expression changed. He sat down and pulled his chair up close to the table. Instead of looking menacing, he looked weary. He leaned toward DeShawn like he was about to tell him a secret. DeShawn prepared for the truth of the ruse to come out.

"Just admit you did it, DeShawn. You admit it, you make everything better for yourself. You'll feel better. I promise. You're still a minor. You show remorse, tell the judge Malcolm Davis was touching you, hitting you, whatever. You'll only get a few years. Ten, tops. You'll be out in your twenties. You'll be a young man. You're a strong kid. You'll survive inside. Ontario? You keep saying it wasn't you, and he's going away. And let me tell you—kids like him don't do well inside. He'll never be the same. They'll eat him alive. The guards in juvi got reps. They like to play with the young ones. . . ."

"Stop it!"

"I'm telling you how it is, son. How it's gonna be for your brother if you don't man up here."

"I know what you're doing," DeShawn said, his voice a whine, a plea.

"What am I doing?"

"You're trying to . . . you're trying to scare me. I get it." The cop pressed a button on the tape recorder. "I'm sorry. I'm sorry I fucked up."

"It's okay, son. Everybody makes mistakes. You're sorry?"

"Yeah."

"I need you to say it, DeShawn. Then this will all be over."

"It wasn't Ontario."

"It was you that killed your parents?"

DeShawn let his head nod. Any second now, he thought. He imagined Sabrina enfolding him in her soft arms. He imagined the cocoa scent of the buttery yellow cream she put on her skin. He imagined drifting off to sleep in his bottom bunk, the sounds of her and Ontario cooking in the kitchen. Pots and pans and the little radio playing Stevie Wonder.

"I need you to say it, DeShawn. It was you that killed your parents."

"It was me."

CHAPTER THIRTEEN

I am outside City Hall waiting for a press conference about asbestos in schools to begin when my phone rings showing a blocked number.

"You have a call from an inmate at Coxsackie Correctional Facility," says an automated voice.

I accept the charges, pull out my notebook, and find half a bench beneath a tree just away from the crowd.

"Hello?"

"Rebekah? This is DeShawn Perkins. I got your letter."

"Hi, DeShawn. How are you?"

"Doing good, thanks. And yourself ?"

His voice is so upbeat I almost laugh.

"I'm okay. Thanks for calling."

"Thank *you*. You said you saw Ontario? How's he doing? He doing okay?"

"He seems good," I say. "He's married. They have two little girls. And he's a chef."

"*Man,* that makes me feel good. He was a sweet kid,

but you never know. Every once in a while I'd see some-body in here that looked like him. *Pheew*. Did a number on me, you know? I was really hoping he'd stay outside. Give him my best, will you? Tell him I'm always thinking about him."

"Sure," I say. I decide not to tell him Ontario seems pretty convinced he killed their family.

"So you think you might write about my case?" he asks.

"I'd like to try." Do I say I know one of the cops who arrested him? "I talked to LaToya and she was pretty ada-mant that you were together the night they died. But she said she never testified. Did you tell your lawyer about her?"

"I told everybody. But they just thought I was trying to cover my ass. At first I didn't want to get her involved. They had me all turned around. I didn't know what I was saying. I just wanted to go home."

"Did they tell you if they ever interviewed her?"

"The cops didn't tell me shit. I asked my lawyer about it a bunch of times before the trial. He kept putting me off, and then he was like, oh yeah, she changed her story so she's some kind of 'unreliable witness.' "

"In your letter you said the detective tricked you into confessing. Was anyone else there? Did they record the interview?"

"He pressed record right at the very end. All he got on tape was me saying, yeah, I did it."

"And no one was there with you?"

"Nah," says DeShawn.

"I'd love to talk to your lawyers," I say. "You said in your letter they weren't very effective."

"My first one was like a hundred years old. He dropped dead, and I got a young guy. We only met one time before the trial. And the prosecutor lady, the one that's all up in the news now, she was really good. My guy was bush league compared to her. My appeals lawyer was better. She tried to argue I had ineffective counsel, but the judge was focused on the confession. And the witness."

"What do you remember about the witness?"

"She was a crackhead," he says. "She must have been confused. But she stuck with her story."

"Is there anything else I should know? Anything that might, I don't know, point to someone else who could have done it?"

"Someone was threatening Malcolm and Sabrina."

"How do you know?"

"For a couple weeks before they died somebody kept calling the house. Calling and hanging up. And there was some graffiti, too. Malcolm never figured out what that was about. Then one day I came home from school before anybody else was home. The mail lady used to drop the letters through the slot in the door and there was one that didn't have a stamp on it. I remember thinking it was weird, so I opened it and it had cutout letters. You know like a ransom note in the movies? It said something like 'I'm watching you.' I asked Malcolm later but he wouldn't tell me anything. He tried to play it off like it was a prank from his kids at the Y, but I know Sabrina was scared."

"And you told your lawyers about it?"

"Yeah. But they said the cops didn't find anything."

"Did you testify?"

"I wanted to, but my lawyers both said it was a bad idea. They said the DA would trip me up and make me look even more guilty."

An automated voice breaks in: "You have one minute left on your call."

"I'll call your old lawyers," I say, rushing. "Maybe call me back in a couple days? Is what you sent me all you have on the case?"

"There's a couple more things, motions and stuff."

"Great, send that."

He agrees, and I give him the address for the *Trib*.

"You didn't ask if I did it," he says.

He's right. Somehow it seems . . . inappropriate. But that's ridiculous.

"Did you?" I ask.

"No. I swear. They offered me twenty years if I pleaded guilty. They were like, you'll be out before you're forty. I'd be free now. But I wouldn't do it. I'm not a killer. I would never hurt Sabrina and Malcolm. They were the only family I had."

I don't necessarily believe him and I don't necessarily

not believe him. The uncertainty, I realize, is both totally unacceptable and totally unavoidable. No attorney, no judge, no juror can ever really know if the person they are dooming to prison—or releasing onto the streets—did the crime they are accused of. I suppose one of the nice things about being a reporter is that you don't have to make that decision in the same way. You find facts, you reveal them, others take action (or don't). It's a potent but limited position. Our power comes in the choice of focus. I picked DeShawn because of Saul, not the merits of his plea. I have to remember not to let that cloud my judgment, either way.

The automated voice comes back. "Your call has been terminated."

According to the file DeShawn sent Amanda, a lawyer named Bob Haverford was the man who originally defended him in court. I search around on LinkedIn and find that the Bob Haverford who worked at Brooklyn's Legal Aid Society from 1990–1993 is now a "principle" at Haverford & Haverford Associates, a real estate company on Long Island. According to his profile, Haverford attended Hofstra University, then CUNY Law. He is the vice president of the Suffolk County chapter of the New York Real Estate Professionals Association and was voted "Broker of the Year" by the same chapter in 2006.

The Haverford & Haverford Web site lists his office and cell number. There is still no sign of anyone official at the asbestos press conference, so I try the cell and he picks up on the first ring.

"Haverford!"

"Hi," I say. "Is this Bob Haverford?"

"Sure is. What can I do for you?"

"My name is Rebekah Roberts. I'm a reporter with the *New York Tribune*."

"Love the *Trib*! Only paper worth reading."

I've lost respect for him already.

"Thanks," I say. "I'm actually calling about an old client of yours. DeShawn Perkins?"

"Shawn what?"

"DeShawn. You defended him on a triple murder back in 1992."

Silence.

"Hello?"

"I'm here," says Haverford. "Hold on." I hear a car door slam. "Okay. What can I help you with?"

"Well, I was hoping I could talk to you a little about the case."

"That was more than twenty years ago."

"I know," I say. "Are you practicing law anymore?"

"No."

"I spoke with DeShawn earlier today, and he said you only met once before his trial. Is that right?"

"Are you really writing an article about this?"

"Maybe," I say.

"Well, I don't want to be quoted."

"Right now I'm just looking for information. DeShawn says he's innocent, and I talked to a woman who says she was with him that night but that the cops didn't believe her."

"You're asking me to remember one case twenty years ago."

"It was a pretty big case. Three people shot in their bed. A three-year-old."

He sighs. "I know. I'm sorry. I'm on my way to a showing. This isn't a good time."

"Fine. I'll call you back. Or we can meet. Whatever works."

"I've got your number now," he says. "I'll be in touch."

He hangs up just as the Schools Chancellor and half a dozen Department of Education staffers make their way to the podium. *Yadda yadda* we will investigate *yadda yadda* we will mitigate *yadda yadda yadda*. I call Mike with the relevant *yaddas*, and while I wait for another assignment, I get on Google and discover that I actually know DeShawn's appeals attorney, Theresa Sanchez. Or rather, I've interviewed her. Now a judge, Sanchez worked as a prosecutor in the Kings County DA's office after her time as a public defense attorney. Since 2008 she's presided over the Brooklyn Community Justice Center, which is where I met her last year when I was helping one of the Sunday reporters get information for a story about alternative courts. Usually, when I am sent to cover trials or observe hearings around the city, it is a sobering assignment. The people waiting outside the courtroom are curled over nervous legs on benches, huddled in corners, whispering into cell phones, snapping at children, biting their nails, adjusting ill-fitting suits, and scrutinizing the contents of thin folders as if inside they might find the solution to the predicament that landed them there. The muffled weeping and strained conversations echo along the wide, mirthless hallways.

The Justice Center, by contrast, felt more like a YMCA than a courthouse. They have a day care center for people appearing before the court, and my tour guide let me peek into one of the classrooms used for GED prep, computer literacy, and various other educational opportunities that defendants are "sentenced" to take part in. The halls are decorated with framed children's drawings and thank-you letters from people who passed through the court. Photographs of smiling men and women with their arms draped around Judge Sanchez, giving the thumbs-up sign as they pose picking up trash or delivering food or painting over graffiti while wearing "Brooklyn Community Justice Center" T-shirts.

When I called to schedule an interview, Judge Sanchez invited me not just to observe an hour of the court's session, but to sit with her behind the bench, so she could chat with me about the various cases before her. The Center didn't handle felonies, she told me, so most of what she saw were drug cases, plus some theft, prostitution, and "quality of life" violations like urinating in public and bicycling on the sidewalk. I remember being astonished by Judge Sanchez's demeanor; she spoke to the people who appeared before her like a social worker. She asked them what they needed to stay out of trouble, and when they spoke—even when they rambled a bit—she listened. She was no pushover, though. Near the end of my hour, a man with a star tattooed on his nose was called to stand.

"This guy is a regular," she said, swiveling back toward me, pointing to his file. "Usually it's drugs, but today it's misdemeanor assault. He served time for attempted murder in the nineties. And he hasn't shown up to any of the interventions we set up for him."

She swiveled back and, despite the wild-haired man's twitchy pleas, sentenced him to three months in jail and two years probation, adding drug counseling as part of his post-release plan.

"It can take ten, twenty times for some people to get clean," she told me after a guard escorted the man out. "Not everybody can do it. We've lost people. But you can't stop giving them chances."

I call the main number for the Justice Center and introduce myself, reminding the woman on the phone that I visited last year and saying I'm interested in talking to the judge about an old murder case.

"Just a minute. I'll check if she's available."

Less than a minute later, Judge Theresa Sanchez picks up.

"Rebekah, how are you?"

"I'm good," I say.

"One of my staff gave me your piece on Roseville in

American Voice," she says. "You write beautifully."

"Thanks. That means a lot."

"Still at the *Trib*?"

"I am," I say. "I'm actually researching a story about a case you worked on back in 1993. DeShawn Perkins."

"Remind me."

"He was sixteen, from Crown Heights. Convicted of murdering his foster parents and sister . . ."

"Oh, yes," she says, her voice lower. "Really horrible crime. The girl was, what, three?"

"Yeah," I say. "Did anything about the case strike you as odd?"

"Odd?"

"DeShawn insists he didn't do it. He says the detective coerced his confession. And I talked to his girlfriend at the time. She says she was with him all night."

"If I'm remembering it right, the case always felt weak to me. That confession was a big hurdle, though. We raised that he didn't have an adult present, but his voice on tape saying he did it—that's hard to argue with. At least back then. And they had a witness, I think."

"Do you remember anything about her?"

"I remember thinking that she didn't seem particularly trustworthy, but that doesn't mean she wasn't telling the truth. Or at least what she thought was the truth."

"You worked on his appeal, right?"

"Right. It was one of my last cases before I went to the DA's office."

"He sent me some of the documents in his file but I'm wondering if there's anything more."

"After the appeal we send everything we have to the defendant. What are you looking to write about?"

"I'm working with the Center on Culture, Crime and Media on a wrongful conviction project. All the stuff that's come out lately about eyewitness testimony and false confessions made me think there could be something there."

"Like I said, the case felt thin. It was such a heinous crime. Shooting a toddler in the face? DeShawn didn't strike me as the kind of person who would do that. And I don't think the cops did much investigating after they honed in on him. Try calling the precinct's administrative lieutenant to ask if they can help you track down their file. I'll make a call to my old office and see if I can locate what we had. I've still got some friends at the courthouse, too. They might have an old copy somewhere."

"Thanks. I really appreciate that."

"Are you looking to try and get the case reopened?"

"I don't know," I say. "Maybe?"

"You should know, unless that witness recants, there's probably not much you can do."

I almost add that I know one of the two original officers on the case and could seek his advice, but instead I just say thanks and tell her I'll call her tomorrow. Why haven't I called Saul yet? Typically, if you have a personal contact that might be able to illuminate something about a story you go straight to them. But going to Saul means going to my mother now, and I am not myself around my mother.

We hang up, and since I still haven't heard about a new assignment from Mike, I call the 77th precinct and ask for the administrative lieutenant.

"Lieutenant Graves," says a female voice.

"Hi," I say. "My name is Rebekah Roberts. I'm a reporter with the *New York Tribune* and I'm trying to get a copy of a homicide file from 1992."

"1992?"

"Yes."

"That's a long time ago."

"Yeah, I know."

"Hold on."

I hold. She comes back.

"You're going to have to call the Department of Records down at One PP."

"Okay. Thanks."

I Google "NYPD Department of Records" and find a Web site with instructions for mailing in a request for documents, but no phone number. There are few things more obnoxious than government agencies and corporations that don't list their direct contacts on their Web sites. I bet I've lost a week of my life searching online for phone numbers for city departments and public relations officers. I'm always clicking around, grumbling, thinking, I'm *going* to find the fucking number, you assholes, and when I do, I'll be pissed and less sympathetic to your point of view than I would have if you hadn't tried to hide it from me. After a few minutes, I give up and I dial the main NYPD switchboard to ask for the Department of Records. I am transferred.

"Goooood morning, Records!" trills a man's voice.

"Hi," I say, almost laughing. "How are you?"

"I'm just great, how are you?"

"Pretty good," I say, thinking, happy people are almost always more helpful than unhappy ones. I introduce myself and tell him I'm looking for a homicide file from 1992.

"Ah," he says. "You got the wrong records room." Shit. "You should probably call the legal bureau. They handle FOIL requests."

FOIL, the Freedom of Information Law, is wonderful in theory, but often useless in practice. There aren't enforced rules about how long a department can take to "process" your request for information, and if they deny it, they don't really have to explain why. You can appeal, but good luck with that. One thing I miss about Florida is the fact that my home state has some of the best open records laws in the country. Pretty much every government document is fair game. Even as a college reporter, I could call the Gainsville PD and get an incident report or arrest warrant e-mailed to me the day after it was filed, and often police departments would just post the documents on their Web sites as a matter of course. It's paradise for a reporter. New York City, on the other hand, makes it as difficult as possible to get information as simple as whether a person was arrested or not.

The nice man at Personnel Records transfers me to the FOIL office, where a less nice woman answers.

"Legal."

"Hi," I say. "I'm a reporter with the *New York Tribune* and I'm looking to get information about a 1992 homicide case. I'm hoping to get a copy of the original police file."

"The file? You mean the incident report?"

"That," I say, "and anything else that's available. Witness statements. Evidence inventory."

"We won't provide the report."

"Okay," I say. "So, the file isn't available?"

"I didn't say it wasn't available. I said we won't provide the report."

Shoot me now.

"What about the rest of the documents in the file?"

"You need to talk to DCPI for that."

Fuck. The Deputy Commissioner for Public Information is the NYPD's media relations arm and it is a complete black hole. At crime scenes, the DCPI officers stand sentry, blocking access instead of providing it. E-mailing a request to the office—which you are always asked to do—yields a response only about 50 percent of the time. And only about 50 percent of those responses actually include the information you've requested.

The FOIL woman gives me DCPI's e-mail address,

which I already know by heart. I e-mail my request into the abyss.

At two o'clock, Mike calls and tells me to come into the office to help with rewrite for the rest of the day. Three hours later, I get an e-mail from DCPI:

You need to contact the FOIL office.

I e-mail back: *Already did—they directed me to you.*

Almost immediately, DCPI emails back: *DCPI is the media office that focuses on breaking news. We are unable to accommodate requests for historic files.*

DeShawn wouldn't call his case historic. He's living it every day.

CHAPTER FOURTEEN

It wasn't until he saw the newspaper article that DeShawn actually believed Malcolm and Sabrina and Kenya were dead. He signed the piece of paper the cop gave him, but instead of his foster parents walking through the door to take him home, two men in uniform appeared, slapped cuffs on his wrists, and walked him out the side door of the precinct and onto a bus bound for Rikers. Even that first night, awake in his cell, the screams and cries of hundreds of boys bouncing off the walls, echoing through the bars, he thought maybe it was all part of a plan to frighten him into straightening up. He shuffled through the line with a tray at breakfast and threw his entire meal in the trash. At lunch, he spotted a copy of the *Tribune* lying open on the floor by a garbage can: "Psycho Son: Cops Nab Foster Kid in Brutal Triple Murder." His knees buckled and he stayed there, kneeling, as he read the article that told him his family was gone.

He used his phone privileges to call Toya, and by some

miracle she picked up and accepted the charges.

"You know I didn't do it, right? I was with you all night."

"I know," she said. But she didn't sound sure.

"I didn't wanna get you in trouble, but I had to tell them I was with you. I'm sorry. I don't know if they believed me, though. Can you call the police and say we were together? Can you call Michael? He was high but he knows we were there. I don't remember the cop's name but it was the precinct on Utica."

"I'm scared," she said.

"Me, too." He wanted to ask her to come visit, but how could he? Some girls bragged about their boyfriends in lockup, but Toya didn't date thugs. She respected herself. It was one of the things he loved about her.

"Who do you think did it?" she asked.

"I don't know. The paper said Ontario is okay, though. Can you ask around about where he is?"

"Okay," she said.

A male voice broke in on the line. "Who's this?"

"I'm on the phone," says Toya.

"Who is this!"

"Winston . . ."

The line went dead. He called her back the next day. The recording announced a call from Rikers Island: "Will you accept the call?"

"Fuck no!" said Winston. "Toya don't want nothing to do with you. Call here again and I'll report you for harassment. Add some rape charges to your murder rap, motherfucker."

For a week he waited, certain she'd sneak away and come see him, assure him she'd gone to the police and provided an alibi. He moved from his bunk to the cafeteria to the yard and back to his bunk with his head down, the bewilderment turning to fear, the fear like a fist in his throat, turning his blood thin, his muscles soft, his bones brittle. Where was Ontario? His brother was a mama's boy, glued to Sabrina's legs since the day he joined the family. Was he getting picked on—or worse—in a group home somewhere? Could they have put him back with his mother? The one who gave him the burn on his arm?

And then, one afternoon, someone called his name.

"DeShawn!"

It was Freddie Anthony, the son of two parishioners at Glorious Gospel. Like DeShawn, Freddie had stopped going to church, but his mother and father were diehards. DeShawn hadn't seen Freddie in probably two years. They were a year apart in school, and Freddie dropped out when DeShawn was a freshman. DeShawn didn't know for sure, but he thought Freddie had gotten mixed up in a gang—one of the local crews affiliated with the Bloods.

"Fuck, man," said Freddie. "You look like shit."

DeShawn had been avoiding the metal plates that served as mirrors in the bathrooms.

"What are you in for?" DeShawn asked.

Freddie shrugged. "Possession with intent. But what the *fuck*, man? What even happened? Was Malcolm, like, *doing* something?"

"No! I didn't do it, Freddie. No fucking way."

"I heard you confessed."

"*Bullshit,*" said DeShawn, almost shouting. "That cop lied to me. Got me all mixed up. I got an alibi! I was with my girl."

"Fucking cops will do anything to close a case," said Freddie. "But you up a creek, man. You got a lawyer?"

"No."

"They'll appoint one, but you gotta get your alibi together. They're not gonna play around on a triple murder. You should call Pastor Green. He helped me out some the first couple times I was in here. He might could help you get a better lawyer. Your girl talk to the cops yet?"

"I don't know. Her stepdad won't let her talk to me."

"You gotta get on that shit. Fast. Longer you stay in here, the easier it is for everybody outside to forget you. They all thinking you blew your family away! If you didn't do it, you need to call everybody you ever known. Get them to go to the cops. Get them to talk to your lawyer. Otherwise you'll just be another murderin' nigger that deserves the needle. You feel me?"

DeShawn felt him. And Freddie's talk woke him up. He called Glorious Gospel, and two days later, Pastor Redmond Green made the trip to Rikers.

"I didn't do it, Pastor Green," said DeShawn as soon as

they sat down. "You believe me, right? You gotta help me."

"The police have told me you confessed, DeShawn," said Pastor Green. "They've told me they have a witness who saw you running from the apartment, carrying a gun, late that night."

"They're lying!"

"You didn't confess?"

"No . . . I mean, that cop, he tricked me. I thought . . . he said they were gonna charge Ontario. He said . . ."

"Ontario? I don't think so, DeShawn. I think the best thing for you to do now is plead guilty and try to focus on getting right with the Lord. You can still be forgiven. You can still do some good. . . ."

"I didn't do it, Pastor Green. You gotta believe me. I *couldn't* do it. I love Malcolm and Sabrina. They've been nothing but good to me. . . ."

"I know *exactly* how good they were to you, DeShawn. And how good they were to Ontario, and Kenya, and anyone else who needed anything from them."

DeShawn remembers that Pastor Green's voice shook as he spoke, and that he had trouble making eye contact across the hard plastic table. The pastor had been part of DeShawn's life for more than a decade. DeShawn knew the inside of the little storefront that Glorious Gospel occupied as well as he knew his home. He knew the mop bucket and cleaning supplies tucked behind the plastic curtain in the shower stall; the art supplies in plastic bins in the storage closet; prayer books and hymnals stacked neatly atop the folding wooden shelves along the far wall of the pastor's tiny office. He knew that on Sunday morning, the sanctuary—which Malcolm told him had previously been a men's clothing store—would smell like coffee and cologne, until it began to smell like the sweat the worshipers leaked as they swayed and sang, rejoicing in Jesus Christ, the saving of their souls, the forgiveness of their sins.

"What about forgiveness," whispered DeShawn.

"Jesus forgives those who repent," said the pastor. "Are you ready to tell the truth?"

"I *am* telling the truth!" DeShawn slammed his hand down on the table, frustration and misery rising as rage inside him. How could Pastor Green think he was capable of murdering his family? What had he ever done but smoke some weed and swipe some cash? "I was with my girl! LaToya Marshall. Ask her! Please! I'm not lying!"

Pastor Green stood up.

"I'm sorry, Pastor Green . . ."

"You need to be a man now, DeShawn. You made your choices and now you need to live with them. Though, Lord knows I don't know how you will. Your church family will be here for you if you repent, but there is nothing we can do for you until you do."

When he got back to Brooklyn after visiting DeShawn, Pastor Green called his wife from the church office and told her he would not be home for dinner. For two hours, he sat in the creaky leather swivel chair and cried like a child. Redmond Green had been surrounded by violence his entire life. He had seen his father choke his mother into unconsciousness in the kitchen of their apartment on Throop Avenue. Had heard her head slam into walls and her arms and legs tumble over furniture behind the door of his parents' bedroom. He had watched his brothers and cousins join gangs and attack other boys in the neighborhood for walking on the wrong side of the street, collecting bats and chains and knives from school storage rooms and empty lots and kitchen drawers, suiting up for battle like soldiers before they could properly grow a mustache. Uprising and anger was everywhere: on the streets, in the schoolyard, on the news. Assassinations, riots, war. Redmond avoided it all as best he could. Enduring taunts about being bookish or a Goody Two-Shoes was nothing compared to the terror that the violence—its perpetrators and its victims—conjured inside him. Once, when he was nine or ten years old, he saw a man stab a woman on a street corner, just blocks from where he would later open Glorious Gospel. Other people saw it, too. He remembers the groan the woman emitted when the knife went into her stomach a second time. He remembers the blood; that it ran down her bare leg and onto the sidewalk. He remembers the way the people walking by barely paused as the man tore the life from her. And he remembers that once he got home, out of breath from the fear and the running, his mother told him to mind his own business, and that the woman probably deserved what she got.

When he was thirteen, Redmond's oldest brother was shot to death in Manhattan. At twenty-one, he watched his mother die of stomach cancer, coughing blood into handkerchiefs and water glasses at home because she refused to "be anybody's science experiment" in the hospital. Yet, after all of this, Redmond Green was not prepared for his best friend's murder. Malcolm Davis, the only son of a city bus driver and a homemaker, moved from Harlem to Crown Heights in 1970. He'd earned a scholarship to Hunter College and graduated with a degree in psychology, then found a job at the Boys & Girls Club in Flatbush. Redmond Green, who was working at the program and attending seminary at night, was the one who hired him. Malcolm was single, and at a Labor Day BBQ in Prospect Park, Redmond's then-fiancée, Barbara, introduced him to her childhood friend, Sabrina Carlyle. Sabrina was, as Barbara put it, "a prize," and Redmond knew he'd be in hot water if he encouraged an introduction to anyone who would break her heart or treat her wrong. But after a few months of working together, Redmond was convinced of Malcolm's good character. And he wasn't surprised when Malcolm and Sabrina were married less than a year after meeting. It was as close to love at first sight as he'd ever seen. Sabrina was confident and beautiful. Tall and slim and stylish, she did some modeling in high school but quit, Barbara told him, after one-too-many photographers asked her to model nude. Sabrina put herself through secretarial school and got a job with the city, hoping the stable profession would put her in a position to meet a reliable man. Because all Sabrina Carlyle had ever really wanted was a family of her own. Her father, a barber, died of a heart attack when she was eight. Her mother began drinking and didn't stop until her liver failed when Sabrina was seventeen. She lived alone in their Flatbush apartment for most of her senior year, skirting child welfare authorities until her eighteenth birthday. The money from modeling paid the rent, and she ate lunch at school and dinner at friends' houses. Sabrina used to tell Barbara how much she envied her noisy, full life, sharing two bedrooms with four siblings and two engaged, if harried, parents. When she wasn't pregnant a year after their wedding, Sabrina began to worry. After two years, she went to the doctor and discovered that she had an abnormally shaped uterus and would never bear children.

It was Redmond who suggested they apply to become foster parents.

"You don't have to make any long-term commitments," he said to Malcolm one Sunday after church service. The tiny flock he was assembling met in Red and Barbara's living room then. They didn't need much. Everyone had their own Bible, of course, and Barbara led songs on a Casio keyboard. Worship led to Bible study, which led to what Pastor Green called "community action." The congregation was mostly couples with young children looking for a church that preached a living gospel, a gospel that encouraged civic engagement. Pastor Green's parishioners weren't going to leave the fate of their community to the drug dealers or the police officers. They knew that they had to be organized and active to make a difference, and as they sipped Maxwell House and nibbled baked goods while the children napped, they discussed how to best focus their efforts. Everyone had a bugaboo: graffiti, prostitution, substandard housing, crumbling school buildings, easy access to drugs. They started small. One Sunday afternoon in May 1974, Pastor Green led about a dozen people with garbage bags and gardening gloves and sandwiches through St. John's Park, and together they picked up trash and passed out peanut butter and jelly to the men on benches and beneath trees. They repeated their mission each week, and the work brought the congregation closer to each other and to God. As the months and years passed, they named themselves Glorious Gospel and focused their efforts on improving the physical environment around their homes, and supporting and educating the next generation.

"I don't say this lightly, Malcolm," Redmond said. "But perhaps God has chosen you and Sabrina to be caretakers for children who are not your own. For children whose own parents cannot be parents."

Malcolm shook his head. "I don't know," he said. "Sabrina adores every child she sees. And they adore her. But I don't know if I can love somebody else's kid."

"I'm not saying it wouldn't be a challenge," said Redmond. "But I wouldn't suggest it if I didn't think you were capable. Think about it, will you? There are so many children in need, Malcolm. It would be a sin for two people as righteous and strong as you and Sabrina not to share your love."

Six months later, the Davises brought home their first foster child, a seven-year-old boy named Philip who was taken away from his mother when he arrived on the first day of first grade weighing less than a child half his age. The school called child welfare, and when social workers went to the boy's apartment they found bare cupboards, rat droppings, and three people packaging heroin into baggies in the kitchen. When they were approved as foster parents, Sabrina painted the spare bedroom mint green— suitable for boys or girls—and Malcolm assembled a bunk bed. But the Davises soon found that many of the children they opened their home to ended up sleeping in their bed, driven from sleep by nightmares and unable to soothe themselves. DeShawn had done the same when the Davises first took him in. And Kenya, of course.

Sitting in his office after visiting DeShawn at Rikers, Pastor Green couldn't help but wonder if he wasn't to blame for what happened to Malcolm and Sabrina and that beautiful, innocent little girl. He knew becoming foster parents would be difficult, but it never occurred to him that it would be dangerous. The Davises had been fostering for more than a decade when they brought

DeShawn home. He was six, and had been in a group home since watching his mother's boyfriend crush her skull with a cast-iron frying pan. The poor boy stayed with her body for three days before finally knocking on the neighbor's door when he ran out of food. Sabrina and Malcolm found him a therapist, and by fifth grade, he was reading at two years above grade level and playing third base for the neighborhood youth league. It took a while, but DeShawn blossomed into the kind of funny, caring kid Pastor Green imagined Malcolm and Sabrina would have created had God blessed them with their own children. But when DeShawn turned fifteen, things began to change. Malcolm and Sabrina had never parented a teenager. Most of the children they fostered were young and ended up back with their parents or a relative appointed by the courts. They decided to begin adoption proceedings when DeShawn was twelve. It took two years to find his father, and when they did, the man put up a stink. He wanted to see the boy, but missed every scheduled appointment. Finally, he demanded money to sign over parental rights. DeShawn pretended the man's machinations didn't bother him, but when his grades started dropping, Malcolm and Sabrina knew they were taking a toll. And this time, DeShawn was old enough to refuse the therapy they arranged for him.

Pastor Green blew his nose and filled a big glass of water in the church's bathroom, drank it down in front of the mirror. He had gone to the precinct and spoken with the Italian detective as soon as he learned they arrested DeShawn. He listened, mute, as the man told him a witness picked the boy he had known for ten years out of a lineup and that DeShawn had changed his story multiple times before finally confessing. When he got home that night, Barbara was in the living room with Abel and Dorothy Norris. They were planning the funeral, making lists of people to call, arranging for burial and flowers and agonizing over what would happen to Ontario. Redmond relayed what the detective told him, and they all held hands to pray. As they lay in bed that night, he and Barbara whispered in the dark. Should they have seen this coming? It wasn't unusual for teens to break away from the church—and their parents—as they struggled to forge their own identity. And it wasn't unusual for teens in Crown Heights to do some of the things DeShawn had been doing: smoking pot, skipping school, even stealing. But Malcolm hadn't said anything about DeShawn getting into fights. Where could this violence have come from? What could possibly have sparked such an insane slaughter? He knew Malcolm was frustrated with DeShawn, and concerned, but had he been afraid of the boy in his home? And would he have said anything if he was?

Pastor Green wasn't sure what he expected, seeing DeShawn at Rikers. He felt obligated to visit the boy, of course. He owed him that. And yes, perhaps he was hoping for some sort of explanation—as if there could be any reason to do what he had done. He expected, at least, that

DeShawn would show remorse. Beg forgiveness. Weep and shake and repent and wail that he'd smoked some of that crack that was everywhere and just gone crazy. What he really wanted was for DeShawn *not* to have done what the detective said he did. And yet, when the boy professed his innocence, Pastor Green could not believe him. Who else could have done this? Malcolm and Sabrina had no enemies.

CHAPTER FIFTEEN

At a little after noon on Saturday, my phone rings with a 917 number I don't recognize.

"Hi, it's Rebekah," I say.

"Rebekah, it's Ontario Amos. You came by my work a couple days ago."

"Hi, Ontario. How are you?"

"Tired. Listen, if you want to know what was going on with Malcolm and Sabrina, you should talk to the people at Glorious Gospel. Pastor Green's retired but he's still around. His son, Red Jr., is the pastor now. Him and Dorothy Norris probably knew them better than anybody."

I grab a pen. "Dorothy Norris?"

"She was the church secretary. She took me in for a little while, after."

"Are you in touch?"

"Not really," he says. "But I think she still lives in the same place."

"Would you mind giving me her address?"

"I'll give you her phone number," he says. "If you talk to her, tell her I said hello. Tell her I been meaning to call."

"I will."

"I been thinking a lot about that night since you came by. We spent the day in the park and I got a stomachache because I'd eaten a bunch of junk food. Cotton candy and popcorn and soda and stuff. Sabrina always read to me before bed, and that night I remember she sat with me and rubbed my belly, too. She was a real good mom. She was always patient. And we weren't easy, you know? I told you about Kenya. She would have these screaming nightmares. Wake everybody up. And I was really hyper. And DeShawn. I mean, he was always in a bad mood. Always saying mean stuff about Sabrina's cooking or something. Now that I got my own kids, I don't know how she put up with some of the shit we did when we weren't her blood."

"Was Malcolm that way, too?"

"Yeah. I remember feeling like I was really important 'cause I was in their family. Like, they'd picked me so I must be pretty, I don't know, almost special. I don't remember a lot. But I remember feeling that way."

I scribble what he's saying into my notebook.

"Have you thought any more about whether you think DeShawn might not have done it?" I ask.

"Yeah, but . . . I don't know. I didn't like him. I mean, I did at first. But by the time I was starting school he was making things real hard in the house. I remember

I tried to be really good. Helping Sabrina in the kitchen and cleaning up my room. I see it in my kids, too. When me and Tammy fight, they get all sweet. They just want calm, you know?"

"When we talked at your restaurant, you said DeShawn scared you. Did he ever threaten you? Did you ever see him, like, get violent?"

"No. He was just . . . unpredictable. Like I said, always in a bad mood."

Sounds like a teenager, I think. Or, I suppose, a murderer.

"Thanks for calling," I say. "I'll reach out to Pastor Green and Dorothy Norris."

"You really think DeShawn didn't do it?"

"I don't know," I say. I can't tell Ontario that half the reason I'm looking into his family's murders is that I need a project—and that my mother happens to be dating one of the cops who actually saw their bodies. "I think it's worth asking some questions."

The Web site for Glorious Gospel is impressive, with video elements and tabs for worship and Sunday school, events, prayer, and a newsletter. I click into the August newsletter and scan. At the corner of the second page is an advertisement for The Davis-Gregory Activism Fund. A short paragraph below reads:

The Fund in honor of Malcolm and Sabrina Davis, and Kenya Gregory, seeks donations and volunteers to further Glorious Gospel's mission

of peace and social justice in our community. For
more information on the Fund's current projects,
contact Pastor Green.

I call the main number for the church and a woman
answers.

"Glorious Gospel."

"Hi," I say. "My name is Rebekah Roberts and I am
a reporter with . . . the Center on Culture, Crime and
the Media. I'm working on an article about Malcolm and
Sabrina Davis and I was wondering if I could speak with
Pastor Green."

"The Center on what?"

"Culture, Crime and the Media," I say. "It's a non-profit
organization. I'm a freelancer. I also work for the *Trib*."

"All right. Let me see if I can find him. Can you hold?"

"Sure," I say.

Two minutes later: "This is Pastor Green. How can I
help you?"

"Hi, Pastor Green, thanks for taking my call. I'm
working on an article about the deaths of Malcolm and
Sabrina Davis, and their foster daughter." I decide not
to go into detail about my specific angle. "I was hoping
maybe I could speak to you—or your father, if he's available. Ontario Amos, the Davises' foster son, told me that
he and a woman named Dorothy Norris were close with
the Davises and that they were very kind to him after
their deaths."

"How is Ontario?"

"He's good," I say. "I don't know if you've read about it, but the restaurant where he cooks has gotten a lot of praise. And he's a dad."

"That's wonderful."

I wait. After a moment, he continues.

"What sort of information are you looking for?"

"I just wanted to get a sense of what kind of people they were. What things they were involved in. I saw the church has a memorial fund in their name. I'd love to learn about that."

"And you say you'd like to talk to my father and Dorothy Norris?"

"That's who Ontario suggested."

"Would your article make mention of the Davis Fund?"

"Um, sure," I say. "I could probably do that."

"It's not essential. But we're doing a lot of positive things. Your readers might be interested in getting involved."

"Totally," I say.

"I'll contact Mrs. Norris and my father to see if they're willing to talk to you. Of course, I can't promise anything."

"Of course," I say. "I really appreciate it."

Two hours later, Pastor Green calls and invites me to come to Glorious Gospel tomorrow at noon, after worship.

I take the R train from my apartment and transfer to the 3 at Atlantic Terminal. At the Kingston Avenue station

I climb the stairs up to the street and find myself at the corner of Eastern Parkway, and on the sidewalk in front of the World Headquarters of the Chabad-Lubavitch movement. I've spent almost two years reporting in the Hasidic world, but I don't know much about Chabad. I've heard them described as the evangelicals of the Jewish world. They wear the black hats and wigs like my mom's family in Borough Park, but aren't quite as insular or as contemptful of modern life. Their mission is to bring non-practicing Jews back into observance, so they routinely interact with people outside their sect. I actually follow a Chabad PR guy on Twitter. He posts a lot of inspirational quotes from Rebbe Menachem Schneerson—who died in the 1990s but is still their spiritual leader—and articles about the gentrification of Crown Heights. Apparently, just as the black and Latino and Chinese residents of Bushwick and Bed-Stuy and Sunset Park are being pushed out, the Jews of Crown Heights are finding it harder and harder to rent apartments in "their" neighborhood, too.

And indeed, here at the intersection of Eastern Parkway and Kingston Avenue, it's like an advertisement for the new Brooklyn melting pot: women in long skirts and flat shoes pushing strollers outside the Jewish Children's Museum; construction workers carrying drywall from a brownstone undergoing renovation (and, according to the sign out front, being offered for sale "exclusively" by Corcoran); a skinny white boy in pristine high-top sneakers carrying a leather satchel and sporting Beats by Dre headphones over his CROWN HEIGHTS ball cap; a black man with waist-length, half-gray dreadlocks selling water bottles out of a cooler; yeshiva students in black hats and pants, walking in packs; a modern Orthodox businessman talking into his Bluetooth headset; a light brown-skinned woman, bra-less and stunning in a maxi dress and gold jewelry, looking around and then down at her phone, lost apparently, hand over her eyes to shade the brutal sun. Bakeries and banks, cafés, cell phone stores, taquerías. I fucking love it, but living here doesn't come cheap. Iris and I looked at listings in Crown Heights last year when we were deciding whether to renew the lease on our shitty place in Gowanus: $2,500 for a two-bedroom walk-up; no laundry.

North of Eastern Parkway the black hats all but disappear. The bodegas advertise lottery tickets and beer instead of kosher food, and the rowhouses are far less pristine than those just a few blocks south. Glorious Gospel is a stone building on a corner lot. There is a gated playground on one side and a handful of parking spaces on the other. At my dad's church in Orlando, people wear flip-flops and shorts to Sunday service, but the men and women filing out here have put real effort into their appearance. Dresses, hats, heels, even suits on a day that's forecasted to reach a hundred degrees. I enter the door marked OFFICE and a woman behind a desk tells me to wait.

"Pastor Green should be here shortly," she says. "He always has a little coffee and some cookies after worship."

About ten minutes later the office door opens again and an impeccably dressed thirty-something man enters, followed by an older man and an older couple.

The youngest man extends his hand.

"You must be Rebekah," he says. "Pastor Redmond Green Jr."

"Nice to meet you," I say.

He takes out a key ring and unlocks an unmarked door, motions for us to enter. Inside is a small conference room: blue carpet, a dining room table and chairs.

We all sit down and Pastor Green makes the introductions.

"This is Dorothy and Abel Norris," he says. "And my father, Pastor Redmond Green Sr."

"Thank you all so much for taking the time to meet with me," I say. "As Pastor Green probably told you, I'm working on a possible article about Malcolm and Sabrina Davis. I spoke with Ontario Amos recently, and he said that if I wanted to know what was going on in their lives, you were the people to talk to."

Dorothy Norris is sitting up very straight at the edge of her chair, her elbows tucked to her chest and her hands folded on the table in front of her. Her gray-and-black hair is swept up from her face and cut short. I can picture her sleeping in pink foam curlers beneath a scarf like my grandma does, combing and fluffing each morning. Her dress is a tan-and-blue flower print with tiny buttons running from the prim collar to her shins. She wears a gold cross around her neck and small gold hoops in her ears. Pastor Green Sr. is in a gray striped suit with a blue tie. His hair is thinning, and mostly gray.

"I noticed you have a fund in memory of the Davises," I continue. "Maybe you could tell me a little about that?"

"The anniversary has just past," says Dorothy. "Is there some specific reason you're interested in this now?"

So much for my plan to ease in.

"Well," I say, "DeShawn Perkins wrote me a letter." Dorothy raises her eyebrows. Pastor Green Jr. makes a sniffing sound. "I'm sure you know that he says he didn't kill them."

"I believe the boy confessed," says Pastor Green Sr.

"Right," I say. "But he says he was coerced. He says the detective threatened him and that he was kept in the interrogation room for hours without an adult. He says he signed the paper because he just wanted to go home."

No response.

"What did you all think when you heard he'd been arrested?"

The people at the table exchange glances. After a few moments, Pastor Green Sr. speaks. "I think we were all surprised. But you have to understand, there was a lot of violence in our community then. It was a terrible time. People like Malcolm and Sabrina, they were working hard to provide stability and positivity for young people, but especially when the weather got hot and school let out, there was a lot of temptation to run wild."

"And how could you blame them, really," says Dorothy. "Most of the adults in the community were no better. Smoking crack in the middle of the street, shooting each other over nothing. Our little girl, Shirley. That same summer some woman mugged her on the way to summer camp. Stole an eleven-year-old's backpack! How can you even explain that to a child?"

"Had DeShawn been in trouble with the law before?"

"I believe he was arrested once or maybe twice," says Pastor Green Sr. "Marijuana, I think. Or it might have been stealing."

"I spoke with him over the phone a few days ago and he mentioned that his parents were getting threats."

"Threats?" says Pastor Green Jr.

"He said people—or someone—had been calling the house and hanging up. And he said he found a letter that said something like, 'I'm watching you.' He said that when he asked Malcolm about it he told him it was nothing, but that Sabrina was worried."

"Come to think of it," says Abel, "I think Malcolm did mention something about hang-ups. He was considering changing their number."

"You didn't tell me that," says Dorothy.

"Didn't I?"

"No!"

Abel turns his head toward his wife but doesn't make

eye contact. He is picking at his fingernails, leaning forward, legs spread wide. He wears a silver Medic Alert bracelet around one wrist.

"Did he say anything about who he thought might be doing it?" I ask.

"No," says Abel.

"What did the police say? About the phone calls."

Abel scratches his throat. "What do you mean?"

"You didn't tell the police?" asks Dorothy.

Abel looks down at his hands, plays with his wedding ring. "You were the only one they interviewed, Dorothy. I'm sure you remember I was taking care of the girls. And then Ontario came to stay. . . ."

He trails off, avoiding his wife's glare.

"So you weren't interviewed?" I ask, looking at Abel and the elder pastor. They shake their heads. "Did that seem odd? That the police didn't talk to people who were close with the victims?"

"Yes and no," says Pastor Green Sr. "They arrested DeShawn very quickly. And once they had a confession, and that witness, I suppose they thought—we all thought—they had their man."

"Did any of you know the witness?"

Head shakes all around.

"Were you at the trial?"

"We all went," says Pastor Green Sr. "We felt it was important to represent the victims in the courtroom."

"Do you think DeShawn got an adequate defense?"

There is a pause, then Dorothy speaks up. "I'm not sure we're qualified to say. We were mostly concerned with Ontario, to be honest. I'm just speaking for myself here, but when word got around that he confessed, and that there was a witness . . . well, that's pretty convincing, isn't it? I never thought of DeShawn as violent, but what happened to Malcolm and Sabrina and little Kenya was just so shocking. I remember thinking that if he was really innocent he would have asked for our help. He would have shouted it to the rooftops."

"He told me he wanted to testify but that his lawyer said it was a bad idea."

I wait for a response but there is none. Every person in the room is grimacing.

"Was there anything else Malcolm and Sabrina were involved in that might have made people angry?"

"They were involved in a lot," says Pastor Green Sr. "We all were. Trying to keep the community safe. Turn it back into a place people might actually be proud to call home. It's hard to say it now, but I voted for Giuliani the first time he ran. I thought his idea about cracking down on the so-called 'quality of life' crimes was a good one. Public urination and turnstile jumping and what have you. If we don't show our children that we respect our neighborhood, how can we expect them to behave? Malcolm and Sabrina helped with sweep-up Sundays. After worship we'd take brooms and garbage bags and try to clean things up a little. If a business had a broken window or some graffiti they wanted help with, we'd make that the day's mission.

"Of course there were bigger things, too. We worked against the gangs. We had midnight marches through some of the nearby housing projects that used to make some people angry. And the Crown Heights Alliance."

"What was that?"

"I'm sure you've read about the riots?"

I nod. I've heard the term "Crown Heights Riots," of course, but I really only have a vague sense that it involved a clash between black and Jewish neighbors and took place around the same time as the Rodney King riots in Los Angeles.

"It was an ugly time," continues Pastor Green Sr. "There was a lot of hatred. A lot of misunderstanding. Glorious Gospel and a few other congregations began a monthly dialogue session with some of the Lubavitchers. It was informal. We were trying to find common cause."

"How did that work out?"

"It wasn't particularly well-attended, on either side," he says, looking at Abel. "But it was very important to me. It's so easy for people to forget their history. All Christians were once Jews. And the Jews were on our side during the civil rights struggles."

"Different kinds of Jews," says Abel quietly.

Pastor Green Sr. runs his hands over his pants and inhales through his nose.

"No one came out of those riots looking good," he says. "It was a black eye for everyone. And I was not going to sit by and watch my community burn to the ground because grown people were too stupid and angry to see common humanity in someone who looks different from them."

"It's not just that they look different . . ." begins Abel.

"Abel, I'm not getting into this with you."

Dorothy puts her hand on her husband's leg.

"Many of us thought it was important to channel the anger everyone was feeling into something positive," says the senior pastor.

"But not everyone agreed," I say.

"That's not unusual," says Pastor Green Jr., scooting up toward the table. "And frankly, this isn't the time for airing these past squabbles. Even today, there are disagreements about the priorities of the Davis Fund, as there are with many church priorities. Dad, I don't think Malcolm was even particularly involved in the dialogue sessions, was he?"

"Well, he wasn't opposed."

"Red," says Dorothy, "Abel wasn't opposed, either."

"He could have fooled me."

"Okay," says the current pastor. "Let's move on, shall we? Ms. Roberts, is there anything else we can help you with?"

I want to keep on friendly terms with these people, so I decide it's probably time to go.

"I think I'm good for now," I say. "I'm not certain where this story is going to lead, but I really appreciate your time."

I write my name and phone number on two pieces of paper and give one to Dorothy and one to the senior pastor. His son stands and walks me out.

"My father and the Norrises were very close to Malcolm and Sabrina," he says. "The murders really devastated them. Off the record, I think they feel some guilt for not seeing what DeShawn was capable of."

"Did you know him at all?"

"A little," he says. "He's a couple years older than me, and he stopped coming to church about a year before they died. Malcolm and Sabrina used to drag him along, but he made a scene during one of the Sunday sweep-ups and I think they decided it wasn't worth it anymore."

"What kind of scene?"

"We were picking up trash and he threw an empty beer bottle at Sabrina. I think he just meant to have her put it in her trash bag, but he threw it hard. She ducked and it shattered on somebody's car."

"Do you think he was actually aiming at her?"

"I have no idea," he says. "I just remember everybody was really upset and DeShawn got all defensive and ran off. We went to different schools, so I didn't see him much after that. My mom thought he was a bad influence."

"What did you think when you heard they'd arrested him?"

"It scared me. There were a lot of rumors about him being in a gang, and I got the idea that the gang might go after my dad. I don't know why. I don't think I slept for a month."

"What gang was this?"

"I don't know. I don't think he actually was in a gang. I think people were just trying to make sense of how a kid—I mean, he was sixteen—a kid could do something that horrible. Later on, I heard he was angry because they'd taken in another child. And then I heard he'd gotten kicked out of school and Malcolm was going to send him to a group home. I have no idea what was really true. But none of it explained why he'd murder them all."

"Do you think it's possible that maybe he didn't do it?"

Redmond Jr. takes off his glasses and rubs his eyes. "It's not something I've thought much about. But yes, of course it's possible." He puts his glasses back on. "Lord knows we've see a lot of young black men falsely accused, even now. We had a parishioner whose son was arrested for allegedly stealing an iPhone last year. Fortunately, the congregation was able to raise the money for his bail, but so many others just get stuck in Rikers. The DA dropped the charges. It makes me sick to think that DeShawn's been in prison all this time if he didn't do it. And if it wasn't him, there's someone out there who shot an entire family in their bed. What else has he done?"

CHAPTER SIXTEEN

Afternoon
July 6, 1992
Crown Heights, Brooklyn

Saul found out about the lineup from one of the officers at the precinct.

"Your witness ID'd the son," said Officer Kevin Whitlock. "Kid confessed."

It was 3:00 P.M. Saul was scheduled for a 4–12. He could have come in early for the lineup, but no one called.

"When did this happen?"

"Just a couple hours ago." Whitlock was on desk duty because he had failed to secure his weapon properly and it went clattering to the ground as he ran after a robbery suspect last week. He lost the suspect, his dignity—a group of kids on lunch break from the nearby junior high saw the whole thing—and got demoted to desk work.

"Who took it?" asked Saul.

"Olivetti. I think that's his second confession this week. I should start a pool to see if he can top April. What was that? Six?"

"I don't keep track," said Saul. They'd done it all

without him. He felt himself going sour with anger, as if curdled milk were running through his veins. There had been so many days of feeling so utterly unmoored since he left the community. And yet he had almost always managed to maintain a kind of distance from what he knew his family and former friends were thinking of him, saying about him. He saw the other former Hasids he met at Coney Island come and go, sorrow and bitterness their only guide as they wandered lost and alone through a world they did not understand. Saul once told a group that had gathered for a Shabbos meal that holding on to anger and sadness was like building their new life upon sand. It could only crumble and be washed away. He took pride in re-creating his own life on the solid bedrock of police work; he was a peace officer, a guardian, a problem solver. His new identity gave him self-worth and that— not the hole in his heart that Binyamin's absence created; not the holidays and weekends and nights spent alone; not the weeping phone calls from his mother or the diffi- culty finding camaraderie with his colleagues—was what would forge the foundation of his future. But if his fellow officers didn't even respect him enough to loop him in on a lineup with his own witness, what kind of foundation was it, really? He walked past Whitlock and the detec- tives' desks, seeing the family photos of smiling wives and children looking at their uniformed fathers as if they were superheroes. He'd missed a significant morning in a sig- nificant case, and it was difficult not to dive headfirst into resentment and animus. So difficult it made him shiver.

"The rabbi returns!" said Olivetti when Saul found him in the precinct's break room with another detective, Paul Amodino. Saul knew some of his colleagues called him "rabbi" behind his back. He tried not to hate them for it.

"DeShawn confessed?"

"Sure did," said Olivetti. "Didn't have much of a choice after your witness fingered him."

"Where is he now?"

"The kid? Rikers."

"Have you talked to the ADA?"

"She's on her way."

"She?" Saul had only ever encountered male prosecutors.

"The new star," said Olivetti, not even trying to hide his disdain. "Sandra Michaels. She's one of those feminists they brought in for sex crimes. Affirmative action hire. One hundred percent."

"You want me to set up the chair?" asked Amodino.

"Perfect."

The "chair" was how some in the precinct referred to a seat beside a particular desk along the far wall and just below the one air-conditioning vent in the squad room. The vent blew cold air straight down, and some of the men thought it was amusing to sit an attractive woman there on hot days and hope her nipples made an appearance. Almost to a man, his colleagues spoke openly, and crassly, about sex, something Saul was unaccustomed to. Frum couples had sex, of course, but he never spoke about his body, or his wife's body, with anyone. As a child, in yeshiva, there was some talk, and yes, he had more than once encountered the gauzy, baffling photographs in a friend's stolen skin magazine. But it was all surreptitious; undoubtedly forbidden. At the precinct, officers taped naked and half-naked photographs of women inside their lockers. Even when female officers were around, the men bragged and teased constantly. He never joined in, and people noticed. It was yet another way he stood out.

While he waited for the ADA, Saul went outside to smoke, something he had begun doing occasionally. Half the time he didn't inhale, but he liked the way he felt holding a cigarette: serious, perhaps even a little dangerous. If the yarmulke set him apart from his fellow cops, the cigarette, he imagined, helped him blend in.

He was about to go back inside when he saw Naftali Rothstein get out of a cab across the street. Rothstein and Saul had not known each other growing up. Rothstein was a Lubavitcher, while Saul's family was Belz and lived in Borough Park. Like many haredi, Saul found the Lubavitchers odd. They wore short jackets, spoke English instead of Yiddish, and stood around the city on street corners asking clearly unobservant people if they are Jewish. He had to give them credit, however, for their tenacity. And since working in Crown Heights alongside members of the Chabad movement, he'd come to admire their general willingness to extend themselves for those outside their community—a trait Saul believed was in too short supply among haredi.

Saul also admired their practicality. Since the 1960s, the ballooning Lubavitch population—made up of survivors of the Holocaust and Soviet oppression, and their offspring—understood the importance of cultivating trust with the police. Most officers and even the top brass had little love for their ways, but because the sect wanted to keep their people safe from the street violence that had become as commonplace as gum on the sidewalk— and keep official eyes averted from issues they wished to handle inside the fold—a hand was extended, and relationships formed. Rothstein worked in the Crown Heights Jewish Council's nascent media office crafting press releases about events major and minor—the beating of two yeshiva students from Israel by "neighborhood thugs"; the dedication of a child-care center. He completed the Citizens Police Academy and signed up for a monthly ride-along, usually to the chagrin of those tasked with having him in their backseat. He was also one of those pressuring the NYPD's recruitment officers to invite Jews to the academy, so when Saul graduated, Rothstein introduced himself. Although most Lubavitchers lived in the vicinity of the 71st precinct, after the riots Rothstein began coming around to the 77th, the precinct where Saul was stationed and that policed the predominately black area north of Eastern Parkway. He told Saul that he believed a presence there would be helpful in the ongoing quest to have the community's voice and situation understood by the outside world—especially since that outside world was just blocks away. The more police saw Jews as people worth protecting, the better, Rothstein reasoned. And in the past year, his face had become a familiar one around the precinct.

"Saul!" said Rothstein as the cab drove away.

Saul raised his hand in greeting and crushed the unsmoked half of his cigarette beneath his shoe. The men shook hands. Sweat dripped down Rothstein's brow, dampening his thin black beard. Saul ran his hand along his own face, thankful it was no longer covered in fur.

"You must be trying to lose weight standing here in the sun!" said Rothstein. "Don't tell me the air conditioning is out inside?"

"Just taking a break," said Saul. "You are well?"

Naftali sighed. "Zelda took the children to the country last weekend. I should have gone with her."

"Why didn't you?"

"I should have!"

Rothstein had a habit of not quite answering questions posed to him.

"Please," said Rothstein, shading his eyes from the sun. "Talk inside?"

Saul did not mind Rothstein—he found the hyper little man's attempts to ingratiate himself with officers and commanders irritating at times, but appreciated his desire to educate himself about the challenges of policing Crown Heights. What he did not like, however, was being called "rabbi," and it seemed to Saul that each time he was seen with Rothstein the nickname spread further, dug deeper.

Saul followed Rothstein through the front doors of the precinct and up the stairs into the waiting room. Rothstein took off his wide-brimmed hat and fanned his face, pulled a bit at the chest of his white oxford shirt.

"Terrible thing about that family on Troy Avenue. Some days I think perhaps the neighborhood is turning around. And then something like that happens. A little girl!" He shakes his head. "There has been an arrest?"

Saul nodded again. He could hear Olivetti laughing from behind the swinging door that led to the detectives' desks.

"Something to do with gangs? Drugs?"

"Looks like a family problem. We brought the teenage son in. A witness picked him out of a lineup. And we got a confession."

Saying the words made the whole scenario seem more plausible. Most homicide victims were killed by someone they knew. Stash houses were dangerous to bust in on because the people inside tended to be armed, but domestics could be just as risky. Angry husbands and girlfriends and even children went at officers and each other with kitchen knives and baseball bats and all manner of household objects, propelled by years of dysfunction or shame so overwhelming they could barely control themselves. Was it really so far-fetched to think a kid like DeShawn could kill his foster family? They weren't even his blood.

Rothstein made a clucking nose and shook his head. "Every little bit you do, Saul. Every little bit. It makes a difference."

Saul didn't respond, and once Rothstein stopped sweating, he bid his fellow yid farewell, and wandered into the back of the precinct to find the shift commander.

Sandra Michaels was greeted by whistles in the squad room. Like any sane person, she'd taken her jacket off, exposing a high-collared but sleeveless blouse. Olivetti made a big show of pulling out a chair for her, and while she dug into her briefcase, he coughed, prompting snickers from everyone else in the room. She blushed, then looked at her armpits.

"It's fucking brutal out there," she said.

Of course, the men weren't snickering at the wet half-moons beneath her arms, they were looking at her nipples.

"*Brutal,*" said Olivetti.

Sandra fanned herself with her hand and pointed her face up toward the vent.

"Thank God for AC," she said.

"Thank *God,*" said Olivetti.

Sandra wasn't stupid. She knew she was being laughed at—she just didn't know why. Saul watched her eyes scan the room, looking for a clue, then hardening. Back to business.

"What do you have for me?" she asked.

Olivetti set a thin file in front of her and explained that it contained DeShawn's confession, as well as statements from Henrietta Eubanks, Dorothy Norris, and the Davises' neighbor.

"Should be a slam-dunk," he said.

Sandra glanced through the documents. "Was an adult present while he was being questioned?"

"You mean other than me?" asked Olivetti.

"You know what I mean, Detective."

"Well, Ms. Michaels, he *murdered* his foster parents. So, no, they weren't available to hold his hand while he cried about it."

"Could be a problem at the trial," she said.

"If anyone can convict him, Sandra, it's you."

The men in the squad room snickered again and Sandra Michaels stood up.

"I'll be in touch," she said, and walked what must have felt like many, many steps to the door.

Not fifteen minutes after that, the desk sergeant hollered for Olivetti.

"You back on rotation?"

"Yup."

"Congratulations," said the sergeant. He handed over a piece of paper with an address on it. "Stabbing on Park Place. One dead, one likely."

And they were off. Malcolm, Sabrina, and little Kenya now yesterday's victims. Their deaths just three more in the city's annual homicide count. DeShawn just another collar.

CHAPTER SEVENTEEN

Night
July 7, 1992
Bushwick, Brooklyn

He came through with the money: one thousand, cash. As usual, he arrived on foot. Hunny watched him walk up the block from the subway at the corner of Gates Avenue. Or at least that's where she figured he was coming from. She had no idea where he lived, if he owned a car, had a family. For all she knew he sunk into the center of the earth when he left and popped back up on their nights together.

He set the money on the sofa and told her to watch as he undressed, then instructed her, as usual, to fold his clothing and set the pile on the coffee table. They did it there in the living room, she bent forward over the sofa and him behind, barely making a sound. The bedsheet curtains she'd nailed above the windows billowed in the hot air. After he finished she went to the bathroom to clean herself, and when she opened the door he was standing, still naked, with a handgun pointed at her face.

"I should kill you now," he said. He pushed the barrel

against her forehead, then drew it down, over her nose, and pushed it into her mouth. She tasted blood. Was there blood on the gun? Or was it her own? The barrel felt bigger than it looked. Her jaw locked around it. She'd lost two teeth that year and remembered hoping, ridiculously, that the hard steel wouldn't knock loose any more. It was difficult to see his face with her mouth spread wide, head tilted back, her eyes beginning to water. She felt a little bit of urine run hot down the inside of her leg.

They stood there, both naked and sweating, for what seemed to Hunny like a very long time. She thought about Gina finding her with her head blown open in the bathroom. She wondered if he'd leave the money and, if so, whether Gina would use any of it to bury her. Her jaw began to tremble. Could it actually come unhinged? Saliva built up in her mouth and her tongue tried to swallow, closing off the back of her throat. She gagged, pulling air in through her nostrils, feeling the wet snot and tears begin to leak out and slide down her face.

"I should kill you," he said again. He pulled the gun from her mouth. She coughed and wiped her face with her forearm, her eyes wide, searching his face for a sign of what to do next. Beg? Run? But he was no longer looking at her. She stood as still as she could manage while he dressed, and when he was finished he came to her again, putting the gun beneath her chin this time. He dropped down the safety with his thumb.

"I won't be far," he said.

He let himself out, and she ran to the window, watching as he walked back toward Gates.

For years after, she saw him in the profiles of men on the street, on the subway. She'd catch a glimpse and taste the metal in her mouth. It was never him. Or, if it was, he passed without a word or a glance. But the sightings took their toll. In the more than twenty years between the summer day he walked out of her door to the summer day he walked back in, she never once felt safe.

CHAPTER EIGHTEEN

On Monday morning, while waiting for my assignment, I call Amanda and fill her in on what I learned from the people at Glorious Gospel.

"Have you talked to DeShawn yet?" she asks.

"Over the phone."

"Do you think he's full of shit?"

"No," I say. "But I guess I don't know if I'd know, you know?"

"So, what's your next move?"

"I need to try to find the witness. It's a long shot, but maybe if she's less sure now that could be something. The issue is that she hasn't lived at the address I got from the *Trib* library for years."

"Did they run a national search?"

"I don't know. I guess I assumed so."

"It's not much more effort, but you have to click a couple more boxes to get non–New York info. Ask them to run it again. If they can't find it let me know, I've got some database access through the Center. You gotta find that witness. If she tells a different story now, that's a game changer."

After we hang up I e-mail the library and have them run a national search on Henrietta Eubanks. Fifteen minutes later they send me a phone number and address in Atlantic City, New Jersey. I tell Iris and she decides it's the perfect excuse for a weekend road trip.

"I'm not officially on assignment," I say. "We'll have to pay."

Iris opens her laptop. "I just saw a Groupon for Atlantic City. They're practically giving rooms away." *Click-click-click* and she finds it. "One hundred fifty bucks for two nights at a hotel called The Coastal. We'll get a Zipcar and I can just wait outside while you interview her. I'll be, like, security."

I can't be sure Henrietta is still at the address from the library, but I have better luck getting people to talk to me when I show up in person than when I'm just a voice on the telephone. Plus, Atlantic City could be fun.

"You could invite your mom," Iris says when I hand her my credit card to enter into Groupon.

"My mom?"

"It might be fun. When was the last time you saw her?"

It's been a while. Months, I think. We had brunch in Park Slope one Sunday back in . . . April? May? When we finally met last year, I initially felt relief. It was like I'd been squinting at her all my life, and now she was in focus and I couldn't stop staring. Everything I learned about her was thrilling, and I was ready to forgive. She's endured a lot—being homeless in Maryland, friendless in Israel, shunned by her Brooklyn family, caring for her troubled brother—but instead of these experiences turning her into a gutsy free spirit, Aviva is conservative in middle age, even a little cowed. She leads a quiet life and seems almost allergic to attention. I know she was invited to join the interfaith nonprofit some of the people in and around Roseville established after the shooting. The goal was to create a foundation for understanding between the haredi and their upstate neighbors, and they reached out to a lot of people like Aviva who had left the ultra-Orthodox world. But she never went to a meeting. When I asked her about it, she wrinkled her nose. *They have lots of important people. They do not need me.* I tried to convince her that her experience in both worlds could be valuable, but I got the sense that she didn't think she deserved to have her voice heard. I felt bad for her until I realized that she was judging me for thinking that I do. At that last brunch I told her about a story I was reporting on a West Village landlord who planned to tear down a hundred-and-fifty-year-old tavern to build luxury condos.

"She's totally dodging my calls," I'd said, finishing my mimosa. "And she won't even admit she owns the building. It's all hidden behind an LLC."

"If she does not want to talk to you, why do you keep calling her?"

"What do you mean?"

"If she owns the building she can do whatever she wants."

"She *can*. But it's fucked up. F. Scott Fitzgerald used to drink at this place. And Dorothy Parker. It's history. The neighbors want to preserve it. And the last thing we need is more condos for rich people."

Aviva raised her eyebrows.

"What?"

"Nothing. It would make me very uncomfortable is all."

"What would make you uncomfortable?"

"Bothering people."

"I'm not *bothering* her. I'm trying to get her to admit the truth. That's the whole point of my job. If nobody asks people doing shady stuff to explain . . ." I stopped myself. Aviva was no longer listening; she signaled for the check.

"We've only got one hotel room," I tell Iris. "Three people is too much. And I seriously doubt she's into gambling."

Iris does not say that neither of us are into gambling, either, which is true. She's made her point, and she knows when to stop pushing.

I pick up the Zipcar—a sapphire blue Kia Rio—after my shift on Friday and meet Iris on Canal, a couple blocks from the clogged entrance to the Holland Tunnel. Traffic leaving the city is monstrous, but a few miles out we're doing sixty. After about two hours, the highway becomes a boulevard lined by crab shacks and board rentals and fishing charters. The air is cooler and the breeze smells of seagulls and sand.

"There it is!" says Iris, pointing to the glass towers rising in front of us. Atlantic City looks a lot more impressive from afar than up close. Half the storefronts along the first street we turn down are boarded up, and more people on the sidewalks are pushing shopping carts than pulling luggage.

The plan is to door-knock at Henrietta's in the morning, so we drive straight to the hotel. The pink neon sign outside and lobby décor (zebra-striped pillows on white leather settees) attempt to convey a kind of art-deco look, but the effort is half-assed. The king-sized bed in our room has an enormous pink pleather headboard that rises halfway to the ceiling. Our window looks out over the parking garage.

Iris pops the bottle of prosecco I picked up at the wine store down the block from us in Gowanus, and I take a glass into the shower with me. We blow-dry and I borrow a Rag & Bone dress Iris got at a sample sale, then we stroll the boardwalk, lose a few dollars at the slot machines, and spend two hours at a "lounge" sipping cocktails, munching on coconut shrimp and fried calamari, people-watching, and occasionally getting up to dance. Just after midnight, I yawn and Iris laughs.

"We're so old!"

"Sorry," I say.

"Honestly, I'm ready to go, too."

The next morning, we turn the Rio into the parking lot outside a two-story apartment building about a mile off the main drag. Half a dozen children run around, spraying each other with water guns, squealing and shouting. Two women sit on the curb, drinking from giant 7-Eleven mugs, watching the children and chatting. Spanish music pumps into the air from the open window behind them.

"The library printout said it was apartment eight," I say as I turn off the engine.

"I might fall asleep," she says. "But I'll turn my ringer up loud. Call if you need anything. Or scream."

"I'll be fine."

I climb the concrete exterior staircase and knock on door eight. I see movement at the peephole, and then a woman's voice.

"Who is it?"

I hate introducing myself from behind a door. "Hi," I say. "My name is Rebekah Roberts. I'm sorry to bother you. Do you have a minute?"

"I don't need any subscriptions."

"No," I say. "I'm not . . . I'm a reporter. I'm looking for a woman named Henrietta Eubanks."

A pause, and then I hear the dead bolt turn. The woman who opens the door is wearing black pants and a black polo shirt with TRUMP TAJ MAHAL embroidered on the breast pocket.

"Hi," I say. "Are you Henrietta Eubanks?"

"How'd you get this address?"

"I . . . just looked it up. It's pretty easy nowadays."

"What you want?"

She's not angry, which is nice. Just suspicious.

"Sorry, are you Henrietta Eubanks?"

"I was. I go by Day now. Henrietta Day."

"Oh. Okay. But you used to live in Brooklyn?"

"What's this about?"

"I'm looking into an old case, from 1992, in New York."

"A case?"

"A homicide. Three people shot in their home in Crown Heights. You testified that you saw their son leave the house that night."

Henrietta's mouth falls open slightly, and she flinches, almost as if I've come at her physically.

"I was wondering if I could ask you a few questions."

For a moment, Henrietta just stares at me. It's hard to tell how old she is. Fifty, maybe? She has a long face, so oval it's practically rectangular, and a mole above her left eyebrow. I sense she's about to slam the door, and am ready to blurt out *Are you sure it was DeShawn you saw that night?* but instead she steps back, inviting me inside.

The tiny apartment looks more like a motel suite than a home. The sofa, eating table, bed, and kitchen—a sink and a mini-fridge with a hot plate atop it—all share the same space. The only interior door is for the bathroom.

Henrietta takes a pack of Merit cigarettes from the kitchen table and lights one, then stands silent, arms crossed below her heavy breasts, looking at her bare feet.

"So," I say, "I've been working on a story about the murder of Malcolm and Sabrina Davis, and a little girl, in Crown Heights back in 1992. I guess you were a witness?"

Henrietta brings her cigarette to her lips, and I can see that she is trembling. She takes a shallow pull, then sits down at the little table. I sit, too.

"That was a long time ago," she says, the words coming through her teeth.

"I know," I say. "And I'm really sorry to bug you. I got a letter from DeShawn Perkins. He's the boy—well, man, now—that got convicted." I pause to see if she recognizes his name. Her lips pull back slightly. It's not a grimace so much as a brace. Like: what next? Hit me. Make it quick. "He insists he didn't kill his family. I know lots of people in prison say they didn't do it, but he didn't have any history of violence. I talked to one of his lawyers who said she thought the evidence against him was weak. And his girlfriend swears he was with her all night. She says the cops got her confused and the prosecutors didn't believe her."

Henrietta's face seems as though it is actually losing surface area. It's almost like she is shrinking as I speak. Her cigarette burns between her fingers, her eyes are unfocused.

"But obviously, your ID was pretty convincing," I say, slowly, not wanting to sound accusatory. "I guess I just wanted to know if you ever had any second thoughts about whether it was him you saw."

Henrietta puts her barely smoked cigarette out into a Taj Mahal ashtray, crushing it over and over, continuing to press it into the hard plastic long after the ember is extinguished. Smashing it for so long the white wrapping paper tears and what's left of the threads of tobacco inside spill out.

"Who you work for?" she asks.

"I'm freelance."

"What you mean?"

"I write for a few different places. The *New York Tribune*. A magazine called *American Voice* . . ."

"The *Trib*?" She almost smiles. "I miss that shit. But I definitely don't want to be in the *Trib*."

"Okay," I say. "We can talk off the record."

She furrows her brow, considering something.

"You recording this?"

"No," I say. "Totally off the record right now."

She nods, stares at the ruined cigarette. Finally, she says, "I didn't see nothing."

"What?"

"I didn't see nothing."

"I don't understand. You picked DeShawn out of a lineup, right?"

She nods.

"But you *didn't* see him coming out of the house that night?"

She shakes her head. "I didn't see nothing."

"I'm sorry, I don't mean to keep repeating, but, like, how did you pick him out then? Your statement said . . ."

"I lied."

"You lied? About seeing him?"

"I wasn't even in Crown Heights that night. I was up in Williamsburg with my roommate."

I stare at her a moment, my mouth open, my heart beating in my ears.

"Did. . . ? But . . . you testified . . ."

"I lied, okay."

"Can I ask you why?"

"None of this is going in your paper."

"Right," I say, thinking: how can I get this in the paper? "We're off the record."

"I had a trick," she says. "He paid me a lot of money to say I saw somebody running out of the house."

"He told you to pick DeShawn?"

"No," she says. "He just said to say I was there and saw a black guy running out."

"Why did you choose DeShawn in the lineup?"

She shrugs. "I was waiting in the precinct and they brought him in in handcuffs. I figured, you know, he'd done something."

I pause, not wanting to seem too enthusiastic.

"I know you don't want this in the paper," I say. "But, what about going to the DA? DeShawn retracted his confession. I think the only real evidence they had against him was your ID. He's been in prison for more than twenty years. You could get him out."

Henrietta pulls another cigarette from her pack. She looks at it between her fingers, twists it, brings it to her lips, lowers it.

"I'm sorry about that boy," she says. "It may not look like much in here, but this place, this job I got, this is more than I ever thought I'd have, okay? I been clean almost eight years. I got a church. I got a man, even."

The air-conditioning unit below the front window clicks on, blowing the thick curtains above it. I look at her and she looks at her cigarette. I suppose she doesn't have to explain. Even if they can't—or won't—prosecute her for making false statements, DeShawn could sue her and take everything she has. I decide that, for now at least, it's not my place, nor would it be effective, to try to convince her to "do the right thing"—because there are probably a lot of ways that it's not the right thing for her. I try another tactic.

"This trick," I say, "do you think he was involved in the murders?"

"I mean, I never *asked*, but yeah, obviously. That's what I thought."

"Are you still in touch with him?"

"Fuck no."

"Is he why you changed your name?"

"Partly. I had a felony record. Couldn't get no straight work. Not even cleaning rooms. So I can't be in the paper.

I'll lose my job. Probably go back to prison on some paperwork shit."

"Do you know if he's still in Brooklyn?"

"I don't think so. He used to send me postcards. Before I moved."

"Where were the postcards from?"

"A bunch of different places. Florida. Chicago. Boston."

"Is there anything you remember about him that you could tell me?"

"He was Jewish."

"Jewish?"

"You know, one of those guys with the black hats."

PART 2

CHAPTER NINETEEN

The first uniform he wore was for football. His mother signed him up for Pop Warner when they were still living in Fullerton. He put on the big plastic shoulder pads, and the jersey with the number, and the shoes with the blunt spikes, and he thought: this is who I am now. I am a Wildcat. He liked the fangs on the red and orange mascot and he wore the jersey to bed and to school so that the other kids would see and know. In school, everyone had their "thing." Some of the girls carried baby dolls and pretended to be moms. Boys aligned themselves with professional sports teams or players that they imagined matched their personality: the more aggressive liked the Detroit Pistons; the preppies liked the Chicago Bulls. Even the teachers had costumes. Mrs. Ellis wore silver rings on all her fingers. Mr. Williams had a thick mustache he dyed orange for Halloween and pink for Easter. Mrs. Ito exposed her toes in Birkenstocks no matter the season. His father's Ford Mustang, his mother's diamond earrings, his sister Jessica's stupid blue eyeliner—they were advertisements, he understood. They signaled membership in a group of like people.

The boys in the Wildcats weren't really like him, but they had a common goal and a common language, and that was enough for a while. He ran fast and hit hard, and his teammates and coaches cheered him on, patted him on the back, said "atta boy." He liked that. If he knew what people expected, he performed well.

The anger was always there, though, and there wasn't always someplace to put it. He was nine when he clamped his hand around Jessica's throat after dinner, pressing her into the wall of the bathroom they shared and squeezing, telling her in a steady voice that if she told anyone that he was still wetting the bed he could put a pillow over her head in the middle of the night and she would never wake up. He'd come up with the idea for the pillow when he pressed his own into his face the night before, nearly suffocating himself to silence the screams. If he hadn't screamed he knew he would explode. But if everyone heard the screams he would have to explain. *What's wrong?* It was not always a question he had an answer to.

His displays of aggression were never public. Other boys got into playground fights, sloppily swinging at one another, sweating and shouting, red faced, clothing askew. He cringed when he saw those fights, embarrassed for the boys who rendered themselves so clumsy and out of control. Did they think they were scaring anyone? Did they think their careless display did anything but reveal their weakness?

His father got the job at USC in July and their move to Los Angeles was rushed. He missed football tryouts and had to start seventh grade in a new school knowing no one. On the first day, he sat down alone near the back corner in science class, and a boy wearing a yarmulke took the seat next to him.

"I'm Ethan," said the boy.

"I'm Joe," he said. "I'm Jewish, too."

Ethan smiled.

"What shul do you belong to?"

"Shul?"

"Synagogue."

"You mean temple? I don't know. We just moved here." Joe's family went to temple once a year, on Yom Kippur. His sister complained that it was boring, but Joe didn't mind. He liked the way the Hebrew sounded, and he liked that he got to wear the little satin hat and she didn't. He'd never seen anyone wear one outside of temple, though.

"You should come to our shul," said Ethan. "It's cool."

When he got home, he told his parents he knew what temple they should join.

"I don't think so," said his mother when he said the name.

"Why not?"

"That's an Orthodox temple," she said. They were

eating dinner at the dining room table, boxes piled around them. Dinner was important in the Weiss family. His mother, Nora, read books about raising children and believed that eating dinner together helped create a strong family and healthy children. The meals weren't fancy, or particularly tasty—macaroni and cheese, fish sticks, tacos, spaghetti—but she made an effort seven nights a week.

"My friend Ethan goes there. He said it was cool."

"Temple is not cool," said Jessica. She was so predictable.

"They're really strict, bud," said his father.

His parents hadn't been getting along since the move. His mother complained that his father worked too much and neglected to help her establish themselves in their new home. She wanted shelves and paintings hung, and she wanted her husband to hang them. Joe offered to help but she told him that it was his father's responsibility. Joe loved the new house. He got his own bedroom, which he was very thankful for. His mind was always going and he needed a private place to sit quietly and listen. Plus, there was a pool.

"What do you mean, strict?" Joe asked.

"I mean there are a lot of rules they think God wants you to follow every day."

"Like what?"

"Well," said his father, searching, "there are a lot of rules about food."

Andrew Weiss was raised in San Francisco by what Nora joked were "commie pinko Jews." His parents were professors—him of European history, her of American literature—who fled New York City, the story went, after a political meeting they attended was raided by police wielding batons. Joe's grandma and grandpa were atheists, and so was his father, but his mother believed in God. Before they got married, his father agreed to "raise the kids Jewish." Most of it was harmless, he figured. All the "King of the Universe" stuff rubbed him the wrong way, but he kept his feelings to himself.

"And you'd have to wear a yarmulke all the time," said his mother.

Joe shrugged. "That wouldn't be so bad."

"Are you kidding?" said Jessica, disfiguring her face the way only a teenage girl can. "Literally *no one* would be friends with you. You know that, right?"

"That's stupid," he said. "My friend Ethan wears one."

"Your friend? You just met him. Let me guess, he was the only one who would talk to you?"

"Shut up," said Joe.

"Stop it, you two," said his mother.

"He's the one that said shut up! What did I do?"

"Yom Kippur is soon, right?" asked Joe. "Couldn't we just go once?"

Joe looked to his father. He wanted him to make the decision. But his father looked to his mother.

The family "tried" Ethan's temple the next week, and

everyone except Joe was in agreement afterward: this was not the temple for them. The service was too long, and there was too much Hebrew and not enough music. His sister pronounced all the kids "dorks," and his mother kept harping on the fact that she was the only woman wearing pants.

"It doesn't make sense to belong to a temple where we're so different from everybody else," she explained.

"I don't think I'm so different. I liked it."

"What did you like about it, bud?" asked his father.

"I thought it was cool how everybody was all into it. Did you see how they rocked back and forth sometimes?"

"Totally *freakish*," said Jessica. "It's like they're in a cult."

Joe wanted one of his parents to correct her. Sure, the rocking was a little weird, but if they were actually Jewish, why did it embarrass them? If they were gonna be Jewish, *be Jewish*. The way they tiptoed around their supposed identity was annoying. It made him think they were weak.

The decision was made. The Weisses "didn't feel comfortable there," but if Joe wanted to go with his friend, that was fine. So the next weekend, Joe spent the night at Ethan's house—which was much nicer than his—and in the morning they went to Hebrew school together. Ethan introduced Joe, telling the rest of the class that he had just moved from Fullerton. Joe appreciated that Ethan didn't mention that his parents had tried, and rejected, their temple. The Hebrew school teacher asked Joe if he was bar mitzvahed.

"No," said Joe. "Isn't that when you're thirteen? I'm twelve."

"You have to study a lot first," said Ethan.

"I don't mind that."

After class, the teacher introduced Joe to the rabbi, who said that he was welcome to join the class, but that he'd have to come for extra tutoring sessions to catch up. When he announced his intentions at home, the reactions were frustrating. His father said he wished he'd pick something more physically active as an after-school activity; his mother told him not to expect "one of those big crazy bar mitzvah parties;" and Jessica predicted he'd drop out within a month.

But he didn't drop out. He had always been good in Spanish class and the Hebrew came easily. His mother took credit for his apparent knack for languages. She studied abroad in Florence and took great pride in "keeping up her Italian." More than once he heard her tell someone "he gets his ear from me." Joe liked that she was proud. Feedback was important to him. It was hard to know how to feel without cribbing off other people's faces.

As part of the bar mitzvah curriculum, the rabbi took the class to visit different shuls—that was the proper word, Joe learned, not temple—around Los Angeles. In May of 1985, they visited the Chabad House. A bright-eyed young man with a wispy beard and a neat, black-brimmed hat gave them a tour. Joe thought the man, whose name was Shimon, was very impressive. His hat made him look important, and his wife, who gave the girls a tour, was pretty. He liked that they separated the girls and the boys when they went inside the shul for a prayer service. But in the backseat of the van on the way home, Ethan said he thought the Chabad people "went a little overboard."

"What do you mean?"

"All the men wear exactly the same thing," he said.

"So?" said Joe.

"They don't go to regular college, either."

"I don't care about regular college."

"You don't? I'm going to Yale, like my dad. Or maybe Dartmouth."

Joe shrugged. He didn't spend much time thinking about the future.

After his bar mitzvah, Joe started wearing a yarmulke every day. He told his parents he was joining the language club after school, but instead took the city bus to the Chabad House three afternoons a week. Most of the people riding with him were black, and he liked that his yarmulke marked him. He wasn't just a white kid. He was a Jew. He was proud and learned and powerful.

He planned his first attack for more than a month. He'd just begun his freshman year and the boys who teased him and Ethan in junior high were newly bold. One in particular, a blond kid named Matt who was popular because he made the varsity baseball team as a freshman, seemed to take particular pleasure in tormenting them. He made a game of trying to knock their yarmulkes off, sneaking up on one of them and whacking them across the top of the head in the parking lot, by the lockers, on the brown-grassed quad. He got Ethan's far more often than Joe's, but when Joe asked Ethan if he wanted to help him hurt Matt, Ethan said no.

"What do you mean, hurt him?"

"I mean punish him. Make sure he stops doing it."

"I told you I don't want to tell," said Ethan. Matt's bullying embarrassed Ethan; it emboldened Joe.

"I'm not talking about telling, I'm talking about doing."

"I don't want to get in trouble."

Joe didn't push. He didn't need Ethan.

The idea for the padlock came from his father. About a week after Joe decided he was going after Matt, someone broke into two garages on the street where the Weisses lived. His father came home with a bag from the hardware store that included a lock for the broken side door.

"This'll do until I get someone out here."

Joe's mother had been complaining about the door for months. She muttered sometimes that she wished she'd married a man who could fix things. After the handyman came, Joe took the lock from the junk drawer in the kitchen and put it inside a sock. He trailed Matt for two weeks and discovered that the time he was most likely to be alone was after baseball practice. Matt might play varsity, but he was only fourteen, so he couldn't drive. Occasionally, he caught a ride home with an older player, but at least a couple times a week, big, bad, blond Matt Simmons could be found sitting on the curb outside the Language Arts building staring at the entrance to the south parking lot, waiting for his mom to pick him up. Joe simply stepped up behind him and swung. Matt must have turned slightly because the lock hit him in the eye. He grabbed his face and screamed, falling forward onto the blacktop. There was blood immediately, and Joe stood for a moment, watching the red pour through Matt's fingers. His screams were high-pitched. He sounded like a bird—*caw caw caw!*—and his feet kicked and kicked.

Matt was out of school for a month. When he returned he wore a black patch over the space where his eye had been. He was no longer on the varsity baseball team. Matt was never able to tell the police anything about whoever attacked him, but the story going around was that it was part of a gang initiation. The news was full of stories about the Bloods and Crips, and later that year the school amended the dress code to prohibit anyone wearing all red or all blue.

Maiming Matt satisfied something inside Joe. He felt calmer, more confident, and he dove into his studies at the Chabad House, telling his parents that he was joining the debate team in addition to the language club. Shimon wanted to meet his family, but Joe made excuses. He said his parents were atheists and had threatened to disown him if he continued to "waste his time" with religion. He wanted to try on Chabad without having to explain it to anyone, especially his father, who was always so reasonable, so sincere and inquisitive, so genuinely interested in Joe, and so desperate to connect. But Joe did not want to connect. He told Shimon that his father had a temper and that his mother was vain and materialistic.

The next Passover he told his mother that he was no longer going to eat "traif."

"Where did you learn that word?" asked his father.

"It's Yiddish. It means food that's not kosher."

"I know what it means. Did your friend Ethan teach you that?"

"No," he said. "God gets insulted when you don't keep kosher." Joe didn't care whether God—if he existed—felt insulted. He figured that if there was some sort of omniscient, omnipotent entity in the sky he wouldn't find silly humans like Jessica and his parents important enough to be insulted by. But Joe liked to stand out. He was different, and although he couldn't advertise his real difference, he wanted his family to see him that way.

"Who told you that?" asked his mother.

"Shimon."

"Shimon?"

"From the Chabad House." He prounced Chabad with a guttural flair.

"The *Chabad* House? How do you know someone at the Chabad House?"

"What's the Chabad House?" asked Jessica.

"I don't like living in a home where God is always being insulted."

His parents looked at each other.

"What's the Chabad House!"

"It's for Hasidic Jews," said his father.

"Hasidic?"

"You're so fucking stupid, Jessica. How can you know *nothing* about your heritage?"

"My *heritage*?"

"Do not call your sister stupid, Joe. And don't swear."

"She's ignorant. That's the same as stupid."

"Jessica is not ignorant," said his father.

"Obviously she is." He knew he would get nowhere with his family, so he dropped the subject. But he stopped hiding his trips to the Chabad House and he began preparing his own meals. By the end of his junior year he rarely ate at home. Shimon and his wife, Sarah, had him for Shabbos dinner most weeks, and after the couple's two small children were in bed, Shimon and Joe would talk late into the night. It was Shimon who suggested Joe apply to the yeshiva at the Chabad World Headquarters in Brooklyn.

CHAPTER TWENTY

Henrietta tells me that she knew the man who paid her to lie as "Joe."

"Sometimes a week goes by and I don't think about him," she says. "Then I'll see something—every once in a while those Jews come into the casino—and I get all jumpy. I still don't know why he didn't kill me. I don't know what stopped him. Maybe he just liked knowing he *could,* you know?"

"Do you think he was the one who killed the Davises?"

Henrietta shrugs. "Maybe. Or maybe he was working for somebody who did."

"Do you remember where he worked?"

"I never knew."

"How old was he?"

"Not old," she says. "Twenty, maybe, back then."

We both fall silent. I have to get her on the record.

"I don't want to, like, pressure you," I say. "But, this kid, DeShawn. He's been in prison for twenty years. All you have to do is tell police what you told me, and you could set him free."

Henrietta shakes her head. "And I'd go to prison."

"Not necessarily . . ."

"I'm gonna tell the NYPD I lied? I watch *Law & Order*. You can go to jail for perjury."

"I think maybe there's a statute of limitations on that," I say.

"Did you not hear me when I told you he put a gun in my mouth? He was watching me. Those postcards. Sometimes they came every couple days. Half the reason I moved and changed my name was 'cause of him. Last thing I want is Joe—or anybody from back then—knowing where I am. I don't mean nothing to him. If he can shoot a little baby girl, what he gonna do to me?"

I decide to leave it there. I know DeShawn didn't do it. And I have a lead on the man who might have. I write my phone number down for Henrietta, and she reluctantly agrees to give me hers.

Iris is asleep in the driver's seat when I open the door.

"How'd it go?" she asks, rubbing her face. "Are you ready to head back to the hotel? I think I'm hungry."

"Drive," I say, pulling my notebook out of my purse. "She basically told me she completely lied to the cops."

"Holy shit!" she says. "So, you've got your story!"

"Not really," I say, scribbling. "She won't let me use her name or anything she said. And she says she won't go to the cops. But it gets better. Or worse, actually. She said a guy—a Jew, like, a black hat—who used to be one of her johns, paid her to lie. I gotta get all this down before I forget."

"Wait, like, one of your mom's Jews?"

"That's what she said."

"Jesus, you can't get away from this shit, can you?"

Right?

"Just drive," I say.

By the time we get back to the hotel I've got four pages of notes, everything I can remember about our conversation: what she said about Joe's schedule, his approximate age, why she picked DeShawn in the lineup, and where she said she was the night of the murders.

Iris heads to the boardwalk for food and a little beach time. I tell her I'll join her in an hour or two. I want to call Amanda and figure out what to do next.

Amanda picks up after three rings. Children are crying in the background.

"Hold on . . . Jonathan—can you deal with them? I gotta talk to Rebekah." Footsteps, and a door closing. "Okay. I'm safe in the bathroom. Tell me everything."

I do.

"Two things strike me. First, most of the time people get killed by somebody they know. And with this case it definitely seems personal. Nothing was stolen, and he shot them in their *bed,* for fuck's sake. So my question is, how did the Davises know a Hasid?"

"The people at Glorious Gospel mentioned something

about, like, an interfaith dialogue thing with the Jews in the neighborhood after the riots."

"Go back to them. You can't use what Henrietta said in print yet, but you *can* tell people what she said. It's gonna be really hard for anybody who actually knew them to ignore all this now. They know DeShawn has always said his confession was coerced, they just didn't believe him. Add this, and unless they're total assholes, they're gonna want to get involved and help make it right."

"Totally," I say. I scribble: *call pastor green, dorothy morris* into my notebook. "What was the other thing?"

"The other thing?"

"You said two things struck you."

"Oh! Yeah. Shit. I forget! Oh my God, my brain on pregnancy . . ."

I laugh. "It's cool."

"I'll remember and call you back, I promise."

"I really appreciate your help," I say.

"I can't believe you got that woman to admit she lied. That's pretty awesome."

"I'm not sure how much good it'll do," I say.

"I bet she comes around. Seriously. You've planted the seed. In my experience, people can't live forever with lies."

We hang up, and just as I'm stuffing a hotel towel into a beach bag, she calls back.

"I remembered the other thing! Did she tell you the guy's name? The one who paid her?"

"Yeah," I say. "Joe. But who knows if that's even his name."

"Well, it might be his name. What kind of paperwork do you have on the case?"

"So far just what DeShawn sent you, which isn't much. He said he's sending me more, though. And Judge Sanchez was going to help me get the appeal file."

"Good. There might be something in there—maybe they interviewed someone named Joe, or he was a neighbor or something. And keep in touch with this woman, the witness. If you go interview her again, bring donuts or something. Call her every few days to check in. She may not agree to talk to the police, but I guarantee she'll be thinking about it. And the more comfortable she feels with you, the more likely she is to go on the record."

I find Iris lying on her stomach, bikini straps undone, reading a W magazine. I set my towel down beside her and sit, pulling my knees to my chest like it's cold.

"Anxious?" she asks.

I nod.

"What does Saul say?"

"Saul?"

"This was his case, right?"

"Right. But I haven't actually told him I'm looking at it."

"What? Why?" She turns over and props herself up on her elbows, holding her top with one forearm.

"I was waiting until I knew more. I didn't want to make a big deal out of nothing."

"Don't you think he deserves to know? I mean, it affects him, clearly."

"Yeah."

"I don't get it. I thought the whole point was that this was something he could help you with. You said the blog girl gave you files from a bunch of different people. Were they, like, less interesting?"

She does get to the heart of it, doesn't she?

"No," I say.

For a few moments neither of us says anything. I look out at the ocean and watch a woman with a parrot tattoo that covers her entire calf stand still, letting the water carve out sinkholes for her feet. I remember that it seemed like a big secret when my dad showed me how the tide could make your toes disappear. I never stood still long enough to get buried to my ankles like he and my brother did, though. The wet sand felt constrictive, and I always hopped out of the slippery pockets with a feeling like something was chasing me.

"This is about your mom, isn't it?" says Iris. She sits up, fastening her top with one hand. "You're not calling because you don't want to talk to her."

"I don't know," I say. "I feel like . . . I don't think she likes me very much."

Iris sighs, pulling her sunglasses down over her eyes and turning her face away from me. "It doesn't fucking matter if she likes you. Or if you like her. She is yours. You are hers. Like what you can, focus on that. Focus on the fact that you found her. She's *alive*."

Iris's mother died of breast cancer when we were in college. Back then it would have been inconceivable that one of us would reject a mother should she somehow appear. But that's exactly what I'm doing. And I haven't given a thought to what it must feel like to Iris.

"I'm sorry," I say, putting my hand on her leg.

"You don't have to be best friends," she says. "But you can't avoid her so hard it, like, *negatively* impacts your life. This is your work. Your fucking career. You could be missing something major by not talking to Saul. If it wasn't for your mom you would have called him, right?"

Right.

CHAPTER TWENTY-ONE

Instead of telling Saul about Henrietta over the phone, I text and ask him if I can come by Sunday night after Iris and I get home. He texts back that I'm welcome for dinner, and that my mom is going to be there, too.

She's looking forward to seeing you.

I get off the Q train at Brighton Beach at a little before seven. It's probably at least five degrees cooler out here by the ocean. At the entrance to Saul's high-rise, a half-dozen wispy-haired women in visors sit on low beach chairs fanning themselves with magazines.

"Is that Rebekah or Aviva?" says the woman in the open-toe terry cloth slippers.

"It's Rebekah, Evie! Jesus!" says the woman with the root-beer-colored hair.

"What, what? They look so much alike!"

Does it make me a bad person that I have no desire to

learn the names of these women?

"Rebekah," I say, pushing out a smile.

"That's what I said!"

"I heard you!"

"Enjoying the sunshine?" I ask, because, polite.

"Oh, we are!" says cloth slippers. "Tell your handsome man to come visit with us sometime. We never see him!"

"He's not her handsome man! She could be his daughter!"

"She knows what I mean! You know what I mean!"

"I do," I say. "I'll let him know."

Saul calls the ladies "the force." There is a security desk in the lobby, but I've never seen anyone behind it. Saul says the ladies are better guards than a bored former transit cop any day.

I can smell the meal the minute I get off the elevator. Aviva cooked for me a couple times at her house in New Paltz, and she really gets into it. My mother is kind of an all-or-nothing person. She either brings home fast food for dinner or spends all day in the kitchen fixing half a dozen elaborate dishes that she'll freeze or give away.

It's been almost three months since I've seen either of them, and I hesitate before knocking on Saul's door. Part of the reason I didn't call when I read his name in DeShawn's file was because I liked the feeling of knowing something he didn't. Saul and Aviva have always been a couple steps ahead of me. He knew my mother was alive and in New York weeks before he told me. And for two decades she had the power to appear in my life anytime she wanted. It wasn't until Iris reacted with such surprise to the fact that I hadn't been communicating with Saul about the case all along that I realized I'd probably made the wrong decision by avoiding him—not to mention, for the wrong reason. It's time to come clean.

Saul answers the door to 16H wearing a mildly ridiculous pair of mirrored aviator sunglasses.

"Nice glasses," I say.

"Your mother got them for me," he says. Saul has lost weight since he and Aviva fell in love. I don't think she specifically encouraged it, but I get the sense that he feels lucky to have a girlfriend who is ten years younger than he is, and he wants to keep himself fit for her. It's kind of cute.

I relay the ladies' message, and Saul escorts me into the kitchen where Aviva, barefoot and dressed in denim shorts and a Coney Island Mermaid Parade T-shirt, is stirring a pitcher of iced tea. She smiles when she sees me, but waits for me to come and hug her. I do.

"Smells amazing," I say.

"You'll have to take some home. I made too much. Tea?"

"Sure," I say.

"There is wine, too."

"Tea's good for now," I say.

"Everything's all ready if you and Saul want to go sit down. I'll bring the borscht."

"Can I help?"

"No, no," she says. "Just make yourself at home. I'll bring the borscht right out. Do you like borscht?"

"That's soup, right?"

"Cold soup. There is sour cream or horseradish to put on top."

"Sounds good," I say.

Saul picks up the pitcher of tea, and I follow him to the table on the balcony. He goes back into the kitchen and I sit, looking through the metal bars at the ocean. Someone I can't see is flying a kite—a big orange and red bird with long streamers flapping behind it. Tomorrow is a workday, but there are hundreds of people still on the beach; blankets and umbrellas and little nylon tents stretch into the distance in both directions. I can see the Ferris wheel and the parachute jump, and hear the rumble of the Cyclone and the screams of the passengers as a train of cars rushes down the old roller coaster's rickety track.

Saul returns, and while we wait for Aviva to bring dinner, we chitchat about my job and his. He's still doing freelance private investigation work. He talks more than I do; it's probably apparent I'm a little nervous.

"Save room," says Aviva, carrying bowls of pink soup onto the balcony. "I've got brisket and asparagus, and sweet kugel for dessert."

"You hit the jackpot didn't you, Saul," I say.

"I'm a lucky man." He looks at Aviva and smiles. She waves him off. Aside from the time I saw them embracing on the grounds of the school where Connie Hall shot seven people in Roseville last year, I've never seen Saul touch my mother. Nor, for that matter, have I seen her touch him.

After we eat the brisket, I decide it's time to bring up Henrietta.

"So," I say to Saul, "I actually wanted to talk to you about a possible story." I tell him about the Center's cocktail party, and meeting Amanda. "I've been looking for something interesting—a feature, you know, something more than the day-stories at the *Trib*. Anyway, I've been reading a lot about wrongful convictions. People getting exonerated now that we have DNA evidence and stuff. So this girl, Amanda, we were talking and she gave me some letters she's gotten from people who say they're innocent." I lean over and pull DeShawn's envelope out of my bag. "She gave me this."

"You'd like an ex-cop's eye?"

"Well, yeah. But . . . it's a case you worked on."

"Ah." He bends forward and pulls the papers out of the envelope. "Just a minute," he says. "I need my reading glasses." He gets up and while he's gone Aviva takes our plates to the kitchen.

"Let's see," he says, sitting back down, putting on his glasses.

"I hope you're not . . ."

"It's all right, Rebekah," he says, not looking up. "I'm not offended."

Aviva returns with three small plates of kugel. I pick at mine while Saul reads DeShawn's letter, then glances at the reports.

"I remember this case. The day after the Fourth of July. Horrible, *horrible* scene. It was the first murdered child I'd ever seen."

"So what do you think?"

"What do I think about the letter? I think this is a man with nothing but time on his hands. There was an eyewitness in this case. That's hard to argue with."

"What if I told you the witness lied."

"Lied?"

"I tracked her down. She's in Atlantic City now. She said somebody paid her to lie."

"And you believe her?"

"I think so," I say. "I'm not sure why she'd lie now."

"She lied then," says Aviva.

I look at her. "She says the man who paid her threatened her. She said he put a gun in her mouth. She also said he was Hasidic."

Aviva rolls her eyes. "Of course she said that."

"What do you mean, of course?"

"I mean the blacks hate us."

" 'The blacks?' "

"Oh, please, Rebekah. Don't you see she's just trying to stir up trouble? It is trendy to make the police look bad now. And anti-Semitism is a very big problem. Have you been reading about what is happening in France?

The Jews are all having to leave! Just like before the Holocaust."

My mother has gone from Henrietta to Hitler in two sentences. I look at Saul. "Is that what you think, too?"

"I have no way of knowing." He looks at the file again. "The boy confessed."

"Right," I say. "But he says the detective—this Olivetti guy—coerced him. That's what happened with the Central Park Five kids, right? And you know there's been a lot of research about how common false confessions are, especially with teenagers. DeShawn was only sixteen. I can't tell if he had a lawyer present, but—"

"I don't know about any research," says Saul, interrupting me. He closes the file and takes off his glasses. "How much money are those Central Park boys getting? Millions, right? I'm sure there are a lot of people in prison who see that and think, maybe I can get some, too."

"You don't think they deserve some compensation for spending ten years in prison for something they didn't do?"

"They may not have done the rape, but those kids were up to no good in the park. We know that."

"Up to no good? What does that mean?"

"I mean that the officers didn't just pluck them out of thin air. They were running around the park, assaulting bicyclists, terrorizing people."

"But . . ."

"I know, Rebekah," he says. He takes a deep breath.

"I'm sorry. I don't like what happened to those boys any more than you do. But things were very, very different in New York twenty-five years ago. I don't think it's even possible for you to imagine what it was like. Every single day there were at least five murders. Five! Now we go days, sometimes a week, without even one. And murder was just part of it. Stabbings and shootings and rape and robbery and assaults. Constantly. *Constantly*. People could barely keep a business open in parts of Brooklyn for all the smash-and-grabs and the fires and the drugs. We were working fourteen-, sixteen-hour days. It was a tidal wave. Nonstop."

I wait for him to continue, but he doesn't. I suppose I shouldn't be surprised that he is reacting defensively to my looking into an old case, but I can't help being a little disappointed. When I met Saul last year all he seemed to care about was justice: a woman had been murdered and he believed that her insular religious community would cover it up. He wanted to get to the truth, no matter the cost. Is it possible he doesn't think the Davis family deserves the same thing? What kind of person does that make him?

"Okay," I say. "I hear that. I just . . . what does that have to do with whether this guy—or anybody—is innocent or not? I mean, it makes sense that with so much coming at you things would get . . . mistakes might get made. Right? I mean . . ." I trail off, hoping he'll agree, but he doesn't. "I talked to DeShawn a few days ago and he said their family was getting threatening letters. And there'd been some vandalism at their house. That's another lead. Do you remember that?"

Saul sniffs, wipes his mouth with a paper napkin, and sets it down. For a moment I think he's about to leave the table.

"Everything pointed to this boy," he says, and begins ticking points off on his fingers. "He was a messed-up kid. He had a history of arrests. He ran from us when we tried to interview him. I don't think he had an alibi. . . ."

"I actually talked to a woman who says she was his girlfriend," I say. "She says she was with him all night but that the police didn't believe her."

"I don't recall a girlfriend. But how do you explain that this witness picked him out of the lineup?"

"She told me she saw him in handcuffs and figured he must have done something wrong."

Saul is trying to appear unmoved—his back is straight, stiff, as if to project confidence—but he's not looking at me. There is doubt somewhere.

"She's not taking the easy way out saying all this now," I continue. "She basically admitted to lying to police, and lying to the court and sending a kid to prison for the rest of his life. She could face a lot of shit for what she did."

"People say a lot of things," says Saul. "Maybe she is looking for attention. She was a drug addict, am I right?"

"So what? She's clean now. She's got a job and an

227

apartment, and she's just living her life like the rest of us. And she's fucking *scared,* Saul. There's some crazy Hasidic murderer . . ."

"Rebekah!" says my mom.

"What? Oh, now you're all protective? This is exactly the kind of shit I thought you guys hated. You don't think it's *possible* she's telling the truth? Why? Because she's black?"

Saul sighs and looks at the sky. "Rebekah . . ."

"Don't patronize me, Saul. I don't deserve it. I may not be a cop but I'm not an idiot. If DeShawn didn't kill his family someone else did. Someone else walked into that home and shot three people—a little girl—in bed. That is a person that needs to be locked up. That is a person who has probably killed again. Right?"

Saul doesn't say anything. Part of me wants to storm off. But storming off is juvenile. Storming off won't make anything better. And I could really use Saul's help.

"People make mistakes, Saul," I say. "It doesn't mean you were a bad cop."

"Of course he wasn't a bad cop," says Aviva.

I ignore her, look at Saul. "You know what I'm saying."

"Yes, Rebekah."

"What if she's telling the truth? Without her ID the case would have been a lot weaker, right? I mean, maybe that confession would still have convinced a jury and the appeals judge, but maybe not. And just the idea that a Hasidic man paid her to lie—that's a real lead. I mean, was there any indication the Davises even knew people from the community?"

"Not that I recall."

"That opens up a whole line of investigation. If she'd told you this back then you would have at least tried to find out who this guy was, right?"

"Yes."

I can tell by the way he says yes that I've made my point.

CHAPTER TWENTY-TWO

Joe arrived in Crown Heights one week after the riots. His mother watched the coverage on the evening news and read the articles in the newspaper out loud to him.

"They are *literally* killing Jews there," she said. "Why would you want to walk into that?"

Joe didn't tell her that he was excited to be walking into what the paper called a "war zone." In their Shabbos talks, Shimon told Joe that Rebbe Menachem Schneerson, the revered leader of the Lubavitch-Chabad movement, said a Jew must be a master of his emotions, that the mind can channel and control the passions of the heart. *Emotions are like oxen,* Shimon explained. *They are unruly and destructive when left alone. But yoke them and they can plow a field.* Joe knew his emotions were unruly and destructive. He tried to yoke them with his mind, but his mind was just as disorderly. Perhaps what he needed was a place to channel them. He was ready to get out of his quiet California neighborhood and into the fires of Crown Heights.

But once he got to Brooklyn, Joe was stuck in a class-toom. The yeshiva kept the boys busy. He spent his days improving his Hebrew and learning to read Aramaic—endeavors that quickly became tedious. Shimon had advertised the yeshiva as the place where the brightest young Jewish minds went to discuss big ideas. But Joe was stuck doing grammar exercises. The first time he was able to go even five blocks from the Eastern Parkway head-quarters was when Daniel Grunwald, the neighborhood mentor he'd been matched with, invited him to Shabbos dinner with his family. At that dinner, Joe met Daniel's uncle, Isaiah. Isaiah Grunwald, Joe learned from his new friend, had been born in Israel and fought in the Six Day War. This impressed Joe. When they discussed politics or even the Holocaust, Shimon always reminded him that the Rebbe taught his followers to use their voices, not their hands, to respond to violence. Joe found this edict frustrating: would the six million have perished if they had taken up arms? Shimon never had an answer that satisfied him.

After dinner, Daniel and Joe and Isaiah lingered at the Shabbos table.

"How are you getting along with your studies?" Isaiah asked.

"He is bored," Daniel answered.

"I was speaking to Joseph, Daniel."

"It's true," said Joe. "I thought I would be *doing* something."

"Would you like a job?" asked Isaiah.

"What kind of job?"

Isaiah explained that he owned about a dozen buildings in Brooklyn and that Daniel sometimes helped him evaluate complaints and do light maintenance work.

"The yeshiva won't like it," said Daniel. "You are not supposed to be doing anything except studying, especially your first year."

Joe shrugged. "I don't have to tell anyone."

"It is dirty work," warned Isaiah. "Many of my tenants live like animals. Do you understand what I mean?"

"I think so."

In Los Angeles, Joe saw crime on the news, but in Brooklyn it was up close; the smells and sediment of it inescapable. Police vehicles rolled down the streets, but the officers stayed in their cars, ignoring the men openly imbibing liquor and smoking marijuana, the prostitutes propositioning every passing pedestrian, the boys spraying their gang names on buildings and tossing glass bottles into the street, the drunks urinating into gutters, onto buildings, behind Dumpsters. It was the dirtiest place he'd ever seen. It was lawless.

Isaiah started Joe in the office. The landlord had a file on each tenant and kept them in two drawers: one for addresses south of Eastern Parkway, where Jews lived, and one for his other properties, which were, he told Joe, mostly populated by blacks. Joe's first job was to go through the latter pile and use red flags to mark the files of tenants who were behind on their rent or had paid late more than once. When people in this pile called to report problems—clogged toilets, mold, broken radiators, vermin—Isaiah would know that fixing the issues was not a priority. Those tenants, Isaiah said, were taking advantage of his generosity. Isaiah understood that sometimes money was tight, but his Jewish tenants at least respected his property. In Isaiah's opinion, if you could not pay your rent *and* you treated the home your landlord was providing you as a dump, you were not entitled to have the owner of your building—the owner who you might as well have been stealing money from—attend to all the problems you caused.

And there were, Joe learned quickly, lots of problems with Isaiah's buildings. Every day there were calls. Rats were the biggest complaint, but nonfunctional toilets and sinks, as well as crumbling ceilings and walls were common. Raisa, the woman who answered the phones, spoke with the tenants and passed their messages to Joe. Joe identified the tenant by his or her file and informed Isaiah of the day's complaints. Isaiah had a small group of handymen—a mix of *goyim* and Jews, including Daniel—who worked for him, and several mornings a week the men came to the office to receive a list of repairs they were to accomplish. Isaiah tended to prioritize issues that, if left untouched, could further degrade the value of the buildings. Roaches and rats he shrugged off as either encouraged by the tenants' poor sanitation habits or an inevitable part of urban living. Burst pipes always got attention, as did crumbling façade—anything that could fall and harm a passerby and spark a lawsuit or a visit from one of the city's agencies.

About two months after he began working, Isaiah suggested that Joe accompany Daniel to a building where the tenants were complaining of a leak in the ceiling. The building was in Bushwick, a barren, industrial wasteland where Isaiah owned two four-story buildings across the street from a Department of Sanitation garage. They parked in front of a fire hydrant and Daniel told Joe to take work gloves and a paper mask from the box behind the driver's seat. A line of garbage trucks, apparently awaiting repair, stretched down the block, fetid juice dripping from their exposed bellies. The door to the apartment building was propped open with a shoe, and inside the hallway Joe smelled cooking grease and feces. He covered his nose and mouth.

"What did I tell you?" said Daniel. He knocked at apartment 1F, and a dark-skinned woman wearing a dress three sizes too small answered.

"It's about time," she said. There was a gap between her two front teeth and a gold cross pendant inside her massive cleavage. Joe felt a surge of blood to his groin. None of the girls in his high school were interested in him after he began wearing his yarmulke, and the girls he met at the Chabad House were saving themselves for their husbands. For a while, he convinced himself that sexual

235

discipline was an important part of his new identity. If he was to belong—and he wanted to belong—he had to live by the rules, even if they meant nothing to him. He didn't crave intimacy, so porn magazines sufficed. But standing in the doorway that afternoon, inches from this woman whose clothing said, clearly, *come and get me,* he decided that he would no longer force himself to suppress his desire to do just that.

The woman let them into the apartment and pointed them to the bathroom, which was the first door past the living room off a narrow hallway. The carpet was soaked halfway back toward the bedrooms, and an inch of filthy water pooled around the base of the toilet and sink. Someone had used towels to try to keep the damage contained to the bathroom, but they lay, soaked through and useless, on the floor. Part of the ceiling was open—melted, apparently, by a cascade of water from upstairs. A cascade now turned to a trickle, browning the wall behind the toilet.

"You know I've been calling about this leak for a month, right? If y'all had come the first time—"

"We're here now," said Daniel, cutting her off.

The woman put one hand on her hip and one hand in the air. "Don't you *even* get mouthy with me," she said. "I pay my rent. I got rights. I should be calling the city to report your asses."

Daniel told the woman they would be back, and when they left her apartment he whispered to Joe that she was a prostitute and wouldn't be calling any authorities.

A mentally retarded man answered the door at the apartment upstairs. His head lolled sideways and his tongue hung between his lips. There was food on his chin and the zipper of his pants was open. On the sofa behind him was a middle-aged woman attached to an oxygen tank. The galley kitchen was swarming with flies; food containers and dishes were piled on every surface, and bags of trash covered the floor, rendering the room unusable. Applause and laughter and ringing bells screamed from a game show on the television. The volume was turned up far too loud.

"Turn that down," Joe said to the woman.

"Uh-uh," said a voice from down the hall. "You don't get no say in how Mom watches her TV."

A shirtless man appeared from inside one of the bedrooms. He had, judging by the creases on the side of his face, just woken up. He buttoned his jeans and ran his hand through his hair. His chest and arms were muscular and there was a tattooed image of a praying woman on his left bicep and a Puerto Rican flag across his pectoral muscle. Joe could smell marijuana coming from either the man's breath, or the bedroom.

Daniel did not argue with the man; instead, he turned his attention to the bathroom, which was worse than the kitchen. The toilet was full of paper and feces; days' worth without a proper flush. Someone had actually defecated on top of the clogged pile. The tile that had presumably once lay between the base of the toilet and the tub was gone and the floor beneath rotted away. Joe knew from his time spent with the files in Isaiah's office that his boss had only owned these two Bushwick buildings for three months. How long had these people been living like this? It was a disgrace. Renting an apartment owned by someone else was a privilege. These people were guests. The woman should be in a hospital, the retarded man should be in a home, and the drug-smoking shirtless man should be in jail. And yet here they were, standing around useless as Isaiah paid Daniel and Joe to fix their mess.

"We been calling," said the shirtless man. Daniel ignored him and kneeled to examine the hole in the floor. "This isn't something we can fix today."

"When you gonna fix it then? Shit!"

Daniel stood up and began to leave the bathroom. The man stepped closer to him, got in his face.

"I want this shit fixed *today*."

The man didn't expect Joe to push him, and just a shove sent him tumbling, his bare feet useless on the slick floor. He fell spectacularly, stumbling first into the tiny vanity, his tailbone landing audibly on the tile, his arm splashing against the mountain of shit in the toilet.

They were all silent for a moment. The man was stunned, shaking his head. Before he could get up, Joe and Daniel left. Neither spoke for the first half of the ride back to Crown Heights. When they crossed Eastern Parkway, Daniel asked, "Do you think he's hurt badly?"

"No," said Joe. "He just slipped."

CHAPTER TWENTY-THREE

I call Judge Sanchez first thing Monday morning to tell her about Henrietta.

"I can't believe it," she says. "I mean, I *can* believe it. I do believe it. That poor boy. I tried to argue that she wasn't reliable because of her drug habit, but . . . I should have sent someone to scour her neighborhood. She wasn't even in Crown Heights! We might have found that roommate if we'd tried. *Fuck*."

I almost say, it's not your fault. But I don't.

"But she won't go to the cops?"

"No, at least not yet."

"If you could get her to write down what she's saying and sign it . . . it might not be admissible. But it might be enough for the DA to at least take a second look at the case. They're starting to do that—reexamine old cases."

"I can try," I say. "I was going to call her again today or tomorrow. I don't want to be too pushy, you know. She's scared of this guy, Joe."

"Joe. Could you get a more common name? And it's probably not even his name. She thinks he's Hasidic?"

"Yeah," I say. "Well, at least that's how she said he dressed. Black hat and the whole thing."

"Unreal. Do you have any idea why the Hasids might have been interested in the Davises?"

"No," I say. "But I'm going to call their friends at the church and ask."

"Good," she says. "Keep me in the loop."

When I call in for my assignment, the *Trib* receptionist transfers me to Mike, who tells me there is mail waiting for me in the newsroom.

"It's from the Coxsackie Correctional Institution," he says. "This for a story?"

"Maybe," I say. I didn't want to give a convicted felon my home address, so I had DeShawn send everything to the *Trib*. This, I realize now, was stupid. I haven't mentioned the story to anyone at the office because I've been working on it in the hopes that the Center might give me a grant. But I can't tell Mike that. "It's sort of preliminary. A possible wrongful conviction on a triple murder in Crown Heights back in 1992."

"Oh, yeah? Morgan's been asking about investigative stuff. He wants us all to bring ideas to a meeting on Friday. Can you have something for me by then?"

"Um, maybe?"

"Give me the gist."

"The guy who the packet is from was only sixteen

when he got convicted. He says the detective on the case manipulated him into confessing—you know, like the Central Park Five?"

"That's it? Everybody says that."

And then my ego gets the better of me.

"I actually tracked down the key witness who flat-out told me someone paid her to lie to the cops."

"That's on the record?"

"No," I say. "Not yet. She's scared of him. She changed her name and moved, but she's worried she'll get in trouble for lying if she comes forward now."

I can hear Mike typing.

"Mike. It's not on the record."

"What?"

"You're typing."

"I'm taking notes, Rebekah." More typing. "Okay. Things are a little slow. Come to the office and see what he sent. I might have to send you out, but you can work on this in the meantime."

I hang up the phone and head to the bathroom. The conversation has alighted my anxiety and when it hits these days, it always hits in my guts—literally. Iris knocks on the door.

"Should I do my makeup in the living room?" she asks.

"Yeah," I call out. "Sorry. I might be a minute."

"Everything okay?"

"I told Mike about Henrietta, and now he wants to pitch the DeShawn story to Morgan on Friday. I don't trust him not to, like, exaggerate what I've actually got. Which is nothing—at least not on the record."

I finish in the bathroom, light a match, and get dressed. Iris and I ride the F train into the city together and just as I'm about to push through one of the four revolving glass doors into the midtown high-rise where the *Trib*'s newsroom is, Aviva calls.

"Hi," I say, plugging my ears against an ambulance screaming up Sixth Avenue.

"Rebekah? Can you hear me?"

"Yeah. Sorry. I'm in midtown. Are you still in the city?"

"Yes. I am driving back to New Paltz today. I would like to talk to you. Can we meet?"

"I'm working all day," I say. "What's up?"

"I would like to see you in person."

"Is something wrong?"

"I would rather discuss it in person."

What doesn't she get about *I'm working*?

"I can probably take lunch," I say. "But if something comes up and they send me out, I have to go."

"I understand."

We agree to meet at a deli around the corner from the *Trib* building at twelve thirty. As I ride the elevator upstairs to the newsroom, I dig through my bag for my bottle of anti-anxiety pills. For twenty-three years my missing mother existed exclusively inside me. She was a feeling: a fist around my heart, quicksand in my stomach; real, but not real. And she had tremendous power. I always figured that if I met her

I could take that power back. That it was the mystery of who she was and why she left that debilitated me. But now, as I pop a pill to dull the dread of seeing her in a few hours, I have to confront the idea that having her in my life creates as much hurt as it heals. And all that hurt, the new and the old, it isn't like some tumor I can just excise. The fact that it didn't just drop out of me when I learned the secret of where she'd been and who she was means it's wormed its way into all my corners and pockets. It's in my body like a virus.

The packet DeShawn mailed to the *Trib* is thin. I pull out the paperwork and the handwritten note attached:

Dear Ms. Roberts,
Here is everything I have on my case. I got it all
from the office of the woman who did my appeal,
Theresa Sanchez. I had a friend in here who found
information in the prosecutor's file that wasn't
given to his defense attorney, so in 2009 I filed a
Freedom of Information Act request to get my file
from the Kings County DA. I waited and waited
and when they wrote me back they said my file was
burned up in a warehouse fire in 2001.
Thank you very much for taking an interest in
my case. I am innocent of this crime. Somebody else
shot my family. Someday, I hope I find out who.
Sincerely,
DeShawn Perkins

Aside from the confession and Henrietta's statement, which DeShawn already sent to Amanda, the packet contains mostly copies of motions filed by his attorneys, including a request for a delay after his first attorney died (denied by the judge), and a motion requesting that DeShawn's confession be thrown out (denied by the judge). There is a short summary of an interview with someone named Virginia Treble, who apparently lived above the Davises; boilerplate motions about DeShawn's appeal and the judge's ruling (the original verdict stands); the Kings County DA's response to DeShawn's FOIA. No crime-scene photos or sketches, no ballistics reports, no autopsy reports, no more interviews.

I call Judge Sanchez and give her the inventory. "DeShawn says he FOIA'd the DA for their copy, but they told him it was destroyed in a warehouse fire."

"Huh," she says. "I guess that's possible. There's definitely more than what he sent. He said he got it from my office?"

"Yeah."

"They're supposed to send everything, but honestly, back then the office was ridiculously understaffed. It still is, but now there aren't quite as many cases. Whoever filled his request was probably rushing and figured they'd cut some corners at the photocopy machine. I'll tell you what. Let's go to the courthouse. I can't do it tomorrow. Can you meet me first thing Wednesday?"

"I think so," I say. I'm scheduled to work a shift, but I'll figure something out.

"I'll call and ask them to get the file up from storage if they have it. Meet me in records—it's on the fourth floor."

"Thanks," I say.

"Thank *you*, Rebekah. Most people don't give a shit about guys like DeShawn. We chew them up and spit them out every day. I've lost sleep thinking about what kind of defense the people I represented could have gotten if they'd been able to pay for it. And once you're convicted that's pretty much it. Reporters are the ones who've done the work getting people out. Well, reporters and lawyers. But honestly, I like reporters better." She laughs. "Not much of a compliment. I like you better than a lawyer."

"I'll take it," I say.

I spot Aviva from across the street. She is standing outside the deli on Forty-Sixth Street wearing the same shorts and T-shirt as she was at Saul's, plus dirty white running shoes and socks with little green balls at the heel. Her red hair, brighter now that she started using drugstore color to cover the gray, is drawn back in a rubber band. As I wait for the light to change, I watch a woman wearing filthy clothing far too heavy for the weather approach her. The woman speaks and Aviva listens, then she reaches into her purse and hands the woman a dollar.

"Hi," I say. Neither of us moves to hug the other.

"Saul was very upset after your visit."

"Okay."

"I do not know if you know this, but Saul was going through a divorce when this case you are talking about happened. It was the worst time of his life. His wife was very angry and spiteful and she used his son against him. Those memories are very, very painful now that his son is dead. Saul feels he did not do enough. He feels responsible for his son's death because he chose to leave the community."

"I know."

"I understand that you are doing your job," she continues, "but perhaps you can find a different story?"

I lift my hand to shade my eyes from the sun. I want to say, I don't have time for this, but instead I sigh. "Can we go inside, please? It's too hot."

"All right."

We enter the deli and I walk straight back past the hot-and-cold lunch bar, stuffed with fifteen long feet of salad toppings and rubbery pasta and steaming fruit cobblers, to the first metal table I see. It was stupid of me to suggest we meet somewhere with food; seeing my mom makes me queasy enough.

"I'm sorry this is tough for Saul," I say when we sit. "Really. But, honestly, it's a lot tougher for this man who's been sitting in prison for twenty years for something he didn't do. He's been locked up more than half his life, and I'm the only person who's taken the time to actually do anything."

"I just don't see why it's your responsibility."

"It's not my *responsibility*," I say. "Did Saul ask you to come talk to me?"

"No. I am looking out for him. You have not had the kind of hardship in your life that he has, and I think it is important that you understand how terrible this time was for him."

This is the second time my mother has asked me to lay off reporting on someone she loves. Last year, she didn't want me to tell my editor that her brother might have been involved in a shooting. She pleaded that he endured miseries I couldn't possibly understand because I grew up in such a loving, stable family. Since then, I've had imaginary conversations with her in which, instead of silently acquiescing, I say that while it might make her feel better to focus on my father's strengths and the family he built in her wake, I grew up battling some pretty significant psychological and emotional trauma, too. Trauma she caused when she decided to slip out the back door while we slept.

"Like I said, I'm really sorry this happened when things were bad for Saul. But he had a job to do. Being a policeman is a powerful position. It's a responsibility. You can really screw with people's lives if you don't do it right. I'm not saying he did anything wrong on purpose. But if he has to endure a little bit of discomfort in order to help get an innocent person out of prison, I think that's an okay trade-off."

"I think you are being very selfish, Rebekah."

Oh, you have *got* to be kidding me.

"Look, if you knew me at all—which you don't because

you bailed on me before I could speak—you would know that there is literally no fucking way that I am going to not report a story because you think it's going to hurt your boyfriend's feelings."

"Rebekah . . ."

"This is what I do. Okay? This is who I am. I am a reporter. And guess what? I'm good at it. It's a hard job— it's an *important* job—and I'm good at it. Most moms would be proud of their children for doing the kind of work I do."

"I'm not . . ."

"Right, I know. You're not really a mom."

I stand up and walk out, though I can barely feel my legs. When I get outside I start walking north toward Central Park. I need shade. I need a bench. I need a place to cry.

I spend the rest of my shift doing rewrite, and just as I am about to head into the subway to go home, my phone rings.

"Hi, this is Rebekah," I say.

"Rebekah, this is Bob Haverford. You called me last week about someone I represented back in the nineties. DeShawn Perkins."

"Yeah," I say, "thanks for getting back to me."

"I'm sorry about . . . how I reacted before. Listen, I'm in the city. Do you have time to meet right now?"

An hour later, I meet Bob Haverford at a café in the

West Village. He is there before me, sitting at a tiny bistro table on the sidewalk. I recognize him from his photo on the Haverford & Haverford Web site: ashy blond hair with a boyish but sun-worn face. He is wearing a striped oxford shirt, dark blue jeans, and expensive-looking European-style loafers. A nearly empty martini glass sweats on the tabletop.

"Bob?" I say.

"Rebekah, how are you?"

"Good," I say, dropping my purse under the table and sitting, carefully, on the chair beside him. Our entire setup is atop the metal door into the basement. I've been avoiding even walking over these things since we did a story in June about a woman who died after an improperly latched one on Second Avenue gave way beneath her; she broke her neck falling down the concrete stairs below. Hopefully that won't happen this afternoon.

The waiter comes and asks what I'd like. "The coldest beer you have," I say.

Bob makes a noise like a chuckle, but can't muster a smile.

"I basically haven't slept since you called." He presses his thumb and forefingers into closed eyelids, wincing. "I want to help you but. . . . Can we talk off the record?"

Ugh. "Okay." Build trust, I think. Build trust and the quotes will come.

"That case, DeShawn—it was the low point of my life. My wife was leaving me. She was the whole reason I'd started at Legal Aid to begin with. We were dating and I did it to impress her. Make myself look like I was some do-gooder. Which I'm not. I mean, I'm not a bad guy. But you have to be a saint to do the shit I was doing. We had, like, thirty cases at a time. And it wasn't as if we had money to hire investigators or spend any time actually researching anything or tracking people down for interviews. Most of the time we just pled shit down as best we could.

"Anyway, we'd only been married two years, and she basically came home one day and was, like, I'm not sure if I was ever in love with you."

"Ouch," I say, but I doubt I sound terribly sympathetic. Aviva is trying to get me to excuse anything Saul might have done wrong because it was a tough time in his life, and now this guy. Tell it to DeShawn, I think. Tell it to his dead family.

"It was all I could do to get out of bed."

The waiter brings my beer, and as he sets out a napkin, Bob finishes his martini.

"I'll take another," he says.

I sip my beer and Bob blows an exhale like he's trying to expel something ugly, and rubs his hand over his mouth.

"I should never have been assigned the case to begin with. They always give homicides like that to people with a lot of experience. But the original attorney had a heart attack about a month before trial and they had to divvy up all his cases really fast. I tried to get the trial post-poned but the judge wasn't having it. The whole system was backed up. I mean, every day we each got another five or six clients. Seriously. And this was a tough case to begin with, okay? The kid had a record, and the cops had an eyewitness and a confession. That's basically insur-mountable. Or it was back then. They didn't have much in the way of physical evidence. They never found the gun. But, honestly, DeShawn wasn't a lot of help. He kept getting into fights at Rikers. Twice I went to see him and they turned me away because he was in segregation for some infraction."

"What about the girlfriend?" I ask. "She said she was with him the night they died."

"I think she flip-flopped. Told the cops she wasn't with him, then said she was. She wasn't reliable. Putting her on the stand wouldn't have helped DeShawn."

"The jury believed the witness," I say, "and she was a crack addict."

"Yeah, but at least she told the same story the whole time."

I nod. "Did you check it at all?"

"Her story? Not really."

"I just visited her in Atlantic City a few days ago. She told me she lied. She wasn't even in the neighborhood that night."

Bob's eyes go wide, his mouth slack. He takes a deep breath and rests his head in fingers.

"I brought up the fact that the woman had a record. But like you said, the jury believed her. I guess, to tell you the truth, I believed her, too."

CHAPTER TWENTY-FOUR

When his wife and children were not at home, Naftali Rothstein often ate Shabbos dinner with the yeshiva students in the basement cafeteria of one of the dorms just south of Eastern Parkway. He was inspired by their youthful energy and enjoyed engaging in the impassioned discussions about Talmudic law. When his father died suddenly of a stroke, the then twenty-year-old Rothstein had cut his formal studies short to begin earning money to help support his four brothers and sisters who were still living at home. He couldn't bring himself to completely leave yeshiva life, however, and found work first as a secretary to the man who coordinated visas and housing for students coming to Crown Heights from across the United States and abroad. Rothstein quickly established himself as an enthusiastic advocate for the community. He was a natural multitasker, and if the phone cord was long enough, he could photocopy, file, and type up meeting minutes while reminding a skeptical mother that, yes, the area surrounding the yeshiva was dangerous, but sending her son into the fray—as it were—was a mitzvah. But in 1986, when a student from London was robbed and beaten so badly he spent three weeks in a coma—a story that made international news in part because the young man's father was a cousin-in-law of Shimon Peres—Rothstein began to wonder if the future of Chabad was actually imperiled by the "bad" neighborhood in which Rebbe Schneerson had planted his flag.

And so, Rothstein went to his superiors at the Crown Heights Jewish Council with a proposal: allow him to create a public relations and development office. It took some convincing, but after a few weeks of meetings, he was granted permission to call himself the Council's Community Relations Manager and to spend some of his time forming relationships with reporters and civic leaders in New York City in order to advance the interests of the movement and better protect the population.

But he could only spin the situation in Crown Heights so far. The police needed constant reminding that the tax-paying, law-abiding citizens of the neighborhood were watching when they rolled past corner drug deals and let thefts and assaults and vandalism go virtually uninvestigated. It took two months for the commander of the 77th precinct to agree to meet with him. The relationship was not a warm one, especially now, a year after the riots, when the neighborhood had become an international symbol of ineffective civil authority and citizen unrest. It didn't seem to matter to Commander Greg Harbrook that it was the blacks—not the Jews—who destroyed entire blocks with fire and baseball bats. Let it burn, seemed to be the precinct motto. Harbrook actually said as much in an emergency meeting with Rothstein and senior Chabad leadership the day after Yankel Rosenbaum was murdered in the street.

"We don't have enough manpower to control every angry nigger in Brooklyn. And now with Sharpton bringing his people in . . ." He shook his head. "Let them get it out of their system. It'll die down eventually."

Rothstein did what he could to use the riots to build support for community. And in some ways, the experience created a kind of lore around the Lubavitchers of Crown Heights. The Jews on the Upper West Side had fled to Westchester in the sixties, and as the blacks moved into Brownsville and East New York, those Jews moved to Long Island. But *not even a virtual civil war* could uproot the men and women of the Chabad movement. Donations began to pour in from as far away as Russia and as close as Prospect Park West.

Isaiah Grunwald was one of those donors. Rothstein knew many of the men who owned buildings in the neighborhood, but Isaiah was not particularly active in the community, so when the stocky Israeli appeared in Rothstein's office in the fall of 1991, Rothstein didn't recognize him. Isaiah handed him an envelope and said that he could count on the same donation each quarter.

Naftali opened the envelope and saw a check for five thousand dollars.

"You know that my wife and I have not been blessed with children," said Isaiah.

Naftali nodded. It was a great sorrow for a Lubavitcher couple to be childless, but some were, of course. Naftali did not know Isaiah's wife, and he wondered if she, like other chassidish women who were barren, felt out of place in the community. It occurred to him that it would be a mitzvah to use some of Isaiah's donation to create a group for those couples. A monthly meeting space, perhaps, to share and comfort. He made a mental note to ask his superiors about the idea.

"We cannot raise Jewish children of our own," continued Isaiah. "We would like to help the community educate and care for the students who come here to learn."

Isaiah did not stay long. Unlike many donors giving far less than he was, Isaiah did not appear to want Rothstein to flatter him, or to arrange a special seat in shul or a one-on-one meeting with the elderly Rebbe. In fact, while the checks came each quarter, Naftali did not see Isaiah until nearly a year later, a few weeks after the Davis murders. Rothstein was in his office working on his monthly newsletter when Isaiah appeared in the doorway.

"Good Shabbos," said Rothstein, inviting the man inside.

"Good Shabbos," said Isaiah.

The two men asked after each other's families and

made small talk of the upcoming trial of Yankel Rosenbaum's murderer, the Rebbe's health, the weather. There was nodding, and then Isaiah lay an envelope on Rothstein's desk.

"Hashem has blessed me with a particularly profitable year. This gift is in addition to my quarterly contribution." He gestured to the envelope, encouraging Rothstein to open it. Inside was a check for ten thousand dollars.

"This is very generous," said Rothstein, clearing his throat in a bumbling attempt to mask a wide grin. Rothstein had recently approached the Council's leadership for a raise. His wife was pregnant with their sixth child, and in May his father-in-law lost his entire retirement in a bad land investment in New Jersey, forcing Rothstein to step in to make mortgage payments so his wife's parents didn't lose their home. Leadership promised to take his request into consideration at the monthly financial meeting, scheduled for next Tuesday. A surprise ten-thousand-dollar addition to the quarterly balance sheet, thought Rothstein, might just make the difference.

"I wonder if you might be able to assist me with something," said Isaiah.

"Anything."

"One of my tenants has come to me for assistance. His brother was murdered in July. Shot to death in his home on Troy Avenue, along with his wife and daughter."

"Yes!" exclaimed Rothstein. "I remember the case. A horrible, horrible tragedy."

"Unthinkable. My tenant's only consolation has been that the murderer—the man's own son, if you can believe it—confessed."

Rothstein nodded.

"But now, it seems, the murderer has changed his mind. He is pleading not guilty."

"No!"

"Yes. And my tenant is concerned that the prosecutor might be lenient because he is still a teenager. They are not wealthy people, but they have scraped together enough money to hire a private attorney to ensure that the family's interests are represented.

"I know that you have developed a relationship with police, and I am hoping that perhaps you might be able to help the family obtain the documents the police have on the case. I believe there was an eyewitness, for example."

Rothstein nodded his head. "It is very generous of you to help this family," he said. "As it turns out, I am friendly with one of the officers involved. Let me see what I can do."

Isaiah stood up. "I knew I had come to the right man." He reached forward and squeezed Rothstein's hand. Rothstein saw that Isaiah was missing the tip of his right index finger. He had heard that Isaiah fought in the Six Day War, and although he was certainly not one to fetishize violence, at that moment he felt a surge of respect for his donor. There were many in the community who disliked Isaiah Grunwald. They felt he was insufficiently pious, and there was talk about his business practices. The Rebbe instructed his followers who were able to help establish housing for Jewish families: apartments with more than three bedrooms, two sinks for kosher cooking; buildings with outdoor space suitable for building a sukkah. Isaiah Grunwald had done this, and then, people said, he got greedy, and bought crumbling buildings in other areas, looking for a quick profit. But who was Rothstein to say? And while some would have seen Isaiah extending himself for a black family as suspect behavior, Rothstein, who believed that peace with their goyish neighbors was in the best interest of the community, admired it.

"I will look forward to hearing from you," said Isaiah.

Rothstein wasted no time. Shabbos did not begin for another two hours, so he donned his hat and jacket, set the newsletter aside for Monday, placed Isaiah's check into his locked desk drawer, and set out for the 77th precinct. September was a beautiful time of year in Brooklyn, and Rothstein, feeling particularly optimistic, decided to take a chance and walk up Utica instead of hailing a taxi. The yeshiva students were all outside, too, holding their binders and books, laughing, smoking cigarettes on the benches along Eastern Parkway. Rothstein envied the young men, and some days the envy soured him. But today, with ten thousand dollars in his desk drawer and a mission to assist a grieving family, he felt as if the work he was doing was helping to strengthen this place he loved. Perhaps, he thought, people like Isaiah and himself, people some might call too modern, too involved with those outside the community, perhaps they were playing an essential role in protecting the Jewish community, in allowing it to thrive in this hostile place. Perhaps the fact that he cut his studies short was a blessing for the community, even if it felt like a burden to him. He would do well to adjust his attitude toward that part of his past, he thought. He looked forward to expressing this new idea to his wife at dinner.

He smiled and nearly skipped across Albany, noticing but not despairing in the overturned garbage can and broken beer bottles at the corner. The black people on the street watched him, but he did not feel afraid. If someone threatened him, he imagined himself saying, *I am on an errand to help your brother! We are neighbors, all of us!* In the imaginary encounter the imaginary black man shook his hand and patted him on the back, sending him on his way.

He arrived at the precinct at shift change. Uniformed officers, some with handcuffed men in tow, filled the two front rooms. Rothstein caught the desk sergeant's eye and the cop waved him past. What a fortunate man he was, to be known and respected here. He found Saul Katz at a corner desk, poking at a typewriter with two fingers. He looked weary, his shoulders hunched over, and Rothstein noticed that Saul's head was bare, his *kippah* laying atop a stack of folders.

"Good Shabbos," said Rothstein.

Saul looked up and returned the greeting, then turned his attention to his typewriter.

"You will have to excuse me," he said. "My shift commander wants this report . . ."

"Absolutely!" said Rothstein. "I see it is a bad time. I have a question but it can wait." He patted his breast pocket where he kept his copy of the Tehillim, the Book of Psalms. "I will busy myself until you are available."

"It shouldn't be long," said Saul. "Thirty minutes."

"We have plenty of time before sundown," said Rothstein. And then: "Saul! Do you have plans for Shabbos dinner?"

"Naftali . . ."

"Yes, yes, I know, you are busy. But please, would you join us? It would be an honor."

"Fine," said Saul. "Now . . ."

"Say no more!" Rothstein made a gesture like he was zipping his lips. He wrote his address on a slip of paper. "Can you make it by nine thirty? I will meet you after shul."

Naftali's wife had prepared a roast chicken for dinner and was delighted when Saul appeared in her dining room.

"Wonderful!" she exclaimed. "Someone to appreciate my cooking!"

"Your husband is not enough?" gasped Naftali playfully.

Zelda waved him off. "My husband will eat anything,"

she said, beaming at Saul. "He is not at all discerning. I could serve boiled fish every night and he would be pleased. It is no fun to cook for him."

"It smells delicious," said Saul.

Zelda ushered the men into the tiny dining area, where the table was set neatly with tall white candles burning in silver candlesticks, paper plates, paper napkins, and plastic utensils. When their fifth child was born, Zelda announced that she was finished washing three meals worth of dishes for seven people. Cookware and serving plates and the baby's bottles were enough. Naftali knew enough not to argue—even if, as the Rebbe instructed, he occasionally rolled up his sleeves to help her at the sink. The dining chairs were upholstered in pink and yellow fabric, and covered in plastic; the table was overlaid with a mauve oilcloth. Like many chassidish families in Crown Heights, the Rothsteins were poor. Furniture and clothing was second- or third-hand, meals were simple, utilities carefully conserved, brand names unheard of. But, as Naftali motioned for his guest to sit next to him, Saul could see that their poverty was material, not spiritual. The apartment was cluttered, but there were tracks in the carpet from a recent vacuuming. Zelda yelled for the children, and all five came running: three boys and two girls, ages three to fourteen. One of the girls brought the challah to the table, then returned to the kitchen to bring a plate of salmon and crackers. Another brought a bowl with salad, and finally Zelda appeared with the chicken.

Over dinner, Zelda quizzed the children about what they had learned in school. It was the second week back, and there were many stories about new teachers and new rules and new students. Saul filled his plate twice—he could scarcely remember the last time he ate a homemade meal—and marveled at the lively discussion. When Zelda told the children their guest was a police officer, the kids went wild, asking if he got to arrest people, asking if they made him shave off his beard, asking if they could see his gun.

"Why aren't you with your family for Shabbos?" asked the eldest boy.

"Mendel!" shushed Zelda.

"It's fine," said Saul, smiling at Zelda. "I was working late. Your tatty came to see me and told me how wonderful your mommy's cooking was. I simply had to eat some myself!"

The boy furrowed his brow. He was not satisfied by Saul's response, but did not press him further. Saul took a sip of wine and saw Naftali and Zelda exchange a smile. How he envied them. Why had he been cursed with such doubts? Such discontent? Such blasted contrariness? Look, he said to himself, look what you could have had. And yet he knew he and Fraidy would never have been like Zelda and Naftali. When she gave birth to Binyamin, Fraidy had nearly died, and the doctors had to do an emergency surgery to remove her uterus. The shock of it stunned them both, and neither had the emotional tools to comfort the other. They sought help from their rabbi, who suggested prayer, of course, but they simply could not come together. And so each sought solace separately. Fraidy turned to her sisters, bringing Binyamin to meals and playtime with his cousins, sometimes staying for days in New Jersey, obsessed with the idea that he should become as close to them as he would to the brothers and sisters he would never have. Saul, working then at her father's hardware store in Borough Park, turned to his radio, finding meaning and moments of joy in the music, but also the voices of the men and women who read the advertisements. Their excited sales pitches occasionally carried him off into another world. A world where a new mattress or a trip to Atlantic City could change everything. He tried to tell Fraidy the way the radio made him feel. How the news reminded him that they were not alone in their suffering, and how the music reminded him that there was still beauty in Hashem's world. But she would not listen. The radio was forbidden. That—not her husband's misery, his loneliness, his bumbling attempts to soothe himself—was what she cared about. She was a small-minded woman. And he began to hate her.

After dinner, Zelda and the girls cleared the table and cleaned the kitchen while the boys disappeared into a bedroom. Saul asked Naftali what he had wanted to speak about when he came to the precinct that evening.

"I was hoping you might be able to help me obtain what I believe are public documents," he said. "Do you remember the family that was murdered on Troy Avenue in July? Mother, father, and a little girl."

"Yes," said Saul. Truthfully, he hadn't thought about the Davis case in a while. After working with Olivetti, he was moved to the newly created sex crimes unit. Homicide had been difficult, but he would have gladly returned to it after just a week on this new rotation. The depravity he encountered each day seemed to know no bounds. He had seen children—*babies*—literally torn apart, ripped open by ravenous monsters masquerading as human beings. Dead bodies could not recount the moment their killer pulled the knife or the gun, could not describe the fear, or the feeling of the hammer on their skull, the bullet in their gut. But these living victims, with their still-bleeding wounds and their shame, they burdened his soul and tested his sanity in ways he could never have anticipated. Each day seemed to bring an attack more vicious than the last, a victim more stunned and debilitated. Saul knew, looking at the women lying in their hospital beds, that the justice he was there to help mete out was not likely to comfort them. Many refused to cooperate with the official investigation. Their attackers were often friends or family members, and even if a jury convicted—which was rare—they would never, truly, be free of them. By the time he appeared at their bedside, or in their home, the victims were so fundamentally altered by what had happened to them that Saul felt he was no better than a newspaper reporter, picking at their pain in the name of "the job."

"The son confessed," said Saul, "if I remember correctly."

"Yes," said Naftali. "But he has decided to plead not guilty and take the case to trial. One of my most generous donors is a landlord, and apparently one of his tenants was related to the victims. The family, as you can imagine, is distraught. They have hired an attorney to represent their interests but have been unable to arrange a meeting with the prosecutor. They are concerned the murderer may be treated lightly because of his young age." Naftali made up the part about not being able to meet with the prosecutor. He was on a roll. "They are hoping to get a copy of the case file to make sure that everything is being done properly—all the *i*'s dotted and *t*'s crossed."

It seemed like a reasonable request, and as Zelda brought slices of homemade cinnamon babka to the table, Saul said he'd be happy to make a photocopy of the file.

"Why don't you come by Monday," he said to Naftali.

The next Monday afternoon, Naftali collected the file from Saul, and that evening Isaiah Grunwald collected it from Naftali.

CHAPTER TWENTY-FIVE

Wednesday morning Judge Sanchez is at the records office before me, arguing with the clerk, a young Latino man with a sliver of a beard shaved across his jaw.

"Let me talk to your boss," she says.

"She's not going to tell you anything different," says the man. "Everything before 1995 was in storage in Red Hook and got destroyed in Sandy."

"Well, that's remarkable, since we've already been told this particular file was destroyed in a fire in 2001."

"I don't know what to tell you," he says.

"Just get me your boss, please. Tell her Judge Theresa Sanchez is here."

The clerk disappears and Judge Sanchez turns to me.

"The incompetence is un-fucking-believable. Please tell me you brought DeShawn's file."

"I did," I say, digging into my bag. I open the manila envelope and pull out a letter explaining that the prosecutor's file on DeShawn's case was not available because it was in storage in a warehouse that caught fire in 2001. The letter is signed by the Kings County Clerk, Chris Hancock, and dated April 2010.

"I can't wait to see how they explain this."

"Me, too," I say, thinking, if nothing else, this might be a story in itself. How many other people are being told their files were destroyed?

After another minute, the clerk returns with a woman who looks about eleven months pregnant. Her arms and legs are tiny, but her belly is shocking—it's hard to figure how she's upright.

"How can I help you?" she asks.

"My name is Judge Theresa Sanchez, I run the Brooklyn Community Court. This is Rebekah Roberts with the *New York Tribune*. We'd like to take a look at a case file from 1992."

She sits down at the computer. "Do you have a case number?"

Judge Sanchez turns to me. I read the case number off the letter DeShawn sent me and she types it in. *Click click click.*

"Your assistant here said that everything pre-1995 was destroyed in Sandy," says Judge Sanchez.

"Much of it was."

"But what's odd," I say, "is that the man whose file we're looking for was told back in 2010 that his paperwork was destroyed in 2001 in a warehouse fire."

"Obviously it's not possible for both things to have happened," says Judge Sanchez.

"Obviously," says the clerk, not the least bit rattled by Judge Sanchez's indignation.

"The clerk who signed this letter was named Chris Hancock," I say. "Is he still here?"

The clerk shakes her head. She's still looking at the computer, scrolling with a mouse. Finally, she speaks. "It's possible that this file is in our basement storage."

"Unbelievable," says the judge.

"I said it's possible," says the woman, looking up. "We *have* had files destroyed in both fires and flooding. And prior to 1997, very little was computerized. This may never have been properly entered into our database, which may explain why it has been difficult to track down."

Judge Sanchez isn't having it.

"What a reasonable excuse," she says. "I'm sure the people sitting in prison being told their files are gone will be pleased to know how difficult your job is."

"Would you like Andre to show you to the storage room?"

"That would be wonderful," says Judge Sanchez. "And can we get your name?"

"My name is Anna Brannon."

I write that down.

"Did you replace Chris Hancock?" I ask.

"Yes."

Andre walks us to the elevator bank and escorts us to the basement of the courthouse. We follow him down a long hallway and through an unmarked door.

The cardboard file box with DeShawn's case number scrawled in Sharpie on the side is smashed beneath a much heavier box. I pull it down and Judge Sanchez and I walk toward the front of the storage room to a desk that looks like it hasn't been occupied in a decade. The files inside don't even fill half the box. It's kind of unreal to think that this measly pile of paper is everything the state had on DeShawn—and it was enough to take his life away.

We start pulling files and comparing them to the paperwork DeShawn sent me. I open one unmarked manila envelope and find two things inside: a police report and a Ziploc bag. According to the typed summary on the police report, Malcolm Davis came into the 77th precinct on June 2, 1992:

Complainant alleges that his family is the victim of vandalism, specifically the word "SNITCH" spray-painted on his front door.

"Check this out," I say, handing Judge Sanchez the report. As she reads, I open the Ziploc bag: inside are three envelopes. One, postmarked June 14, 1992 in Brooklyn, is addressed to Malcolm Davis at the apartment on Troy; there is no return address. The other two were not mailed, apparently. I open the postmarked envelope and unfold the piece of paper inside. Just as DeShawn described, the text is made up of letters cut out from magazines: YOUR FAMILY WILL SUFFER.

"Look at this."

The judge looks up from the police report.

"What the fuck?" She reaches for the paper, then stops. "Put that down."

I do.

"We didn't have *any* of this."

"When we talked on the phone, DeShawn said somebody was threatening his parents. He said they were getting hang-up phone calls and letters like this. But he said his original defense attorney told him the cops never found any."

"Well, clearly *that's* not true. Jesus. *Jesus!* They just didn't turn this shit over. We need to get these letters tested for fingerprints, first of all. And DNA. They might be able to find something from whoever licked the envelopes."

"What about the police report? You didn't have that?"

"Definitely not."

"Sandra Michaels prosecuted this case," I say, my voice low.

"Yes, she did. Un-fucking-believable. Honestly, I wouldn't have expected this from her. I thought she was a straight shooter."

"Do you think it's enough to get the case reopened?"

"It might be," she says. "It should be."

I pull out my cell phone. "I'm gonna get pictures," I say. "Just in case."

"Oh, I am *not* letting this shit disappear," says Judge Sanchez, pulling out her own phone. "One of my best friends is still a prosecutor. She does sex crimes. I'll have her send someone down. We will not leave this box until it is safe in her office."

"You're sure you can trust her?"

"Absolutely. We grew up together. She's gonna hit the roof. Especially once she finds out I've got a *Trib* reporter with me."

I take photos of the first letter, the envelopes, and the police report, then follow Judge Sanchez and a clerk from her friend's office back upstairs. Her friend, ADA Felicia Castillo, is in court, but she's told her clerk to let us wait in her office.

"I wonder how many other cases Sandra Michaels withheld evidence on," I say.

Judge Sanchez shakes her head. "They're going to have to look back at everything. Two *decades* of convictions. What a shit show. This could end her career."

"Can I quote you on that?"

"No," she says. "Not that. But I'm on the record saying we didn't have any of what's in that file. The letters and the report, I mean."

Felicia Castillo returns to her office at a little past noon.

"Whose case was it?" she asks Judge Sanchez.

"Sandra's."

Felicia doesn't even attempt to hide how the news makes her feel. She drops into her seat.

"I don't know what's worse," says Judge Sanchez, "that she withheld all this from the defense, or that this office has been telling the defendant that the files we just found in about five minutes were destroyed more than a decade ago."

"None of it's good," says Felicia. She's staring at the box like she's never seen one before. For a moment, no one speaks, then Felicia comes out of her trance and looks at me.

"This meeting is off the record," she says to me. "I have to figure out what the fuck is going on."

"Okay," I say. "But I'm obviously going to want a comment from Sandra Michaels."

"Are you planning to run this tomorrow?"

"Maybe," I say. I need to talk to Mike, but my guess is he'll want copy immediately. This morning, DeShawn's story was just a possibly interesting feature idea that could pad Mike's pitch list at a meeting. Now, it's the center of a legit scoop on a powerful woman whom everybody in the city is already talking about. Was it just Sandra Michaels who withheld evidence? Or was that how the Kings County DA did business back then? How many DeShawns are there?

"I'm due back in court at one," says Felicia, looking at her watch. "I'll have someone call you."

Outside the courthouse, Judge Sanchez tells me to call her if I don't hear from the DA's office by tomorrow.

"Can you get in touch with DeShawn?" she asks.

"He has to call me, I think. But I'll try the prison and see what happens."

"He's, what, forty years old now?"

"Almost," I say.

"Un-fucking-believable," she says again, raising her hand to hail a cab. "I don't know how a guy like that doesn't go completely insane after all this time. Maybe that's why so many of them get religious. Let go and let God. Me? I'd wanna burn it all down."

Ninety minutes later, I'm with Mike, Gary, and Larry Dunn—the paper's longtime police reporter—in Albert Morgan's office on the eleventh floor of the *Trib* building. The *Trib*'s leadership structure is absurdly male. There are plenty of female reporters, but almost no one making editorial decisions has a vagina. I wonder, standing there, if it's because the boys like it that way, or if they've actually tried to get women on board but they're smart enough to know what this place will do to them long-term.

"I hear you have another scoop for us, Rebekah," says the managing editor from behind his enormous desk.

"I do," I say.

"And it doesn't even involve Jews," says Mike.

I decide it is not the time to mention that Henrietta told me the man who paid her to lie was Hasidic. For one, I don't think it's immediately relevant to the Sandra Michaels angle of the story. But even more, that particular piece of information feels dangerous. I've done a lot of reporting in the haredi world in the last two years and, frankly, I've never come across—or even heard about—anyone cold-blooded enough to behave the way Henrietta says this man did. Not that it's not possible. I just know how cavalier the *Trib* can be, and the last thing I want to do is start a rumor that incendiary based only on the word of an admitted liar who won't go on the record.

"Do we have a comment from Michaels on this?" asks Morgan, after I've briefed him on DeShawn's case and the evidence Judge Sanchez and I found.

"No," I say. "I literally just came from the courthouse. I'm waiting on a call."

"Gary, can you spare one of your reporters?"

"Sure."

"Get somebody calling defense attorneys. See if anyone else ever accused Michaels of anything like this."

Gary nods.

"Tell him about the eyewitness," says Mike.

"She told me—off the record—that she lied."

Morgan raises his eyebrows. "Good work, Rebekah. Are you still freelance?"

"Yeah," I say.

"Gary, aren't you hiring for your desk?"

Gary avoids looking at me. "We actually just brought Jack Owens on . . ."

"Who?"

"He, um, he's been here about six months. Columbia j-school."

"Hm," says Morgan. He moves on. "So, we've got two

parallel stories. There's DeShawn's case with the lying witness, and there's the Sandra Michaels-withholding-evidence story. I want to focus on Michaels. It has implications for Kendra Yaris, and that's what's trending now. If she didn't turn over evidence in this case, how many other cases did she withhold on? Is she still doing it? What else is she doing? Does the NYPD know? Are they colluding?" I start scribbling, thinking, those are questions you could spend three years trying to answer. "Write up what you have and get it to Mike. I want our first story to run tomorrow. If we can get it online earlier, even better."

The last time I was in this room, I was terrified. I'd made a couple really big mistakes and was pretty certain I'd lose my job. Today, I feel differently.

"I can get some of those answers," I say, "but it'll take a couple days. There's not a huge rush. No one knows I was looking into this case. The missing evidence—that's totally exclusive. Plus, I can't call DeShawn. He has to call me. If we could just wait until tomorrow I might be able to—"

"No," interrupts Morgan. "Michaels could call somebody at the *Times* who's sympathetic and get her side of the story out first. This is too big to sit on. We can fill in the holes later. This story is going to get picked up, and I want every news outlet in the city to have to say, 'as first reported by the *New York Tribune*.' "

CHAPTER TWENTY-SIX

When I wake up the next morning, my article is online. It doesn't get top billing (that goes to the cover story on a round-up of arrests after a man dressed as Cookie Monster and another dressed as Elmo got into a brawl in Times Square), but it's number three on the site, with a red banner reading TRIBUNE EXCLUSIVE atop the headline:

SANDRA MICHAELS ACCUSED OF WITHHOLDING EVIDENCE IN TRIPLE MURDER
by Rebekah Roberts

The woman many expect to be the next Brooklyn DA is accused of withholding critical evidence in the triple murder trial of DeShawn Perkins, a teen convicted of killing his foster parents and sister in 1992.

"It's a disgrace," says Judge Theresa Sanchez, who was Perkins' appeals attorney.

Perkins was 16 years old when he was convicted of shooting Malcolm and Sabrina Davis, and 3-year-old Kenya Gregory, on July 4, 1992.

Sandra Michaels had been with the Kings County DA's office less than a year when she prosecuted Perkins. She won praise for putting the supposedly violent teen behind bars.

And she may have cheated.

Buried in a case file in the Kings County Courthouse basement, the *Trib* found bizarre letters sent to the victims in the months before their deaths, and evidence that family's home had been vandalized.

But none of this evidence was ever turned over to the teen's defense attorneys.

Perkins is now 38 years old, and has spent more than half his life in prison.

"I did not kill my family," Perkins told the *Trib*.

Perkins retracted his original confession, which he says was coerced and made without an adult present. But the jury believed the witness—an admitted crack user and prostitute—who said she saw him leave the scene of the crime.

Other than that, Sanchez says the case against him was "thin."

Perkins has been stalled in his quest to have his conviction overturned because the Brooklyn DA's office told him his case file was destroyed in a 2001 fire.

But when a *Trib* reporter requested the file on Wednesday, she was told it was destroyed when a Red Hook storage warehouse flooded during Super Storm Sandy in 2012.

Neither was true.

The file Perkins wanted was in the basement of the Kings County Courthouse—along with the missing evidence that might have freed him.

Richard Krakowski, the spokesman for the Brooklyn DA, says the office is investigating the situation.

Judge Sanchez, who now presides over the Brooklyn Community Court, has vowed to get the case reopened.

"What else are they hiding?" asks Sanchez. "How many people are sitting in prison because the prosecutors lied?"

With DA Stan Morrissey undergoing treatment for cancer, Sandra Michaels is now running the office. She is currently under pressure to indict NYPD Detective Jason Womack in the shooting death of Kendra Yaris.

The *Trib* was the first to report that Womack has a history of use-of-force allegations.

Attorney Andrew Perlstein, who represents Yaris' family, told the *Trib* that he isn't surprised the DA's office is accused of withholding evidence in a case against a young black man.

"Even in supposedly liberal New York City, black defendants and victims simply don't get real justice," he said.

"If Kendra Yaris had been white, her killers would have been indicted immediately, without a doubt."

Additional reporting by Jack Owens

No one ran the quote from the Yaris family attorney

by me. Apparently Jack couldn't find anybody who had accused Sandra Michaels of tampering with evidence, so they just decided to throw in a link and a nod to the story that's currently getting the most clicks on the site. Just as bad, Mike added that the witness against DeShawn was a drug addict and prostitute, which wasn't necessary and will likely piss off Henrietta and make it harder to convince her to go on the record. It would be awesome to work for an editor I could trust.

My phone rings at 9:00 A.M.

"This is Rebakah," I say.

"Hold for Mike."

I hold.

Mike comes on. "Sandra Michaels is doing really well on the site. We need a follow for tomorrow. Have you heard from the kid?"

"DeShawn? No. Hopefully he's not pissed we ran the story without checking with him."

"Try to get in touch," says Mike, ignoring my concern. "Call the prison. And go down to the courthouse to see if you can corner Michaels. We need a comment from her. Larry's gonna look into the precinct, see if there were shenanigans there around the same time. Call me back at noon so I can give an update at the meeting."

"You made some changes in the Michaels story," I say. "What?"

"Henrietta isn't going to trust me if I called her a crackhead in the paper."

"You said she was a crackhead."

"I said it but I didn't write it. Can you ask me next time before you make changes like that? Please?"

"I can't run every edit by you, Rebekah."

"I'm not asking you to run every edit by me."

"Fine. Call me at noon."

I'm pretty sure I just made the situation worse. I call the DA's spokesperson and leave a message requesting an interview with Sandra Michaels. Just after I click off, my phone rings with a blocked number.

An automated voice says, "You have a call from the Coxsackie Correctional Facility. Will you accept the charges?"

"Yes," I say.

"Rebekah?"

"DeShawn?"

"I saw the article! You have to be kidding me!"

"I know," I say. "I'm sorry I couldn't run it all by you. I'm so glad you called."

"I can't believe they had those letters all this time! My lawyer said the cops never found nothing."

"Well, somebody lied."

"Ms. Sanchez is a judge now?"

"Yeah," I say. "I don't know if I would have found this stuff if it weren't for her. She's on the warpath." It's time to tell him about Henrietta. "And there's something else. I tracked down the eyewitness. The woman who picked you out of a lineup. She's clean now, and she's moved to New Jersey and changed her name. She wouldn't let me quote her, but DeShawn, she says she lied. She says she wasn't even in Crown Heights that night. She said somebody paid her to make up a story, and she picked you because she just happened to see you in the precinct that night."

Silence at the other end of the line.

"DeShawn?"

"I'm here. I'm just . . . she really said she lied?"

"She did. But I don't have it on tape. And she says she won't go to the cops. She's afraid of this guy who paid her."

"Who is he?"

I could tell him what she told me, but what if Aviva is right? What if Henrietta just said the man who paid her was Jewish to settle some old score? Until I have more than her word, I decide to keep that part to myself.

"I don't know," I say. "She won't tell me. I'm going to keep trying, though. I'm gonna call her and tell her what we found and basically beg her to come forward."

"I don't even know what to say," says DeShawn.

"I'm working on another story for tomorrow. What would you say to them—to the DA—if you could?"

"I'd say they should all be ashamed of themselves. I was just a kid. I didn't know nothing. And they're gonna lie and cheat just to make some case? What the hell? They took my whole life, man. My whole damn life."

I scribble the words he says into my notebook, but I

wish I could scribble the way he says them. At the beginning of the conversation DeShawn was energized. But after I told him about Henrietta, he deflated. I don't know what he is thinking, but I know what I'm thinking: the last twenty-two years of his life spent locked in a cage weren't just some random, awful twist of fate. They were the result of machinations by people for whom the truth of what happened the night someone slaughtered his family was less important than a win—or in Henrietta's case, some cash. Whatever faith in humanity DeShawn managed to hold on to these past two decades has probably been hard won. This shit—I imagine it's enough to undermine that entirely.

"Judge Sanchez thinks there's a good chance they'll reopen your case now," I say, trying to sound hopeful. "I mean, if it's not prosecutorial misconduct, it's definitely negligence." I don't really know what I'm talking about, and before I can make any more empty promises, a recorded voice breaks into our call and says we have ninety seconds remaining.

"DeShawn?"

"I'm here."

"I know this is a lot to lay on you."

"I been dreaming about something like this for so long. I just . . . I don't want to get my hopes up, you know?"

"Totally," I say. "But listen, you've got people behind you now. The DA's office knows they fucked up. And I won't let this drop. Neither will Judge Sanchez."

"Okay."

"Call me tomorrow? Same time?"

"Yeah," he says. "Thank you. No matter what happens now. Just this article . . . thank you."

And the line goes dead.

DeShawn isn't the first person to thank me for reporting a story—people who loved both Rivka Mendelssohn and Pessie Goldin told me they were grateful someone outside the insular haredi community was looking into their deaths. But Rivka and Pessie were dead. My efforts to bring them justice would never change the essential fact that their lives were over before I'd ever heard their names. DeShawn, on the other hand—if I do this right, he could walk out of prison and live for fifty years in a world he would never have seen had I not opened his letter to Amanda. That feels good.

I get dressed and brush my teeth, and at a little after ten, I call Saul. He doesn't pick up.

"Hey, Saul," I say to the voice mail. "I just wanted to see if you saw my story today. Give me a call when you can, 'kay?"

My next call is to Henrietta, but she doesn't pick up, either. I leave a message, and as I do another call comes in. I click over.

"Hi, it's Rebekah."

"Rebekah, this is Richard Krakowski at the Kings County DA. I can get you ten minutes with ADA Michaels this afternoon. Come to the third floor at one thirty."

CHAPTER TWENTY-SEVEN

Sandra Michaels looks like shit. She doesn't appear to have slept, and without the soft Plaza lighting and armor of an elegant suit and professional blow-out, what you notice about her are the prominent tendons in her skinny hands, the hurried eyebrow pencil, the sunspots.

For a few seconds she doesn't speak, she just looks at me.

"Do we know each other?" she asks finally.

"No," I say. "I mean . . . I was at the Plaza the other day."

"I know that. That's what I'm talking about. Did I *do* something to you?"

"I don't understand."

"You did that story about my ex, and now this shit from, what, 1992? Do you have something against me?"

I don't bother protesting that I didn't actually write the story about her ex. I'm the face she associates with it, and splitting that hair will probably aggravate her even more. I decide to focus on DeShawn. "A lot of people are looking into old cases. . . ."

"You think I don't know that!"

Her face contorts dramatically and without all the makeup she was wearing last week I can see that she's had work done. The way her face moves doesn't make sense. The skin beside her eyes scrunches up, but the skin below doesn't budge. Plastic surgery makes me sad, especially on accomplished women. What does it matter what a prosecutor looks like? Maybe I'll think differently when I'm thirty. Or fifty. "Just so I'm clear: this isn't personal? I didn't prosecute your boyfriend or something?"

I shake my head, waiting for more hostility, but she changes tack.

"You're going to have to give us some time on this," she says.

"What do you mean?"

"I mean we have to figure out what happened."

I sense weakness and decide to exploit it. "What happened with what? That the office has been saying the file was destroyed? Or that DeShawn's attorney says she never saw the evidence inside it?"

"She *says* she never saw it. Do you know definitively that it wasn't in the appeals file?"

No.

"Of course not," she continues.

"Are you saying you did turn it over?"

"I'm not saying anything. That's not true. This is what

I'm saying: I have never knowingly withheld evidence in a case. That's on the record. You can print that. Everything else is off the record. As Richard explained." She pauses. "You realize this is going to effect the Kendra Yaris case, don't you?"

I decide I don't need to answer.

"That's all I've got for you," she says.

I am dismissed. Outside the courthouse I pull out my phone and am about to call Mike with Sandra Michaels' quote when I get an incoming call from a 718 number I don't recognize.

"This is Rebekah," I say.

"Rebekah, this is Dorothy Norris. We spoke last week at Glorious Gospel."

"Hi, how are you?"

"I saw your article this morning. I hadn't put it together before, but I remembered something that might be useful. Before they died, Malcolm started collecting signatures against a landlord. I don't remember his name, but he owned several buildings in the neighborhood that were in terrible condition. I think one of Malcolm's kids from the YMCA might have lived in one. I believe he complained to the landlord in person—on their behalf—but if I recall correctly, he'd been frustrated by the response. Or lack of response."

"Do you remember the landlord's name?"

"No," she says. "I'm sorry to say I don't. But he was Jewish. I remember that because Malcolm didn't want to tell Pastor Green about it. Like he told you, Red felt it was important for us to get along with our Jewish neighbors, especially after the riots. He was very embarrassed by the way the community behaved. Red does not have much patience for violence or law breaking. Not that I do, either, of course. And Malcolm certainly didn't. But I suppose we were a little more sympathetic to the frustration, especially among the young people then."

"Do you know if Malcolm ever talked to anyone at the city? Maybe made a formal complaint I could look up?"

"Well, Sabrina worked in the city's housing department."

"She did?"

"Yes. I don't know if she was involved, though."

"Okay."

"If DeShawn really is innocent, my husband and I want to do everything we possibly can do help him."

It's about time, I think.

I call Mike and fill him in on what DeShawn, Dorothy, and the DA had to say.

"The vic was collecting signatures against a Jewish landlord?" he asks.

"She thought so, but she didn't have a name."

"More fucking Jews. You're like a magnet."

"Thanks."

"You didn't find signatures in the box with the letters?"

"No," I say.

"Okay, ask the DA's office if they know anything about

that. What about the witness?"

"I'll call her. She's in Atlantic City," I remind him, "so I can't just door-knock."

"Okay, Morgan's more interested in the Michaels angle anyway." I know. I was in the meeting, too. "Send me whatever you have by four."

I end the call and find a Starbucks to start plunking out a draft of what I have so far. I splurge on an enormous Frappuccino and text Saul:

Just got a tip that Malcolm Davis may have had some sort of conflict with a Jewish landlord before he died. Any thoughts?

CHAPTER TWENTY-EIGHT

December 1991
Crown Heights, Brooklyn

Two months after the man with the tattoos fell into the toilet, Daniel invited Joe to a meeting on Albany Avenue.

"What sort of meeting?"

"Wait and see," said Daniel. "I think you will find it interesting."

The apartment was on the top floor of a two-story home. By the time Joe and Daniel arrived there were already four men there. Three were standing at a dining room table eating pastries out of plastic bags. One man sat on the floor, fiddling with a radio.

"Avi," said Daniel to the man on the floor, "this is Joe."

Avi rose. He was easily six foot three, with broad shoulders and red hair. He shook Joe's hand and invited him to sit, then called for the rest of the men to gather around the coffee table.

"Did Daniel explain our mission?"

Joe shook his head.

"We came together last year after Shmuli's sister was

attacked." Avi looked to the dark-haired man sitting on the far end of the sofa. Beneath his beard, Shmuli's face was red and mountainous with acne. He cast his eyes down when Avi mentioned his sister.

"I will not offend you with details, but she endured violence no woman should endure. Shmuli's family contacted the police, but as I am sure you can imagine, they were useless. Shmuli took matters into his own hands several weeks later. His sister was brave enough to return to the street where the incident occurred, and she identified the man. Shmuli followed him home, and the next day Eli and I accompanied him to the address, where we were able to detain the man when he came outside."

"Detain?"

Avi smiled. He leaned sideways and unhooked a pair of handcuffs from his belt. "We did not wait for the police to come get him. We brought him to the police. Not surprisingly, the man was on probation for another crime. He is now off the streets."

Avi explained that as students they were not allowed to join the neighborhood's official *shmira,* or patrol group. But even if they could, Avi said, the men in the room believed that the assiduously law-abiding shmira were ineffective. Reactive, not proactive; not willing to, as Avi said, "get their hands dirty."

"You are new to Crown Heights, yes?" Avi asked.

Joe nodded.

"When you read about the riots at home, what did the newspapers say?"

"What do you mean?"

"Did they say that blacks and Jews were fighting? Killing each other?"

"I think so. I don't remember exactly."

"The newspapers had it all wrong. Jews and blacks weren't fighting each other. Jews were being attacked. And we didn't raise a hand! But did that matter? No. The story was that everyone resorted to violence. We were all at fault. Al Sharpton and his people talking about how unfair life is for the blacks. How the police target them and treat the Jews so well. Ha! Who was burning the city? Not Jews! Who was stabbing and beating people in the street? Not Jews!"

Avi shook his head.

"No more. The Rebbe says not to raise hands in violence. But if the world already thinks that is what we are doing . . ." He paused. "You see what I am saying?"

Joe saw. He stayed at the apartment until very late that night, and volunteered to patrol with the group the next evening. It was December, and Joe's first experience with temperatures below freezing. The cold made him feel limber and clearheaded. The air was stimulating, like a shot of adrenaline. He met Daniel, Avi, and another man called Barry at the bakery across the street from Isaiah's office. Daniel handed him a foot-long metal pipe.

"Don't start trouble," Avi said. "But don't run from it, either."

The foursome split into twosomes; Joe and Daniel went west, Avi and Barry east. They would reconvene at midnight. The first hour was uneventful, but Joe felt powerful with the pipe in his jacket. At about seven thirty, they heard glass shatter near the corner of Albany Avenue and Union Street. Two black men ran past. Joe and Daniel started after them, but when the men darted into the traffic on Eastern Parkway, Daniel stopped.

"It's not worth the risk going north after dark," he said. "Even with two of us. They have guns and we don't."

"Why not?"

"Why don't we have guns?"

"Yeah."

Daniel, somehow, seemed to be considering this for the first time.

"I suppose they aren't very easy to get. And we're the good guys. Guns are for bad guys."

Joe found Daniel's response ridiculous, but did not say so. They walked back to the street where they had heard the glass break and found a woman standing beside a minivan with two of the windows smashed.

"Did you catch them?" she asked.

"No," said Daniel. "But we will make sure to add this street to our patrol."

The woman made a disgusted sound. She peered into the vehicle. "This is the third time since Sukkot these same men have broken into cars on this block. I told my husband not to buy another radio after the last time. It only encourages them!

"Do you know how many times I have called the police? They don't even bother to come unless they steal the entire car!"

The rest of the night was busy. They shouted at three men urinating in public, confronted the drivers of two cars obviously trolling for prostitutes, and, brandishing their pipes, broke up two clear drug deals. At just after 10:00 P.M., a young haredi woman, barely out of her teens by the look of it, came running up to them on President Street. Three men had just attacked her husband and he needed help. When they got to the man he was sitting on the curb, his lip split and his white shirt stained with blood. The woman explained that they had been walking home from her parents' apartment when the men came from behind and grabbed her purse.

"Ezra went running after them," she said, breathless. "I screamed for him to stop but . . ." She looked at her husband, who was rubbing his jaw. "One of the men punched him right in the face and then the other one began to kick him. I screamed and screamed and finally they ran off."

"They took our money," said the man. "And now, with her identification, they know where we live. When will they be back for more?"

Neither Joe nor Daniel had an answer for him.

They split up at midnight, and instead of returning home

immediately, Joe walked north, toward Eastern Parkway. He hailed a taxicab and told the driver to take him to Bushwick. He was wide awake. Since seeing the prostitute in Isaiah's building, he had been nearly unable to control his desire for a woman like her. A woman with no dignity; a slab of meat to bite and lick and explode inside of. In the taxi, he put his brimmed hat in his backpack and replaced it with the Dodgers cap he'd brought from California. He directed the driver to a corner a few blocks from the building with the leak in the ceiling. As much as he wanted to knock on the big-breasted woman's ground-floor door, he knew he had to find someone else, someone who could not connect him to his life in Crown Heights.

With his backpack over one shoulder, he strolled, scanning the street for women. He walked two blocks up one side of Wilson Avenue, then crossed to the other side and walked the same two blocks in the other direction. He approached a bodega in the middle of the block, its piss-yellow awning torn, its windows fogged with filth and dusty canned goods, a neon Budweiser sign blinking. Outside stood a woman in an oversized military-style coat, her legs bare, feet stuffed into high heels. He slowed.

"You want a date?" she asked.

It was that easy.

Ten minutes later, around the corner and up the stairs into a sparsely furnished apartment, Joe no longer needed to control himself. He pulled down her shirt and squeezed, then sucked, lost, as if in a dream. It was finally real. He told her to take off her shorts, and she did. He told her to get on her knees, and she did. He came in her mouth. He roared, excited by the volume of his voice. Who could hear him now? Who could stop him from doing exactly what he wanted?

The prostitute took her clothes into the bathroom and he heard the water running. She was dressed when she came out.

"No," he said. "We're not done."

He told her to take off her clothes and sit on the sofa. He told her to open her legs so that he could see what was there. He looked, intrigued and appalled.

Afterward, he gave her twenty-five dollars, five more than she had told him it would cost.

"Next week at the same time."

The woman nodded. "I'm Hunny," she said.

"Joe."

A week later, he was back on the street with the patrol group, this time paired with a small, bespeckled man named Lazer, with whom he quickly became exasperated. Just fifteen minutes after beginning their patrol, the pair spotted two skinny, filthy men huddled in the doorway of an abandoned storefront on Brooklyn Avenue. They were smoking crack. Joe began to jog toward the men, but Lazer grabbed his sleeve.

"What are you doing?"

"I am going to tell them to move or we will call the police."

"They could be dangerous. Avi says, don't start trouble."

"I'm not starting the trouble. They're the ones doing drugs."

He shook Lazer off and pulled the metal pipe from his waist. The men in the doorway did not see him until he was standing just a few feet away, and when he kicked one in the stomach, the other was so startled he didn't even run. Joe kicked the man again, and then brought his pipe down on his ribs. The man vomited blood.

"Stop!" screamed the second crackhead, throwing himself toward Joe's feet. Joe stepped back calmly, disgusted at the display.

"This is my neighborhood," said Joe. "I will kill you if I see you again."

The men nodded frantically, like children. The friend took the injured man's hand and together they lumbered north. Joe watched the men go, their pants falling off their skinny hips, their sneakers scratching along the sidewalk. When they disappeared around the corner of Bergen, Joe turned and waved Lazer over.

"You have a kit?"

At first, Lazer appeared not to hear him. He looked to Joe like one of those tiny dogs the Puerto Ricans kept; twitchy and useless.

"Lazer!"

Lazer dug into the knapsack slung across his chest and handed him a pair of work gloves and a small broom and dustpan. Joe swept the glass from the broken pipe into the plastic dustpan. He handed the dustpan to Lazer, then, when his partner turned to dump the glass in a garbage can, Joe picked up a tiny plastic bag with what he assumed were two pieces of crack cocaine inside. Rocks, he had heard them called. He put the plastic bag in his pants pocket, and later that night, he gave the bag to Hunny and asked her to smoke one before they had sex.

He didn't have to ask her twice. She pulled a glass pipe from her purse—it was just a little tube, really—put the rock at the end, and flicked a lighter. The smell was chemical and sour, and Joe was impressed with the white cloud of smoke she blew after her inhale.

"How does it feel?" he asked her.

She leaned back on the sofa and spread her legs. "It feels like I wanna get to fucking."

The next day, Joe dozed off in his morning Hebrew class. The droning of the students' recitations entered the dream: he and Hunny were walking in Bushwick. It was summer and he was wearing shorts, a T-shirt, flip-flops: the clothing of his childhood. The men in black hats were all around them, crowding the sidewalk, their mouths moving, moving, moving. He had to push them aside like overgrowth in a forest. First with his hands, then he had a pipe. *Smack*. The instructor's hand on the desk where his head lay. Joe startled awake, felt the cold wet of drool on his chin. The instructor stared down at him, performing disgust for his obedient, obnoxious pupils. Joe didn't think, he just swung: fist to chin, and the man fell.

301

CHAPTER TWENTY-NINE

December 1991–February 1992
Crown Heights, Brooklyn

Daniel brought the news of Joe's expulsion to Isaiah. The second floor was busy that morning. A Lubavitcher couple and a black woman sat on folding chairs in reception, and the secretaries darted around, apparently unable to find whatever paperwork was necessary to attend to them. Isaiah yelled from behind his desk and when Daniel poked his head in, the landlord said he would have to wait. An hour later, Daniel closed the door behind him and relayed what the yeshiva's principal had described.

"Does he deny it?"

"No," said Daniel.

Isaiah raised his eyebrows.

"What do you think of him?" Isaiah asked.

"Think of him?" Daniel considered this. He was reluctant to say that he didn't really know Joe any better now than he did when they were introduced in August. His mentee was friendly and articulate. He was polite and he expressed reasonable opinions about the Talmud and the neighborhood and the collapse of communism across Eastern Europe, but every time they interacted, Daniel couldn't help feeling as if they had just met. They ate meals together, worked together, walked the streets of Crown Heights together, but there was no intimacy between them. Was that abnormal? Daniel didn't know. They were from very different backgrounds, after all.

"Were you surprised when you learned what he'd done?" Isaiah asked when Daniel did not seem to be able to come up with an answer.

"No," said Daniel. "I have seen him be aggressive. But against blacks."

Isaiah nodded. He explained that he was getting pressure from his partners in the UK to turn a bigger profit on his buildings and may have to start evictions in order to replace his current tenants with people who would pay more.

"I need someone to accompany me on what are occasionally unpleasant visits."

Daniel understood. "I think he would be good at that."

The next day, Isaiah summoned Joe to his office.

"Would you like to stay here in Crown Heights?"

"Yes," said Joe.

"Good. I have been looking for someone with a certain skill set. As you know, some of the people who live in my buildings are very different from you and I. They do not understand what it is like to have to make a living. They do not understand the responsibility of owning something." He paused. Joe sensed Isaiah needed a nod, so he nodded. "Of course, we always conduct ourselves as best we can. We try not to draw attention."

"Of course."

Isaiah paid Joe a month's wages upfront, in cash, so that he could rent a furnished apartment. With a job and a place to stay he did not have to go home. With a job and a place to stay he could deflect his parents' anxious inquiries. With a job and a place to stay he could live exactly as he pleased.

Typically, Isaiah was vague about what he wanted. He told Joe that the building on Bedford had only three apartments still occupied, and that without heat it would be very difficult for the remaining tenants to stay through the rest of the winter. So Joe went to the building and took a wrench to the boiler. When the tenants called to complain, the women at the office took a message. By spring, the building was empty.

And then Malcolm Davis came along.

At first it was just phone calls requesting a meeting.

"Is he a tenant?" Isaiah asked the receptionist one morning when she informed them that there was another message on the machine overnight.

"No," said Goldy. "He says he is calling on behalf of someone on St. John."

"On behalf?"

"Listen to the message, why don't you!"

"Press the button," said Joe.

This message is for Mr. Isaiah Grunwald. My name is Malcolm Davis and I have called several times on behalf of Roberta Wilcox. Ms. Wilcox has a ten-year-old son with asthma and the mold in the apartment is making him very sick. She is going to begin withholding her rent until the problem is fixed. She will be filing a complaint with the Department of Housing.

"Let her complain," said Isaiah. "If she does not pay her rent, we will evict her."

Two weeks later, Isaiah got a call from Gabriel Sachs, the son of a fellow former IDF solider. Gabe worked in planning at the city's housing department.

"There is a woman here who is trying to convince my superiors to open an investigation into your business," Gabe told Isaiah.

"A woman?"

"Her name is Sabrina Davis. She is a secretary. Apparently her husband works with children and some of their families have made complaints."

"Should I be worried?"

"Possibly. Most complaints never trigger an inquiry, but much of the time it is haphazard. You don't want someone bringing up your name constantly."

"And that is what she is doing?"

"Yes."

That afternoon, Isaiah informed Joe that the Davises seemed to have become fixated on him.

"We need to avoid an investigation."

CHAPTER THIRTY

The follow-up story on Sandra Michaels withholding evidence isn't much. Just a "no comment"/"we're looking into" placeholder. Jack Owens got a quote from a defense attorney whose client was exonerated in 2013 after serving twenty-eight years for a murder ("Some prosecutors will do anything to get a conviction") and on Monday morning the office issues a statement announcing that ADA Michaels has been taken off the Kendra Yaris case "pending investigation into allegations of past mishandling of evidence."

Mike calls and directs me to Crown Heights to get reaction from the Yaris family. But just after I get off the subway at Nostrand, Judge Sanchez calls.

"I'm at Felicia's office," she says. "They think someone slipped that evidence we found into the file recently."

"What makes them think that?"

"Apparently somebody came in asking about the same file a couple days before we did. And they have him on surveillance video."

Forty minutes later, I'm in ADA Felicia Castillo's office with Judge Sanchez and Richard Krakowski, the DA's spokesman.

"Before we go any further, we need to set some ground rules," says Krakowski. "Our official statement is that the prosecutor who tried this case *did not* have the evidence you uncovered—the letters and the police report—at the time of the trial. We are actively investigating whether what you found is authentically part of the case and, if so, how—and when—it was put into the case file."

I scribble what he's told me into my notebook.

"Now, we're going off the record," says Felicia. "I want you to know, I would never—*never*—give this kind of access to a reporter if Theresa were not involved."

"I told her I want someone outside this office—someone outside the court system—to see this," says Judge Sanchez. "If this video disappears . . ."

"It's not going to disappear," says Felicia.

"It better not."

The four of us gather around Felicia's desktop computer. Krakowski opens a plastic CD case and slips a disk into the drive. He clicks open the icon that appears and up pops a black-and-white image with a time and date stamp in the corner. The camera is mounted above the doorway leading into the storage room Judge Sanchez and I were in together.

"We don't get a lot of people asking for paperwork this old," explains Krakowski. "I talked to the clerk this morning, and it turns out she was sick early last week. She asked her people and was told that a man came in on Monday looking for the same file. Her replacement had an assistant escort him downstairs, and the assistant told me he brought the box down for the man, but left him alone after he showed an ID from the PBA."

"The police union?" I ask.

Krakowski nods, then clicks the video image, and after a few seconds we watch two men walk into the room. Because of the angle of the camera, we can't see their faces.

"That's the assistant," says Krakowski, pointing at the first man.

The two disappear out of the camera's range. About a minute later, the assistant appears again—he's facing the camera, so we see his face—and walks out the door. Another minute passes, and the second man walks back into the frame.

"That's him," says Krakowski, pausing the video. "In the sunglasses."

Mirrored aviator sunglasses. It's Saul.

"Do we think he's a cop?" asks Felicia.

"If he's not a cop he was pretending to be one," says Richard.

"If he's a cop, though, why show a PBA card? Why not his shield?"

Because they took his shield away, I think.

"What does the assistant say?" asks Judge Sanchez. "It looks like he wasn't alone long."

"Long enough to slip something into the box," says Krakowski.

"How many people have seen this?" I ask, trying to keep my voice steady.

"The clerk and the assistant. And ADA Michaels."

"And nobody recognizes him?"

"The sunglasses make it hard, but we'll print up a still image and start asking around. I've got a call in to the original detective on the case."

For a moment, everyone is silent, staring at Saul's frozen image.

"This doesn't show anybody actually slipping anything into the file," I say.

"No," says Krakowski. "But obviously, we need to talk to this man."

Yeah, I think. So do I.

Outside the courthouse in the blazing sun, I stare at my phone. Who do I call first? Mike, to tell him we have an exclusive on the fact that the DA suspects someone—someone only I know was one of the officers who arrested DeShawn—slipped crucial evidence into the Davis file two decades after the case was closed? Or Saul, to give him a chance to explain? But what possible explanation could he have for being in that storage room the day after I came to visit *other* than to fuck with the file? And if he did fuck with the file, that's a crime. It might be a bunch of different crimes. Even if Henrietta never comes forward, what Saul did might be enough to get DeShawn's conviction overturned. If that happens, the DA is going to shout Saul's name from the rooftops. DeShawn and some lawyer will sue the shit out of him. He might even go to prison.

And maybe he should.

CHAPTER THIRTY-ONE

Saul was taking his daily walk along the boardwalk when he received Rebekah's text about the landlord: *Just got a tip that Malcolm Davis may have had some sort of conflict with a Jewish landlord before he died. Do you remember anything about that?*

He put his hand on the railing and found a bench. How could he have been so stupid? He closed his eyes and saw Fraidy's spiteful face; he heard Binyamin's voice saying "I don't want to see you anymore;" he smelled the mildew in the lonely room in Coney Island. He had come so far from the misery of that time. But what he had done—and what he had not done—lived on. Rothstein wanted that file for a landlord. And he gave it to him. No questions asked.

Until he received the text, Saul had forgotten about the favor entirely. What sent him to his basement storage locker was what Rebekah said about the eyewitness. Her identification made it easy to do what he had done.

The Ziploc bag was inside a cardboard box of mementos from his life on the force. A certificate from the academy; a photograph of Saul shaking hands with the commissioner at graduation; a ribbon for placing in the NYPD 5K; his white dress gloves; a letter from a rape victim whose attacker he'd helped convict. He brought the box upstairs. Aviva was back in New Paltz and he had the apartment to himself. What would she think of what he'd done? Probably she would understand. Her daughter, on the other hand, would not. Aviva's moral code was less rigid that Rebekah's. Perhaps it was a function of her age. Saul once thought he had a rigid moral code. It was that code, ironically, that told him putting the letters and the police report in the Ziploc bag was the right thing to do.

It was a week after they handed the Davis case to the ADA. Saul was sitting at a desk in the precinct, going over his statement about why and how he had shot and killed a twenty-seven-year-old named Eric Overland the day before. Overland was the suspect in the double stabbing that he and Olivetti had been called to on Park Place. The scene was more gruesome, even, than the Davises'. The mother, forty-five-year-old Pauline Rodriquez, died in the apartment. Her daughter, Lisa—who had been dating Overland—was nineteen, and died at the hospital. Both had been tied up, sexually assaulted, and stabbed and slashed so badly that pieces of their bodies were severed. They found Pauline without nipples. Lisa arrived at Kings County Hospital unconscious, the four-month-old fetus

314

inside her exposed by the gaping wound in her abdomen. Olivetti and Saul tracked Overland to his cousin's house on Staten Island three days later.

"Keep your hand on your weapon," Olivetti had told him before they stepped out of the car. "This guy is a sneaky motherfucker."

What they'd learned about Overland was that four years earlier he'd been acquitted in the choking death of his seventeen-year-old girlfriend. When Saul talked to the ADA who prosecuted the case, he said the defense created reasonable doubt by introducing love letters from one of the girl's classmates. Overland's attorney speculated that it could have been this lovesick high school boy—not the girl's older boyfriend—who'd murdered her out of jealousy. If not for those stupid, harmless letters, Overland would have been in prison, and Pauline and Lisa Rodriguez would be alive.

Before they even knocked on the cousin's door, Saul sensed this arrest was going to go badly. The front window was open and he heard shouting, then a crash, like a piece of furniture being knocked over. Olivetti drew his weapon; Saul did the same.

The detective banged his fist on the front door.

"NYPD!"

Heavy footsteps, and then the door swung open. A man held his hands up and said, "He's upstairs."

Olivetti pulled the man onto the home's little front porch.

"Cuff him," said Olivetti. Saul obeyed.

"Is he armed?" Olivetti asked the man.

"He's got a knife. And my sister's in there."

"Why didn't she come out?"

"She's trying to talk to him. He showed up last night. Drunk as shit. I fucking *told* him to leave."

"But you didn't call the cops."

"Come on, man, that's my cousin."

"Your cousin stabbed a pregnant woman and her mother to death."

"He said it wasn't him."

"And you believed him?"

The man didn't answer.

"Put him in the car," said Olivetti. "Hurry up. And radio for backup."

"What'd I do?" asked the man.

"You harbored a felon, for starters."

Saul sat the man in the backseat of the cruiser. He got on the radio and gave their address, said they were preparing to apprehend an armed murder suspect.

Back on the porch, Olivetti was itching to get inside the house.

"If there's a woman in there she's in danger."

As if on cue, they heard a scream inside.

Olivetti kicked open the screen door, his gun pointed in front of him. Saul followed.

"Eric!" shouted Olivetti.

Another scream, and Eric Overland appeared at the

top of the staircase just inside the home. He held a young woman in front of him, a knife to her throat.

"Drop the knife, Eric," said Olivetti. Olivetti seemed calm, but Saul's hands were shaking. When they crossed into the house, Olivetti stepped right and Saul left, which put him at the foot of the stairs. His vision narrowed; everything surrounding the man and the woman above him became blurry.

"Stay the fuck down there!" shouted Eric.

Saul heard the words, but they sounded as if they were coming from far away, inside a tin can. Both he and Olivetti had their weapons pointed up, but there was no way they could shoot and not risk hitting the woman. She was silent now; a knife at her neck and two guns pointed at her.

"Let your cousin go," said Olivetti.

"Shut up!"

"Your family's been good to you, Eric," he said. "You're gonna need them. Let her go, drop the knife, and we'll talk. Just talk."

"Fuck you! I ain't stupid."

"Let her go, Eric. We can help you if you let her go. If you don't let her go, things are going to get really bad really fast."

In the distance, sirens.

"Let her go, man," said Olivetti. "Those sirens are for you. When those sirens get here all hell is gonna break loose. You're gonna die and your cousin's gonna die. Let her go and we can still talk."

The cousin started wimpering. Eric pushed her sideways and started down the stairs, the knife held strong out in front of him, pointed at Saul.

Saul pulled the trigger. Later, they told him he fired five shots. Four of the bullets hit Eric Overland.

No one thought he'd done anything wrong. The suspect was coming at him with an edged weapon. But in one instant, Saul became a man who had killed another man. Even in those first hours afterward he knew that fact would change him in ways he could only begin to imagine. He hated Eric Overland for that. He hated the cousin who didn't call the cops. And he hated the twelve members of the jury who had let Overland off four years earlier.

So when the woman from the evidence collection team found him in the precinct that mid-July afternoon and handed over the "possibly relevant" items they had taken from the Davis home, Saul made a decision. He was not going to be responsible for letting another murderer go free over some bullshit reasonable doubt. They had the confession. They had the witness. They had the perp.

If Saul is honest, and when Rebekah texts him twenty-some years later he has lost whatever ability he once had to be dishonest with himself, he has to admit that he hadn't thought once since about the papers he tucked into a drawer in his room at Coney Island, and then carried around from apartment to apartment in a box, until her visit. When he finally did think about it, he knew he'd done wrong. But, he thought, maybe I can make it right. Let Rebekah look into the case. Let her find the evidence—meaningless or meaningful. Let the truth come out, whatever it is.

PART 3

CHAPTER THIRTY-TWO

Once Joe had their phone number, finding the Davises' address was simple. He started with spray paint, something dramatic: big red letters across the front door. He hand-delivered the first letter, hopping quickly onto the porch after watching the family leave in the morning, then mailed the next two, thinking better of being seen on their street.

The letters were vague: *YOUR FAMILY IS IN DANGER* and *YOU ARE BEING WATCHED.* No details that could be traced to Isaiah.

He made the first phone call at dinnertime and a woman answered. Children's voices in the background; pots and pans.

"Hello?"

He was silent.

"Hello? Who is this?"

He called again a few days later and a boy answered.

"Davis residence, this is Ontario speaking."

In the background a woman asked: "Who is it, Ontario?"

"Who is it?"

The woman—Sabrina, he assumed, the wife who was complaining to her bosses at the housing department—came to the phone.

"Hello?"

He hung up.

He called every other day, at different hours, from different pay phones. If Malcolm answered, he hung up. If it was Sabrina or one of the children, he remained on the line, listening as their confusion turned to frustration and then to fear.

"Stop calling here!" begged Sabrina one evening.

"You are being watched," he said.

"What is this about?"

He decided he could tip his hand on the phone. No hard evidence, just a voice saying words no one else would ever hear.

"Stop bothering Isaiah Grunwald."

"Who? Isaiah . . . you mean . . . Oh my God. Malcolm!"

He hung up.

If they had just done as he asked, it would have ended there. But Malcolm Davis got self-righteous. One of Isaiah's handymen stopped by the office about a week later and informed them that a black man named Malcolm was knocking on doors at one of the buildings in Bushwick, asking people to sign a petition.

"What kind of petition?"

"I didn't get a look at it, but something about failure to maintain the building."

"Who does this man think he is?" shouted Isaiah. "What is this obsession with me? What have I done to him?" He turned to Joe. "I thought you were taking care of this?"

"I am," said Joe. "I will."

"This family needs to know that nothing good will come from challenging me like this."

Joe began to watch the Davises, to learn the patterns of their life. They attended church on Wednesday evening and Sunday morning, and went grocery shopping at the Associated market on Utica on Saturday. On Sundays after church they went to Prospect Park, sometimes with a larger group, sometimes alone. Sometimes they stopped at a restaurant and bought food for a picnic, sometimes they brought Tupperware from home. Mommy and Daddy and a little girl and boy. Sometimes a teenager was with them. Malcolm and the boy played catch, and Sabrina sat with the little girl, reading to her on a blanket, or watching as she climbed on the playground equipment.

He got the gun from a man who worked at the bodega on Hunny's block. All he had to do was ask, and hand over the cash.

"Have you shot one before?"

Joe said he hadn't, and the man suggested he take the gun on the Metro-North to a range outside Peekskill.

They won't ask you for paperwork, he said. You should be fine.

Joe took the train from Grand Central Station and spent the day shooting at paper targets in a field. His aim was good for a beginner. And the small pointers the instructor gave—pull the trigger on the exhale, be prepared for the kick—helped. But he was astute enough to realize that it would take time to become truly proficient with the weapon. And he did not have time.

On the ride home, he noticed his ears were still ringing. The noise and his inexperience with the weapon were liabilities. He needed to attack while the family was as helpless as possible—and as isolated. On the street, they could run or fight back. On the street someone could intervene. Ideally, he would shoot the couple in their home. Ideally, he would be hiding somewhere and wait until they were asleep. But gunshots in the middle of the night would alert neighbors quickly. The train stopped to pick up more passengers and that was when he saw the red, white, and blue bunting.

TARRYTOWN ANNUAL FOURTH OF JULY PARADE!

Gunshots could be mistaken for firecrackers.

It was June thirtieth. He had five days to prepare.

When he got back to Brooklyn that night, he walked from the subway to the Davises' address. They lived in a small house that was separated into two apartments; ground floor and above. Several things about the home worked to his advantage: it was the last house on the block, and there was a small alleyway behind it, meaning there were multiple ways in and out. The most promising entrance appeared to be a window he could reach with just a little boost. He found a paint bucket a few houses down and used it to peek inside: bunk beds and strewn clothing and posters on the walls. The window was open for the breeze, he guessed. But what kind of parents did not have bars on the window in their child's bedroom? More proof, Joe thought, that they deserved what was coming to them.

The paint bucket gave him the idea to disguise himself as a handyman, just in case anyone asked him what he was doing in the almost entirely black neighborhood. On July second, he tested the costume: work boots, paint-dusted pants, a roller, and a small tarp, all taken from one of Isaiah's vans. He watched as the family left their home in the morning, then laid the tarp under the window—cracked open again—climbed onto the bucket, and let himself in. No one said a word. He took his shoes off once inside. The house hummed softly; a refrigerator, or maybe an air-conditioning unit on the floor above. He walked down the hallway to what was obviously the master bedroom. A pile of laundry sat unfolded in a basket on the bed. There were framed photographs on the bureau: a wedding day, a visit to a tropical location, school portraits. A jewelry box. A mirror with a corsage of dried flowers hanging from one corner. Matching bedside tables with matching lamps. On the woman's side was lotion, a datebook, Kleenex. On the man's side there was a clipboard with a piece of paper on it, and on the piece of paper, signatures. He snatched the clipboard. They would think they had misplaced it, and in two days they would be dead.

There was a clothes closet in the bedroom, but it was small, with two sliding doors—not a good hiding place. The hall closet was also unsuitable, filled with built-in shelves that held linens and cleaning supplies. He could curl beneath the lowest shelf, but if someone opened the door, he would be cornered. Nothing presented itself in the second child's bedroom, either. He had two choices: a small space between the wall and the living room sofa, or beneath the master bed. Both were risky, but the living room seemed more so. If the family came home and sat down to watch television, the kids might run around and find him. The bedroom, he decided, was less likely to be a center of activity. Yes, someone might look under the bed for something, but a decision had to be made. He would enter the house while the Davises were at the Independence Day festivities—he made the assumption that they were the kind of family that would take the children to some sort of celebration—and shoot the parents in their bed once the family was asleep. From inside, he could unlatch and lift the window in their room, hop into the alleyway, and walk home.

He visited Hunny the next night and gave her a hundred dollars cash, and the addresses of the Davises' home and the precinct on Utica Avenue.

"Say you were in the neighborhood after the fireworks and saw a black man running out of this house. Say you saw him carrying a gun."

"I don't talk to cops," she said. She had smoked her drugs before he arrived; he could tell because of the way she kept licking her lips, and she couldn't stop moving.

"Sit down," he said.

She sat, knees bouncing, eyes moving around the room like she was following a fly. When she was like this she would fuck him more than once for the same price. But she wasn't as attractive to him as she had been when they first met. She'd lost weight, and didn't bother fixing herself anymore. Her apartment smelled like garbage, and she had turned lazy. At the beginning, she took charge of their nights, giving him new experiences and allowing him to relax and enjoy. But now he had to ask her to do every little thing. When this was over, he would stop seeing her.

"I don't talk to cops," she repeated.

"Five hundred dollars," he said. "And you aren't helping the police. You're lying to them."

He wasn't sure if she heard him. Or if she heard him, he wasn't sure she understood. If he had thought it might help, he would have hit her. But he did not want to risk her becoming angry and stubborn. Hunny did what she did for money, pure and simple. Enough money and she'd do anything.

"One thousand dollars," he said. "All you have to do is go to the precinct and say what I told you."

"A thousand?"

He nodded.

She picked up the twenties from the table between them, flipped through them like she was counting, but her eyes were unfocused.

"You trying to jam somebody up?" she asked.

He didn't answer. He didn't need to. She didn't really want to know. He stood up and began to unbutton his shirt, thinking, as he did, that the next time he was in this ugly little room he would be a killer.

The Fourth of July fell on a Saturday. He couldn't have planned it better. The streets near the Davises' house were swarming with people running amok, throwing bottles and blasting music, shouting and laughing. He kept his head down and his hands in his pockets as he walked up Utica from Eastern Parkway. No one noticed him. He had hidden the paint bucket in the alleyway, and he was ready with a response should someone question him as he popped the screen on the window and slipped inside. *I work for the landlord. They're having a problem with the latches.* But there were no questions. Before he slid under the bed to begin waiting, Joe used the toilet in the hall bathroom. He peed and flushed and put the seat down, using his knuckles so as not to leave fingerprints. There were three toothbrushes in a plastic cup on the sink and a sticker on the mirror, an *S*—the symbol for Superman. He smiled as he looked at himself beside the emblem. He pulled his handgun from his waistband and posed, pointing it at the mirror, moving his wrist around and watching the way he looked with the weapon in his hand. In the planning, he had not allowed himself to indulge in excitement. What he was doing was not about him, or what he wanted; it was about his commitment to Isaiah. But, he decided there in the Superman mirror, there was nothing wrong with taking pleasure in his work.

From beneath the bed, Joe felt the floor shudder when the Davises came in. Children running. A woman's voice.

"Ontario, will you help Kenya with her shoes please?"

"Kenya! No shoes on the carpet!" said a little boy.

"Gentle," said Sabrina.

Adult footsteps came into the bedroom. Joe saw gym socks. Malcolm Davis switched on a lamp.

"Do you want me to run a bath?" he called.

Sabrina came in. Bare feet, toenails painted pink.

"I think we can skip it tonight. It's late. If you do teeth and pajamas, I'll get them down."

"I thought maybe he'd be home," said Malcolm.

"I know," said Sabrina.

"I don't know what to do anymore. Does he even want to be here?"

"I think he does. I think he's just . . . having a hard time."

"I'm worried about how all this is affecting Ontario. It's exactly the wrong thing for him to see right now."

"I know."

Malcolm sat down on the bed.

"Red thinks he has a girlfriend. He told me she's nice. A track star. Why wouldn't he want to share that with us?"

"Maybe he will."

"He can't stay out all night. We can't just let this go."

"It's only eleven. He might still come home."

"And if he doesn't?"

"I don't know, Malcolm. If he doesn't we . . . talk to him."

"It's not enough. It's not *working*."

"What else can we do? I'm not giving up on him."

"I'm not saying we should give up."

"I know what you're thinking."

"We have to consider all the options. We have to consider Ontario, and Kenya."

"Giving up our son is not an option," said Sabrina. "I don't want to talk about this anymore tonight. There is nothing we can do. Stay here. I'll get them ready. Try to relax. Try to see the big picture. He's sixteen. He hasn't hurt anybody. . . ."

"He's hurting me! He's hurting you. He's hurting this family."

"Shh!"

From down the hall the little boy shouted, "Kenya needs help on the potty!"

"It's going to be okay, Malcolm," said Sabrina. "If we keep loving him, it's going to be okay."

Sabrina left the room, and Malcolm sat on the bed.

It was very hot. Joe's armpits and forehead itched. He heard the children talking, water running. Outside, the celebrations were ongoing. Shouting and pops; sirens, car horns. Malcolm switched on an electric fan and went into the bathroom. He brushed his teeth and changed his clothes, then got into bed. Soon, Sabrina came in and did the same.

"We should think about an AC unit for the boys' room," she said. "He doesn't complain, but even with the fan, it's uncomfortable in there. He's been opening the window, which makes me nervous. Should be sales coming up soon. I wouldn't mind one in here, either."

"Sounds reasonable."

"What are you reading?" asked Sabrina.

"Abel recommended it."

Bodies adjusted on the bed.

"You want a little lovin'?" asked Sabrina.

"Not really," said Malcolm. "I'm just . . ."

"It's fine."

"I love you."

"I know you do."

"I can't stop worrying about him."

"I think he's going to be okay," said Sabrina.

"The way he's been speaking to you . . ."

"He's testing us, Malcolm."

Malcolm sighed. More adjustments on the bed. Quiet. After about ten minutes, the bedside lights switched off.

"I love you," said Malcolm again.

"I love you."

He needed to wait until they were asleep, so he lay there in the dark, listening to them breathe. He would shoot Malcolm first, then Sabrina. When he heard the snoring, his stomach clenched. It was time. And then there was a scream. It came from down the hall.

"I'll go," said Sabrina.

"Just bring her in," said Malcolm.

Sabrina climbed out of the bed and Joe realized he would have to kill the girl, too. She was young, yes, but it was possible she could tell the police something. Even that he was white would be enough to contradict the story Hunny would tell. And what kind of life would she have anyway, with both parents dead? She would probably never recover. It was, he decided, the right thing to do, under the circumstances.

The little girl and the woman came back. Soon, he heard the snoring again, and decided it was time. He crawled along the carpet slowly, staying low as he emerged from beneath the bed on Malcolm's side. He came to all fours, and then stood, taking relief in the breeze blown by the fan, the cool against his sweat-soaked T-shirt. He aimed the weapon inches from Malcolm's head, face turned toward his wife, mouth slightly open. The bullet entered just in front of his ear, blowing his head apart. Sabrina sat up, sucking air. She turned his way, eyes wide. He aimed at her chest. Two shots and she fell back, slumped over. The little girl dove toward the end of the bed. There was less of her to aim at. Joe jumped to meet her before she could climb down. She stopped and stared up at him. There was a blond princess on her sleeping shirt.

"This is just a dream," he said. "Go back to sleep."

He pointed the weapon at her face, closed his eyes, and pulled the trigger.

CHAPTER THIRTY-THREE

July–September 1992
Crown Heights, Brooklyn; Fort Jackson, South Carolina

The Davis murders did not make the front pages. The morning after the bodies would have been discovered, Joe bought a copy of the *Trib* at a bodega down the street from his apartment and found the article on page four: "Three Dead in Savage Crown Heights Home Invasion."

The article said that police were interviewing a "person of interest." The next day, the paper reported that the Davises' teenage son was in custody. A day after that, the paper said the boy confessed, and that police had a witness who saw him leaving the scene. Each of these days, Joe went to the Kingston Avenue office ready for Isaiah to congratulate him. He did not expect a celebration, of course, but a nod. An acknowledgment. He had done his job. Yet Isaiah said nothing. Joe knew the landlord read the newspaper, and a triple murder in the neighborhood— even if it was on a black block—should have caught his attention, especially once he read the victims' names.

Finally, on the day the newspaper covered the funerals, Joe brought a copy to the office and laid it on Isaiah's desk.

"You have been reading the articles?" he asked.

Isaiah was silent.

"Everything is taken care of," said Joe. He opened the newspaper to the page where he'd slid the signatures from Malcolm's bedside table.

Isaiah looked up, and their eyes met. Joe saw immediately that the landlord was not pleased.

"There is no need to worry," said Joe. "The son confessed."

"Never come to this office again," said Isaiah. "If I were you, I would leave New York."

Joe withdrew what was left in his bank account that afternoon and took a taxi to Bushwick to get drunk and look for Hunny. He told the bartender he'd just been fired, and she poured them both a shot of whiskey.

"To new opportunities," she said.

"Yeah," said Joe. "New opportunities."

By nightfall, he'd forgotten about Hunny. He hailed a cab back to Crown Heights and walked through the streets for the last time, alternately mumbling and shouting about Chabad being full of phonies and cowards and idiots. How he got back to his apartment, he didn't remember, but the next morning he packed a bag and got a hotel room near Port Authority. He slept all day, then followed the crowds toward Times Square at night. And right there, in the center of it all, was the military recruiting station.

The whole process took less than an hour. Two days later, he took the ASVAB. When his score came back the Army recruiter told him that if he passed a background check he could start basic training in South Carolina in two weeks.

"Anything going to come up on the check?" asked the recruiter.

"I was expelled from school for fighting," he said.

"That shouldn't be a problem."

Basic training was more difficult than he expected. What bothered him was not the physical exertion—he had no problem stretching his body's limits—but the demands from his trainers. A year earlier—six months, even—he would not have felt the need to challenge the men barking orders at him. A year earlier, he would have accepted, even respected, the chain of command. He would have found pleasure in keeping his clothing and his bunk tidy, in pleasing his superiors, in conquering obstacles. But what he'd done in the Davises' bedroom changed him. He was more than just a rule follower. More than just a deviant looking for a place to park his problems. He was a man of action. He didn't want to be told what to do anymore. He could survive on his own.

Six weeks into training his marksmanship instructor criticized his shot grouping.

"Where's your control, Weiss?"

Joe turned and looked the man in the eye, then raised his rifle and fired it inches from the instructor's head.

"I'm better up close."

In the brig, he met Lawrence Franklin. Lawrence had gotten court marshaled for driving drunk on post and taking a swing at the officer who cuffed him.

"Fuck this shit," Lawrence said during one of their first nights sharing a cell. "We got skills. Come with me back to Chicago and we can make some real money."

CHAPTER THIRTY-FOUR

"You can't print that picture without warning him," says Iris.

We're on our third round at the cocktail bar down the block. The bartender (excuse me, mixologist), a lanky white boy from California with a man bun and Gothic script tattooed across his collarbone, wants to fuck Iris, so he's making us elaborate drinks, one after the other. Iris is sipping at a stemless champagne flute with pomegranate seeds floating in it; mine is pisco-something. Dinner is the free popcorn.

"I could," I say. "I almost did. If I hadn't recognized him I would have brought the printout to the office three hours ago and it would be online right now."

"But you did recognize him. You have more information, so you have a different responsibility."

"My responsibility is to the truth," I kick back. "Saul broke into that file. At the very least he tampered with evidence."

"You don't know that for sure. You don't have any photos of that."

I would respond, but instead I launch into a coughing fit. The popcorn is peppered almost maliciously. Mixologist brings a glass of water as I right myself, wipe my eyes.

"I'm kind of surprised you're so ready to turn on him," says Iris.

"I'm not turning on him. He lied to me. Again. He was like, I barely remember this case. And he made me feel like shit for questioning him. But DeShawn didn't kill his family. Henrietta proves that."

"You're sure you believe her?"

"Why is it so hard to believe that I believe her?"

"It's just such a crazy story. And she's obviously good at lying. She convinced a jury and Sandra Michaels and everybody."

"I don't get the sense they took much convincing, you know? There were a couple murders every single day just in Brooklyn back then. Now there's one in the whole city, if that. I bet they were like, cool, we got a witness, we got a confession, onto the next."

"I don't see how you confess if you didn't do it," she says, then puts her hand up. "I know, I know. The Central Park Whatever, but seriously. Would you ever say you murdered three people if you didn't? I mean, that's insane."

"The fact that your privileged ass can't imagine doing it doesn't mean someone else wouldn't."

Iris rolls her eyes. "Fine. Fine. Even if Saul lied, even if he somehow fucked with the case, shouldn't you give him a chance to explain before you put him on blast to the whole city? Journalism 101. Get both sides of the story."

"Running the photo doesn't necessarily ID him," I say.

"You're saying you're going to give the *Trib* the photo and not tell them you know who it is?"

"I don't know! I mean, I guess I have to tell them, right?"

"Probably. But talk to Saul first. Just get it over with. Call him now."

She picks up my phone, plugs in my passcode.

"Stop," I say, snatching it back. "I will."

"Your mom will understand."

"I don't think she will," I say, my voice quieter. "I'm trying, I really am. But she thinks I'm spoiled. And selfish."

"Well," says Iris, "she doesn't really know you. And if you keep avoiding her she never will."

I don't respond.

"You need to try to look at it from her point of view. She's gotta be dealing with a shitload of guilt every time she sees you. I'm not saying she doesn't deserve it. It's just . . ."

"We don't have to talk about it," I say. What I mean is, I don't want to talk about it.

"You need to call him."

I suck the last of my cocktail through the little black straw.

Mixologist appears immediately. "Call who?"

"Tell her to call him," says Iris.

"Call him," he says.

"Tell her you won't make her another drink until she calls him."

"I won't make you another drink until you call him."

Does he think this makes him attractive?

"I don't need another drink," I say.

"Just do it," says Iris. She actually pokes me with her finger.

"Do it," says the mixologist.

"Fucking Christ," I say. "Fine."

The story Saul tells is reasonable. Wrong and fucked up, but reasonable. When he is finished talking, his face is red. He hasn't looked me in the eye since I walked into his apartment, where he summoned me promising to reimburse the late-night livery cab fare.

"Why didn't you just give the evidence to me?" I ask.

"Because I was trying to stay out of it."

"That doesn't make any sense! You can't really have thought you could sneak that stuff into the file and no one would notice. And what about Sandra Michaels? You're cool with her just getting blamed?"

"She'll be fine," says Saul. "She is very powerful now. She has lots of friends. And it is just one case. There are many possible explanations for something like this."

I am, for the first time I can remember, stunned to

silence. He was just going to let her take the fall.

"You don't have to use my name to tell your story," says Saul.

"Saul, you *are* my story. An innocent man has been in prison more than half his life because the cop working his case buried evidence in a fucking *box* in his apartment!"

"That is not the only reason he is in prison."

"Saul . . ."

He stands up abruptly, knocking a mug of coffee onto the carpet. We both stare at the floor, watching the brown stain spread.

"I am not proud of what I did, Rebekah. I am asking you . . . They will reopen every case I ever worked on."

"Maybe they should! How many other times did you do this?"

Saul raises his eyes to me. "None. I give you my word. The day that woman from evidence gave me those letters was the most terrible day of my life, Rebekah. I had just killed a man. My relationship with my son was over." He pauses. "He was afraid of me. Can you imagine? No, you do not have children, so you cannot. But please try. He did not want to see me because he had been convinced that I was a threat to him. Me—his father. I would have died for him, suffered for him. And when he learned what I had done. That I had taken a life . . . I knew Fraidy would never let him see me after that. It was the perfect excuse. *Your tatty is a killer. Forget him.*"

Saul waves his hands in front of him like he is trying to

flick something off them. It's a gesture I know well: trying to fling the pain inside out.

"I have to run the photo," I say. "It's not just about you."

Saul does not respond.

"Someone will probably recognize you."

"Perhaps."

"It's only a matter of time, Saul. I can't believe you thought you'd get away with it."

"I took a chance," he said. "In my experience, security cameras in public buildings in this borough are nonfunctioning at least half the time."

I almost laugh. Almost.

"Before you make your decision I want you to come with me somewhere," he says.

"Where?"

"Crown Heights."

Saul and I step off the elevator on the third floor of the Crown Heights Jewish Council just after noon the next day. A receptionist shows us into Naftali Rothstein's office, where two men are waiting.

"I was hoping we could meet alone," says Saul.

"You and Daniel are here to discuss the same problem," says Naftali. He looks at me. "This is Daniel Grunwald. He runs the Crown Heights Shmira."

"Shmira?" I ask.

"It is like the shomrim," says Saul. "A different word for the patrol group."

346

"We are off the record, Miss Roberts," says Naftali.

Figures.

"Fine," I say, thinking, as always, build trust now, get quotes later.

"Do you remember a man named Joseph Weiss?" asks Naftali.

Saul shakes his head.

"There is no reason you should," says Daniel. "He was only in the community about a year."

"Joseph?" I ask. Then look at Saul. "Joe."

"What?" asks Naftali.

"Last weekend I went to Atlantic City and talked to the only witness in the Davis murders. She told me that a Jewish man named Joe paid her a thousand dollars to lie and say she saw a black kid running out of their house that night. Could it be the same person?"

Daniel breathes in deeply through his nose. "Yes," he says.

For the next twenty minutes, Daniel tells us about "Joe from California" who worked for his uncle Isaiah, a landlord, from September 1991 to July 1992.

I hear the word *landlord* and look at Saul. If this Isaiah instructed Joe to kill the Davises to stop their investigation into his business, the story I write is going to confirm every ugly stereotype about Jews imaginable. This is exactly the kind of shit that got nine utterly innocent Jewish students and teachers slaughtered in Roseville last year. What if Ontario, or DeShawn, or even Toya—people whose lives are divided entirely by what happened before the Davis murders and what happened after—get it in their head to get some revenge? It's easy to get a gun in Brooklyn. It's easy to find a Jew on the street.

When Daniel finishes speaking, Naftali looks at Saul, whose face has gone white.

"I know what you are thinking. Yes, Isaiah Grunwald was the man who asked for the Davis file. He lied to me, apparently, about his relationship with the family. Obviously, if I had known he might be involved in some way . . . if I had even *suspected* . . ."

Saul lets him trail off. "I should not have handed it over in the first place."

"What are you talking about?" I ask.

"There is nothing we can do about that now," said Naftali. "I've asked the yeshiva to look for any paperwork they have on Joseph. Daniel wants to go to the police. I would like to speak with Isaiah first."

"Why?" I ask. "He's the one who benefited from their deaths, right?"

Naftali and Daniel look at me.

"What do you mean, benefited?" asks Naftali.

"A friend of the Davises told me that before they died Malcolm and Sabrina were trying to get the housing department to investigate a landlord."

Naftali looks at Daniel. "Did you know about this?"

Daniel nods.

"And yet you said nothing," says Saul.

"Do you remember what it was like here in 1992?" says Daniel, raising his voice. "Can you *imagine* what would have happened if a chassidish man was accused of slaughtering a black family? Jewish blood would have run in the streets!"

I raise my eyebrows, which upsets Daniel.

"You think you are so smart. You have *no idea* what we were dealing with then. Now it is fashionable to live here. When this happened you could not *give away* a home in Crown Heights. My uncle . . ."

"Daniel," says Naftali.

"No. No. My uncle invested in this neighborhood. He may have made some mistakes but . . ." Daniel stops himself. "When this happened, I was not certain that Joe—or my uncle—was involved."

"And now?" asks Saul.

"Now," he pauses, "now I wish I had not been so careless. Or so blind."

Naftali clears his throat. "We are not certain this man committed these murders. And we are definitely not certain Isaiah was involved. If this is just a coincidence, I do not want to bring unnecessary scrutiny to the community. Joseph is a very common name."

"Do you have a picture of him?" I ask.

"The yeshiva should have a class photograph," says Naftali.

"Good," I say. "I know a woman who can tell us for sure."

CHAPTER THIRTY-FIVE

September 1992
Crown Heights, Brooklyn

Isaiah kept the signatures in a safe deposit box along with his birth certificate, his citizenship papers, and $750,000 in gold bars. The bars he had been amassing since the late 1970s. They were the only insurance policy a Jew in this world could rely on. With gold bars, a man need not stay longer than is safe in a country whose leadership has suddenly changed. Gold could get Isaiah and his wife plane tickets and new identities in Mexico, or Indonesia, or South Africa. His mother's entire family perished together in 1941, lined up and shot by Nazis along with 35,000 other Jews at the lip of a mass grave outside Minsk. Somehow, the spray of bullets only grazed eighteen-year-old Sonia Baran. For hours she lay still beneath a thin layer of sand, bodies below and beside and atop her, many still writhing and moaning. At nightfall, she climbed out and ran through the forest. She made it to a suburb where no one on the streets wore a yellow star. What she needed were papers that did not identify her as Jewish. With those, she could escape to Israel or America. For two days, she hid in a storage shed behind a bakery. The smell of the bread coming from the ovens nearly felled her—Isaiah remembers her telling him that she hadn't eaten bread that didn't chip her teeth in a year—but she remained out of sight, watching the proprietor and his family through a crack in the door. The baker and his wife appeared to have only one child, a daughter about her age. On the third night, after two days eating the flour and sugar dust off the floor of the shed, she broke the window of the bakery, stuffed yesterday's bread down her shirt and, while the family was downstairs assessing the damage, snuck into the apartment above. She found the daughter's identification documents folded neatly in a leather envelope on the bureau in her bedroom. For six months, until she got to Israel, Sonia Baran, born in 1923, became Dasha Garmash, born in 1925.

Isaiah was born in Tel Aviv in 1944. Many of his peers' parents had stories like his mother's, and each took something different as a moral. The Rebbe taught that, more important than searching for lessons from the Holocaust, one should guard against despair. If the Jews who survived sunk into despair, they became victims of the Nazis, too. Jews should live with joy; serve God with joy. Isaiah agreed with the Rebbe, of course, but he also believed that after Hitler, a Jew who did not plan for a quick escape was a fool. And Isaiah Grunwald was no fool.

So when Joe Weiss came to work grinning in the days

after the Davis murders appeared in the newspaper, Isaiah experienced not just the shock of what had been done in his name, and the fear of the consequences for himself and his fellow Lubavitchers, but the unmooring knowledge that he so badly misjudged this man. How could he have failed to see what he had let into his life? For two days he did not eat; he lay in bed and could not sleep. He had taken a step—many steps—in the wrong direction. He had crossed lines. He had sinned. The sins had seemed minor; the victims removed from his daily life, the actions not technically his. But there could be no doubt that he set into motion the series of events that led to the slaughter of three innocent people. It mattered little that he had not intended for Joe to commit murder. What had he intended when he instructed him to make the problem go away? A threat. What kind of threat? If he wanted someone to reason with the Davises, he could have tasked Daniel. But he chose Joe. Would he have approved of a black eye? A broken leg? A menacing note handed to a child? Where did what was moral turn into what was immoral? He turned these questions over in his mind until he realized that the answers made no difference. He had not intended the specific outcome, but should have foreseen it. He had encouraged—or at least allowed—Joe and the others who worked for him to think of the people in his buildings as unworthy of the help they would give fellow Jews. If they were lesser human beings, it was just another few steps to barely human at all.

He avoided Joe for three days. The California boy with the handsome face was a monster, and now Isaiah had a decision to make.

When Joe came to his office with the newspaper and the signatures he had taken from the Davis home, Isaiah did not give the speech he had been constructing in his mind. He did not yell or even question. Standing on the other side of his desk, Joe felt to him like a bomb about to explode. The longer Joe remained in Crown Heights, the more likely what he had done would be discovered. And if it were discovered, Isaiah feared that what had happened the summer before—the fires and the stabbings and the mayhem; the hate writ large on every face—would be repeated, magnified. With the match lit by a Jew, he knew that whatever sympathy the police and the goyim of the city had for his community would be obliterated. The death of that poor little boy on Utica Avenue had been an accident. This was murder. And he and his fellow Jews would be made to pay for it.

So Isaiah told Joe to go. Go and never come back.

"You have done the wrong thing," he said as the young man turned to leave his office. If Joe heard his boss, he did not respond. Isaiah remembered that Joe had the newspaper tucked beneath his arm, folded open to the page with the photograph of the mourners. As if he was proud.

When enough time passed that it didn't look suspicious, Isaiah asked Naftali Rothstein for the file on the murdered family and learned that the police did not

354

appear to have anything that could connect him—or Joe—to the crime. After that, he did what he could do, what was all too easy for him: he wrote three checks. One was made out to Glorious Gospel, with the words "In memory of Malcolm and Sabrina Davis, and Kenya Gregory" written on the note line. The second, mailed in the same envelope as the first, was made out to Ontario Amos, "For the care and education of the child." The final check he took to an attorney outside the community. He instructed the man to create a trust for DeShawn Perkins. Invest it, he said, and send a little to his prison account each month. Isaiah knew DeShawn had been sentenced to life, but perhaps someday he would get out. If he did, he would need money.

The checks came from a bank account for "The Canada Fund, LLC," but all a curious soul would find if he went searching for the entity was a PO box on the Lower East Side. A PO box that Isaiah closed once the checks were cashed. He named the fund for Ontario, the little boy left behind. Maybe, he reasoned, the boy's mother had a connection there. Maybe she named him for a good memory.

Over the next few years, he sold his interest in most of the apartment buildings Joe and Daniel had visited. Let his former partners manage the tenants. Let them make those daily decisions that had led to this. By the summer of 2014, when the article about DeShawn appeared in the *Tribune,* Isaiah Grunwald owned only the four-story building on Kingston Avenue that housed his office on the second floor and his home on Crown Street. The rent from the storefront and two apartments at the Kingston address was enough to live on. He was getting old, and the gold bars meant he didn't need more for his family's security. Certainly, he did not deserve more.

CHAPTER THIRTY-SIX

I am sitting in a café on the ground floor of the Jewish Children's Museum on Eastern Parkway when Henrietta calls.

"That's him," she says. "How'd you find him?"

"It's a long story. You're sure that's who paid you to lie to the police?"

"Positive. I almost forgot how young he was. But he scared me good. Little shit." She pauses. I can hear slot machines ringing in the background. "I gotta get off before my shift manager sees me talking."

Henrietta hangs up before I can ask if she'll go on the record. I call back, but she sends me to voice mail.

I look at the photo of this man who I now know likely murdered three people and got away with it. He is, I have to admit, attractive. Large hazel eyes and a heart-shaped face. A man you would feel safe opening the door for. He is smiling at the camera in the portrait. Chin up, like he is proud; preening almost. Naftali and Daniel and the other

Lubavitch men milling around me wear a black-brimmed hat that is slightly different from the ones the men in Borough Park and Roseville wear—it is angled down at the front, more like a fedora than a top hat. It occurs to me that that hat, which always seemed so stodgy and old-fashioned, is also, on Joe at least, almost rakish.

Mike calls at noon, and he isn't happy.

"The *Ledger* just went live with a story about some guy planting evidence in your cold case," he says. "They've got a surveillance photo and a comment from Michaels' office. Why don't we have this?"

"I . . . um . . . I actually had it, but I wanted to confirm . . ."

"You had it? What the fuck! We need to get this up *now*. And we need to advance."

I make the decision quickly. The photo is out there; if someone sees past the sunglasses and identifies Saul, I'm screwed. It'll look like I withheld the information because of my relationship with him. Which, of course, I did.

"I know who it is."

"What? Who? Is it on the record?"

"It's Saul Katz."

"Saul Katz. Why do I know that name?"

"Because he was my source on the Rivka Mendelssohn murder."

"Who?"

"Crane lady."

"Crane . . . oh, Jesus! You're kidding me. The disgraced cop?"

I figure I might as well go all in. "He's dating my mother."

"Fucking fuck, Rebekah. I . . . I'll call you back. Do not call the DA's office. You are off this story."

He hangs up and I sit, listening to the roar in my ears. My face is hot; it feels like needles are poking into and out of my skin.

My hands are shaking as I call Saul's cell.

"Where are you?" I ask. We left Naftali's office only an hour ago.

"I am home."

"You're going to get a call from the *Trib*."

"I see."

"I'm sorry. The *Ledger* has the photo online. Someone in the DA's office must have given it to them. It was only a matter of time before someone recognized you."

"Perhaps."

"Henrietta just called and she ID'd Joseph from the photo Naftali gave us. That's the man who paid her to lie to you. If he didn't kill the Davises, he knows who did."

I expect Saul to respond, but he doesn't.

"Saul?"

"I'm going to have to call you back, Rebekah. I need to make some arrangements."

And he's gone.

I e-mail the *Trib*'s library and ask them to run a backgrounder on Joseph Weiss, originally from California (*He'd be 40-something now. Lived in Brooklyn in 1991–1992ish*), and then pack up and head to Isaiah Grunwald's office. It's a little bit cooler out than the last few days, and the yeshiva students—all male, of course—are lingering on the sidewalks, chatting, sipping sodas, typing on smartphones. Two women, each pushing a double stroller, walk past with purpose.

The door to 318 Kingston is slightly ajar, so I push in. A bulletin board just inside lists Grunwald Management as being on the second floor. Halfway up the stairs, I hear a woman screaming.

"I don't know!" She says something else but I can't make out the words above the howls of another female voice. "Please! Come now! Help!"

I step inside the door marked Grunwald Management and find a woman in the reception area kneeling over a man who is splayed on the carpet, convulsing. Her arms to her elbows are blood smeared, and I can see her underwear beneath her flesh-colored pantyhose. She appears to have pulled off her skirt in order to press it against the man's chest. The man, I realize as I step closer, is Naftali.

"Give me your shirt!" screams the woman when she sees me. I pull my flimsy H&M blouse over my head and hand it to her. She presses it against Naftali and it is soaked through in seconds. She tries to pull her own shirt off, but her hands are shaking so violently she cannot control her fingers to grasp the blood-slick buttons.

"Did you call 911?" I ask.

"Yes! Yes!" The woman turns to her colleague, a much

younger woman—probably a teenager—who has her back pressed against the wall. Her eyes are wide and she is huffing a half-scream half-grunt with each breath. I watch as her face turns from white to purple.

"Hella!" shouts the woman on the floor. "Give me your skirt!"

But Hella can only gasp for air.

I look around for something else to press against Naftali's chest. Through a doorway about ten feet away I see the tail of a black coat. I crawl toward it and realize it is attached to a man. A dead man. Daniel. And he is not the only dead man in the office. An older man is bent backward over the arm of a leather desk chair, his eyes frozen open, a pink ring across his forehead where his hat pressed into his skin.

"What happened?" I whisper, almost to myself.

"He just started shooting!"

"Who?"

"I don't know! I don't know! Hella! Give me your skirt!"

But Hella's skirt won't help. Naftali is gone.

When help arrives, the only person they are able to assist is Hella, who gets oxygen, a stretcher down the stairs, and whisked away in one of the waiting Hatzolah ambulances. Someone brings the other woman, Goldy, a blanket to cover herself. I sit, shivering in my bra until an EMT hands me an FDNY T-shirt that is four sizes too big. The blood is everywhere. I won't be able to get it out of my cuticles for days.

Goldy tells the detectives that Naftali and Daniel came to the office unannounced—probably immediately after meeting with me and Saul—and that the three of them had been behind closed doors when the man with the gun arrived.

"Do you have any idea who he was?" asks the detective, Anne Richter.

"He was frum, but I never saw him before."

I pull out my phone and scroll to the photo of Joseph Weiss.

"Was this him?"

She looks hard for several seconds. "Maybe," she says. "Hella was the one who greeted him. I was at the photocopier."

Detective Richter turns to me. "Who is this?"

I explain, and when they are finished questioning me I call Henrietta, but she doesn't pick up. I leave a rambling message, then boil it down in a text:

Joe might have just shot 3 people in Brooklyn. Be careful.

On my way home in a livery cab, I text Amanda:

I've got some info on a shooting in Crown Heights

CHAPTER THIRTY-SEVEN

Spring 1993–August 2014

He'd been lucky, and smart, and he'd stayed out of prison. He didn't have to do jobs more than three or four times a year to live the way he wanted—which was alone. After Chicago, he rented a house on Martha's Vineyard during the off-season and returned most winters. He walked on the beach for miles and didn't see a soul. The people he met in bars, the girls who came over to fuck—paid and unpaid, though there was overlap—didn't ask a lot of questions.

But in Brooklyn, they had his real name, and they might even have his DNA. He avoided the borough entirely for twenty years; in 2002 he actually turned down fifty grand for an easy job in Bay Ridge because he knew that his first kills had been careless. He kept up on the news, however, and when he saw the article that said they'd found the letters he sent the Davises, he knew he needed to take care of it. Immediately.

He ordered the black pants and jacket and hat online, and two days later, at just after noon, he parked his car—a silver Hyundai; forgettable, dependable, with all the interior bells and whistles, and the registration and insurance up to date—along the eastern edge of Prospect Park. He walked toward Kingston Avenue with his gun in his pocket.

Isaiah and Daniel did not have time to recognize him. The third man, well, that was his bad luck. The woman who asked him to wait at reception must have hidden herself when she heard the shots, and he decided it was not worth hunting her down. The sooner he was out of Brooklyn, the better.

His buddy with the tech job at the FBI had gotten him Hunny's new address. He figured he had less than twelve hours to execute before she got word there'd been a shooting in Crown Heights and got on her guard.

There was a gas station across the street from her apartment complex, and he stopped there to watch. At sunset, she drove into the parking lot and took the stairs to the second floor. She'd gained weight, but not as much as some women. Maybe, he thought, she'd want to fuck him. For old time's sake.

He was taking a risk approaching without being certain she was alone, but he wanted to be south of Richmond by midnight, with Brooklyn behind him forever.

He wiggled out of the Chabad uniform in the driver's seat; donned a plain black T-shirt, cargo shorts, and his Dodgers hat. He knocked twice at apartment eight, and he was raising his arm for a third rap when the bullet pierced his chest.

CHAPTER THIRTY-EIGHT

August 2014
Atlantic City, New Jersey

A lot of things had changed in her life since the summer Joe the Jew stuck a gun in her mouth, but a lot of things hadn't. She made better choices now, but still woke up every morning wanting to get high. She'd accepted that she always would, which was why she went to church, and why she kept fucking poor Marcus Reeves, with his bad knees and dopey anniversary celebrations. But she was no fool. Henrietta Day in 2014 may not do the same things Hunny Eubanks did in 1992, but she had seen the same things and felt the same pain and learned the same lessons. One of those lessons was that when she was sober, her gut was pretty good at detecting danger. And when she read that reporter's story in the newspaper, she knew shit was gonna come home to roost. If he was still alive, he'd have to try to get rid of her.

So she pulled Roger the night janitorial supervisor aside, and he got her a gun. Gina had one for a little while back when they lived together in Bushwick. A guy

365

she used to see came by late one night and asked her to hold it. He didn't even wanna fuck, just needed to stash the thing. After a week, she sold it for a hundred dollars and they got high. Gina was dead now. Long dead. Like most of the people Hunny used to know. But not Hunny. Not yet.

What did she remember about Joe? He was smart, but not street smart—at least not as much as her. That could have changed by now. Either way, he was always going to be physically stronger. So she couldn't hesitate. She watched from the window, and when the white guy in the ball cap came across the parking lot, she pointed her gun at the door and waited for the knock.

After the first shot, she looked through the peephole. He was down, but not out. She opened the door and took three more shots until she was certain.

There was nothing in the apartment she couldn't replace. She could clean for cash anywhere she could get a reference, and there were still a couple people who would help her: a cousin near Savannah; an old classmate in Jacksonville. She knew they would all look for her—the police, the reporter. And maybe they'd find her. But she wasn't gonna give herself up. If they wanted her, they'd have to work hard, just like she'd done all her fucking life.

CHAPTER THIRTY-NINE

I take a livery cab home from Crown Heights, get in the shower to wash as much of the blood off me as possible, then open my laptop and start writing. I write about seeing Saul's name in DeShawn's file; I write about meeting Ontario and LaToya, and about finding the evidence box with Judge Sanchez. I write about the Pastors Green, Dorothy and Abel, and the lovesick Legal Aid lawyer-turned-real estate agent. I find the place in my notebook where I scribbled notes from that morning's meeting with Daniel and Saul and Naftali, and I add that conversation. I keep writing when Iris comes home, and when I'm done, I e-mail what I've written to Amanda.

Want some context on the latest murders?

About twenty minutes later, Amanda e-mails back.

Can you come over tomorrow?

I'm scheduled to work a 10-6 on the city desk, but I e-mail my cadre of fellow stringers and find someone to cover the shift. Everybody needs an extra $150 these days.

I don't sleep much, so at dawn, I start walking to Amanda's. I don my headphones but don't turn on any music. I feel like I have to listen to what's happening inside me, even though I don't know what it is. Is Joe coming for me next? Did I get those men killed? I still haven't heard from Hunny. The consequences of what I've done are so vast I worry that if I stop walking I'll collapse and never get up. Amanda brings two mugs of coffee outside and we talk on her front porch. She sits, but I can't.

"So how are you?" she asks.

"Okay."

"Have you ever seen bodies like that before?"

"Shot? Sort of," I say, remembering the kids beneath white sheets on the playground in Roseville. "Not that close up."

A few seconds pass.

"I can't publish what you sent me," she says. "I can't give these deaths that much more attention than I give everybody else. You know? That's not fair. But it's amazing. I can't believe how much you found out so fast. This shit happened decades ago. I e-mailed my friend at the *Guardian,* and she wants it, with some minor edits. Will the *Trib* let you do that?"

"As far as they're concerned, I'm off the story. Too close to it."

"Yeah, well, their loss. You're not hiding anything with this, and it needs to be out there. But listen, I've got a question for you. I applied for a grant from the

Open Society a few months ago, and I just heard it came through. A hundred thousand dollars to expand the scope of the Project."

"Wow, that's awesome," I say. "What's your plan?"

"I want to hire you."

"Me?"

"I want to be able to write more about the people who die here. I've got all this data and all these contacts, but I'm not the writer you are. And I'm not as good a reporter, either.

"We can work on the details, but I'm thinking, you pick a murder every week, maybe more, maybe less, and do a deep dive. And you can do issue stories, too. Look for patterns in what's happening. Domestic violence, the iron pipeline, mental illness, gangs. How are people really dying in this city, and why? My friend at the *Guardian* might be interested in partnering up, so your stories could have real reach. Which is what I want. It's hard for people to connect with maps and data. I need shoe leather. And narrative."

I look at her to make sure she's serious.

"What?" she asks. "What are you thinking?"

"I'm thinking with that much money you could hire someone away from *ProPublica,* or *The Times*."

"Yeah," she says. "But I want you."

Detective Richter calls a few days after the shootings to tell me (off the record) that the gun found on the man shot to death outside Henrietta's Atlantic City apartment was the weapon that killed Isaiah, Naftali, and Daniel.

"The guy didn't have an ID, so we're still confirming he's who we think he is. Joseph Weiss has exactly zero paper trail since 1994."

I ask her about Henrietta, and she says they're still looking.

"We didn't find anything personal in her apartment. Even her boyfriend says he didn't know her real last name. Her prints are in the system, though. Eventually, she'll show up."

Or not.

The Sunday desk assigns Jack Owens to look into Joseph Weiss's background, but the only story he does is about Weiss getting kicked out of the Army in early 1993. Jack tells me at a happy hour a couple weeks later that he tracked down Weiss's former cellmate from military prison, but the *Trib* didn't think it was worth sending him to Indiana where the guy is incarcerated. So far, I haven't seen any reporting on the last twenty years of his life, except that his parents told the Associated Press they got a phone call from him once a year, on Yom Kippur.

The *Trib* and the *Ledger* and half a dozen other city news outlets send reporters up to Aviva's house in New Paltz where she and Saul hole up after the story of the corrupt Jewish cop who covered up for the Jewish murderer goes live. All three cable news networks cover the triple murder in Crown Heights, but Saul's involvement is too "inside baseball" to make waves nationally. Several papers contact Pete Olivetti, retired and living in Sarasota, but the best quote anyone gets is "Katz seemed like a straight shooter to me." Sandra Michaels maintains she is "looking at options" for charging him with something, and the NYPD calls him a "bad apple" at every opportunity, but Saul tells me his lawyer assures him the statute of limitations for anything that he did in 1992 has long expired. And even if DeShawn decides to sue, the lawyer says he'll almost certainly sue the city, or maybe the state, not Saul personally. The Kings County DA's office creates a "task force"—which consists of two people working a couple hours a week—to examine all of Saul's old cases. So far, they haven't found anything.

The people Saul helped lock up over two decades, however, are getting lawyers. And Aviva blames me. I hear nothing from her for weeks after the murders, and then early one Sunday morning she calls.

"All these crazies! Lawyers coming by the house! Letters from prisoners!"

"What?" I had been deep in a dream about my first apartment in Gainsville. The one Iris and I shared with two other girls sophomore year. In the dream we were throwing rocks into the pool from our concrete balcony. It was dusk and the pool light was on. There was something in the water we were trying to kill.

Saul's voice in the background: "Aviva!"

"She should know!"

Saul comes on the line.

"Rebekah, I'm sorry. This is . . . we need to have a discussion."

"What?"

"Your mother is very angry. . . ."

"You are angry, too!" shouts Aviva.

"Aviva, stop it!"

"Are you okay?" I ask. "Is she okay?"

"Yes. This has gone on long enough, Aviva."

"Where are you guys?" I ask.

"We are in Brooklyn. We drove back late last night. Your mother hasn't slept."

I look at the time on my phone: 5:18 A.M.

"We will come to you," he says.

Iris won't be up for hours, so I tell Saul to meet me at a park near my apartment. The sun is just up and the air is lighter, the pavement cool. This early, it's a different population in Park Slope. There are the runners—on their way to or from Prospect Park, smartphones velcroed to biceps, T-shirts commemorating the most recent race; and parents—men and women pushing strollers, wearing sunglasses, flip-flops, and drinking Venti coffee. I pick up my own coffee at a bagel shop. The woman next to me is wearing a baby strapped to her chest. The child is astonishingly blond and chewing on a plastic corn on the cob with the words JOHN DEERE printed across. I smile. If Iris were with me, we'd laugh and add the scene to our list of hipster details. Someday, we're going to write *Legally*

Blonde: Brooklyn, get Reese to sign on as a perky pro bono lawyer for senior citizens being gentrified out by people like us, and make a million dollars. It feels like the first time I've smiled in weeks. It's hard not to think that a whole bunch of people would be alive today if it weren't for me. DeShawn is probably going to get out; he has one of the best exoneration attorneys in the country. But my mind keeps going to this: is his life worth three other people's? I know it's completely unanswerable, and the wrong question, and obviously unfair, but I can't stop thinking it. Iris and my therapist and my dad say it's crazy to blame myself. But the Davis murders were a case sitting in a dark room until I switched the light on. Would I have started making calls on DeShawn's letter if I had known how Joe Weiss was going to tie up loose ends? And if the answer is no, does that mean I made the wrong choice?

At seven o'clock I find Saul and Aviva sitting on a bench. She stands up when she sees me. He stands up after her.

"Thank you for coming," says Saul. He's a couple days past a shave, which is unusual.

Before I can even ask *what the fuck?* Aviva steps close to me and says, "I think you did this to Saul to get back at me."

I look at Saul.

"I didn't."

"Would you admit it?" asks Aviva. Her voice is tight and her stare fierce. "I don't think so."

373

"Saul? Can you get in here, please?"

"I am asking you a question, Rebekah."

"And I answered it, Aviva."

"See! She is so angry!"

"I'm not sure what I'm supposed to say."

"I want you to tell me the truth."

"You want me to tell you the truth, but you don't want me to tell other people the truth."

"This is not about other people."

"No," I say, "it's not about *you*. It's about three dead people in Crown Heights. And a cop who fucked up. And an innocent kid who wasted his life in prison. And a man who's probably been running around murdering people for twenty years."

"And you are so special you get to decide?"

I know she is barely my mother. I know that the connection we have is little more than biological. I know—or, I guess, I am beginning to realize—that my fantasies about a future of tender friendship between us were foolhardy. She doesn't get me. She barely even wants to. Fine. I can accept that. But the way she asks me if I think I'm special pinches at my heart. If my dad were here he'd stand up for me. He'd say, yes, she *is* special. She is one of a kind.

"All I did was tell the truth," I say quietly. "I'm not going to apologize for that."

"Why do you have to make everything so public?"

"Because I don't like secrets, okay! *You* gave me that. You left us with nothing but questions. If we don't fucking *admit* what really happened—if we *pretend*—the world just keeps getting shittier and shittier."

"And it is your job to change the world? Let me tell you something, Rebekah: the world will always be the same. There are bad people and they will do bad things and there is nothing you can do to change that."

"I don't believe that," I say.

"Neither do I, Aviva."

We both look at Saul.

"Rebekah is a reporter for the same reason I was a police officer. We believe we can make a little difference. And we believe it is our duty to try. I think you used to admire that about me."

"Well, look where that has gotten you."

"Aviva," Saul says, sighing. "You have to stop this. I made a mistake. *I* did the wrong thing. Your daughter, Rebekah, she did the right thing. You can yell and scream all you want, but you won't change that. And I can't imagine why you would want to. Look at this young woman you created. *Look* at her. If you don't see something beautiful . . ."

His voice cracks and I know he is thinking of Binyamin. Here we are, mother and daughter, both alive and healthy, pushing each other away like we will always have time to repair the damage we are doing.

Aviva looks at Saul. She sees it, too.

"I only want for things to be . . . easy between us," she says finally. "We have, all of us, been through so much. I just don't see why we should bring more heartache."

I could say that things will never be easy between us. And I could say that she is the one who made it so. I could even say that she doesn't doesn't deserve an easy relationship with me if she can't bring herself to at least attempt to understand what I've devoted my life to. But instead I put my hand on her arm and say, "I know."

CHAPTER FORTY

DeShawn was snapping green beans when the CO with the terrible breath and the earring came to bring him upstairs.

"Perkins, you got an emergency call."

It was two days before Thanksgiving, and they were deep in the weeds with prep. His boss, Manny, was grumpy because Charles had, once again, neglected to label the jugs of vegetable oil (*"It's obvious what they are!"* / *"That's not the point!"*), and everyone was on edge waiting for the judge's ruling in DeShawn's case.

"Go ahead," said his boss, Manny. "God bless."

DeShawn took off his apron and squinted, red-faced and teary from the sting of the onion air and the heat of eleven ovens. He had been bringing in the articles for months: the withheld evidence; the dead Jewish killer; the still-missing ex-hooker. But nobody was getting their hopes up. The men on the kitchen staff knew that the system that put them in their cages was designed to keep them there. Prosecutors didn't admit mistakes if they

377

didn't absolutely have to. Judges looked for any reason to reject your appeal. If your motion wasn't just so, if the legal rationale not in exactly the right vernacular: *denied*. Justice had nothing to do with it. It was a game of language and egos, and if you couldn't afford a good lawyer—even a good jailhouse lawyer—you didn't stand a chance.

For more than ten years after his conviction, DeShawn was angry about this. *They gonna lock me up for nothing? I'm gonna make 'em regret it.* He fought over nothing and got locked in the box and got even angrier. And there was a lot to be angry about. He never got a letter, never had a visitor. There was a hundred dollars in his account every month, but nobody could tell him where it came from. Was somebody fucking with him? He spent the money on little things—a sweatshirt, a decent razor, snacks—and hustled a little more cash where he could. But a good hustler was friendly, and DeShawn had turned into a man people tiptoed around. He never shook who he wanted to be, though. He never shook Malcolm. So when Manny chatted him up after DeShawn transferred from Sing Sing to Coxsackie in 2004, he let the lifer from Flatbush draw him out.

"You from Brooklyn, right?" asked Manny one night after dinner. Manny was pushing a seven-foot metal cart of food trays through the dining hall, and DeShawn was dawdling, checking out flyers for jobs in the laundry and the library, notices about upcoming movies, warnings about contraband and HIV.

"Yeah," he answered.

Manny pointed to another tray cart. "Wheel that back for me?"

Manny was a talker. He'd killed two people in a home invasion in 1983 and knew he was going to die behind bars. His kids visited a couple times a year, and he had people he could trust inside. He was part of the Brooklyn crew at Coxsackie, and for as long as anybody could remember, Brooklyn ran the kitchen.

At first, DeShawn just listened. But because they were always talking about cooking, pretty soon he told a story about Sabrina.

"She used to give me and the other kids assignments. She'd be like, here's a recipe, now figure out how to make twice as much. Or half as much. She was trying to teach us math, but, you know, be fun about it. One Christmas we were gonna make this gingerbread house, and I was all excited because I was gonna take it to school. I told everybody. But I did something wrong with the baking soda. Or maybe I used baking soda instead of baking powder. So the walls and shit came out all soft and you couldn't stand 'em up to build the house. I cried and Sabrina was like, it's really hard to be good at baking. She said, 'Cooking is an art. Baking is a science.'"

"That's true," said Manny.

"So that was like a challenge to me, you know? Like, I'm gonna be a *scientist*."

Manny and Charles exchanged a look.

379

"Charles been wanting to get out of bread and cake. You game?"

DeShawn shrugged.

"I'm getting pretty sick of watching you shrug, DeShawn," said Manny. "You just gonna shrug the next fifty years of your life away? *I don't know*. Shit."

"Fine," said DeShawn. "I'm game."

It was an easy fit. DeShawn loved the bakery. He loved the smells from the oven—sweet in such a sour place. The crunch of sugar in buttery batter and the way the flour tasted in the air. Some guys inside sold drugs, some sold their law knowledge, some sold tattoos—DeShawn sold cakes. Mostly birthdays and parole, but the cakes tasted so good guys started creating occasions: Danny from the Bronx benched a record; Woodstock Steve finally cut his stupid fucking braid. The endeavor gave his brain something to focus on. He could charge more for lettering on the frosting, or carrot cake instead of plain yellow. And the more creative he got, the more people ordered. If he got everything done for the kitchen and they had leftovers—which they always did—Manny was cool with it. The CO's, too, as long as DeShawn dropped everything to whip up something pretty for an almost-forgotten anniversary.

Over the years, he sent his letter and the photocopies of his case file to hundreds of lawyers, hoping somebody would take his case. In 2012, he watched a program on TV about a group of journalism students in Chicago who got people exonerated. So he started sending letters to reporters.

The lady from the *Trib* was the first person who wrote back, and just a few months later the whole world looked different. He had a lawyer with a Manhattan office, and what everybody in the kitchen thought was a damn good chance of eventually getting out. As soon as the shit went down in Crown Heights, he started getting letters himself. LaToya wrote, and Dorothy Norris, and Pastor Green. There were apologies, and explanations, and promises. He wasn't sure what to do with it all. Ontario was the only one who actually came to see him. The nine-year-old DeShawn remembered was now six inches taller and a hundred pounds bigger than his older foster brother, but he cried like a baby in the visiting room. Poor kid didn't know what to think. He blamed himself, sure he must have pointed the finger in some way. DeShawn let him get it out, and when he composed himself they started talking food. Ontario said that he might be able to get him a job at a restaurant. Once that was in the air, DeShawn couldn't help but hope. He'd never really been able to see himself outside again. Where would he fit? In a kitchen, of course.

As he followed the CO up to the phones, DeShawn reminded himself that even if the judge said no now, it wasn't the end. This was only their first try, his attorney had assured him. There were always other motions and other strategies. With all the new evidence, it was just a matter of time.

He picked up the receiver in the counselor's office. It was his attorney, Harry Blum.

"DeShawn, you ready for some good news?"

"Sure."

"The judge reversed your conviction. And I just got off the phone with Sandra Michaels. Her office isn't going to re-try your case. They sent a messenger to Albany with the judge's order this morning. The paperwork should be at the prison tomorrow. You can spend Thanksgiving with your family."

Ontario, Tammy, and the two girls were waiting in the parking lot. DeShawn felt all kinds of terrible making them battle holiday weekend traffic, and even worse that the situation all but forced them to invite him to Thanksgiving dinner. He started to apologize but Tammy shook her head.

"It's like I told Ontario and the girls. Either you're family or you're not. If you're family, you're family. And Ontario says you're family."

Tammy insisted DeShawn ride up front. She squeezed herself between the carseats in the back of the Maxima, and all three females quickly fell asleep.

They merged onto the Palisades south. It was a clear day, and many of the trees still held their leaves.

"You got a beautiful family," said DeShawn.

"We try," said Ontario. And then a moment later: "I do. I know."

From the George Washington Bridge, DeShawn caught his first glimpse of the city. The city he'd never left until he left in shackles. The towers downtown were gone, he knew that. But what else was no longer there? And what had replaced it? Cars sped by and DeShawn rolled his shoulders back, straightening his posture to face his new life. He wasn't yet forty. He had living to do.

"Kenya's birthday is tomorrow," said Ontario as they crept onto the Brooklyn Bridge from the FDR. "It always gets lost in Thanksgiving. I'm counting on you to surprise her with a cake."

ACKNOWLEDGMENTS

Thank you to my agent, Stephanie Kip Rostan. Your belief in my abilities and ideas has allowed me to live this dream of being a novelist. Thank you to Gillian Flynn for introducing us, and thank you to the entire team at Levine Greenberg Rostan for your hard work and cheerful attitudes.

Thank you to my editor, Kelley Ragland, for being patient while I learned to be a mom this past year. Thank you to Andy Martin, Elizabeth Lacks, Sarah Melnyk, and the entire Minotaur gang for your constant support and encouragement.

Thank you to my friends and colleagues at CBS News: Erin Donaghue, Graham Kates, Michael Roppolo, Susan Zirinsky, Nancy Lane, Dan Carty, and Paula Cohen.

Thank you to Mordechai Lightstone, Shabaka Shakur, Maurice Possley, Eugene O'Donnell, Michelle Harris, and Shulem Deen for sharing your insight and expertise.

Thank you to all the amazing people with the Jewish

Book Council, Jewish Federations, and Hadassah for hosting me in your communities and providing the opportunity to meet with and learn from readers across the country.

Thank you to my Fresno, California, public school teachers: Gordon Funk and Bill Greene at Manchester Elementary; Marty Mazzoni at Edison-Computech Junior High; and especially Robert Jarnagin at Bullard High School who taught me, in the words of Harold Bloom, "how to read, and why."

Thank you, as always, to my family: my father, Bill Dahl, for inspiring me to get interested in the law, but to avoid becoming a lawyer; my mother, Barbara Dahl, for telling me to "bring a book" wherever I go; my sister, Susan Sharer, for being my tireless publicist; my sister-in-law, Lori Bukiewicz, for taking such good care of me and my son while I finished this book; and my husband, Joel Bukiewicz, for everything, but especially for making me laugh every single day. This book is dedicated to my son, Mick, the sweetest soul I know.

The Man who Rained

ALI SHAW

Atlantic Books

London

First published in hardback and trade paperback in Great Britain
in 2012 by Atlantic Books, an imprint of Atlantic Books Ltd.

This paperback edition published in Great Britain in 2013
by Atlantic Books.

1 2 3 4 5 6 7 8 9

A CIP catalogue record for this book is available from the British
Library.

Paperback ISBN: 9-780-85789-034-4
E-book ISBN: 9-780-85789-798-5

Printed in Great Britain by Clays Ltd, St Ives plc

Atlantic Books
Ormond House
26–27 Boswell Street
London
WC1N 3JZ

www.atlantic-books.com

For Iona

The Man who Rained

'These our actors,
As I foretold you, were all spirits, and
Are melted into air, into thin air,
And, like the baseless fabric of this vision,
The cloud-capped towers, the gorgeous palaces,
The solemn temples, the great globe itself,
Yea, all which it inherit, shall dissolve,
And, like this insubstantial pageant faded,
Leave not a rack behind. We are such stuff
As dreams are made on.'

William Shakespeare, *The Tempest*

1

THE CLOUD-CAPPED TOWERS

The rain began with one gentle tap at her bedroom window, then another and another and then a steady patter at the glass. She opened the curtains and beheld a sky like tarnished silver, with no sign of the sun. She had hoped so hard for a morning such as this that she let out a quiet cry of relief.

When the cab came to take her to the airport, water spattered circles across its windscreen. The low-banked cloud smudged Manhattan's towers into the atmosphere and the cab driver complained about the visibility. She described how dearly she loved these gloomy mornings, when the drizzle proved the solid world insubstantial, and he bluntly informed her that she was crazy. She craned her neck to look out of the window, upwards at the befogged promises above her.

She did not think she was crazy, but these last few months she had come close. At the start of the summer she would have described herself as a sociable, successful and secure twenty-nine-year-old. Now, at the worn-out end of August, all she knew was that she was still twenty-nine.

At the airport she drifted through check-in. She paced back and forth in the departures lounge. She was the first in the boarding queue. Even when she had strapped herself into her seat; even as she watched the cabin crew's bored safety routine; even as the prim lady seated beside her twisted the crackling wrapper of a bright boiled sweet; even with every detail too lucid to be a dream, she still feared that all the promises of the moment might be wrenched from her.

Life, Elsa Beletti reckoned, took delight in wrenching things from her.

Elsa's looks came from her mother's side of the family. The Belettis had given her unruly black hair, burned-brown eyes and the sharp eyebrows that inflected her every expression with a severity she didn't often intend. She was slim enough for her own liking most months of the year, but her mother and all of her aunts were round. At family gatherings they orbited one another like globes in a cosmos. She feared that one morning she would wake up to find genetics had caught up with her, that her body had changed into something nearly spherical and her voice, which she treasured for its keen whisper like the snick of a knife, had turned into that of a true Beletti matriarch, making every sentence into a drama of decibels.

Her surname (which she gained aged sixteen, after her mother had kicked her father out) and her physique were all she had inherited from the Belettis. She had always considered herself more like her dad, whose own family history existed only in unverified legends passed down to him by his grandparents. One ancestor, they had told him, had been the navigator on a pilgrim tall ship. He had coaxed the winds into the vessel's sails to carry its settlers over unfathomable waters en route to a new nation. Another was said to have been a Navajo medicine man, who had survived the forced exodus of his people from their homeland and helped maintain under oppression their belief in the Holy Wind, which gave them breath and left its spiral imprint on their fingertips and toes.

Elsa's mum said that her dad had made both of those stories up. She said he had done it to pretend that his sorry ass was respectable.

She said his ancestors were all hicks and alcoholics. She said it all again on the rainy afternoon when she kicked him out of the house and he stood in the falling water like a homeless dog.

Then, this spring, he had left them for a second and more final time.

The plane took off with a judder. At first all Elsa could see through the window was grizzled fog. She pinched her fingertips together to keep herself calm. Then came the first tantalizing break in the grey view. A blur of blue that vanished as quickly as it had come, like a fish flickering away through water.

The plane rose clear.

If the world that she left below her had looked like this, she could have been happier in it. Not a world of packed dirt under cement streets and endless houses, but one of clouds massed into mountains. As far as she could see white pinnacles of cloud basked in the bright sun. Peak after peak rose above steamy canyons. In the distance one smouldering summit flickered momentarily like a blowing light bulb: a throwaway flash of lightning some two hundred miles to the south. She wished it were possible to make her home in this clean white landscape, to spend her days lying on her back in a sun-bright meadow of cloud. Since that was impossible, she was giving up everything for the next best thing. Somewhere remote, where she could rebuild herself.

'Ma'am?'

She turned, irritated, from the view of the world outside to that of the aeroplane aisle and the air hostess who had disturbed her. After the majesty of the cloudscape, the domesticity of the plane infuriated her. The plastic grey cabin and the air hostess's twee neckerchief. People loafing in their seats as if in their living rooms, reading the airline's free magazine or watching whatever came on TV. A little girl wailed and Elsa thought, *Yes, me too.*

The air hostess outlined the choice of set meals, but Elsa told her she wasn't hungry. The hostess smiled with good grace and pushed her trolley further down the aisle.

The plane turned away from the country of her birth, from the glass-grey city blocks and the gridlocked avenues, from the concrete landing strips, from the ferry terminals and the boats jostling in the cellophane sea. She felt no sadness in saying goodbye to all that, although she had bitten back tears before boarding. Against Elsa's wishes, her mother had appeared at the airport to wave her off, sobbing into a handkerchief. She had brought with her another unwelcome sight: a pair of presents wrapped in sparkling red paper. Elsa had tried to refuse them – she wanted to leave her old life behind her entirely – but had ended up cramming them into her luggage regardless.

It had been years since Elsa had properly connected with her mother. Their telephone conversations were dutifully recited scripts, both of them dutifully reciting their lines. Their infrequent meet-ups took place in an old diner, where her mum would order Elsa the same muddy hot chocolate and slice of pecan pie which she had consumed greedily as a child. These days, the mere sight of that glistening slab of dessert felt fattening, but Elsa always forced it down. She hoped that by playing along, she might, some day, bring this repeating scene to a close and let the next commence. But they had been stuck in the same tired roles ever since her mum had kicked her dad out; and Elsa feared that her mother had thrown the remaining acts out into the rain along with him.

This past spring, the first sunshine and the cherry blossom had brought with it news that had shattered her life as she had known it. Her cell phone had rung, hidden somewhere in Peter's Brooklyn apartment. She and Peter had searched for it, lifting up cushions and rummaging in pockets, while it teased them with its disembodied tone. At last Peter had found it beneath a pile of magazines and tossed it to her. She had been breathless when she answered.

'Is this Elsa Beletti?' A slow, Oklahoman accent.

'Yes. Yes it is.'

'My name is Officer Fischer of the Oklahoma Police Department. Are you on your own, Elsa?'

'No. My boyfriend's with me.'

'Good. That's good.' And then a deep breath. 'Elsa, I am terribly sorry to have to tell you—'

She'd hung up and dropped the phone. After a second it had started ringing again, vibrating and turning around on its back. In the end Peter had answered and talked briefly with the officer, and then hung up and wrapped his arms tightly around Elsa.

Her dad had been found in the wreckage a tornado had made from his car – his lungs collapsed, his femurs shattered – a hundred miles west of the windswept little ranch on which he had raised his only child.

A jolt of turbulence and the seatbelt signs lit up. The plane was entangled in clouds. Elsa gazed out at the grey view. After a long while, it fissured open and she could see a line of ocean like a river at the bottom of a crevasse. Then the plane shot clear, and below it the wide sea shuffled its waves.

For some hours the world stayed unchanged. Then abruptly the sea crashed against a tawny coast. The land below was a devastated wild country, with drought-dried hills and pockmarked plains. A settlement passed beneath, its scattered buildings like half-buried bones. A tiny red vehicle crawled like a blood spider between one nowhere and the next. Then, for a while, there was only brown rock and brown soil.

She still had all the letters her dad had written her after he'd been kicked out. He'd stopped writing when he ended up in jail, and people said they found it difficult to comprehend how a man behind bars couldn't find the time to pen a few words to his only child. But Elsa understood him where others could not. She understood how his mind shut down indoors.

She'd seen it as a kid, when an afternoon storm had lifted the gutter off the ranch's barn, twirled it in the air like a baton, then flicked it at him. It broke his leg. Being holed up in the house while it healed made him catatonic. 'I'm weather-powered, see,' he mumbled once, and it was the best way to describe him. One blustering day he decided his broken leg had healed. He rose from his armchair and drove into the empty distance of the prairie. She remembered pressing her hands to her bedroom window to watch the dust trails rise up behind his departing truck. Then the wind scuffed them out. She could imagine him in whichever blasted patch of wilderness he had headed to, stepping out of the vehicle to turn his palms up to the sky, wind and rain prancing about him like dogs around their master.

Her dad had raised her to love the elements with a passion second only to his, but life in New York had weatherproofed her. Only at her dad's funeral, as the spring winds wiped her tears dry and carried his ashes away into the air, did it feel as if that passion had been uncovered again. It was her inheritance, but it had knocked a hole through her as if through a glass pane. All summer long she had been dealing with the cracks it had spread through the rest of her being.

A pylon came into hazy view below. Then another. Then more, running in a little row towards the dimming horizon. Then came lights all aglitter and white, avenues of the first trees she'd seen in many hours, a wide blue river, roads chock-a-block with cars. Then everything reverted to rocks, plains and hilly land that looked like a sandpit from this high up. Dusk came. The speakers crackled with an announcement from the captain: they were coming in to land.

The airport floors were mopped so clean that Elsa's spectral reflection walked with her, sole to sole across the tiles. Heading for work in New York, she used to catch her reflection in traffic windows or corner mirrors in subway stations. She would pretend she'd glimpsed another Elsa, living in a looking-glass world where life had not become unbearable. *Now,* she thought as her suitcases slid on to the luggage roundabout, *I'm one of them.* A new Elsa. For a minute she was paralyzed by delight. She squeezed the handles of her cases so hard she heard her knuckles pop.

By the time she reached the arrivals lounge, jet lag had set in. She stared at the row of bored cab drivers and wondered how on earth she'd find Mr Olivier. To her relief she saw a man holding a handwritten sign that bore her name. He'd left himself too little space to write it, so its last three letters were crushed together like a Roman numeral. He was a tall black man with a self-conscious stoop, wearing the same ghastly multicoloured jumper he'd worn in the photo he'd emailed her so that she would recognize him. His hair curled tightly against his scalp and was flecked with grey. When he saw her reading his sign he smiled with toothy satisfaction and proclaimed in a voice that sounded quiet, even though he raised it, 'Elsa Beletti? You're Elsa Beletti?'

'Mr Olivier?'

'Kenneth to you.'

Funny to think that she'd first 'met' this man two months back, when she was in an Internet café in Brooklyn, bright sunlight filling her computer screen and making it hard to read the word she'd typed into the search engine: *T-h-u-n-d-e-r-s-t-o-w-n.*

The computer returned a single match – an advert for a bed and breakfast. *I'm looking for somewhere to stay in Thunderstown,* she'd written in her email, *and I'm thinking of staying for quite some time.*

Mr Olivier had emailed her back within minutes. In the space of the following hour they'd exchanged nine or ten messages.

He described how he'd left St Lucia for Thunderstown in his late twenties, about the same age as she was now. He didn't ask her why, precisely, she desired to exchange New York for a backwater of backwaters, a forgotten and half-deserted place many miles from any other town. She returned the favour by not asking why he'd chosen it over the Caribbean. She fancied she understood his responses instinctively, and that he understood hers, and that his offer to turn bed and breakfast into more permanent lodgings would prove amenable to them both.

In the arrivals lounge he greeted her by clasping both his hands around her outstretched one. His palms were warm and cushioning. She could have closed her eyes, leaned against him and fallen asleep there and then.

'I'm here,' she said with tired relief.

'No,' he laughed. 'Not yet. There's still a long drive ahead of us.'

She nodded. Yes. Her mind was wilting.

Gently, he muscled her hands off her suitcases. He carried them as he led the way to a dark car park, eerily quiet compared to the concourse. Here he crammed himself in behind the wheel of a tiny car. Elsa climbed into the passenger seat and breathed deeply. The car smelled pleasantly of wool, and when she reclined her head against the seat she felt soft fleece covering it. 'Goat pelt,' he said with a smile. 'From Thunderstown.' She turned her cheek into it, and it was downy and gentle against her skin. He started up the car and drove them slowly away from the airport complex into the frenetic urban traffic and parades of street lamps, lights from bars, illuminated billboards. Then, slowly, they left these things behind them.

The steady passing of anonymous roads made her head loll. She opened her eyes. The dashboard clock told her that half an hour had passed. They were on a highway, a line of red tail lights snaking into the distance, catseyes and gliding white headlights in the opposite lanes. Kenneth hummed almost inaudibly. Elsa thought she recognized the song.

What felt like only a moment later she opened her eyes to find the clock had rubbed out another hour of the night, and the windscreen wipers were fighting rain bursting out of the darkness. The traffic had thinned. Another car sped up as it overtook them and vanished into the distance. She rested her head back into the fleece.

When she opened her eyes again the rain had stopped. Through a now-open window the night air flowed in, fresh-smelling. Ahead appeared the giant apparatus of a suspension bridge, with traffic darting across it and its enormous girders yawning. Left and right Elsa could see winding miles of broad river and lit-up boats bobbing on creased waves. A wind hummed over the car and struck the pillars of the bridge like a tuning fork. All around them the metal hummed. Her head drooped forwards.

She dreamed about being with Peter, before he did the thing that sent her over the edge and made her realize she had to leave New York. In her dream she listened while he made white noise on one of his electric guitars, back in his Brooklyn bedroom. She sensed all the tenements, all the nearby shops and offices and the distant skyscrapers of Manhattan packing in close around them. Every window of New York City straining to eavesdrop.

She opened her eyes. The traffic had vanished and Kenneth's was the only car on the road. The only visible part of the world was locked inside the yellow wedge of the headlights. The road had no boundaries, no walls or hedgerows, and the car rocking and bouncing over potholes and scatterings of slate kept her awake. A forever road, as if there were nothing more in the universe than car and broken tarmac. Then it turned a sudden bend and for a half-moment she could see a steep drop of scree, and sensed that they were at a great height.

The road straightened and the surface evened. Her head lolled.

She opened her eyes. The headlights shimmered across nests of boulders and trunks of stone on either side. No grass, only slates splitting under the weight of the car, each time with a noise like a handclap. Eyes closing, opening. The clock moved on in leaps, not ticks. Either side of the road were trees bent so close to the earth they were barely the height of the car, growing almost parallel to the shingly ground. A wind whistled higher than the engine noise.

'Awake again,' said Kenneth jovially. But she was asleep once more.

Awake again. The moon lonely in a starless sky. Swollen night clouds crowded around it. And beneath those the silhouettes of other giants.

'Mountains,' she whispered.

'Yes,' said Kenneth with reverence. 'Mountains.'

Even at this distance, and although they looked as flat as black paper, she had a sense of their bulk and grandeur. They lifted the horizon into the night sky. Each had its own shape: one curved as perfectly as an upturned bowl, one had a dented summit, and another a craggy legion of peaks like the outline of a crown.

She lost sight of them as the car turned down an anonymous track. The only signpost she had seen in these last few awakenings was a rusting frame with its board punched out, an empty direction to nowhere.

They had followed that signpost.

'One more hour to go,' Kenneth said.

Saying anything in reply took more effort than waking up a hundred times. She drifted off again.

When she came to, the car had stopped and Kenneth had turned off the headlights. 'What happened?' she asked, rubbing sleep dust from her eyes.

He pointed past her, out of the window. She turned and

straightened in her seat, suddenly wide awake. She could no longer see the mountains in the distance. Stars were brightly visible, but only in the zenith of the night. She could not see the mountains in the distance because now she was amongst them.

Through gaps in the clouds moonlight glistened like snowfall, brightening mountain peaks where it landed and illuminating their bald caps of notched rock. Elsa could feel the mountains' gravity in her skeleton, each of them pinching her bones in its direction. Yet they were not what Kenneth had parked to show her. Ahead of them the road descended dramatically into a deep bowl between the peaks, so steep that she felt they were hovering high in the sky.

At the bottom of that natural pit shone the lights of Thunderstown.

The first time she had seen those lights had been from a plane a few years back, a passenger aircraft like the one she'd disembarked from tonight. She'd been sitting beside Peter on a second-leg flight, en route to what would prove to be a crappy holiday. He and the other passengers had slept while she leaned her head against the window and watched the night-time world drift by beneath her. And then she'd seen Thunderstown.

Viewed from the black sky, the glowing dots of Thunderstown's lights formed the same pattern as a hurricane seen from space: a network of interlocked spirals glimmering through the dark. And at the heart of the town an unlit blot – an ominous void like the eye of a hurricane. Peter had despaired because on the first few days of their holiday she'd wanted to do nothing but research the route of their flight, until at last she came upon the town's name and repeated it over and over to herself like the password to a magic cave.

Kenneth restarted the engine and they began their descent. As they drew closer to the little town, the view slowly levelled, turning the glimmering spiral into an indistinct line of buildings and street lamps disappearing into the distance. Then the road bent around a towering boulder that jutted up from the earth. Its grey bulk hid the approaching town for a second, and the headlights opened up the jaw of the night.

There was something out there in the darkness. She saw it and let out a startled cry.

The lights picked out two animal eyes. Fur and teeth and a tail. Then whatever creature it all belonged to ducked out of the beam and was lost.

'It's okay,' said Kenneth.

'Was that a *wolf*?'

He laughed. 'Just a dog, I think.'

They cleared the boulder and the buildings drew close enough to make out individual windows and doors.

'Here we are,' said Kenneth. 'Home.' He spoke that word with deliberate heaviness. An invitation as much as a statement. Elsa had never been to Thunderstown, but – sitting bolt upright, wide awake now and stiff with anticipation – she did feel a sense of homecoming.

In the first street they entered many of the houses were boarded up. They were terraced slate cottages, with rotted doors and windows locked by hobnails. 'Nowadays there are more houses,' explained Kenneth, 'than there are people to live in them. We cannot keep them all in good order, especially when the bad weather comes. Nobody lives on this road any more. But don't worry, we're not all dead and buried in Thunderstown.'

The car bumped along the road's broken surface. The final tenements in the street weren't so derelict, yet there were still no lights inside. It was late at night, but these houses would not be coming to life at dawn. Their doors looked like they could no longer even be opened, shut as tightly as the doors of tombs.

In the next street the houses were taller but still seemed strangely cowed, as if they had been compressed under the weight of the sky. Their walls had been plastered and painted, and outside one front door a lantern fended off the shadows with a reassuring glow.

Beside the lantern hung a basket full of wild mountain flowers, winking orange and yellow like the lamplight. The shutters on the ground floor had been flung wide, and through the window Elsa saw a sitting room lit by a chandelier. A thin mother in a nightgown rocked a baby in her arms, and stroked its forehead. It was a welcome sight after all the decay. The mother looked up as the car drove by, as if it were the first motor vehicle in an age of mule-drawn carts.

They passed a bar, the Burning Wick, with outer walls of sooty slate and an interior panelled with caramel wood. A bare light bulb shone inside, but the bar had long since shut for the night and its stools were stacked on its tables. Nevertheless, in the doorway an old man in a raincoat remained, cradling a bottle of something wrapped in brown paper. He wore a leather rain cap, the broad brim of which flopped down at the sides like the ears of a spaniel. He stared up mournfully at Elsa as the car passed, and then the road turned and he vanished from view.

More houses followed, some of their slate fronts painted in muted colours that brought tentative life to the streets. Then the road curved into an enormous square lit by antique lamp posts, save in a few instances where their glass heads had shattered.

Suddenly Elsa gasped. At first she had missed the square's principal landmark. It loomed so large that her tired eyes must have skipped over it, mistaking it for an intrusion from a dream.

'The Church of Saint Erasmus,' whispered Kenneth, and slowed the car down. 'Patron saint of sailors, among all things.' He chuckled. He had a habit of closing his sentences with a chuckle instead of a full stop. Elsa wound open the window to poke out her head and look up, then up further.

It was gargantuan, disproportionate to the needs of the tiny town; a massif of stone to rival any cathedral. And it was entirely unlit. The night air around it looked displaced, as if evicted from its rightful position by the immense bulk of the building. She thought of the cathedrals of New York, and how at night their chiselled stone faces were celebrated by brilliant lamps. The Church of Saint Erasmus was lit by nothing. And she could tell, even in the gloom, that it would be a very different kind of spectacle if it were. Its awe was in its darker-than-nightness, its graceless silhouette, its sad blunt steeple hardly taller than the highest point of its roof, its broad sloping sides built for girth rather than height. More like a titanic pagan megalith than a Christian church.

They turned out of Saint Erasmus Square and drove along more streets of hunched terraces and town houses. She caught some of the names: Auger Lane, Drillbit Alley, Foreman's Avenue. 'There were mines here once,' explained Kenneth. 'In fact, the whole town is built on them.'

Then they turned into Prospect Street, a name she recognized. Here, at number thirty-eight, Kenneth parked the car and turned off the engine.

It was a four-storey house, crumbling but charming. Kenneth confessed that he spent most of his life in it watching cricket matches on television. He joked that cricket and lashings of rum were all he had cared to hold on to of his old life in St Lucia. The keys he gave her for her room were large and warm, like the hand he clasped around hers when he placed them in her palm. He let go slowly, giving her fingers a squeeze.

'You are here now,' he said in a formal voice, clearly aware of how momentous the occasion was for her. A kick of adrenaline perked her up. Yes, here she was. At the start of starting over.

She grinned and left Kenneth smiling after her from the bottom of the stairs, while she ascended to the uppermost floor. Kenneth had explained how he had converted this space into a one-bed apartment some years ago, when his fully grown son came to live here and wanted a place of his own. Here stood the door: a panel of rich, varnished wood like the lid of a treasure chest. She weighed the key in her hand: its head was the size of a medallion and satisfactorily heavy. She pushed it into the lock, pausing to enjoy the tarnished brass of the door handle and the flecks of rust on the hinges, then she reached out, pinched her finger and thumb around the head of the key, and began to twist.

The mechanism of the lock made a noise like a quarter dropped into a wishing well. She opened the door and listened to the hinges sing.

She closed her eyes and remembered all the beds she'd called her own down the years. The bed she'd had as a kid, on which she used to sit with her duvet piled over her, reading with a torch the cloud atlas her dad gave her; the bed in her college dorm that she'd shared with various bugs and boys; the bed in her New York studio, narrow as a pew; Peter's bed and its soft white sheets; stretches on sofas and floors.

She opened her eyes.

Beyond the door a dark stretch of hallway into which she walked so excitedly that she half-expected the air to crackle. She felt along the wall for the light switch and clicked it on.

The walls were papered grey, with a pattern that might once have been artful but was now as broken as aeroplane contrails. In places the wallpaper peeled up where it reached the skirting boards, which ran around a floor of bare wood. At the end of the hallway hung a full-length mirror in a silver frame, like something from a fairy story.

She left her cases in the hall under a row of coat pegs, took another deep breath and closed the door to shut herself in. On either side of the mirror were two closed doors and she walked down the hallway and opened the one on her left.

So this would be her latest bedroom. A high ceiling, a wide bed with grey sheets and an antique wooden wardrobe. Big enough to fill a whole wall, its doors had been engraved with spiralling patterns that threaded hypnotically around each other. In each outer corner of the door was carved a round-cheeked face, and it was from the puffing lips of these that the swirling patterns originated. She grinned, remembering her dad clowning around in her bedroom when she was very young, flapping his arms and huffing through his impression of the great north wind. She opened the wardrobe to the smell of wood polish and the jingle of dancing coat hangers. A bunch of dried flowers hung upside down from the rail within. She opened her suitcase to unpack her clothes, but immediately had no energy to do so. Unpacking could wait until the morning, although she did deposit the presents her mum had given her (still unwrapped and in their carrier bag) into the wardrobe, before firmly closing the door. She did not want her old life coming with her to Thunderstown, however well intentioned her mother had been.

Back through the hallway, the other door led to a sitting room with a kitchenette crammed into one corner. On a small table, Kenneth had filled a vase with fresh mountain flowers, their florets all buttery yellow. A wicker armchair by the window overlooked a courtyard lit by a lamp post. Beyond its far wall were more houses, and in the distance, a triangle of something darker than the rest of the night. She hoped that the morning would reveal it to be the low spire of Saint Erasmus.

She heard a faint tinkle outside the window and pushed open the glass.

A charm dangled lightly from a rusty nail wedged into the outside sill. She unhooked it and held it in her palm. A medley of trinkets, all bound by a dirty thread: silver-barked twigs; a pair of copper coins with their faces disguised by green patinas; a bent feather and something ... Suddenly she jerked her head away and dropped the charm to the floor. A canine tooth, flecks of blood dried to its roots. She reached down and retrieved it. The tooth clinked against the coins.

She tossed the whole thing out of the window and watched it fall to the courtyard below, where the old twigs snapped on the flagstones.

She yawned and returned to her new bedroom. She permitted herself to test the mattress.

Within moments she was sound asleep.

In the cold dead of night a strange sound at her window awoke her. A snuffling like some wild creature. She rolled over. Probably nothing more than the sounds of an unfamiliar house. Probably just the weather making its night-time noises.

She put it out of her mind, and sleep dragged her back into her dreams.

2

AN EXECUTION

Elsa woke to a bird chirruping on the window sill and a bedroom filled with sunlight. She blinked sleep away and yawned.

Then she remembered she was not in New York.

She propped herself up on her elbows. The clock on the wall had just struck half-past nine. She sank back on to the pillows and smiled. Finally. Finally she was a world away.

When she got out of bed she stood for a while at the window, taking a long look at her corner of Thunderstown. A morning haze made the street look like a faded photograph. A yellow film of sunlight masked every crumbled facade and dusty flagstone. She smiled, washed, dressed and discovered the groceries Kenneth had thoughtfully left in her otherwise empty kitchen. After a breakfast of muesli and an apple that crumbled as sweetly as fudge on her tongue, she ventured out, ready to explore her new home. The haze was lifting, although it still hid the sun in a radiant quarter of the sky. In the east, small clouds marred the blue of the atmosphere, and the warm day seemed powerless to polish them away.

The slopes of the rolling mountains that encompassed Thunderstown had been chewed back by centuries of biting wind, until their naked slate showed through. Where grass or scrub did grow, the late summer had roasted it golden. Dried-out soil had given way to rockslides that had exposed sheer tracts of black and brown earth.

Of these mountains, four imposed themselves on the town beneath, one at each cardinal point of the compass. The largest was a crumple-peaked summit in the east. During her email exchanges with Kenneth, she had excitedly posed every question she could think of about Thunderstown, and he had told her that this massive mountain was named Drum Head. It was particularly dominating due to the way the sun caught its slopes: light threw its rocky sides into a relief like the man in the moon, so that on bright days it wore a gentle and stupefied expression made from untold tonnes of rock.

Opposite Drum Head, in the west, Old Colp climbed in a steep curve like the arched back of a cat. Its slopes were dense with a species of mottled heather that the locals called tatterfur. In the north, Old Colp's foothills gave way to the ragged lower ranges of the Devil's Diadem, a mountain with no single peak but a cluster, the points of which jabbed upwards like the teeth of a mantrap. Kenneth had said that two centuries back the Devil's Diadem had been called Holy Mountain, but he had long since forgotten the story of its rechristening. There were too many legends in Thunderstown, he had said, for anybody to remember them all.

The southern mountain was more discreet. A haze shrouded it like smoke around a bonfire. This was the Merrow Wold, piled up with so many boulders and so much stony rubble that it resembled not so much a mountain but the largest cairn ever erected. Goats had made it that way, gnashing at the soil and plant life until the earth shrugged up no more flowers and shoots, only pebbles and slates. The Merrow Wold was the most barren of all the mountains and the hardest to climb; its ground slipped and crunched underfoot like the shingle of a beach.

These four were each too giant to ever be ignored by the little town they cupped between them. Their scale made Elsa feel so slight as she wandered the flowing roads with no fixed destination, letting their tributary alleyways and shadowed passages carry her. She felt at once enclosed, as if in a maze, and exposed, as if on the plains of her childhood. A narrow street would course along between the tall walls of houses, around a tight bend, narrow and narrow further, then terminate in a dead end. Just when she'd begin to think she might wander this labyrinth forever, a sharp turn or a run of steep steps would eject her and she would be released into a brilliantly lit courtyard, wildflowers bursting up between its flagstones. But wherever she found herself, one of the four mountains would always preside.

There were more residents in Thunderstown than first met the eye, but they were furtive, like pill bugs found under a lifted slab. They were absorbed in themselves, always in a hurry to be elsewhere. She couldn't comprehend their dress code: even in this late-summer warmth the women wore shawls and the men raincoats and broad-brimmed leather caps, as if such garments were the vestments of a religious order.

The wind stalked Elsa through the town, brushing over her face and bare arms before dying away and leaving the air still. Otherwise it danced at crossroads and raised miniature whirlwinds out of the dust of poky courtyards, so that it did not feel like one wind but many, each wrestling to claim its own space and territory. At a stall where a butcher sold dried meats, the wind played the part of his assistant, brushing the purpling flesh of his meats free of flies. In another place the wind helped a woman hang out her laundry, unfurling the smocks and breeches she took from her basket to hang on the line.

In one of his emails, Kenneth had potted as best he could the town's history. He had told her of a devastating flood that once ransacked these buildings. In the dry Thunderstown streets it was difficult to imagine water bucking and roaring between the houses, but Kenneth said that great fathoms of old floodwater still lurked deep and dormant beneath the lanes and alleyways, filling old tunnels where once miners had toiled. Elsa pictured this undertow as she explored, pretending it determined her course, and in doing so she made a discovery: all of the town's roads led back to the Church of Saint Erasmus. She had to tread with determination to avoid circling back there. Streets that first appeared to bypass the church turned a corner at the last minute and offered her up to it.

Another fact remembered from her email education was that, not so long ago, an excavation in Saint Erasmus's vaults had unearthed evidence of older buildings on the site, thought to be long-lost temples to long-forgotten deities. When next her route returned her to the church, she had the spine-tingling sensation that the distant past remained close in this place. She stared up at the bluntly steepled belfry and its crucifix dark as two crossed sticks of charcoal. It was the centrepiece of an array of metalwork adorning Thunderstown's rooftops. Weathervanes in their hundreds glinted from the ridges, some depicting bestial figures, some depicting human faces with lips pursed to blow forth a breeze. Winds skipped nimbly from eave to eave, tinkering with the weathervanes as they went, like engineers toying with the dials of a complex machine.

She began to walk around the edge of the church. Then, up ahead against one of its walls, she saw a small crowd of people, all raincoats and shawls, making quite a hubbub. When she reached them, one or two heads turned to regard her, but the thing they were crowded around seemed more pressing. People murmured to each other in low, serious voices. 'Hold my hand,' asked someone of their partner. 'I can't bear it,' confessed someone else. 'Whenever will Daniel be here?' 'Yes, where's Daniel?' Elsa budged into the throng to see what the fuss was all about. A creature cowered against the blackened church wall. A dog, growling uncertainly, frightened by the townsfolk who had backed it up against the stone. Elsa couldn't tell the breed, but it was something akin to an Irish wolfhound: tall and of elegant limb, with a tousle-haired coat and silver whiskers. Its snout and ears were fox-like and she was surprised by the coincidence of its eyes, which were blue and brown-grey, just like today's sky and indefinite clouds.

The beast wore no collar, and judging by the dried dirt in its fur, Elsa guessed it was either a stray or wild. It did not seem to pose any threat, yet when it moved even a fraction towards the crowd, a man swished his walking cane so violently that it whimpered back against the masonry.

A sigh of relief rippled through the crowd and the people parted for a tall man in a broad-brimmed rain cap to pass. He had a black beard, dark eyes and a Roman nose. He carried his large frame with an authority affirmed by the gathered townsfolk, who all relaxed upon his arrival. His coarse beard began at his cheekbones and hung in black straggles down to his nape. In addition to his rain cap, which he removed as he approached the dog, he wore scuffed britches, high leather boots and a brown chequered shirt with the sleeves rolled up, showing off his brawny forearms.

The dog stopped very still upon seeing him, as if in recognition. The man crouched down so that his head was level with the dog's, whisker to whisker. He stared for a while into its peculiar eyes, then began to make a deep rumbling noise in his throat like the sound of a distant rockslide. The dog seemed relieved, bowed its head and then pushed it forwards, nuzzling it against the man's chest. The man's arms came up gently to hold the dog, one hand stroking along the flat space between its ears, the other itching the soft fur hanging from its throat.

Then his grip turned a right angle and the dog's neck snapped with a click.

The crowd took a step back, leaving Elsa foregrounded and shocked. The man stood up, punched his hat back into shape and squashed it on to his head. He crossed himself. The crowd followed suit, then gave him a brief ripple of applause while the dog's corpse flopped on the flagstones.

It lay there staring hollowly up at Elsa while she stared back in horror and disbelief. Then, as she tried to comprehend what she had just seen, a strange thing happened. Its blue eyes darkened. Its irises changed colour like paper blistering in a fire. In seconds they had charred from sky blue to singed black. A sudden breeze passed over and she shivered from confusion and fright all at once.

One or two of the crowd thanked the bearded man or clapped him on the shoulder. Then they disbanded with satisfied chatter, as if exiting a theatre.

The tall man crouched over the dead body, lifted it off the dusty floor by its ears, then hefted the carcass over his shoulder and stood up. The last of the crowd had dispersed. Elsa was alone with him, uneasy but indignant. It was the first time she had seen someone murder an animal for no reason. The man turned towards her quizzically, dog draped around his neck.

'Ma'am,' he said, and ducked his head in a half-bow.

'What … why …' she began. 'What did you just *do*?'

'It was wild, ma'am,' he said, as if it were self-explanatory. He tried to step around her, but she sidestepped to block him.

'You should have taken it out of town or to a kennel … or … or *something*!'

He frowned. He seemed to her more like something blasted from rock than something that could grow up from a child. She stood her ground nevertheless.

'You are distressed by this?' He sounded confused.

She nodded as if he were stupid, but his voice was gentler than she'd expected and he seemed to be giving serious if bemused thought to her position, all the while with the corpse lolling over his shoulders and the dog's changed eyes upturned in their sockets.

'It was wild,' he pronounced again.

'It's –' she flapped her hands, '– it was a living thing!'

He frowned, like he was preparing to disagree, but instead he said, 'You are not from Thunderstown? I would know you and your family if you were. But it is a pleasure to see a new face here.'

She clenched her fists. 'Where I'm from has nothing to do with it.'

The dog's drooping tongue and dangling legs were becoming too much, as was the man's thoughtful face amongst all that dead fur.

'My name is Daniel Fossiter,' he said softly, 'and I am pleased to meet you.'

'Elsa,' she snapped, then felt all the more infuriated for becoming even this familiar with this cruel man.

'I should explain, Elsa, about this particular species of—'

She raised her palm to him, defiantly. It was a gesture she hadn't made since high school, where it meant she didn't want to hear what he had to say, but in the wide church square Daniel Fossiter only looked intently at her palm as if he were reading it. Embarrassed, she cringed away as fast as she could. Only at the end of the road did she look back, to see him watching her patiently, the dog still slung over his shoulders as if it weighed no more than the air itself.

By the time she returned to Kenneth's house she still hadn't recovered her cool. The stairs to her apartment passed the door to his sitting room, which he had left open as he loafed on the sofa, watching a cricket match. He had pulled the curtains closed to keep the sun's glare from the television screen, but the light was too strong and brightened the room regardless, projecting the fabric's peach hue on to every surface.

Kenneth had kept the furnishings simple: a plain bookcase full of yellow-spined almanacs and a cushioned footstool in front of his deep two-seater sofa. The empty seat of that sofa was as smooth as new, but when he stood to greet her, a depression remained where he'd been sitting, imprinted by years of cricket-watching. Elsa might have thought him lazy, had not one final detail of the room given her a hint of an explanation. On top of the television was a framed photograph of a young black man, probably the same age as Elsa, wearing an orange t-shirt and jeans. He had been snapped in the middle of a fit of laughter. His hands were plastered all over with clay, a large quantity of which appeared to have just that moment exploded across his body.

'He was a potter,' said Kenneth, noticing Elsa's attention to the photo. 'Michael. My wonderful son.'

Before Elsa could say anything he frowned and tugged open a curtain. The sunlight, which had seemed so powerful projecting through the curtains, turned coy through the glass, making only the window sill lambent. Then, as clouds moved across the sun, the room became darker than it had been before.

'You look mighty unhappy, Elsa.'

She told him about the dog.

He listened with the comforting expression of a counsellor, which made his response all the more surprising. 'Elsa, I don't want to upset you further, but you must understand. It is good that the dog was killed. Such dogs bring foul luck to the town.'

'*Foul luck*? It was just a dog! A beautiful dog with blue eyes!'

'Ahh, yes.' Kenneth chuckled awkwardly. 'The eyes, you see, are the giveaway. Find one of those wild dogs at sunset and its eyes will be pink or red.'

Elsa remembered the way the blue had charred out of them upon death. It made her shiver and fold her arms.

'Tell me, Elsa. The man who killed it, was he tall? With a black beard?'

'Yeah, that was him. Daniel something-or-other.'

'Daniel Fossiter. That man is very well respected in Thunderstown. His family have been cullers as far back as anyone can remember. It would be wise to remain in his good books.'

'Cullers?'

'Mostly he kills mountain goats. He keeps the population in check to stop them destroying the plants or wandering down into town. Believe me, they will eat anything they can lay their teeth on. But his role is also a ceremonial one. Daniel is expected to kill other ...' he faltered, '*creatures*, too.'

She pictured Daniel Fossiter again. There had been an air of power about him that felt animalistic. Like a lion in the wilderness. Not wicked like a human being could be, but menacing by nature nevertheless. 'I didn't like him.'

'To tell you the truth, Elsa, I must admit that I too am sometimes uneasy around him.'

'Yeah. Exactly. Uneasy.'

She went upstairs to her apartment and sat in the wicker chair looking out across the rooftops. The clouds were all oblong lumps, nothing more than blockages to the daylight. She had liked Thunderstown better before she had encountered Daniel Fossiter in it and she wished she had not chanced upon him. She could use a day without uneasiness.

There had been no such day all summer. After her dad's funeral she had felt like she was a vase full of hairline fractures, straining to contain water. Then, one day, a month ago now, the pressure finally became too much to bear. One final crack had branched through her and she had shattered into a thousand pieces.

Peter had done it. Lord knows he was probably still searching his soul over it, for she had not been able to explain to him that she had been breaking for a long time and this was just the tipping point. She hoped he would get over it quickly. He deserved that much.

His idea had been a long weekend outside of the city. 'Let's take a tent and head out west. A breath of fresh air might do you good.' He'd organized everything, and when they made their camp late on a sunny afternoon in a woodland glade in Pennsylvania she thought yes, this is precisely the good I need. Resting her head on his shoulder, watching the flames play among the cindered logs of the fire they had built, she took deep breaths of the timber smoke and felt the luxurious heat of the late lazy sun, the quick heat from the flames and the inner heat she'd absorbed from the bottle of red wine they'd shared as they set the logs to burning. Peter opened another bottle, freed the cork with a whoop and filled her glass. The leaves swayed, feather-light. Two squirrels whirled from trunk to trunk. A bird whistled as it flapped through the glade. And then he did the thing that broke her.

'Elsa,' he said, as he reached into the pocket of his jeans. He pulled his fist out, clenched around something. He opened his hand and a ring lay there in his palm.

'Elsa ... will you marry me?'

She stared at that small golden loop. Its diamond eye stared back. Her eyes followed the band's circumference, round and round and round. When she picked it up the world seemed suddenly very heavy. Leaves and blades of grass lay flattened, weighty as ornaments. She looked through the ring as if it were a spyglass and saw the woods leaning in, the twigs scratching, the bird leering beady-eyed from a bent branch. Her stomach lurched. The world changed, realigning like a dial.

'Elsa?'

She dropped the ring back into Peter's palm and choked back a sudden barrage of tears.

His eyebrows knotted. 'Elsa ... Elsa, I love you.'

She wept. When they had first started dating they had agreed with cool cynicism that love was just chemical flushes and electrical signals flowing through the brain, something tacky that belonged in souvenir shops. 'Love,' she had declared once to Peter, 'is just the heart on an I Heart NYC baseball cap.' And he had agreed with her.

Yet here and now he was deadly serious about it, down on his knees and looking up at her.

And she did not love him, even if she cared for him deeply, and she did not know whether she even believed in love, and she had lost her father, and she wanted to go like he had, up with the tornado to see him in whichever place he had left the earth for, and she could not explain that to Peter and could not explain why she was falling apart like this, and she did not know anything about herself any more.

3

CLOUD ON THE MOUNTAIN

The next morning, in the scorched front yard, Elsa found Kenneth Olivier hard at work digging out weeds with a trowel. He stood up straight when he saw her, dusting the bleached soil from his fingertips.

'Off exploring again?'

She nodded. She had her sunglasses and a thick layer of sunscreen on, as well as a water bottle in a bag hanging against her hip. 'I'm going up to the mountains.'

He looked reflective. 'Which one?'

She paused, then pointed. 'That one.' Three of the four peaks were visible from here. The fourth, the Merrow Wold, was hidden behind a low cloud in the south. The rest of the sky remained an unbroken blue, but that cloud above the Merrow Wold was bleached like ash. In the north the broken pinnacles of the Devil's Diadem glimmered in the sunlight, while to the east the face of Drum Head was slowly emerging. Elsa, however, pointed to the western mountain, the hump-backed rise with slopes as dark as soot.

'Old Colp,' said Kenneth.

'Yeah, that's the one. On your map it says there's a viewpoint. Near to a windmill, if my map-reading's any good.'

'Hmm. That windmill's not there any more. The wind it was milling saw to that.' He chuckled uneasily. 'Be careful up there. These mountains are full of old mine entrances. Some of them are only half-sealed.'

'Don't worry. I might look like a city girl, but I grew up in a spot even more remote than this.'

He nodded, although she could tell she hadn't convinced him. He looked embarrassed. 'I beg your pardon, Elsa, I'm just an old man, fretting. I've been fretting a lot ever since Michael went away.'

She put a finger to her lips. 'Don't worry about it.' She moved towards the street then paused. 'Where did he go? Your son, Michael?'

He smiled. It was an awkward, unhappy smile. 'I wish I knew the answer to that question. All I know is he went out for a walk in the mountains.' He cleared his throat. 'There is a bit of local folklore about how these mountains come to be here. It is said that, long ago, four storms became weary from whipping and raging through the air. So they came to settle on the earth, right here, to rest for a while. They soon fell asleep, and while they slept they began to crust over and calcify. By the time they awoke, the four storms of the sky were rock, welded solid to the ground. It's a superstitious way of explaining that there are places up in the mountains that aren't as stable as they look. Places, as the story would have it, that have kept something of their stormy origins. We found Michael's clothes folded on the bank of a mountain lake. That was the last we knew of him. We dived and dived to try to find his body, but he had just … vanished.' He sighed and rubbed his brow. 'I am sorry, Elsa. Now I have made it tough for you to go up there. But you must because you want to and the views are magnificent. And you will be perfectly safe, of course.'

'Sorry,' she said, 'to hear all of that.' She had hoped to offer more sympathy, but no sooner did she think about her own loss than a lump filled her throat.

Kenneth chuckled sadly and retrieved his trowel. 'Thank you. Now you enjoy your walk, and don't worry about any of these things.'

The lower reaches of Old Colp were covered in tussocks of grey grass or knotted heather in coarse carpets. Blossoms flowered in the tangle, and Elsa assumed they must be poisonous because the mountain goats had left them alone.

Halfway up the foothills she stopped to admire the view of the town below. The sun found the metal of the manifold weathervanes and lit them up like a bay of prayer candles. Still the windows of the Church of Saint Erasmus remained indomitably dark. The sky had sullied, thanks to the dusty cloud she had seen earlier above the Merrow Wold, which had now smeared itself northwards across the heavens.

Further uphill, the path led around a shoulder of the mountain that obscured the town. All signs of civilization were erased. Dark slates sat up like rabbits between the parched grasses and occasional contorted tree. Several times she glimpsed real hares, or rodents she didn't quite recognize, hopping after shady burrows. Then later she saw her first Thunderstown goat, a stony white creature with horns that doubled its height, peering down at her from a natural turret of boulders. It brayed as she passed, and the noise was like the echoes of long-gone landslides.

From this height she could see the rest of the mountain range, running in a jutting line of yellow and brown like an animal jawbone still full of sharp teeth. Caught between some of those peaks were twists of grey and white cloud, and when at one point she passed along a valley top, she saw a puff of mist climbing the far slopes, as sprightly as one of the goats.

When she came to the windmill it was indeed ruined. A piebald cylinder of bleached plaster and blackened stone, prized open in places by the weather. Between the path and the ruin stretched a meadow of springy brown grass, across which it looked as if a storm had blown apart the mill as if with dynamite. Some thirty feet from the main structure a broken-off sail arm had been fastened to the ground by the grass. A layer of something covered it, as dried out and leathery as a gourd. The stained canvas of the sail itself stuck hard and dark to the frame.

As a viewpoint it was everything she'd hoped it would be, offering an unparalleled panorama of Thunderstown and the surrounding mountains. They leaned in above the roofs below like card players around a table. She inhaled, and the air going into her was so clarified compared to that of the city that she burst out laughing. What relief, that her plan had come good like this. Not since she first moved to New York had a change of place so delighted her. Back then she had felt drunk at the sheer sight of Manhattan, its chaos and its possibility. This time she had feared that relocating was what her mum had warned it was: escapism. She had never been good at knowing the difference between running away and running forwards and she reckoned that with her they were probably one and the same thing. When faced with any challenge or fear she knew only to run, and only in retrospect could she tell whether she had charged in headlong or fled for her life. She wondered if this was what her dad had really meant when he described himself as weather-powered. To be in constant upheaval. Finally, she turned away from the view to investigate the ruin. An assortment of cogs and ratchets poked out of its snapped top, growing red dreadlocks of rust. She walked its circumference and found, covered in mosses that brushed loose with the lightest motion, a door so small it came up only to her breastbone. She tried the handle, assuming it would be locked, but it budged an inch before wedging against its own frame. Age and water had bent it out of shape, but she shoved it hard and it lurched open.

She ducked through the door and forced it closed behind her, its woodwork groaning as she did so. Inside the ruin it was cool, and beautifully lit by beams of sunlight bouncing between the rusted gears and splintered timbers above her. It felt like entering a shipwreck. Brighter light shone in thin shafts through chinks in the wall, drawing glowing threads in the air. Knobs of fungus protruded from bricks and beams, steeped in the orange pigment of the rust that fed them.

She stood there enjoying the noise of the fluting breeze in the decrepit mechanisms above her. She soaked up the atmosphere. She lost track of time.

Then she heard a voice.

When she got over her surprise, she tiptoed to the wall and peeked out through one of the chinks in the masonry.

A man was standing there on the grass, taking in the view of Thunderstown.

The first striking thing about him was that he was there at all. The second was that he was not only bald but entirely hairless. He had a bony, wary face without any eyebrows, eyelashes or any indication of stubble. Despite this lack of hair he still looked young, and she guessed he was several years her junior, probably twenty-three or twenty-four. He stood firmly over six feet tall and was broadly built, but his size came from neither muscle nor fat. She had the impression that his body was more like that of a sea lion, as if it were a design from a different habitat in which, if it were to return there, its shapelessness would be its grace.

He wore a shirt with the cuffs rolled up, jeans worn through at the knees and a pair of shoes so battered that his toes poked out through open lips. She had no idea how long he'd been standing there. He was all alone and talking to himself. 'I wonder what would happen to me,' he said, 'if I just let go?'

His voice was slow and nasal and deep. He looked at the windmill for a second and she caught a full view of his face and drew back from her spyhole. His eyes were close together, deep and dark. His nose was smooth and straight like a piece of folded paper. She hoped he couldn't see her through the tiny crack in the wall.

He began to pace around on the grass, moving with light grace despite his size. He stopped for a moment to gaze down at the town made miniature beneath the mountain and as he did so he looked forlorn, as if he were marooned on a desert island and staring out to sea. 'There's only one way,' he said, 'to find out.'

He took a deep steadying breath and ran his hands back over his bald scalp. He bent his back and stared up at the sky. His evident distress made Elsa feel guilty about spying. She wondered if she could sneak out of the mill and away down the mountain path, so as to allow him the privacy he must surely have come up here to find.

Then the man began to undress. Elsa looked away out of instinctive politeness, but after a moment looked back.

He disrobed methodically. With light fingers he unbuttoned his shirt and tossed it to the grass. He tugged undone the buckle of his belt, then the zipper of his fly, then kicked off his trousers. He pulled down and stepped out of his underwear.

His body was as smooth as a weathered pebble on the sea shore. He had very little complexion: he was not so much a white man as a grey one. He had a flat pair of buttocks and skin as hairless as that of his head.

He stood on the ridge between her viewpoint and the sun. His tall body was an eclipse and the light was a corona behind it. He spread his arms to strike a pose of dejected surrender.

Then, very gradually, he began to dissolve.

Like chalk washed into a blur by the rain, his outline began to distort, and almost imperceptibly he lost his form. One minute he was a man and the next he was a blurry grey silhouette. His skin became a coat of mist. The sun shining from behind him lit him up and edged him with its brilliance, wherein he stopped looking man-shaped and instead resembled a cloud formed by chance into the posture of a human being.

He broke up. His head caved in, becoming nothing more than a dented sphere of fog. His chest tore apart and the blue sky and bright sun shone through the place where his heart should have been. He disintegrated, every second less like a man and more like a cloud.

She yelled wordlessly. She fought the windmill door for a panicked, precious second, then rushed out across the meadow. She slowed to a halt only a few paces from the cloud. She had no idea what she was doing; she was only aware of her heart pounding in her ears.

'Please wait,' she whispered.

The cloud flickered with light. She jumped backwards in alarm. A fine filigree of electricity shivered through the vapour. For a second she thought it made up the shapes of arteries, the network of a person's veins. Then in a shimmer the lightning was gone.

She reached up to her cheek because something cool and moist had touched it.

Rain. It was scattering out of the cloud in a drizzle.

In her bewilderment she had forgotten to breathe. She gulped for air and in doing so let out a pent-up cry.

Then the cloud began to contract. It puckered backwards into shape. Its ragged outline either dispersed in the air or else smoothed down into flesh, covering once again a frame of arms and legs. It rebuilt the man she had spied on, and when he returned into definition he coughed and screwed up his eyes. He teetered off balance before doubling up to spew crystal-clear water on to the grass.

He whimpered, and she could tell that for the first time he was aware of her presence, and consequentially, that he was entirely naked in it. After a moment – she was still shocked – she remembered enough formality to look away while he retrieved his clothes. She heard his drenched jeans squelching on.

She turned back to him as he buttoned up his shirt. 'Um …' she began, but had no idea what to say. 'Um, what …' Her heart was thumping. 'What just happened?'

He didn't reply. He looked as if he didn't know how to.

'What, I mean … oh my God, are you all right?'

He nodded. He licked his lips. His irises were grey, and tinged with the same moody purple as a thundercloud. 'I can't explain.'

She gaped at him. She felt like she deserved an explanation. A raindrop dangled on his chin. Two more hung from his earlobes. 'Tell me,' she said, 'that I'm not going mad.'

He looked down awkwardly at the grass, the leaves of which balanced so many caught raindrops that it looked as if a diamond necklace had broken there. 'I can't tell you anything,' he muttered.

'But … but … I saw you …'

'I let go. There, now you know. I let go. Then I heard you calling to me and that made me come back.'

The drip on his chin fell free and dashed off the broken lip of one of his shoes. In the distance of the sky behind him, a flake of cloud was blowing north, towards the saw-toothed heights of the Devil's Diadem. *A moment ago,* she thought, *you were a cloud just like that.*

'I don't understand,' she said.

He bit his lip. 'I'm not sure we should be having this conversation. You shouldn't be talking to me. We should be frightened of each other.'

She pressed her hands over her worried heart. 'I *am* frightened!'

He deflated. Now he sounded crestfallen. 'Really? For a moment I thought that you weren't. I'm sorry I frightened you. Am I really frightening?'

She felt dizzy and had to sit down and stare at the grass, where a little golden ant was nibbling through a leaf. She felt as if, in that instant, the world had grown as limitless as it must appear to an insect. 'I'm going crazy, aren't I?'

'No. I explained. I let go.' He waited for a moment, and then he began to fidget. When he spoke again he sounded alarmed. 'Please don't tell anyone in Thunderstown that you've met me.'

She rubbed her eyes. 'It was as if I saw you turn into a cloud.'

'Yes. Yes, that's exactly what you did see. And you have to promise never to tell a soul.'

'I don't think anybody would believe me.'

'They might. In Thunderstown, they might. And they might try to get me.' Again he became worried. 'I should go now.' He hesitated, then began to walk away from her.

'Wait!'

He looked back.

She stood up. 'You can't just *go*. Not after that!'

He looked at her sadly, opened his mouth as if he wanted to say something else, then turned and kept on walking across the meadow.

'Hey! Wait! Hey!' She stomped after him. 'What am I supposed to do now?'

'Just … leave me alone, okay? Pretend you never met me. Go back to doing, I don't know, whatever you were doing up here in the first place.'

She stood there, stupefied in the sunlight, watching him walk downhill towards a stretch of the mountain full of furrows and knotted boulders. Three times, lately, life had so surprised her that she felt as if the planet itself had stopped spinning. First the news of her dad's death, then Peter's unexpected proposal, then – perhaps strangest of all – a startled minute during which she had watched a man become a cloud.

When, at the bottom of the meadow, the bald man reached the place where the path veered out of sight, he paused for a second and looked back at her over his shoulder. Then he vanished around a stack of boulders.

No sooner had he gone than she felt the urge to run, although she didn't know whether she should bolt for the safety of Kenneth's house or chase the man to get some answers. For a long minute she stood on the spot, held perfectly taut by two opposing forces. But she did not want to wonder about him forever. She set off in pursuit, the soft ground putting a spring into each pace. Past the boulders the path dropped into a gully, in which there were a great many squares and triangles of slate, but no sign of the man. Then she spotted a wet blot on one of the stones, then another, and since the sky was bare she reasoned that these must have come from his soaked clothes. She followed their direction until their clues dried up, then pressed on until she came out on to smoother slopes that were scattered with lonely trees and heads of rock. Here she stopped with her hands on her hips, surveying the mountain for some sign of him.

As she paused she saw a little house built from uneven stacks of slate and tiles, camouflaged by the shadow of a gnarly old bluff it backed up against. It was a bothy, a tiny bungalow, with just one door and one window, a wilderness shelter similar to the ones she had seen in the Ouchita Mountains, which provided mountaineers and rangers with emergency reprieve from the weather.

She approached it cautiously, for she felt sure the man would be inside. Its walls were plugged up with warty grey lichens, except for in one corner which was furred with a moss as orange as a mango. It had a stubby chimney bearing the most delicate weathervane she had seen since arriving in Thunderstown: a fox or wolf with paws stretched out mid-leap and snout raised to scent the wind. Above it the vane branched out into art nouveau curves that drew, in iron, the shape of a cloud.

She knocked on the door but got no reply, so tried the handle and found it to be locked. She thumped the wood with the flat of her palm. 'Hey!' she yelled. ' Can we talk some more?'

No answer, so she went to the window and peered in.

Someone had clearly been living there, although right now she could see nobody inside. Instead there was a table with a plate on it, and on the plate was the core of a pear, brown but not yet rotten. There were two chairs, and most remarkably given her initial assumption that this was a shelter and not a home, there were mobiles hanging from the ceiling. She twisted her head to try to get a clear view. The ceiling was thick with them. Dangling configurations of wire hung with white paper birds.

'Hey!' she yelled again, tapping on the glass. For a moment she considered breaking it, and turned around to locate a stone, but then a cold wind blew past her and she thought she heard a bark. She looked back up the mountain and saw a silver-furred animal slinking over a heap of rocks in the near distance. It vanished into a ditch before she could get a good view of it, and it did not re-emerge. Still, it had made her feel uncomfortable, and she chewed her thumbnail.

Then, because it was the only way to feel safer, she turned and picked her way back towards Thunderstown.

4

A HISTORY OF CULLERS

It had been many days since Daniel Fossiter had last seen Finn Munro, the strange and weather-filled young man whom he protected in secret. Daniel had been to the bothy on Old Colp once or twice in that time, but had found the stone shelter to be empty. Probably Finn was out wandering the mountains, or lurking in one of his many dens in the foothills, and Daniel had been relieved not to have had to endure one more awkward encounter with him.

He trudged now down the path from the dusty Merrow Wold, with a dead goat slung over his broad shoulders. He had shot fifteen that morning, before the winds started digging at the shingly soil and clawing up swathes of dust that trapped him for hours in their powdery fog. By the time he had picked his way clear the best of the afternoon was behind him, but he was untroubled. It excused him from looking in on Finn for one more day. Because it was tough, just being around him. He and Finn were two leftover corners of a triangle that could no longer be drawn.

Eight years had passed since Finn's mother left Thunderstown, during which time Finn's voice had deepened and he had grown taller even than Daniel. Yet being a man was about more than gender and age. That was something Daniel's father and grandfather had always been at pains to remind him of.

He sighed and adjusted the weight of the goat on his shoulders.

The gravelly earth of the Merrow Wold crunched under his boots. Every step required his concentration, for centuries of ravenous goats had turned this soil into a slide of rubble. People had fallen to their deaths on the gentle inclines; all it took was one slip, and they would find themselves skidding and rolling down a mountainside that offered no friction or solid space to arrest their fall. They would be scraped and grated apart by pebbles.

'Betty,' he whispered. It did not lessen, his ache for her, even after those eight years. His grandfather would have mocked him for it. His father would have turned away in resigned disappointment.

On the morning she left Thunderstown, Betty had appeared at his door and asked him to look after Finn. 'Take care of him for me,' she'd said. 'You're the only one I trust to do it. And anyway, I'll be back soon.' As if there were any chance he might forget her, she sealed the request with a kiss to his lips. Often he lay awake at night remembering that kiss, the lightness of her skin, the smell of her lipstick, the tension in the muscles of her neck as she went up on tiptoes to reach him. Sometimes it seemed that the only thing in the world worth holding on to was the memory of that kiss.

Anything anyone could call 'soon' had long since passed. Eight years with no sight or sound was not 'soon'. All the same, he could not be angry, for to be angry with her he would have to conclude that she had deliberately not written or called, and he could not bear the thought that she might have discarded him so casually. Then again, he could not bear the alternative, which was that something had befallen her to prevent her from making contact, and so he did his best to skirt around such speculation. All he could allow himself was this simple, painful, longing for her return.

He plodded downhill, soles crunching on the loose earth. If you found a handful of grass up here you were lucky, and if you pulled that grass even lightly it would uproot, so thin was the Merrow Wold's dirt. The stink of goat droppings and fur were ever present in the dry air, but hard evidence of the culprits who had ruined the landscape was hard to come by. On the other mountains it was easy to spot signs of them: hoof prints pressed into baked mud or the naked blonde trunk of a tree they had stripped of bark. Here there was neither mud nor trunks. In making the Merrow Wold barren, the goats had made themselves nigh on impossible to track.

His grandfather had believed that on the fifth day the Lord had created every animal on land except for the goat. This he left to the devil, who made them in his greedy image. Upon seeing how they gobbled up the apple trees of Eden, the Lord gave them tails like knotted ropes, and these caught and snared the goats in the undergrowth. The devil was outraged, but the goats were relieved – the Lord had spared them from temptation, and for this they were grateful. This the devil could not bear. He bit off their long tails and licked out their eyes and he feasted upon them, and when he had eaten his fill he replaced their eyes with his own, so that they would never know the difference between restraint and indulgence.

More often than once, Daniel's father, the Reverend Fossiter, had told that story from the pulpit of the Church of Saint Erasmus. Should any of the congregation have needed further proof of the tale's wisdom, they needed to look no further than the way the goats' long teeth tortured the trees. Putting up shoots was an ordeal in the face of the weather that befell these mountains. Even the sun could be the enemy of leaves in need of water. Trees that survived up here bent their trunks close to the soil. Branches grew thrust out like arms in a plea for mercy. A hard enough life, then, without the goats who came to chew away what protective bark they could grow. Daniel had taken it upon himself to guard the saplings whenever he came upon them, erecting fences of ringed razor wire. Still the goats would come. He would find the razor wire red with blood where the animals had chewed it, ignoring the pain it caused them.

Once he found an old nanny dead with her jaws clenched around the blades of the fence, her beard a brownish red from the blood that had flowed from her mangled tongue. And under the shade of the tree slept her plump little kid, who had scrambled on to her rump and used her neck as a ladder to clear the fence and chew so deeply on the sapling that it hung like a snapped straw. A kid like that did not deserve to die quick with a bullet between its eyes. It deserved to suffer with a bleeding belly, to ruminate on its deeds. But Daniel was weak-willed. His father and grandfather had always said so, and he conceded it was true. He had shown the kid the mercy it had not offered the tree, and killed it with one quick squeeze of his trigger.

Daniel loved the trees. Their blossoms in the spring were as silky and fragrant as rose petals. When the winds blew the blossoms loose they rolled through the air and reminded him of that day when he and Betty stood side by side in a swirling cloud of them, and two symmetrical petals had landed on Betty's nose, for all the world like butterfly wings.

He snorted, and spat out a wad of phlegm.

He had done as she had asked and taken care of Finn, even though the boy was so unnatural that Daniel sometimes feared he was damning his own soul by doing so. He only prayed it would mean something to Betty if she came back and found he had kept his promise.

'Ah, *ahh*,' he said to himself. 'Now there's a telltale sign in your thinkings.'

If, he had thought. *If* she came back.

When she first left he had been so certain of her return. There were some things, he'd told himself, that were fated, and his and Betty's love was such a thing. Star-crossed, they had been. He had divined it from the feeling of his bones – just as his grandfather had read signs in goat entrails (and charged a shilling for the service).

He no longer felt such certainty. These days, his heart felt like a broken compass, always spinning after a direction it could no longer find. These days, it was as hard to maintain his belief in Betty as it was to hunt for a goat on the Merrow Wold. These days, there was just the mountains, the weather, and the stink of pelt and old dung.

He left the main path and took a tussocky fork that would skirt the edge of Thunderstown to reach the south road, where the Fossiter homestead had stood for over two centuries. Not for the first time was he letting guilt gnaw at him. True, he could not bear to consider the reasons for Betty's long absence, but he could always bear to torture himself with what he had and had not done during those eight years.

He had done as Betty had asked and looked after Finn, but he had not done so happily. He was a love-smitten fool who was incapable of refusing her, but that didn't mean he was ready to forgive Finn for being the thing he was. At best Finn was a freak of nature. At worst he was touched by the devil, just as the ravenous goats were.

Every Fossiter man back through the generations had been a culler such as he. Only his father had bucked the tradition. Whereas previous generations had been heavy drinkers, meat-eaters and womanizers, Daniel's father was a teetotal vegetarian, and as spiteful as a hornet.

Throughout Daniel's childhood his father and grandfather did not speak to one another, and when Daniel's father died of a sickness they had still not reconciled. Daniel was fourteen when that happened, and after that his grandfather raised him and recommenced in earnest the Fossiter tradition for raising boys. He taught Daniel how to shoot, how to work his way upwind of a goat, how to use the curved knife that peeled softened fat from the hide. How to cleave the meat, drain the blood without spoiling the pelt and how, once Daniel's fifteenth birthday came around, to drink. He had made Daniel eat for the first time in his life the flesh of an animal, and it had tasted as seductive and vitalizing as it had immoral.

He taught Daniel the characters of the mountains, the methods and charms for appeasing them and the ways in which a canny goat could exploit the landscapes to hide from a culler. He instructed him in the preparation of traps, the spring-loading of iron jaws that would snap clean through a leg. He taught him to carry goat droppings in his pockets to dupe the foolish beasts into trusting him as he stalked the mountainsides.

He taught him, too, about the roamy goat, the one that could only ever be sighted when the mists hung over the mountains. The one goat he must not shoot.

Nobody had ever seen two roamy goats together. Logic said there must be more than one – there had been roamy sightings for centuries. Or perhaps they were a genetic anomaly, like a white hart, born to a normal buck and its nanny. Or … or perhaps, as Daniel's grandfather vehemently maintained, it was one of a kind, an ancient beast still alive and unthreatened by cullers.

It was twice as large as a normal goat, almost the size of a bullock. Its features were nobler, its tread delicate as a deer's. Its horns were a marvel, patched grey, white and iridescent like flint. Its fleece was threaded with indigo and steel-coloured hairs, so that the shadows of its coat were a moody purple and the outline bright like a cloud's silver lining.

It would mean, his grandfather used to insist with rare vitriol, a curse on your family to shoot that goat.

Daniel's father had always taught him to obey his elders. So, after his father died, Daniel did all he could to adapt to the lifestyle his grandfather pressed upon him. Yet the character of his father had also been strong. Daniel feared God, even if he did not always believe in him. He was at times, he could admit, terrorized by God.

As a teenager he would sneak off to the Church of Saint Erasmus when he knew his grandfather would not notice, to sit in its vaulted silence staring ever upwards at the black shadows of the ceiling. There he would feel a terrible despair, barren and biblical like this land of the Merrow Wold. He would repent of all the things his grandfather had encouraged him to do, the drinking and the brawling and the savage talk.

Likewise, when he was nineteen, Daniel had wept heavily at his grandfather's funeral, even though every other tear was one of relief that at last he was free to pick up the pieces of the previous two generations and try to understand how to be the descendent of both men at once. That was a puzzle that would prove difficult to solve.

On the night before the funeral he had wolfed a steak so rare and bloody it was near raw, then, after the burial, resumed the vegetarianism of his childhood. He had consumed the meat both in homage to his grandfather and in fear for the dead man's soul. Looking back, he could never comprehend how his grandfather had shrugged off talk of his impending torment. 'You only think that'll be,' he had once said with a wink, 'because you think you yourself are so special. But look at the goats. They think they're special too, and we cullers know that ain't true. Living by instinct only. No control over what they do and don't do. And if you think we ain't the damned same as them, well … then you're more of a fool than anyone for thinking there's a bed made up in hell for the likes of me.'

Daniel was approaching the homestead now. It was a long building constructed from sturdy beams, more like a feasting hall of old than a home to be at peace in. A sturdy fence marked out the territory of its yard, on the far side of which were an outhouse, a workshop and a disused barn. Although Daniel had lived here since his father's death, his childhood years spent at the vicarage meant that the homestead, in which so many of his ancestors had dwelt and died, had never felt his own. In fact, for a few blissful years he had left it to rot. That was when he lived with Betty in her house in Candle Street.

He had met her on the Devil's Diadem one day, while he crouched with his hunting rifle. Stalking like that, in no hurry to make the kill, was an experience as calming as the long hours of prayer his father had encouraged. The Devil's Diadem, that far up and that far wide of the path, was a deserted place. He had never encountered another human being among its barbed trees and narrow boulders. So, when the woman stepped into the clearing he had been aiming his rifle at, he very nearly placed a bullet between her eyes, as he would have done had she four legs and dainty hooves.

She screamed when she saw him, and the noise stayed his trigger finger and made him blanch.

'Please!' she cried out. 'Please don't! Please just don't!'

When he realized it was the gun she was frightened of, and that she had completely misread his intent, he dropped it and stood up slowly with his hands raised. He wasn't a man of words, but a man of doings. People often mistook him for a simpleton, thinking the same had been true of his grandfather and all the Fossiters before him, but he had his father the Reverend Fossiter's mind and his father's thinkings. Indeed, it was thinkings that hampered his tongue. So thick and flavoursome that when they came down to his mouth to be spoken it was hard to make the sounds of them, like talking with a mouthful of honey.

He managed, after stumbling over and over, to tell her his purpose. 'This gun is only for goats, ma'am.' He pointed to himself. 'I am a goat culler.'

She laughed. So lightly and freely that he sensed it was all right to smile back, then laugh too. On such rare occasions when Daniel started laughing, out came a great booming laugh that rocked back his shoulders and bent his spine and opened wide his big bearded jaw to let the deep bass laughter out, like the noise of an avalanche echoing in a chasm. They laughed together for several minutes, and later he would try to conjure that sound in his head again and again.

A friendship began between them. Unlikely, someone at church remarked. For Betty was at odds with Thunderstown, while Daniel had it in his bones. Betty often said that the place was so provincial, so small that she couldn't understand why she didn't return to the metropolis she'd come from. As for Daniel, he was so rural he found even Thunderstown's size intimidating. But this was the thing they had in common, this displacement. Two people who found it hard to belong wherever they found themselves.

Daniel had been her confidant. He had been there to listen in giant silence when she told him of the urges affecting her. She wanted a child, she would say, then would say it again. She wanted a child wanted a child wanted a child. Someone she could raise right, make fit in right, fit into the world and live a full life because of it. In response he would scratch his head and try to explain that he wished she wouldn't talk as if she were some botched job. He feared it when she talked like that, because she made it sound like all she longed for was to replace herself. He could never convey how queasy it made him, for the slowdown between his thinkings and his speakings always let the proper moment slip. All he could do was listen, confused by his sympathy, as she told him of her attempts at pregnancy, and of all the subsequent ways in which her body and medicine had failed her.

She looked as fragile as a thing made from bird bones when she told him what the doctors had said. Infertile. She spat out the word like blood and Daniel at least understood, as he watched the sobs make her jerk like a marionette, that it would have been far better for her to lose a limb, or an eye, or all her teeth than to lose this thing. Then she stepped into Daniel's arms as if walking over a cliff, and he'd wrapped them around her and sensed that if he squeezed her even in the slightest she'd be crushed to salt.

After she had confessed all this to him he climbed up on to the Devil's Diadem with just his rifle and his thoughts for company. It was a day of mists: he could see barely a stone's throw through the cloud.

Then he'd glimpsed for the first time the roamy goat, the one with silver eyes and horns like flint. The one that trod with a gentleness of spirit other goats did not possess. The one whose bleat was like an infant crying. It emerged from the mist with a faint breeze blowing in its blue-hued fur. Its eyes twinkled and its fur sparkled and it was as if there were a bond between them. It cried out and the noise reached inside Daniel's chest and squeezed his heart in ways he could not understand, and made the mist become a silver world that only they shared. He chewed for a while on nothing, and the goat chewed too, and the pinks and ambers in its iridescent horns gleamed. Then Daniel let out a great choking sigh, raised his rifle and shot the goat between the eyes.

Within minutes, the mists had cleared.

He'd carried the roamy goat dead down to the homestead, letting the weight of the animal describe itself on his shoulder blades and the spike of one of its horns tease his jugular. Down he plodded from the mountains, and once at the bottom he threw it on the counter in his workshop and he skinned it and treated the fur and did all he could to cut the shape of it well, so he could present it, finally, weeks later, to Betty as a birthday gift; a shawl of silver-blue wool that she took from him gingerly and smiled at, then wrapped around her neck. Quilted in blue goat fur, she pressed herself up against him and drew his hands around her waist, helped his broad fingers slide under the soft fabric of her skirt and along the even softer surface of her skin. She led him indoors into her house on Candle Street and undressed him. Then, when he could not make his fingers do the work, she undressed herself, the goat shawl and her skirt and her underwear dropping one by one on to her bed. They lay down on that deep pile of clothes and fur and he drowned in the feel of all her flesh pressed under all of his own.

At the memory of all this he shook his head like a stunned boxer. He blinked moisture out of his eyes. He let out a harrumph. He had reached the gate of the Fossiter homestead, and he entered the yard and crossed to the workshop, still carrying the goat he had killed that morning on his shoulders. Inside, he used the goat's horns as handles to lower its head on to a chopping block. He collected his old axe from its hook on the wall and whistled it through the shaggy goat neck so that it snicked apart the vertebrae within. He hefted the carcass and left the head staring up indifferently from the block. He hung the empty body from cords suspended from the workshop ceiling and let the blood dribble out of its neck and patter into a stained collecting trough beneath.

Not a day passed by without him remembering that night with Betty. Their lovemaking had been intense and finally ecstatic, but it was their subsequent state that had affected him so profoundly. He had lain on his back with her drifting to sleep against him and he had felt aligned. She had made geometry out of him.

In the morning she'd been in tears. 'I'm so so sorry, Daniel. I've made a mistake. It's not you, it's me. I can't explain. Sex just reminds me of how I can't have a baby. There, I've said it. You shouldn't stick with me, you should have someone better, someone undamaged.' Then he put his arms around her and told her it didn't matter, and smelled her hair while she cried against his throat. He meant it. He did not believe that sex was a prerequisite to the peace he had discovered as they lay together. Sex was just bodies. Peace was spirit. They did not sleep together again.

Yet since that night he had never found such peace. Shortly afterwards, Finn had arrived.

When Betty told him she was pregnant she said, 'I swear to God, Daniel, I swear on my mother's blood, I swear on my father's grave. I went up the Devil's Diadem during the storm, and that was all I did.'

At that he covered his face with his hands. To think – he had been the one who had put that idea into her head! He had told her, without ever thinking she would act on it, a superstition of his grandfather's. The old man had believed that if a childless woman climbed to the top of a mountain during a storm, and there in a whisper petitioned it for a child, and then drank rainwater until she was sick, then, one out of a hundred such times, she might conceive. His grandfather had believed many such things.

Daniel did not know what he found worse. The idea that she had given herself up to some infernal trick of the weather, or the idea that he had planted the suggestion in her mind. 'Betty,' he whispered, 'is there no likelihood that the child is ours?'

'No. Daniel, I'm sorry. I would have been pleased by that, but there's no way. What's happened to me is a miracle.'

Towards the end of her pregnancy he would sometimes catch himself staring morbidly at her belly, while in his own he felt his terrors kicking. He had always been caught between two fears: his father's fear of the judgements of the Lord, and his grandfather's fear of wicked spirits that could conjure squalls out of blue skies. Each man had debunked as superstition the beliefs of the other, leaving Daniel with no middle way save to abandon belief altogether, which would be the most fearful thing of all. In church he stopped praying and forced his mind to think about goats and mountains and camouflaged traps. He did this because he feared hearing the whisper of the Lord in his prayers. If the Lord asked him to do something about the baby in Betty's womb he knew he would be too weak-willed to obey. Better not to hear the command in the first place. He felt removed from God then, trapped from him as though under rubble, and sometimes he would wake up with his heart thumping in the dead of night, having dreamed about a little boy holding his hand.

At last the too-late day came. Her phone call.

'Please, Daniel, no midwife,' she gasped down the line. 'Just you. Listen to me, please. Just you.'

'Betty ... you need ... I don't know ...'

'*Please!*'

He set off at once, at a run, leaving the hide he had been tanning to spoil.

He found her sitting on her bed. At once she grabbed his forearm and squeezed so hard he felt like the bones inside it would break. She was shivering and sweat-drenched. Daniel piled blankets around her, among them the shawl he'd made, but it did no good. She was freezing cold in the hot room. She ground her teeth to stop them chattering. He saw that a layer of ice had crystallized across the bed sheet. It had tiled the fabric in a snowflake's hexagonal patterns. Even as he watched (she squeezed his arm harder still) the ice spread and sculpted itself further across the bed. Icicles creaked over the bed posts and stretched for the floor. Networks of frost coated the insides of her thighs. Then there was a thump at the window and a noise like the calling of an animal, or a wind shrieking, and he crossed himself and she arced her neck and shouted and then the baby began to emerge.

'Help me!'

Daniel went to the foot of the bed and set his jaw. He tried to remember the times in his childhood when he had helped his grandfather birth the livestock. The head came first, covered in a caul of mist. He readied his hands for the body. It followed quickly –

so small and so cold, cottoned in cloud and sparkling like hoarfrost. His fingers tacked to it as if to an ice block. It let out a noise like wind wailing across wastelands. The windows shuddered and the door latch shook. 'My baby,' cried Betty, and it took a moment for Daniel to realize that she meant the thing he held. He deposited it into her outstretched arms. At once the crying ceased. As she placed the child to her breast, the contact released a hiss like a branding iron cooled in a bucket of water. The smell of burned sugar (for all he knew the smell of hell itself) filled the air. As he stood there, dumbly watching Betty as she held and stroked and soothed, the thing seemed to settle. It took on a guise more like that of a real baby, with true flesh instead of hardened ice. Betty gave a shout of pure delight. Daniel crossed himself.

'Hello,' she whispered reverently. 'Aren't you wonderful?' And then she looked up at Daniel and said, 'A boy, Daniel! And I shall call him Finn.'

5

WILD IS THE WIND

Elsa woke in the early morning to the noise of a wind gusting through Thunderstown. Only when she sat up in bed did she realize that she could no longer hear it, that perhaps she had dreamed it. Through a crack in the curtains she could see the sky filling up with the dull half-light that precedes a hot sunrise. The air had closed in overnight. Inhaling felt like breathing through a veil.

She got out of bed for some water. She drank it at the window, pulling back the curtain to gaze out at the sleeping world. Beyond Drum Head's horizon it would already be daytime, but the sun had still to labour up the far side of the mountain before its rays could reach Thunderstown. For now the streets enjoyed the last reposeful moments of the night. Even the white flowers growing up through the cracked paving looked like stars set in a stone heaven.

A breeze came in through the open window and licked the fine hairs on her forearm. She shuddered. She had the feeling she was being watched, but outside there was only the view of the rooftops, the motionless weathervanes, the steadily lightening slopes of the mountains. She tried going back to bed, but the discomforting feeling had stirred her wide awake and after a few failed attempts at sleep she made herself coffee and sat by the window to watch the day begin.

When the sunlight came it overflowed Drum Head and rolled downhill to Thunderstown. Walls turned amber and chimney pots gold. Windowpanes lit up with the reflected dawn.

Then, with a start, she realized there was something down there in the courtyard beneath her window. She sprung up from her chair, her coffee dancing in her mug.

As she looked down she saw a wild dog, padding across the flagstones, its brushy tail snaking behind it. It settled down on its haunches and lifted its silvery muzzle to sniff the air. Then it looked straight up at her, its stare inexpressive and animal.

With a cry she pulled shut the curtains. She paced around the bedroom. She slapped herself on both cheeks at once, told herself how stupid she was being, then reopened the curtains an inch.

The dog still sat there, its pink tongue lolling between its incisors and its eyes fixed on her room.

She didn't know what to do. She poured herself some cereal and stayed away from the window to eat it. She had to put down her spoon when a surge of dread rose up from her toes, overwhelmed her and then was gone again.

Once more she approached the curtains. Her hands trembled so much when she drew them open that the fabric flapped in her grip.

The dog had gone.

With a great sigh of relief she hurried to the bathroom and took a long shower. She dressed and brushed her teeth. Toothpaste dribbled over her lip and pattered into the sink. She buttoned up her jacket and ensured she had packed her keys. She checked the clock. She tried to forget about the dog, just as she had tried to forget about the man she had seen yesterday. After she had come back down from the mountain she had pictured him diffusing into cloud every time she closed her eyes. She had not wanted to be alone, and had bugged Kenneth to share a glass of wine with her.

Today would be her first day in her new job and she needed to hold herself together. She would be helping in a low-key, part-time role at the town's offices. It was a step down from her job in New

York, where she had organized other people's recipes and fashion tips and inspiring real-life stories for a newspaper's weekend magazine. It had been more like collage-building than journalism and she had loved that about it: she had been a compiler of all of America's variety and she had never failed to appreciate it. Only, back then she had been sure of herself. When the cracks started spreading, each hour at her desk became an ordeal. Every story, every snippet, every horoscope and even every word puzzle made her question who she was, confused under the weight of all the people it was possible to be. One mid-summer Monday afternoon she broke down in the office. She found it hard to even work out her notice period.

The job Kenneth had helped her find was exactly the sort of thing she needed. Something to forget about come five o'clock. It was only a short walk to the offices, which stood at the end of a dusty street running west from Saint Erasmus. They rose in a grand old heap of tanned stone, with whiskery grasses poking out of their walls, and culminated in a clock tower that unified the ramshackle wings and annexes beneath, but in which the hands of the clock had frozen long ago. Craning her neck and shielding the climbing sun from her eyes, she could just make out a wooden figure on either side of the face, attached to some kind of clockwork track. The first, a man with a rough beard and broad brimmed hat, a pickaxe held in one hand and in the other a hand bell, thrusting it out into the open air. The second wore black and leaned on a scythe.

Lily, Elsa's new supervisor, met her in a reception hall panelled with dark wood and hung with row after row of trophy goat heads. Lily was nineteen years old and her jaw wagged when she spoke, as if the things she said were chewing gum. She led the way up a flight of wooden steps that tapped under their heels with hollow echoes, to an office with a small desk allotted to Elsa.

Elsa spent most of the day at an ancient photocopier. There the hours passed so slowly that they seemed measured by the broken clock.

'So what in the world,' asked Lily when lunchtime at last arrived, 'possessed you to move here from New York?'

Lily made it sound so ridiculous that Elsa hesitated. Kenneth had treated her decision with something like reverence, so it surprised her to hear someone question it. But in this shabby office it did indeed seem ridiculous.

'I …' she said, 'I …' She was damned if she would belittle herself; Lily could think she was nuts if she wanted to. 'I did it to try to get my head straight. In New York my life just … accumulated. I didn't feel like I'd chosen any of it, only wandered into it and just started living it. Then earlier this year some stuff happened and it made me realize that I needed to live a life I had chosen, to be a person I had considered being. So I came here, I suppose, to have the space to find that version of myself.'

Lily looked at her like she thought she was nuts.

When she stepped out of the offices at the end of the day, the shadow of the clock tower lay across the street. She wandered wearily into Saint Erasmus Square to sit on one of the wooden benches that faced the church. The evening heat was stirred with dust that blurred the details from the rooftops and made the sky look used and flat.

She was exhausted, tempted to lie down right there in the square and sleep, but she was determined to make something from the evening that was emerging, blown full of the scent of wood fires. She got up and walked until she discovered a bar called the Brook Horse, which spanned five storeys. It had a glorious, hand-painted sign hanging above the entrance, in which a horse swam underwater, its mane flowing behind it. A grid of eggshell cracks had split the paint, but the deep teal of the water remained vivid. The horse in the sign was no ordinary equine. Instead of hind legs its body streamlined into that of a fish, its tail fanning out gracefully to propel it through the currents.

Each floor of the bar was a cubbyhole joined to the others by a rickety spiral staircase. A group of girls who would never have been served in the States nursed pots of a sticky-looking beer on the ground floor, while on the next a woman in a raggedy shawl sewed behind a bottle of wine. The top storey overflowed on to a lop-sided balcony where Elsa sat to watch the heat haze sandpapering all sharp angles from the rooftops and chimneys. It filled the distance with its dust, and of all the mountains only Old Colp was dark enough to show through it.

She gazed across the street. A weathervane creaked and turned west. In a gutter a crow jabbed at something yellow-feathered. Further off, a wind tugged at washing strung between two rooftops. It pulled loose one sleeve of a shirt and flapped it about as if it were signalling to her.

She clutched her hands to her face. All of a sudden she was raging inside for the magic of yesterday. A man had turned to cloud and rained before her very eyes. She should have knocked that bothy door down to get answers, but instead she had run back to Thunderstown and photocopied reports for eight hours. She had to go back. She had to know.

She set off at an impassioned pace, out of town and up the broken slopes of Old Colp. She thought of all the questions she would ask the man. She wondered if he would transform into a cloud again. Then, abruptly, she was lost.

Her passion sputtered out. She came to a halt so suddenly that she tripped. She had thought she recognized the track, the boulders and the harrowed trees that leaned like signposts, but she had no memory of the view that opened before her now: a valley full of weathered rocks and beyond them the horny foothills of the Devil's Diadem. She looked back the way she had come at a landscape without milestones. She supposed that dusk was soon due, so she begrudgingly turned to retrace her steps to Thunderstown. Then, to her surprise and horror, the track forked at the base of a valley and she could not remember which path she had come down.

As if in mockery of the morning, when she had watched the sunrise crown Drum Head then rush through the town in a golden outpouring, the dusk was brief and the sunset as fleeting as a smoke signal. A few pink bars flared across the sky while she toiled up the path she hoped would lead her back. Then the light blotted out behind Old Colp's eclipse. She shuddered. She still had no idea where she was or how to get back. The fierce desire that had driven her up here was gone with the evening light. Nearby an animal yipped, and she couldn't tell whether it was bird or beast. She scrambled onwards, pleased that the path had started to ascend, hoping that the higher ground would offer her a view she could use, but when she reached the path's crest she saw only expansive black slopes. In the sky vast clouds had spread like ink spills. The only light was a jaundiced smudge where the sun had died out behind the mountain.

She sat down forlornly on a rock. Darkness drained the land. The visible world became small and black; but beyond sight it ehoed with the tuneless symphonies of the wind. She wondered when she had last been so immersed in a night. Not since her last in her childhood home, when she was fifteen and could not sleep because all of her belongings were taped away in boxes, ready to be relocated in the morning to the new house her mum had bought. Her mother had never really liked living on a ranch in the empty prairie, so when she kicked Elsa's dad out she headed straight back to the city of Norman. It was only when they went to visit the new place, a bright wooden house in a leafy suburb, that Elsa realized how much she loved that ranch in the middle of nowhere. On her final night there, while her mother snored in the adjacent bedroom, she had slipped out of bed and crept downstairs, remembering how she had tiptoed just so as a little girl when she and Dad escaped for morning storm hunts.

That night she had wandered a long distance from the unlit ranch. As she'd sat down on springy earth, the darkness had felt like a sister. The night was kin to the lightless workings of her heart and lungs, the pitch-black movement of her blood in her veins. All of her feelings happened in darkness, in emptiness as immeasurable as the expanse of the firmament above her, of which the stars were but the foreground.

Now, in this night on the mountain, she felt that same darkness inside her again. Without the metropolitan fluorescence of New York she could feel it going into her like a thread through the eye of a needle. It suffused her and reassured her that, lo and behold, it had been in her all along. She was, at heart, just as empty as the night, and despite being so lost she was grateful for the rediscovery.

When the animal call sounded again it startled her out of herself. It howled nearer now and there could be no doubt – it was a wild dog. All at once it appeared. It prowled into the cusp of her vision. Even a few yards away its body was hard to pick out. Its fur was as dark as the night clouds. Its teeth when it bared them were moon-pale. Its eyes were freckled with white like the zodiac.

It padded to a halt and stood in front of her, panting and staring up along the length of its snout.

'Hello,' she whispered pathetically.

Its tongue flickered across its nose. It slinked past her and trotted away a few paces. There it paused and looked back, idly swishing its tail.

She stood up, hesitated for a second, then followed. It loped along at a fast pace, and in her attempts to keep up she stubbed her toes painfully on a stone and tripped through a rut in the earth. It kept moving, weaving down through pathless valleys and up slopes she had to ascend on all fours. When she reached the top of a peak she shrieked to find the dog lurking in wait for her, its muzzle point-blank to her face, its breath rancid and meaty. Then she realized that beyond the dog, at the bottom of a long and easy descent, shone the lights of Thunderstown.

She laughed to see their glowing amber spiral, so welcoming after having been so lost. Then for a second she had to shield her eyes because out of nowhere a blast of wind hit her, kicking up dust from the soil and flapping her hair against her ears. This wind did not smell fresh like an alpine breeze, but grimy like feral fur. Then it was gone and she uncovered her eyes. She turned to the dog to pat or scratch her thanks, but it had already left her. Surprised, she studied the night in every direction. It must have run off, into the darkness.

6

PART WEATHER

The next morning, when she left for work, Elsa found Kenneth Olivier standing on a garden chair in the front yard of his house on Prospect Street, holding a battery-powered radio up to the sky like an offering. To its aerial he had affixed an extension bent from a coat hanger, which he now reached up to tweak an inch to the left. The adjustment changed the tone of the static crackling from the radio's speakers, but still all it would emit was a crackle and a hiss.

'Oh, hello, Elsa,' he said upon noticing her. He kept the radio held aloft. 'It's the heat we've been having, see? It's playing the devil with the reception for the test match. The television's a lost cause and the radio looks to be another.'

She had slept badly, and once she had given in and left the pretence of her sleep, it had taken her five minutes to pluck up the courage to open the curtains, afraid to find another wild dog crouching there in the courtyard. When she had finally opened them the courtyard had been bare, but her unease had persisted.

'Elsa?' Kenneth put down the radio. 'Are you feeling okay?'

'Yeah,' she said. Then, after a pause: 'I wanted to ask you about something. This might sound crazy, but … I keep seeing these dogs …' And she told him about the animals, the one who had lurked in the courtyard yesterday morning and the one who had guided her last night. She didn't tell him about the man she'd seen, although she could tell he was concerned by her ventures in the mountains after dark.

'Listen, Elsa, I tried to tell you about these dogs before. They're not like other dogs. They're different.'

'What do you mean?'

He scratched his head and looked wistfully at his useless radio.

'Come on, Kenneth. You were going to say something more than that.'

He cleared his throat. 'I don't expect you to understand. Part of them is weather.'

'Part of them is *weather*?'

For the first time since she had met him she saw a flash of irritation in his expression, although he quickly buried it. 'Well, of course you should believe in whatever you want. Perhaps this is just another superstition from a superstitious town.'

'Sorry, it's just ... you can't be serious?'

'Look, Elsa, I am just trying to make things clear to you. For my part I have found the world a far more bearable place to live in ever since I stopped trying to assemble a list of things I believe in and a list of things I don't. Instead I have resolved to believe in just a single thing: my own ignorance. The world is bigger than the confines of Kenneth Olivier's head.'

'I'm sorry. I bugged you about it and then I overstepped the mark.'

He chuckled. 'Don't worry. Because if you stay here worrying, you are going to be late for work ...'

They smiled at each other, then she set off for the office and her thoughts went back to her cloud man from the mountain. At work she became quickly reacquainted with the photocopier, but on her lunch break she found a bench in the church square and pulled from her bag the map she had used to find Old Colp's ruined windmill. Tonight she would be better prepared to find the bothy.

No sooner was her afternoon shift over than she had changed into her sneakers and was hurrying up the mountain. Uphill, the world became hushed. The brown mountain grass and the mounds of heather stood as motionless as the ranks of boulders that crested each ridge. The sky was a tinny blue, and barred in the north with diagonal clouds. When a bird of prey whistled overhead it sounded loud as a siren. She looked up in time to see it become a plunging black chevron landing death on some unfortunate mammal.

When she reached the wreckage of the windmill she stopped to catch her breath. She found the spot where she had watched the man turn to cloud and rain on the meadow, and she fancied that the grass was greener there. After her hurried climb it was pleasant to imagine the cool touch of water, but she was too close now to stop and daydream. She set off along the gully she had followed the man down, the slates grinding beneath her footsteps, and before she knew it she was at the bothy.

She approached the front door and rested her fingertips for a moment on its white-painted wood. She had to calm herself before she could knock, for now that she was here she was nervous at the thought of seeing him, and perhaps seeing cloud seep out of him again. It took her a moment to take control of her feelings, for her instinct was to either race away downhill or charge on into the bothy, demanding answer after answer. A measured approach was required, and that had never been her strong point.

She tapped her knuckles lightly off the wood. Her feet were shuffling nervously on the step when the door opened.

His eyes widened when he saw her. A weird pallor of shadow and light rippled across his hairless face, like the shadow of a cloud dappling across a field. She was again struck by his size and peculiar lack of pigmentation, as if he had no blood to show through his skin.

He looked like he wanted to run and hide, but to her delight she had him cornered. 'Hey,' she said.

'It's you.'

'Yes. Me.'

He tried to shut the door, but she stepped quickly forwards to block it. 'Wait! Please. I'm sorry to ambush you like this.'

'Then why are you here?'

She liked his voice. Each word was like the dry push of breath that blows out a candle. 'I suppose … I just want to know what I saw.'

'It's better for you if you don't.'

She swallowed. 'Then you're going to be seeing a lot more of me.'

He sighed and looked past her at the slopes. He was wearing those same broken-lipped shoes he'd worn before, and a pair of jeans whose denim had faded almost to white, and a shirt that had perhaps been red or orange once, but had turned with time to a bleached yellow. 'Are you alone?' he asked.

'Yes.'

'Okay … First you have to make me a promise. If I tell you all I can, will you leave me alone?'

'Sure. I promise.'

'And will you promise not to tell a soul?'

'Okay, I promise that too. I only know one person in Thunderstown, anyway.'

He nodded. Then right away he looked puzzled. 'Wait … you're not from Thunderstown?'

'New York.'

His mouth made an O. 'I'm sorry, I should have been able to tell that from your accent. But I don't hear many voices up here, let alone New Yorker ones.'

'Actually my accent's kinda Oklahoman. That's where I grew up.'

He looked confused. 'Oak-what?' he asked.

'La-homa,' she said, unable to hide her delight that he didn't know the name. It gave her the spine-tingling assurance that she had come as far away from home as she had hoped she would all summer.

'You'd better come in.' He moved inside the bothy and motioned for her to follow him. She held back for a moment on the hearth, then took a forwards step that felt like a leap of faith.

The building's low ceiling and confining walls told of its original function as a simple shelter. The main living space was no bigger than her bedroom in Kenneth's house, but it still managed to cram in a sitting area, including a pair of wooden chairs and a small eating table. A door on the opposite wall opened on to a bathroom, and a wooden stepladder fixed to the wall climbed to a bedroom converted out of a loft.

But it was the man's paper models that caught her attention. She had noticed the quantity and variety of them when she had peered in through the window, but inside she kept spotting more. As well as the countless paper birds that hung on mobiles from the ceiling – which now rippled their wings in the breeze flowing from the door as if they were real falcons riding on the thermals – there were paper animals tucked in every cranny. On shelves where in other houses books or photo frames might have been arranged, proud paper horses and paper dogs posed among paper trees with leaves twizzled out of paper branches. Unfolded sheets were stacked up on the table, and it seemed that she had caught him at work, for alongside them was a work-in-progress model: a half-formed animal she could not recognize.

He pulled out a chair for her, then sat down opposite. He was so big he made his chair look like a child's, but he sat on it as lightly as a balloon on a lap. He examined her for a moment, his gaze more direct than any she had experienced before. If someone had looked at her so directly in New York she'd have freaked out or told them where to shove it, but there was something forgivably curious about the way he regarded her. He had an unfettered manner, as if he were an animal and this was his den.

Eventually he met her eyes and she saw again that his irises were tinged with a stormy purple. Within them his pupils looked imperfect, the black of them mingling with the inner rims of his irises, just as the eye of a hurricane mixes with its cloudwall. Looking into them made her feel like one of the paper birds hanging in the breeze.

'Who are you?' she gaped.

'My name's Finn Munro,' he said.

But she hadn't really meant to ask him his name. She had meant *what* are you? How can you have eyes such as these and how did you dissolve into cloud? 'You're ...' she struggled. 'I mean ...'

'Are you going to tell me yours?'

'Elsa. Elsa Beletti.'

He took a deep breath. 'Well, Elsa, I am not like you. I am not like anybody. I used to think I was, but that was a long time ago now. I can't promise you will understand. I don't think many people could.'

'I'll do my best.'

'Like I say, I'm not normal. Even if I'd started out that way, I suppose I'd have become very strange by living alone for so long like this.'

'How long have you been here?'

'Eight years. I was only sixteen when I came here. Before that I lived in Thunderstown, in a beautiful old house on Candle Street, with my mother and with Daniel. But I did something bad, and for everybody's benefit I moved up here. Since then I've sort of stopped thinking in years, just in seasons. I've given up on birthdays and calendars.'

'Wait. Daniel? Fossiter? I've met him.'

'He was my mother's ... friend. He helped me move up here so I could stay out of trouble. After my mother went away.'

He said those last words as lightly as he could, but she knew how to spot a child's pain at their parent's exit. She wanted to offer him sympathy. My dad left home when I was sixteen, and I can still remember him going, as if it were yesterday. Stuff like that doesn't really get old.'

He looked up at her gratefully. 'Yeah,' he said, 'it's hard to forget what happened. But I have made my peace with it. I only mention it to explain that I've been up here on my own for a long while trying to come to terms with myself.'

'I still don't understand what I saw.'

'Okay, put it this way ...' He laid his hands flat on the table, beside the unfinished paper model he had left there. Up close she realized it was the start of a horse. The long head and fluid forelegs were complete, but the back of the animal remained only half-folded.

'I have a storm inside of me.'

She blinked. 'I beg your pardon?' But she had heard him clearly. Her instinct was to disbelieve it, but she had seen grey mist fuming out of him. She had to lock her ankles together beneath her chair to stop her legs from jittering.

'It's always been that way. Part of me is cloud and rain and sometimes hail and snowflakes.'

'But ...' Her mind hurt, as if she had bitten on an ice cube. Her eyes were drawn again to the half-finished paper horse, and she suddenly realized that she had entirely misinterpreted it. It *was* finished, it was just that its hindquarters, which she had assumed were in need of more folding, were not those of a horse. They were those of a fish. She shuddered. 'That's impossible,' she said.

He laughed ruefully. 'I wish it were. Then I would not have this problem. Because, in a way, it is impossible. Impossible to live like other people do. Like you. I am too ... unpredictable. The weather can change in an instant.'

He looked at his fingers. It took him a minute to continue. 'I grew up trying to be normal. My mother did all she could to make my life like that of any other little boy. In the end it didn't work out.'

'You said you did something.'

'Something happened, yes. And I ended up living on my own in this bothy, trying to keep out of sight. There are people in Thunderstown who might … react badly if they knew what was in me. So I spend all day walking the mountaintops and all evening folding animals out of paper. It's not much of a life. It means I stay safe, but there's always the weather inside of me, reminding me that things can never change. I can feel it, see, in my belly.'

She was sitting forwards in her chair. 'What does that feel like?'

'Well, it's different from day to day. Sometimes it's ice-cold, which makes me apathetic, like nothing matters in the world, and I think I wouldn't care even if I dropped down dead. Other times it's as hot and heavy as a monsoon and I can barely believe there's so much rain inside of me. That's when I'm glad that I'm up here alone, because I get soppy and ridiculous. I bawl my eyes out over the slightest things – a smashed mug, say, or a sad memory – then afterwards I wonder what I made all the fuss about. It makes it impossible to live life like an ordinary person. So, lately, I've started to wonder whether I should keep trying to be a person at all. Would I be happier if I was weather entirely? And that's what I mean by coming to terms wiht myself. With what I really am. A few times now I've built up the courage, but every time something's pulled me back. Just like you pulled me back at the windmill.'

'Me?'

'Yes. You asked me to wait.'

That caught her off guard. She remembered her strong urge for him to stay, but she had put it down to fear. She would never have thought that he would stay because of her.

They sat in silence for a moment. The paper birds flew along their painstaking orbits. The door was still ajar, and the breeze carried in a sudden fragrance of heather blossom. Finn seemed in no hurry to say anything more. She supposed you learned to cope with silence if you lived alone, in a stone hut halfway up a mountain.

'Sometimes,' she said carefully, 'I feel things I'm not able to define. I'm not, um, part weather, but I mean … I feel things I don't recognize, feelings for which there are no words in the dictionary. Sometimes they frighten me, if I'm honest, and … well, I'm not saying it's the same as what you've just described … I guess I'm just saying that, maybe, you don't have to feel so alone about it.'

She scratched her cheek. It was an artificial gesture created to give her hands – turned suddenly fidgety – some occupation. She looked sharply around the bothy. She was not used to talking about her emotions with strangers. In fact, she was not used to talking like this with anyone.

'Did you just try to say,' he asked quietly, 'that you feel like that too?'

A brisk nod. She forced herself to laugh. 'Well, we have become awfully serious, for two total strangers!'

Again he regarded her with that level, scrutinizing stare, so unacceptable in a bar or café or subway car. Hell, even Peter had never had the nerve to look at her as if he could see into her like that, as if she were as insubstantial a thing as she had seen Finn turn into.

'You're different to the people in Thunderstown,' he said.

She shrugged, still embarrassed. 'The world's a big place.'

'Thank you,' he said, 'for telling me that.'

Suddenly she was talking again. 'I just started feeling this stuff. It was a bolt from the blue. My dad died, you see, and that put everything out of perspective. Or into it, I can't decide. He used to have a picture on his wall of a hurricane seen from space. I found it again after he died, when I went through all his things. A little eye of emptiness wrapped up in a whole lot of bluster. That's me, right there, I thought. But I was frightened that, if I let the bluster die away, all I'd be left with was the emptiness at the middle of it all.'

She stopped as abruptly as she'd started. She was surprised to have blurted out so much of herself.

She tapped the table like a judge calling for order. 'This is crazy!' she declared, high-pitched. 'What are we talking about? It's impossible! You aren't made out of weather! You can't be!'

He was taken aback. 'But you saw for yourself.'

'It must have been a trick. One that isn't funny any more. You have to tell me how you did it. Tell me what you did to me!'

He looked hurt. 'I didn't do anything to you. I didn't even know you were there until you asked me to stay.'

She stood up and straightened out her top. 'Look,' she declared, 'this has gone too far. Tell me the truth about what happened and I'll leave you in peace.'

He scowled, then he stood up too, and went to the sink. There in a rack some cutlery was drying in the sun. He grabbed a knife and spun around with the blade raised.

She panicked and backed towards the door.

Then he turned the knife point down and used its tip to prick his forefinger. He tossed it aside and raised his hand. She could clearly see the little cut at the centre of his fingerprint, but no blood welled out of it. Instead, it hissed. It whistled like a punctured tyre. She felt its tiny breeze flowing across her cheek.

'So,' he said curtly, 'all of your questions have been answered. And now you can keep your promise.'

'What promise?' She had more questions now, although she did not know how to phrase them.

'To leave me alone.'

She could see she'd upset him. She wished she hadn't acted in the way she just had, but she had been so suddenly frightened. She tried to apologize but she was no good at it and she only mumbled something ineffectual. In the end she had no choice but to give a feeble goodbye wave and leave the bothy.

A few paces across the scraggy mountainside she looked back and hoped to see Finn at the door watching her go. But he had closed it soundlessly behind her and he was not even at the window.

7

OLD MAN THUNDER

It took the morning sun a long time to light and heat the Fossiter homestead. As it crept westward shafts of it shone in at angles, highlighting the cobwebs and the painted frowns on the portraits of deceased patriarchs. In a pool of such light, Daniel Fossiter was on his knees, saying, 'Are you dead? Have you died, Mole?'

Mole, his dog, lay on the wooden floor with her paws stretched forwards and her good eye firmly shut. Her bad eye – the one in which she had been blind since birth – remained open, marbled black and blue like the shell of a mussel. She had not moved all morning and he could not detect her breathing.

If he was not such a damned sentimental old fool he would long ago have given her one last favourite meal, then led her outside. As it stood, he had let her reach this infirm stage, where every day seemed like her last.

'Mole?' he whispered. 'Are you still in there, Mole?'

Every Fossiter who had ever walked the mountains had owned a dog, a member of a canine dynasty with a pedigree as meticulously charted as that of the Fossiters themselves. They were copper-haired, hardy pointer-retrievers, who rarely barked or played, preferring to slink after scent trails with their bellies close to the ground. Daniel had inherited several from his grandfather, but he also had his father's pair of clumsy house dogs, who had spent their lives bickering in yaps so shrill that the hunting dogs had never dared to hassle them. For some years he'd lived with this motley pack, until the time when, as if in competition, the hunters and the house dogs had each birthed a litter of puppies and he'd feared being overrun. How strange it had felt to be the sole remaining Fossiter of Thunderstown, while all around him the fur-ball progenies of his forefathers' mutts scrapped and bit and barked.

He had sold the dogs then, all bar one puppy from each litter. In truth he no longer required them in order to hunt. Tracking, trapping and sniping had all become so instinctive that he fancied he could do all three sleepwalking. When those two puppies had matured and born mongrel puppies of their own, he kept only the runt: a serious, black-furred little pup with a blind eye and a wrinkled nose. This he christened Mole.

Mole was different from the other dogs he had owned. She was like his shadow. Those other animals he had looked after well, for sure, but only in the way he might look after the upholstery of his house, or polish some inherited antique whose history he had not learned. Mole was quiet, like her hunting ancestors, but thoughtful and sombre like her master. There were times when Daniel and Mole would sit side by side on some rocky parapet in the mountains and look at each other with such reflected heaviness that he would touch his face, expecting it to be canine, and Mole's to be his reflection in a mirror.

He'd been surprised, then, when Betty met Mole and the two had been madcap together. Betty would chase the dog around the yard, and Mole would bounce after Betty, the pair creating such a tumult of yapping and laughing and rolling about on the floor that Daniel could only gape and marvel.

Now here he was, on his hands and knees, pushing a bowl of gruel closer to Mole's elderly snout, wondering if, finally, the day had come when he would need to take up his shovel and pierce the earth of the Fossiter pet cemetery.

'Mole,' he whispered, nudging the bowl even closer, 'Mole, can you hear me in there?'

Her blind eye stared blankly back at him. That eye had never shut. A strange prophecy, he supposed, of the moment when the other would become its empty equal.

She opened her good eye and he breathed out with gladness. 'Mole!' He wiped his forearm across his face.

Mole climbed groggily to her feet, whiffed the gruel for a moment, then clumsily plugged her nose into the bowl and snaffled at the food.

'Mole,' exclaimed Daniel, 'good old Mole!'

Somebody cleared their throat.

He spun around, still on his knees. A man in a raincoat and cap stood in the doorway looking down his nose at Daniel. He had a flabby pink neck which he had tried to bind back with a tight collar. Likewise his belly had been squeezed by his belt into two bulges, one above and one below his waistline. He took off his hat and smeared into place the combed hair that covered his baldness.

'I see you are hard at work, Mr Fossiter, keeping the weather at bay.'

'Mr Moses,' said Daniel, gruff and embarrassed, climbing to his feet while Mole slurped behind him. Sidney Moses had, of late, taken to keeping tabs on him.

'The door was open, so I let myself in.'

'I see that you did. And to what do I owe the visit?'

Sidney cocked his head, and his jowls wobbled down to the collar. 'To the town, Mr Fossiter. You owe it to the town. In whose employment, I might add, I see that you are currently serving.'

He smiled sarcastically and looked down at Mole, who belched upon completion of her meal and sat down in a lump.

'I also see,' continued Sidney, 'that you are still utilizing the fittest, most valiant hunting hounds available to a man of your profession. I'm certain that the goats of the mountains would throw themselves from a precipice rather than face a beast such as this.'

Daniel's nostrils flared. 'What do you want, Mr Moses? I'm sure we would both prefer it if we made this brief.'

Sidney raised his hands. 'Now, now, Mr Fossiter, you know I only jest. But if you want brevity I will cut to the chase. I was expecting your report at the beginning of this week.'

Daniel glared away down the length of the hall, along which his family in portraiture expressed their disdain. He wondered whether they were frowning at his guest or at himself, for none of those men would have suffered a bureaucrat like Sidney Moses.

Thunderstown was full of busybodies, but Sidney surpassed all the rest. He had recently obtained a high-ranking position at the town offices which, much to Daniel's chagrin, had given his interferences an air of legitimacy. Daniel had as little time for him as he would have for a mosquito, but lately Sidney had proven that he had the power to withhold the culler's bursary and had implied he might revoke it entirely.

Daniel stared down at his boots and mumbled, 'I forgot to write the report.'

Sidney sighed. 'You and I,' he said, 'are either going to work through this or come to a head. It is perfectly justifiable that a man financed exclusively by the town be asked to file a weekly report on the results of his working activities.'

'I have shot thirty-eight goats, trapped sixteen and brought down four for meat and hides.'

Sidney rolled his eyes. '*Why* is it so difficult to commit that to paper?'

'Because it is unnecessary. The townsfolk know I do my duty.'

'Nobody is calling that into question.'

Mole harrumphed, and Daniel agreed with her.

'I simply wish,' said Sidney carefully, 'to make things better. How can I explain? Perhaps by asking you: when was the last time you went out into the world beyond Thunderstown?'

He shrugged. 'Once. Thirty, maybe thirty-five years ago. That was enough of seeing the world.'

'Well … it's changed a good deal in that time. Shrunk. And it will come to Thunderstown before long.'

Daniel thought of the American girl who had confronted him in the square.

'Thunderstown,' said Sidney, 'will change. Old ways of doing things will slip away. You, for example, have not taken on an apprentice.'

'I have no son.'

'Quite. But you must have given thought to the question of who takes over when you are gone.'

The truth was that he'd thought about it less than he should have. He could not imagine Thunderstown without a Fossiter. His family had been culling here since the first foundations of the streets were laid, and it seemed impossible that it would fall to him to terminate such an ancient tradition.

'Whether we like it or not,' said Sidney, 'we are approaching a moment when our old ways of doing things will be challenged. That is why I've been pressing you, Mr Fossiter, for reports and schedules. Not to question your sense of duty, but to make the most of it. What if we harnessed this moment of transition, and used it to our advantage? What if the great work of your family could be concluded?' He gestured to the grim-faced oil paintings. 'Think how proud you would make them.'

Daniel shook his head. He knew where this was going. Sidney always came to it eventually.

He looked down at Mole, who was staring into space, and wished she were still young enough to bite and growl. For when Sidney started talking about the future, he became like a fanatic in a trance. Where before he had only irritated Daniel, now he unnerved him.

'Old Man Thunder,' said Sidney in a half-whisper. 'The catch to end all catches. The one that eluded all of your forefathers.'

'Old Man Thunder is a bedtime story.'

'Is he, though? Only last week, somebody told me they'd seen a bald man walking on Drum Head.'

Inwardly Daniel cursed Finn for being so careless. Outwardly he did his best to be indifferent. 'None of us are getting any younger, Mr Moses, and half the men of Thunderstown have watched their hair desert them. It was probably just Abe Cosser, searching for a lost sheep.'

'Abe Cosser was the man who saw him.'

Daniel shrugged. 'If he were real, one of my fathers would have caught him. But not one of them ever even saw him.'

'But what if your fathers never caught him because they never had the tools? If we organize, Mr Fossiter, and if we bring in the newest technologies, I believe we can flush him out. Then, at last, the town will be safe from the weather.'

Daniel stared across the room at the picture of his grandfather. Painted before his hair had turned white and his skin had wrinkled from the bone, he looked in the portrait the spitting image of his grandson. As did every other man glowering from the hallway walls. He remembered his grandfather concluding wistfully that Old Man Thunder did not exist, just as each and every Fossiter before him had concluded it, after hoping it was true and searching for him in vain. Old Man Thunder, the legend went, was a storm cloud that had become a man. He was the master of the wild dogs, the rider of the brook horse, the herdsman of the mountain goats, and more. It was said he once lived, bald and wizened, on the spot where Saint Erasmus now stood, but he had been driven up into the mountains by the first of Thunderstown's settlers. There he still roamed, inciting the weather, scheming to reclaim the land from the townsfolk.

It was said that if the culler were to put a bullet in Old Man Thunder, then the weather would stop forming into devilish beasts and the town would be reprieved. As such, each young Fossiter had dreamed about being that gunman, then in old age called time on the fantasy and declared Old Man Thunder to be nothing but a bogeyman.

Unlike his family, Daniel had been content to dismiss the story of Old Man Thunder from an early age. He had believed in his grandfather's rebuttal, and seen nothing in the mountains to question it. Only when Finn was born did the details of the legend creep back into his thinkings. In the first months of his life, Daniel had watched nervously as Betty nursed this bawling, wizened creature, and he had thought that it matched very well the angry, bald-headed devil of folklore.

Clearly he had done a bad job of hiding such fears, for one night Betty had sat him down and held his hand and said, 'Nothing in the world is ever like you think it's going to be,' and that maxim had dropped into his thoughts like an anchor and he had again put Old Man Thunder out of his mind. Yet here was Sidney Moses, dragging him back out again.

'No,' said Daniel. 'It is a waste of all our times to look for him.'

Sidney had been watching him studiously. For a moment his mouth looked full of venom, but then he managed to smile and gently laid a wad of papers on the homestead table. 'I disagree,' he said, 'and I hope to bring you round. For now, please consider these documents a favour. To help you file your reports.' He put his hat back on his head and tipped it. 'Good morning, Mr Fossiter.'

Daniel nodded, and Sidney left him. He closed the door and bolted it, then took a cursory look at the papers Sidney had left. He had prepared row after row of boxes he expected Daniel to tick. Records of goats shot and trapped. Wild dogs sighted. Expenses incurred. Daniel spat on the sheets and prayed for a rockslide to tip down on Sidney, his report books, and eliminate every final trace of him.

After making sure that Mole was comfortable, Daniel filled a sack of groceries and with this and the fifty sheets of rolled white paper headed out for Old Colp. He did not take the direct path from Thunderstown, but instead embarked south into the Merrow Wold. Only once he was some distance from the town did he turn northwest and climb Old Colp's slopes from that oblique direction. This was his habit whenever he visited Finn, for he did not want a man like Sidney Moses to know where he was going. Should Sidney discover Finn, well … he feared how things would turn out.

When at last he reached the bothy, the sun and the banded clouds dropped stripes of shadow across the dirt and the bluff the cottage backed up against. Crickets rattled in the grass, and when he knocked on the door a yellow bird shot up from the eaves and flew away with a corkscrewing bent.

He crossed his fingers and hoped that Finn would not be home. Then this awkward duty would have been avoided once again. He would leave his delivery of groceries and paper by way of a calling card.

Today he was unlucky. He heard the handle turn, and then the door to the bothy opened.

A lifetime spent tracking beasts had made Daniel keenly observant, so he did not miss the enthusiasm on Finn's face when he answered. It promptly dropped away, as if he had been expecting someone else. They greeted each other civilly, but when Daniel entered the shelter he sniffed the air as if he might smell an intruder. Nothing, and he wished Mole were young and well and with him. He took the groceries straight to the kitchenette corner, wondering why on earth the two of them still did this. Neither could conceal their disdain for these occasions. He dumped most of the supplies directly into Finn's cupboard and vegetable basket, then selected two plates (remembering how he and Betty had once eaten off these plates amid laughter) and carried them to the table along with a bunch of carrots still speckled with soil, a loaf of bread that yesterday had been fresh and springy but today had staled, and a tub of a vegetable pâté he had bought from Sally Nairn in Auger Lane.

They sat down to lunch at the table, but both positioned their chairs askance to it, so that they didn't quite face each other.

'Well,' said Daniel, 'are you going to tell me how you've been faring?'

'Good, for the most part.'

Daniel nodded and broke the bread. 'Dear Lord,' he prayed, 'bless this our sustenance, for which we give thanks.' *And,* he added in his head, *make this wretched hour speed by.*

'Amen,' they both said aloud.

Daniel dipped the end of a carrot into the pâté, sighed, and took a bite. Sally Nairn, he thought, was a fine woman – but whether she laboured over a spread, a pickle or a jam, the result always tasted of chalk and cauliflower.

'And you,' asked Finn, avoiding the spread, 'how have you been keeping?'

Daniel spared his palate with a mouthful of dry bread. 'Little has changed. There is still this business of Sidney Moses.'

'I'm sure you can deal with Sidney Moses.'

'Of course I can.'

The crunching of their molars on carrot was the only sound. Daniel liked to bring carrots to these meetings. Time spent chewing was time rescued from trying to talk. In the early days they had filled such gaps by reminiscing about Betty. She had been their intermediary before she had left, and without her they were like two foreigners abandoned by their interpreter. They had stopped talking about her for two reasons. Firstly, because the time when they expected her to return had passed. Secondly, because they discovered that their memories of her were so very different.

'Someone visited me,' said Finn, out of the blue.

Daniel swallowed his half-chewed mouthful of carrot. It wedged in his throat and he spluttered. 'Who?' he demanded when the coughing had settled.

'An American girl. She was nice.'

He pushed his plate away from him. He was no longer hungry. He had pictured in an instant the light in Sidney Moses's eyes were he to discover Finn. 'I don't much care whether she was *nice*. Surely we don't have to go back over the reasons for being up here. For keeping your own company.'

'I knew you'd take it badly. It doesn't matter, though. She won't be coming back.'

'Good. But really, Finn, you should not have opened the door to her.' He tapped his fingers nervously on the table until his memory finally offered up her face and name. Elsa Beletti, who had objected when he killed the wild dog. He became anxious. 'What did you tell her? What did you say about why you are living up here?'

Finn picked at a piece of bread. 'Nothing at all.'

'Good. That was wise. Nevertheless, I should speak to her.' He combed his fingers through his moustache and beard. 'Yes. I shall warn her not to blab to all and sundry about you.'

Finn frowned. 'She won't blab.'

Daniel bit his lip. And now he remembered the look of excitement on Finn's face when he had answered the door. 'You know who she is and who she is not, do you? You were hoping it was her when I arrived here today!'

'So what if I was?'

In an instant Daniel's head was full of blood. He gripped the table for support. 'So what? Damned well remember what you did to your mother!'

Finn shrank in his chair.

Daniel stood up and took a deep, controlling breath. He brushed with chopping motions the crumbs from his hands. 'I should see about her right away.' He took his broad-brimmed cap from the hook on which he had hung it. 'Good day, Finn.'

Yet even as he charged back down the slopes towards Thunderstown, he discovered that he was oddly grateful to Elsa Beletti. He told himself it was because she'd given him an excuse to cut short his visit, since his other reason unsettled him. Sometimes his thinkings presented him with sudden emotions or opinions that he did not recognize as his, as if they were intrusions from some other mind, carried like a tune into his own. This had been just such an unasked-for feeling, which he now snuffed out: he had been pleased to know that Finn had found somebody to smile about, for when he smiled some angle of his lips reminded him of Betty's.

8

THE LIVES OF THE CLOUDS

Five o'clock in Elsa's office arrived as slowly as Christmas morning to a child. When it came she hurried at once along the winding roads that led to Candle Street and the path out of town. From there she was soon climbing Old Colp, en route to Finn's bothy. As she walked, tiny yellow birds flittered in pairs or trios around her, enjoying the softening heat of the evening. The sky remained a lazy blue, save for a scattering of cumuli in the east and a white band of aeroplane contrails disintegrating high overhead.

'Hi,' she said when Finn opened the bothy door. 'Me again.'

He was wearing a ropey old tank vest and a pair of shorts that had seen better days, as well as his bashed-up shoes with the holes in their lips. 'It's hard to get rid of you, isn't it, Elsa?'

She laughed nervously. 'I didn't really like the way we finished things last time. I thought I should come to apologize. For, you know, freaking out a little.'

He smiled ruefully. 'I suppose it's to be expected. In retrospect I'm amazed that you stayed as long as you did.'

'Well, I wish I'd at least stayed a bit longer.'

'It's probably best that you didn't. Don't take this the wrong way, but you shouldn't come up here any more. It's not that I don't like you – I wish I could get to know you better – it's just that … it's dangerous.'

She didn't want to be asked to leave again. 'Surely there's no harm in a little more conversation?'

He sighed and placed a hand on his chest. 'The harm is in here.'

She laughed. 'What kind of threat is that?'

He put his hands sheepishly into his pockets. One of them was a torn pocket out of the bottom of which his forefinger showed. 'I made something after we talked. I think I'd like to give it to you. Will you come in?'

'I'd love that.'

He turned and she followed him into the bothy.

He had been crafting more paper since last she saw him. Birds formed a mound of wings and white tails on the table. Each, she felt, was a work of art, as delicate and innovative as any origami she had seen, but Finn dug through them as if they were waste paper, sending them gliding left and right down to the floor.

'Here!' he exclaimed, and held up a different kind of model. It was a paper skyscraper, built with a pointed paper spire and a roof of stepped tiers. 'My mother showed me a photograph once, of New York. Is this right? Don't you have towers there?'

'It's ...' she said, but she had to stop because her lip was trembling. She was surprised at how upset she was to see the shape of it. In New York she had barely registered Manhattan's height – she was so used to it after her first few weeks there – but this paper version felt as heavy as its inspiration. It trapped her hands at her sides and she could not move them. She was at once homesick and sick of the reminder of home. 'You don't like it?'

'It's not that.' She spoke through a tight throat. 'It's so very sweet of you, but ...'

'Here.' He held it lightly on his palm for a second, then screwed it into litter. 'Gone.'

After a while she said, 'I'm really sorry. I don't know what came over me. I don't want to seem ungrateful.'

'I understand. Sometimes there are things in life that you would rather forget. I apologize. I should have made you something different.'

'No, it was lovely of you. I'm just … a bit screwed up, that's all.'

He threw the scrunched paper model across the room and into the bin. 'Then you're in good company.'

'Do you know … it's weird, but I felt like I was. When we were talking yesterday.'

He didn't say anything. She still hadn't got used to the silences that he was so comfortable with opening up between them. She supposed they were to be expected: he was, after all, part weather, and weather was not renowned for its verbosity. She waited a minute before he spoke again.

'Would you like to choose a paper bird instead? You can take as many as you like.'

She began to search through the ones on the table, inspecting each with the diligence of an auctioneer. 'How do you get them so lifelike?' she asked when she had chosen her favourite: a broad-winged goose with a neck straight as a ruler.

'I don't really know.'

She laughed. 'That's not a very good answer.'

He looked out of the window for inspiration. He had filled a clay jar on the sill with a spray of wildflowers, including one magnificent specimen whose dappled petals formed a yellow orb, like a world globe made out of gold. He touched its petals lightly as he thought, and she realized that *that* was how he made them, with a rare and gentle precision. 'Okay, put it this way,' he said with a shrug, 'I just fold on a hunch, and I know there's really no such thing as flight. That might sound crazy, but it's true. There's only really a kind of swimming in the air.'

She smiled. 'My dad always used to say the air was an ocean.'

'Yeah, exactly! Just like an ocean, with currents and tides. And people are like … like the crabs and the worms on the ocean floor.'

'That's very flattering.'

'I just mean that people are stuck on the bottom level. But to other creatures those currents and tides can be climbed just like a person climbs a tree or a hill. When you understand how that works, you can fold a paper bird. I've watched a lot of birds surfing the air up here on the mountain. I actually look after a few of them.'

'You keep them? Here?'

'No, farther up the mountain.'

She placed the paper goose gently on to the table. 'Would you show me?'

'Um, I'm not sure I should.'

'Why not? You don't want to?'

'I'd love to, it's just ...'

'Then what are we waiting for?'

After a moment he shrugged and got up.

They stepped outside and she followed him uphill. He walked with a centre of suspension that made him look as if he were gliding. She plodded along beside him and paused now and again to catch her breath. The recent heat had papered the boulders with dust, and so dried out the grass that their shoes left crushed footprints in the turf. In the east, congesting cumuli teased the prospect of much-needed rain.

They walked in the kind of comfortable silence she thought it took people years, not days, to learn. Then, unprompted, he began to describe how last summer a field mouse had made her nest outside the bothy and he had learned to entice her inside with a trail of white chocolate. Once he had lured her in he had crouched beside her to make model after paper model. He said he got good at her tail – a long twist of paper instead of a fold. And then when he had finished the story he fell to silence again, and it delighted her that she could resist her natural compulsion to fill it.

Then they came upon the fringe of a wiry copse. Around the trees a ditch had been dug and around that a perimeter of razor wire coiled. Clumps of fur hung from its blades.

'I'm guessing we'll be trespassing if we go in there,' said Elsa.

'No,' said Finn. 'These defences are Daniel's work. To keep goats out, not us. Goats would devour these trees in a day.'

He picked up a plank of wood and leaned it against the fence to create a rudimentary stile. He hopped over and turned to help Elsa. She enjoyed the smooth touch of his fingers as he took her hand and guided her over the step.

Under the copse's foliage the world immediately cooled and quietened. The leaves had been parched by summer into early autumn's hues, but enough still lined the branches to cast a pied pattern across the floor. Here they stopped, themselves dappled in light and shade.

'Now, just listen,' instructed Finn, holding a finger to his lips.

She heard the chirrup of birdsong, and scanning the intertwining branches saw in several places little yellow birds perched in threes and fours. One swept past her, warbling as it went.

'You see them?' he whispered.

'Yes. Of course.'

He grinned. 'They're canaries. I've put up nest boxes for them. There are thousands of them on the mountains in the summer. My mother told me a story about them once. She said that on the day the floods finished off the mines, a tradesman was selling canaries in Candle Street. The water knocked his stall down and smashed his cages open. Out flew a hundred canaries, and they hatched a hundred more and so on. Ever since then there have been wild canaries in Thunderstown.'

'That's a nice story.'

'But it's not true, because they don't hatch.'

'What do you mean? Of course they hatch.'

'No, they don't. Look over there.'

She looked along the line of his pointing finger, and saw nothing.

'You're too slow, Elsa. Wait … wait … Now! Over there!'

At first she thought it was an optical illusion. A trick of the sunlight playing on the fallen leaves. Then up out of a bright patch of loam shot a canary, to join its fellows in the boughs of the copse. She rubbed her eyes. 'What did I just see?'

'It's happening again! Over there!'

He was pointing to a spot in the leaf litter that seemed more radiant than all the rest. It was as if an ember had touched down there and set the leaves to kindling. As she watched, the glow became intense. It formed a tiny orb of light that made the roots and twigs around it gleam, and left a sunspot in her vision. It began to shimmer and skew, and then the leaves looked like fiery feathers and she heard a bird cry out.

The light rose from the leafy floor with a hiss like a sparkler. Then it shot past her ear and she felt a hot breeze bristling her hair to its roots. Its shine dimmed as it flew, until she could clearly see its wings, a beak and tail feathers steering its ascent. It fluttered on to a branch, where it preened its plumage and tested its song.

'Whuh … what just happened?'

'A sunbeam,' Finn said, 'came to life.'

She had too many questions to ask him any.

He grinned from ear to ear. 'Would you like to catch one?'

'What?'

'They're quite friendly. Come on.' And with that he grasped the lowest boughs of the nearest tree and heaved himself up its trunk.

She was surprised that such a big man could ghost so easily upwards. He grinned down at her from the higher branches and asked, 'What are you waiting for?'

She shook her head, still stunned by what she'd seen.

'We won't catch one on the ground, Elsa. They only like to perch among the branches.'

'I ... I ...'

He glided back down as swiftly as he had gone up. 'I'll help you climb. Here, grab this branch.'

She took hold of its warm bark and stared up through the foliage at a trio of canaries who had squeezed on to a twig, watching her with cocked heads and cooing as if she were the most ridiculous thing in the world.

She hauled herself upwards with no real method, lifting her feet from the ground and pushing them against the trunk to try to find a foothold. She was surprised by how light she felt, then realized that Finn had cupped one hand beneath her foot to give her purchase. For a moment she wanted to leave her foot there. Then she pushed on upwards and got up on to one of the branches, after which it became easier to climb.

Finn floated up the trunk to overtake her and lead her gradually higher, until they sat facing one another on two high wooden arms.

'Now we have to be quiet, and wait for the birds to resettle.'

She nodded, and they sat with the tide of leaves swaying back and forth around them. She knew he was looking at her and smiling, but she did not look back. She supposed that sights such as these were ordinary for him, but the strangeness had made her feel as if they had been through a momentous event together. It had always been her assumption that to connect with a person you needed to have shared so much. Yet here they were, still strangers, and she felt a connection to him as tangible as that between the branch she was sitting on and its trunk. 'Now,' he whispered, 'hold out your hands.'

She did so, wondering if he was going to take hold of them. Instead he produced from his good pocket a sachet of seeds, and placed one fat grain in her palms. Then they waited. A canary bustled through the treetops, springing and zipping from branch to branch, getting closer in stops and starts. It paused for a while on the twigs above Finn's head, leaning its head left and right, its eyes swivelling hard at Elsa. She smiled at it, in case that would help.

Then it flicked wide its yellow wings and whirred down to perch on her hands. She felt the pin-tip of its beak tapping against her skin as it gobbled up the seed.

'Catch it,' whispered Finn.

Nervously – it felt wrong to touch a wild creature – she slid her free hand over the canary and cupped it to trap the bird in her hold. It burbled at her furiously, and she yelped when its wings whirred and tickled her skin. Still she kept it trapped, and then she felt a change come over it.

'Finn ... something's happening!'

'Don't worry. It can't hurt you.'

The canary had stopped struggling. It crouched still, virtually weightless in her hands. It was getting hot – not just with the compact warmth from its small heart and muscles, but with the penetrative warmth of a summer afternoon. And now around her hands a dim light glowed, getting brighter as she watched it, until golden shafts shone through the cracks between her fingers.

Some fearful switch tripped inside of her and she let go of the canary with a start. But her hands were empty and the bird had vanished, as had the light she had been holding, gone in a yellow shimmer of air. The only evidence that remained was the warmth in her palms, as if she had been holding them to a campfire.

Finn laughed and clapped his hands, but she needed a moment to compose herself. 'I ... I ...' she stuttered. 'I didn't kill it, did I?'

'No, of course not. You can't kill sunlight, can you? It'll come back in a minute or two. Unless the sun stops shining.'

He started to climb down from the tree. She stayed put for a moment, then scrabbled after him.

'Finn, I ... I saw a dog the other night. It led me to a path and then it vanished. There was only thin air and a wind that barged back past me.'

Finn nodded. 'If you know where to look you will see other such things. They exist in these mountains. You might see a horse cantering out of a flood. You might see swifts and swallows vanishing on the breeze. Some will be manifestations of the weather. If we stayed here until sunset we'd see many of these canaries turn red, and if we stayed longer, until nightfall, most of them would disappear.'

She dwelt on this for a moment. 'So … what about you?'

'I …' he started. He looked so crestfallen that she had made the connection that she wanted to retract it.

After a moment she tried to prompt him. 'You said yourself that you are part weather. And I saw what happened to you at the windmill.'

'Yes,' he said.

The canaries trilled and warbled overhead. She wanted, she realized with a thrill like an electric shock, him to be the same as them. She wanted him to be weather entirely.

'You want to know,' he said slowly, 'whether I am any different from the dogs and the canaries. I … I feel like I am, although I'm not sure if that counts. There is one big difference: these creatures have materialized out of thin air, whereas I was born and grew up. There are photos of my pregnant mother, and pictures of me as a baby and a boy. So I must be a man.'

'Of course,' she said, trying not to sound disappointed. 'Yeah, I guess that is different.'

'But … sometimes I don't feel substantial enough to be a person. I feel too light, like I might be blown away at any moment. And I, um … I …'

'You can trust me, Finn.'

'I don't have a heartbeat.'

'But … that's impossible!'

'Is it?'

She held a hand to her head. She had a feeling like vertigo. 'No heartbeat,' she repeated, and she found herself staring at his chest. 'Then what keeps you going?'

He laid a palm on his breast. 'Maybe the thunder.'

She licked her lips. She felt like she was standing on the edge of a precipice, and she had to either back off or let herself fall in. 'Can you hear it?'

'Yes. Sometimes.'

And because she knew no other way, she let herself tip forwards. 'I want to listen.'

She held her breath. He looked at her as if she were mad. ' I don't want to scare you again.'

'I won't be scared this time. I know it.'

'Then … all right.'

She nodded, but did not move towards him. She was all of a sudden aware of his height and breadth, and of her own body and her hot pulse intruding through it, of a film of sweat on the small of her back, and of the air between them that had turned into a giant obstacle.

'Now?' she asked, to buy time.

'Y-yes,' he said. 'Whenever you are ready.'

She took a deep breath then plunged forwards, bending in towards his chest so fast she almost headbutted him.

His chest was firm against her ear. She felt him tensing. She closed her eyes and listened.

It was like putting an ear to a conch shell and hearing the sea: through his breastbone she could hear a noise like a distant storm. The steady strokes of falling rain, the whistling of winds, the unmistakable base notes of thunder, then a whiplash fizzle of lightning. She didn't flinch. She was as absorbed as she had been when she was a little girl, her hands and face pressed to her window to watch black clouds scud across the horizon.

'Elsa …'

His voice brought her back to her senses. Senses that were clearer now, clearer than they had been in a very long time. She felt as if she had just stepped in from a long and bracing walk.

'Elsa …' he repeated.

She stood up straight. 'Thank you,' she said.

Then she kissed him.

At first he made a feeble resistance, but she could tell he didn't want her to stop. Then he was kissing her back, wrapping his arms tightly around her even as she slid her hands over his shoulders and thought, *Maybe I'm kissing a storm. Maybe I'm kissing the thunder.*

Finn kissed with his eyes closed, she with hers open. Then after a minute he opened his too and she looked straight into those storm-tinged irises. She lost herself in the rough circles of his pupils, like the centres of a labyrinth, towards which she had been stumbling and lost for a very long time.

9

THE SOLEMN TEMPLES

Sunday morning had come around, and Elsa lay in bed thinking about Finn. She'd hoped to see him again today, but he'd said they should wait until Monday. In Thunderstown, he explained, the Sabbath was still a day of rest and observance, when families would come together. Daniel Fossiter would often materialize at the bothy, driven there by guilt to share an awkward meal. Finn thought it best that, for the time being at least, the culler did not see them together.

Elsa had no intention of letting Daniel dictate who she could and could not see, but his interference was a problem for the future, one she hoped Finn would confront sooner rather than later. For the time being, she let herself be satisfied with a kiss.

A knock at the door. She yawned as she climbed out of bed. She answered, rubbing sleep dust from her eyes. Kenneth Olivier was wearing a crumpled suit with a fresh yellow flower through its lapel. His tie was as gruesomely patterned as one of his multi-coloured jumpers. Elsa was still dressed in her bed boxers and a t-shirt, and he looked embarrassed to see her in such clothes. 'I'm sorry,' he mumbled, backing away from the door. 'I thought you would be getting ready for church.'

'Er ... no. I'm not religious.'

'Oh,' he said. 'Oh, I see. Oh.' His expression fell, not because he judged her on it, but because just yesterday he'd told her with a level of enthusiasm she'd only seen him display before when talking about doosras and googlies in cricket matches that he'd become the church choirmaster, and this Sunday would be the first time his charges would sing in the service. She wished she hadn't said anything.

He blushed, apologized for disturbing her, and turned to shuffle back down the stairs.

'Wait!'

He looked back hopefully.

'The Church of Saint Erasmus?'

He nodded.

She grinned. 'Five minutes.'

She closed the door and hurried to her wardrobe. She immediately caught sight of the presents from her mother, still wrapped and in their bag, forgotten in the wooden shadows. She bit back a wash of guilt that their taped-up paper brought her, but still she would not open them.

Church, then. It had been a while. She couldn't stomach her mother's church, a place she was obliged to attend if a visit home took place over a Sunday. The way that the congregation raised their hands in the air and pulled pained spiritual expressions as they sang made her feel self-conscious, even though she liked the idea that God could be like lightning, that raising a hand might increase your chances of being struck. She hoped the Church of Saint Erasmus, that cavernous minster so closed to the elements, would prove to be different.

She'd have to dress smart, like Kenneth. Her only appropriate clothes were her office skirt and blouse, which she pulled on with regret, since they made her feel like a workday had come around early. She tied her hair up to disguise the fact she hadn't washed it, then hurried down the stairs, still stamping into her unpolished black shoes. Kenneth was waiting in the yard outside the house, whistling a hymn she half-recognized. The noise of a dull bell tolling rang out from the direction of the church. She put her arm through Kenneth's and they set off.

'Daniel Fossiter stopped by earlier, while you were sleeping,' he remarked as they walked.

'Why? I mean, are you guys friends?'

'Not really, no, although we get along all right. But this morning he had actually come looking for you. He said he'd heard I had a guest. And that she was an American girl. He's going to come back later, but perhaps you'll see him at church.'

'That's all? He was just paying a friendly visit?'

'Yes. I suppose so.'

They turned off Prospect Street and into Bradawl Alley, where the walls wore a green stain like a tidemark and every so often the pavement hopped down a few chipped steps.

'Weird,' she said. 'He didn't seem like the type.'

Kenneth frowned. 'You're still thinking about the dog you saw him kill. I don't think you should judge him too harshly for that. Daniel is dependable and decent. You'll find far worse than him in Thunderstown.'

'That doesn't paint a pretty picture.'

He chuckled. 'You wait until you see some of the folk in my choir. I'm afraid that the people of Thunderstown have good reasons for many of their beliefs. Some of the things they think are, frankly, nonsense, but others are born out of very real and painful memories. Lots of people here are old enough to remember the terrible flood that destroyed the mines, and many of them lost loved ones that day. It is important for them to know that a culler is here with them, to protect them from the weather.'

Bradawl Alley ended under a blackened stone arch, beyond which lay Corris Street, whose windows were all shuttered up. Saint Erasmus's belfry poked above the chimney stacks, its tolling bell sounding closer with every step. Behind it, Drum Head watched the town with one sleepy eye.

'What on earth,' she asked, 'could Daniel Fossiter do to protect Thunderstown from another flood?'

Kenneth chuckled. 'Nothing, of course, although the more superstitious residents would disagree. They still hope he'll catch Old Man Thunder.'

'What? Who's Old Man Thunder?'

He cleared his throat. 'Some people blame a sort of devil for the bad weather that has, in the past, devastated parts of the town. Legend has it that he lives somewhere up in the mountains. He's old and bald and wicked, although they say he didn't start out that way. They say he was a thunderstorm once, who got so lonely up in the sky that he turned himself into a man of skin and bones. Only, when he tried to speak, his words were lightning, and they set the meadows on fire. When he tried to touch another person he blew them away with a gale. He became so sad that he could not be a proper human being that he wept, and his tears became a flood that rushed down to the town, drowned the livestock and filled the mines with poisonous water.'

They walked in silence. There was no noise of bird or wind, only the clang of the church bell.

'Kenneth,' she asked warily, 'do *you* believe in that story?'

'Oh no, no. But I can understand it. Sometimes people need someone to blame.'

Corris Street arced into Saint Erasmus Square, and the colossal church appeared before them. The knowledge that she was about to enter it, not just to explore it but to be there with the worshippers, gave the building an even darker aspect. It didn't feel like a church from the modern world but some solemn temple from ancient times.

She shook her head as if to clear out her overactive imagination. It was just a huge stack of bricks and mortar. Inside there would be nothing but empty space and elderly churchgoers.

She was right, and triumphant for a moment as Kenneth led her through the door, then disappointed that there was no mystery within, no soul of the building present like a phantom. The church felt barren, its walls whitewashed and bare, the cold confines of its stone keeping the hot day out. A tuneless organ played as the congregation entered. Depending on how you looked at it, attendance was either exceptional or dire: every uncomfortable pew was full, but there were very few pews in the church. Most of them had vanished along with its statues and gargoyles and, given the rich mahogany they'd been joined from, Elsa suspected they had all been pawned. Surrounding these few rows of worshippers spread a sea of grey flagstones, chiselled with the names and titles of the bodies interned beneath. Mosses sprouted through the cracks, and the stones were smattered with the droppings of those feathered church regulars who lived in the rafters.

Then she saw Daniel Fossiter in the front row, head bowed in piety, a conspicuous space between him and both his neighbours.

Kenneth went to sit with his choir so Elsa found a spot on the end of a back pew, as far from Daniel as possible. She'd been sitting there barely a minute when a diminutive nun wearing enormous glasses sat down beside her.

'New here?' she asked Elsa, in an ancient, impish voice.

'Quite, yes.'

The nun unfolded her hands in her lap. When she spoke her teeth showed, each one whittled away until it was set apart from the next. 'I'm *old* here,' she said. She unfolded her ancient fingers to indicate she was not only old in this church but old in the streets outside, the uplands and the mountains beyond.

'Dot,' she said, and pinched Elsa mischievously on the arm.

'Elsa.'

'And you're staying with Mr Olivier.'

'Yes,' Elsa replied, surprised at what this old lady knew. 'Kenneth, yes.'

Dot tapped the side of her crooked nose with an even more crooked finger. 'Kenneth told me to look out for you. Said you'd sit at the back. So I stuck my bones down here. I won't hear much of the sermon this far away from the lectern, but there's no harm in that, is there?'

Elsa laughed, a little too loudly, and her laughter rippled off the vault of the roof, where wings thrashed in response.

'And how was your journey?' Dot asked.

'We just walked. Kenneth doesn't live so far away.'

'No. Your journey to Thunderstown.'

'Oh,' she said absent-mindedly, 'Beautiful. You know, when the clouds are like a landscape and you want to run across them? And everybody else has their head in a book or their eyes closed and you feel like you're the only one in the world who still thinks there's magic in flying.'

'Look here,' said the nun, reaching into her crisp grey habit to pull out a little pouch. After trying unsuccessfully to remove its contents with her bent fingers, she reached across and took one of Elsa's hands, turned the palm upwards into a cup, and tipped the contents into it. On to her palm fell a fresh red flower like a baby tulip, a big yellow button, a canine tooth and a passport-sized photograph. This last item Dot picked up and showed to Elsa.

'I haven't got a husband to carry in my purse with me,' grinned Dot, 'unless of course you count the good Lord himself, who doesn't pose for photographs. But this is the next best thing.'

The photo didn't show a face but a dark mass of clouds with the sun bursting behind them, so that the cloud edges were lined with a brilliant light.

'It's a silver lining,' Elsa said.

'I've got more, many more.' She began to repack the things into their pouch. 'You should come and visit me sometime.'

Before Elsa could answer, the organ ceased playing and the priest stood and cleared his throat. He was all jowls, and had no hair on his spotted head except for a pair of eyebrows that were thick and black like rat fur. 'That priest,' Dot whispered, leaning so close that Elsa could smell her (and she smelled heady and sweet like pudding wine), 'was young here when this church was glorious. When the windowpanes were still full of stained glass.'

After an opening address and prayer, the priest informed the congregation that it was time for the choir to sing. Elsa recognized one or two of its members from around town, but she now knew all of them by name and vocal range, thanks to Kenneth's enthusiastic descriptions.

That man with the tufty moustache and greased, combed hair was Hamel Rhys, who claimed he had been suckled on bottles of beer instead of breast milk. Behind him stood Hettie Moses, wife of the town busybody Sidney, and alongside her a pair of austere old sisters, identical twins who still lived together. These Hettie had befriended, and she had done all she could to curl her hair and dress as if she were their triplet. The final member of the choir was little Abe Cosser, who kept a flock of sheep on the fields of Drum Head. It was said in Thunderstown that just as a dog resembles its owner, so too a shepherd resembles his flock, and true to form, little Abe Cosser possessed spread eyes and the slanted, reaching teeth of a ewe. Yet he also had a beautiful falsetto, and when Kenneth raised his hands (Elsa could see the nerves jittering in his left leg) and the choir began to sing, Abe's voice fluted mournfully over the amateur tones of the other members, lifting their plain song into a melancholy harmony made almost supernatural by the lofty echoes of the church. Dot closed her eyes and exhaled with pleasure, and when the singing stopped Elsa had a momentary pang of something almost like grief at its ending.

Then came the priest's sermon, addressed to the gathered faithful in his reedy voice. It was a losing battle with the acoustics of the building. The congregation cupped hands to ears to try to make out the words above echoing interruptions from sneezes, cleared throats, dropped hymn sheets and the constant commotion of pigeons up above.

Unable to follow the sermon, Elsa settled as comfortably as she could into the pew and watched the light playing across the plain frosted glass of the windows. Outside, the clouds were passing across the sun, sifting shadows down on to the town.

She remembered waking before first light on a Saturday, the door to her bedroom creaking open, and her dad appearing with a finger to his lips. Slipping out of bed, she'd padded after him and shadowed him down the stairs. There in the hallway he'd dressed her in her coat, and together they'd tiptoed out of the door with him carrying her shoes by the laces. She couldn't risk putting them on inside, in case her footsteps echoed on the floorboards. Dark mornings were different from night-times, especially when you were still brimming with sleep. She'd crept along, hand in hand with her father, obeying the only rule he imposed whenever they did this: this stays our secret, you don't breathe a word about it when we return to the house. But that would happen long after absorbing fleets of altocumulus in the dim morning glow, or the eerie disc of a lenticular cloud, floating like a spaceship above the distant Ouachita Mountains.

She kept their rule. Never told her mother she'd been up and outside long before the day had started. Told her instead that her dad had taken her to dance classes while her mum had snored through her weekend lie-in. She had to learn a few moves now and again to feign a performance, but she didn't feel bad in deceiving her. She knew her mum would go berserk if she found out what they were really doing, and besides, these trips were just as important to Elsa as they were to her dad.

Now, thinking back to it, she wondered why her dad had never come to church with them on Sundays? If he'd done that it could have been a pact: storms on a Saturday and services the day after. She knew right away why he hadn't: he was addicted. On Sunday mornings, too, he'd head out cloud-watching before dawn broke. But to Elsa those Saturday mornings felt more spiritual than the Sunday ones. It was no surprise to her that, once upon a time, people had equated storms with gods. The first time she saw a town that had been sucked up and spat out by a tornado, it broke her heart and made her question the immense indifference of the universe, just as others might question the indifference of a deity. That was what storms were: they behaved with all the splendour and barbarity of ancient deities. Clouds were not just an ornament of godly imagery, clouds were the inspiration for pantheons, awesomely real and intangible at the same time. There were thousands of them swarming across the planet at any given moment, and yet under the shelters of roofs and ceilings it was so easy to forget their existence.

The church of the sky was something she'd so often dreamed of while the hoo-ha of the Sunday service carried on around her. There seemed to her infinitely more God to be found by staring up at the never-ending universe than by looking glumly around a building of bricks and stone.

Her father's holy books were written by meteorologists. His preferred prophet was the lightning: he was on a one-man crusade to explain the inner workings of a lightning bolt to anyone he could, as if they held some revelatory value. Cab drivers, waiters, shop assistants: no one was safe. 'The lightning doesn't strike,' he would tell them, and if they made the mistake of asking him to elaborate he would do so until they managed to excuse themselves. 'It's a connection, you see. The storm reaches for the ground with an electrical feeler, invisible to the naked eye. The ground does the same, and it's like two arms trying to grasp each other in the dark. Then, if they manage to find one another, their connection is so strong it catches on fire, and is hotter than the surface of the sun.'

Not long after Elsa moved to New York, her dad received his first prison sentence. She had been hosting her flat-warming party on the night he phoned her to say he was in trouble again with the police. It was not the first time he had been caught stealing. On previous occasions he had escaped with fines and community service, but this time the judge had ruled that his repeat offences warranted something more severe.

It had been a surreal revelation. She knew he had been broke for years, but he had hidden the extent of it from her. It was because he was a storm junkie. When she was a kid he had worked at a big weather centre in Norman, but his employers had noticed the peculiar pattern of his sick days. Every time he got news of some big hurricane forming off the coast, or some mega-tornado predicted in the prairie, he'd set off in his truck to be in its company. After they fired him he got other, crappier jobs, but these exerted even less of a hold on him and his absenteeism only increased. Eventually he had no money left and stole a bag of candy bars from a mart.

She had wanted to support him at the hearing. She'd been able to see what he'd done in perspective: it was only a damned packet of candy bars, whereas he was her precious father. But he had lied to her about the court location and only subsequently did she learn of his later, escalating crimes, which had culminated in the theft of the purse of a single mother of three.

She was the only one who visited him in jail. Not her mother, not her father's side of the family, not even the storm-chaser friends who – she had always felt – had never been on his wavelength anyway. They were thrill-seekers, whereas her dad had no interest in storms as a joyride. His reasons for following them were more spiritual than that. He was the high priest of the hurricane, the liturgist of the lightning, and this image was the one she clung to, even if she knew it was only a part of the picture that was her father.

Before he was interned, Elsa had hoped that prison would knock sense back into him. Then, on her first visit, when he'd mumbled, 'I'm weather-powered, see,' she'd had a kind of premonition of how he would go to pieces behind bars.

One time, after she'd drunk a little too much bourbon, her mum said she was calling his weather-powered bluff. He was not fuelled by the energies of storms and tornadoes. He was fuelled by the company of his only child, and he had stopped functioning because she had left him for the bright lights of the city. Perhaps she had drunkenly exaggerated, but even so the idea sent Elsa's mind reeling in horror. Could she have destroyed her father through the inevitable act of growing up? She tried to ask him about it, once, in the space between that first jail term and his second, but he was too prickly to speak on the topic.

Remembering this forced her to dry her eyes. She sniffed conspicuously, but there was only the priest's mumbled sermon to distract her from her thoughts, and it had no power to do so. Then, to her comfort, Dot's tiny, buckled hand reached sideways and squeezed hers. She breathed out, bit back her tears, and got a grip. Dot turned her head and gave her a long, studied look. Elsa met it, and the two women regarded each other for a minute before the nun smiled and returned her attention to the rambling priest.

Eventually the sermon was over and the priest was leading a prayer of grace Elsa did not recognize. It was murmured by everyone who was not her, addressed equally to everyone who was not her (save for Dot who turned to her to recite it) and then the service had ended. Spines clicked and creaked as the worshippers rose to their feet, making their way back towards the closed front doors, around which an outline of daylight glowed. Elsa looked over at

Daniel Fossiter at the front of the church. He rose slowly from his seat, stretched out his spine, then glanced back across the pews and caught Elsa's eye. She looked at the ground immediately.

The priest had opened the doors, but had backed up into a slice of shadow, and she shook his frail hand on the way out and wished him well for the week before stepping out hurriedly into the late morning. She wanted to get away from the church doors before Daniel Fossiter strode out of them. The sky had filled with a sheet of grey cloud, binding the town and the surrounding mountains together.

'Altostratus,' she thought, then realized somebody else had said it out loud. It was Dot, emerging behind her.

Dot winked at her. 'You look like you've other places to be. Don't worry, I won't keep you. But we fellow cloud-watchers should never abandon each other. You must come up to see me at the nunnery. Kenneth can give you directions. And don't wait too long about it. I could show you things. More pictures. I have a great many pictures up there.'

'Thank you,' said Elsa, meaning it. 'I'm sure I will.'

Dot nodded, and turned back up the church steps, just as Daniel Fossiter emerged, stuffing his hat on to his head and scanning the assembled crowd until he saw Elsa. He moved towards her as if he intended to speak to her, but then found his path blocked by the little old nun, who cooed about how good it was to see him and pinched his elbow and asked after his health. Meanwhile Elsa seized her chance, and slipped away towards Prospect Street.

10

BETTY AND THE LIGHTNING

In the late afternoon Elsa headed for a little teahouse she had happened upon whilst exploring the town. The Wallflower was reached via a snaking alleyway with walls overgrown with vegetation. Flies and moths buzzed in and out of the leaves, or hovered over gutters whose cracked covers revealed plunging shafts. Overhead, a green roof of creepers stretched from one wall to the other, some of its stems as thick as children's arms. Further along the alley she passed an electric lamp, twinkling in a prison of foliage, and this lit up a sudden memory of a hedge maze her mum and dad had taken her to once, for a birthday treat. She alone had found the centre of that maze, and had waited for a fruitless hour for either of her parents to discover her there.

Eventually the passage opened on to a courtyard enclosed by similarly verdant walls, with trellises dotted with trumpet-headed flowers. Hidden water gurgled somewhere nearby and made the air humid.

There were six small tables and a kiosk, where she ordered the same syrupy honey drink she'd enjoyed when she first found this place. The only other patron was a shrunken old man in his waxy rain cap. She recognized him as Abe Cosser, from Kenneth's choir, but he did not appear to have noticed her. He was smoking a pipe with his eyes in upturned reverie, sedentary save for the puffing of his mouth at the pipe's lip.

She chose a seat and watched an orange butterfly, whose wrinkled appearance suggested it was as old in butterfly years as Abe was in human ones, fly jerkily from flower to flower along the trellis. After a while it swept down to her table, where its wings sagged like damp cloth over its carapace. She used her teaspoon to drop a bead of her drink beside it. The butterfly approached and uncurled its doddery proboscis. It seemed to relish the taste of the liquid, for it took off rejuvenated, swerving drunkenly through the air.

She settled back into her seat and enjoyed a sip of the sticky drink. Then a movement out of the corner of her eye made her look up.

Abe Cosser had come to life. He was suddenly full of action, like those buskers who used to annoy her in subway stations by pretending to be statues, only to burst alive at the drop of a coin. He raised his hand to his head and doffed his rain cap. At first Elsa thought he had doffed it to her, but then she heard a heavy footfall behind her and looked over her shoulder.

She gasped when she saw Daniel Fossiter, then screwed up her fists under the table for being so impressionable. He stood tall in his creased old shirt, his britches, and his boots that were hobnailed and scuffed. 'Miss Beletti,' he declared in a gruff voice, then nodded to Abe, 'and Mr Cosser. A pleasure as always.'

Abe Cosser sprung to his feet. 'All mine, Mr Fossiter. But I was just on my way.' He doffed his cap again and scurried out of the courtyard.

Keep cool, Elsa thought to herself. She didn't feel it.

Daniel motioned to the spare seat attached to her table. 'May I?'

She shrugged.

He eased himself into the chair; it was difficult for him to squeeze his big body between its arms and to find a space for his legs beneath the table. 'I had hoped for the chance to discuss a certain matter with you, Miss Beletti.'

She swallowed. 'And what's that?'

He placed his fists down on the table. He sat rigidly – in contrast to Elsa who suddenly could not sit still – but inside he was shaking. His thoughts had been fully occupied these last few days with how best to intervene. He had prayed on his knees for the right words to persuade her, until the unrelenting church flagstones made the pain in his bones too overwhelming to pray any more. If he got this wrong, if he failed to persuade her to steer clear of Finn, then he was not sure he could cope with the guilt the inevitable disaster would bring.

'I had hoped to discuss,' he said tremulously, 'Finn Munro.'

She was agitated. 'What is there to discuss? You're going to tell me I shouldn't see him any more, and I'm going to tell you that we'll do as we please.'

He sighed and looked down into the broth he had bought at the kiosk. They were kindly to him here, keeping a sour, fermenting vegetable stock in a special jar, even though nobody but him would buy it. 'It is more complicated than you think. It isn't safe.'

'Perhaps it's less complicated than *you* think.'

Elsa wondered whether he had any genuine hold over Finn, whether if she let her anger loose and made an enemy of him he could really make their lives difficult.

For his part, he watched her and observed that she was capable of a hundred thinkings at a time, and in this he could not help but be reminded of Betty, who had been the one to teach him that human hearts were never alike. He had known that to be true between species – the mountain shrew's heart, for example, pounded ten times faster than a human being's – but Betty's had operated at ten times the speed of his own, and he had felt like a glacier around her.

He sipped his broth. Its warmth was reassuring and gave him courage. He cleared his throat and spread out his fingers on the table. He stared at his nails as he spoke. They were grubby with mountain dirt. 'You will think me a tyrant, with no right to make demands on the boy.'

She didn't disagree.

'But, Miss Beletti, you should understand that I am not asking you to stop seeing Finn because of any wrongdoing on your part. On the contrary, I am asking you because I fear for your safety.'

She gave him one of her best sarcastic smiles. 'How very selfless of you, Mr Fossiter, but I've already had this conversation with Finn. He kept insisting he was dangerous. Because of the weather in him, he said. I told him I would be the judge of that.'

Daniel slumped back in his chair, too stunned at first to digest what she'd just said, for Finn had looked him in the eye and promised him he'd told her nothing. 'You mean to say you know what's inside of him?'

'I saw and heard what's inside of him.'

He suddenly felt very cold. The sunlight on his neck and the hot broth in his mouth were icy. Finn had deceived him. 'Do you mean to say,' he asked as steadily as he could, 'that you have seen and listened to the weather in him, and that you *still* wish to befriend him?'

'Yes. Why is that so hard to believe?'

Daniel chewed his thumbnail. It was a moment before he could speak again, and even then it was hard to regulate the anxiety in his voice. 'Have you told anybody else?'

'Of course not. It's far too … personal for that.'

He breathed out. 'Thank heaven for that. At least in that matter you are not so reckless.'

'Reckless? I think you ought to know that just because I haven't told anyone, it doesn't mean I think he should be ashamed of what's inside of him. You know what? I actually think it's wonderful.'

'I am telling you this for your benefit, not his.'

'I don't think he's dangerous. I don't think he could hurt a fly.'

Daniel rubbed his eyes. 'If by that you mean that he couldn't hurt a fly *on purpose*, then we are in agreement. What I am fearful of, Miss Beletti, is what he might do by accident.'

'Both he and I are grown-ups. We can deal with it. You've got to stop treating Finn like he's still a kid.'

Daniel could not see why she was so predisposed to find him patronizing, but as a consequence he was eager to be as straight with her as possible. It did not matter, he supposed, what she thought of him. Only that she stayed away from Finn after this conversation. 'I do not treat him like a child. I treat him as I would a wild beast.'

'Jesus, that's even worse.'

He frowned. 'I find you strange, Miss Beletti. A mystery, if you will let me use the word. I cannot pretend I understand what brings you to Thunderstown, nor why you risk so much by seeing this boy.'

'I don't think I'm risking anything. On the contrary, I think *this boy* and I have everything to gain.'

'Are you quite sure of that?'

'Of course I'm sure.'

'You have not seen what Finn is capable of.'

'Yes, I have. He's capable of sweetness and softness and silence.'

He sighed. 'Perhaps it is because you are young. Only the young put their lives at risk so brazenly.'

She was about to retort but stopped herself. 'Excuse me? What do you mean?'

He narrowed his eyes. ' He has not told you, has he?'

'Told me what?'

'What he did to Bett—' he paused, exhaled; 'to his mother.'

'Please,' Elsa asked quietly, 'tell me what happened.'

Daniel closed his eyes for a second. It was painful to remember and Elsa could see that too. 'I don't know,' he began, 'how much he has described of his childhood, but it was by necessity a sheltered one. To begin with, Betty tried to pretend he was a normal little boy, but not long after he started school the other children began to pick on him. One afternoon in the playground a stone was thrown. It hit him here – ' Daniel pointed to his cheekbone, ' – and a swelling came up. He ran to the teachers to show them the bruise, but when they looked more closely, they discovered it was not a bruise at all. It was more like a patch of dark cloud emerging from his very skin. They were horror-struck – they had no idea what they were seeing. They hurried him out of sight, thank goodness, and eventually the school nurse gathered herself together enough to try to wipe away, whatever it was. But it was useless; more cloud just seeped through the bruise, marking out again the place where he was wounded.'

Daniel shuddered and sipped his broth.

'There was no way Finn could return to school after such an incident, and it took all of my powers to persuade the staff to stay silent. From then on, Betty taught him at home. She kept him safe from other children, and that was for the best. He was happier because he was safe and she was happier because she saw more of him. Yet it did not take away the fact that his body was full of foul weather. I sometimes wonder … if she had not kept him so safely hidden … might there have been warning signs that would have shown just what he was capable of? Might we have been more alert to the dangers? As it was, when it happened, we saw it at full force. One night, when he was sixteen and we were at supper in Betty's house, he revealed that he had met a girl. He said she was staying in Thunderstown for the summer and that she had approached him while he lay in the sun in Betty's garden. He said he did not understand why, but that he had found it hard to talk to her. He said that in her presence he had felt things twisting inside of him, and he did not know whether he had enjoyed the feeling. Betty told him not to worry, and then she looked at me to help explain to him something of what a young man goes through when he grows up.'

He leaned back in his chair with a puff.

'Well,' asked Elsa, 'what did you tell him?'

'I told him that friendship with this girl was not for him, because he and the girl were made out of different stuffs. And I told him that his twisting feeling was like a serpent he should fight. At this advice he became lost in himself. Betty was furious – I knew she would be – but I had only said what he needed to hear.' He stared down into his drink, as if its surface were a screen replaying the past. 'Then our knives and forks began to vibrate, and I could feel every follicle of my body stiffening. I watched the hairs on Betty's head lift. Finn thumped the table and at once the knives and forks flew together and locked as if they were magnets. The very air felt like pins and needles. And then it came out, as if he'd been keeping it all bottled up and something had released inside him. He demanded to know why he had been kept so isolated. Why hadn't he been able to have friends, to talk to girls and keep their company? Why had Betty kept him hostage at home, like some freak in a sideshow? Well, I took exception to this. He'd gone too far. I told him to fasten his mouth. And then ...'

Daniel frowned. 'Things happened so fast. Betty stood up in a rage. Her chair fell over behind her. I thought she was angry at Finn, but she leaned across the table and she struck me across the cheek.' He grimaced and downed the dregs of his broth. 'She turned to Finn, she reached out to him, she tried to embrace him ... he tried to hold her at bay, and then something flashed across his face. I am not talking about an expression, I am talking about a *light*. I just sat there like a damned fool, pitying myself, while Betty tried to embrace Finn again. Then all of a sudden came more flashes of light, but this time coursing through him. Elsa, it was as if he had electricity in his veins instead of blood – I could see every one of them like a branch of forked lightning!' He swallowed. 'There was a wicked, crackling sound, and then the lightning jumped into Betty's outstretched arms. The shock threw her across the room so hard that the impact broke a rib.' He stuffed his wrists into his eyes and gritted his teeth for a moment. 'If only you had smelled her burned skin … Elsa, please. I tell you this for your own safety. You are being too reckless – Finn was not born to live among people. He should not have been born at all.'

He waited for Elsa to take it in, grimly satisfied at her white face and wide eyes. It was right that she should be appalled. He had no desire to see her this way – it gave him no satisfaction. But what his father had told him was true – the most important lessons are the ones that hurt the most.

She drained her honey drink, which had now gone tepid, in one quick motion. 'My dad died last year.'

Daniel scratched his beard uneasily. He had not expected her to say that, nor to look so suddenly composed. 'I … I'm sorry for you.'

She shrugged. 'Thanks, I suppose. It was hard. Until then I thought he was invincible, because he had spent his life walking through storms unharmed. Once he was even struck by lightning.'

'And was he hurt very badly?'

'He was completely fine. He had a blackout, and then was back on his feet. He was storm-chasing again the very next day. So you see, sometimes when it happens, it doesn't always end in hurt.'

Daniel's spirit sunk. He closed his eyes and tried to imagine what her father would have been like. Cavalier, that much was for certain. 'He sounds,' he said, 'either very lucky or very foolish.'

'No!' She jabbed a pointing finger at him. '*You're* the foolish one. If you hadn't made matters worse for Finn, it might never have become as bad as it did!'

He gasped. It had been many decades since anyone had dared to call him foolish, and then only his grandfather, cackling at him from his deathbed as Daniel tried to pray for his eternal soul.

'When I was with Finn yesterday,' she continued, tearful all of a sudden, 'I felt like we were aligned somehow. But you couldn't possibly understand.'

'No,' he said; 'on that we agree.' He shook his head and pushed back his chair. When he got to his feet his legs felt old and weak. He could not find the strength to fully straighten his spine. He was trying not to picture Elsa with the same burns he had nursed Betty through, or worse. 'I have appreciated your time this afternoon, Miss Beletti.' He punched his hat into shape and looked at it wearily. 'I am not a man who needs to have the last word, so this will be the final thing I say. You can have the last word after I have spoken it.' He cleared his throat. 'Everybody thinks that they will be spared. Betty was lucky to survive. Your father was lucky to survive. Not everybody is lucky.' He put his hat on his head, tucked his thumbs into his britches, and waited for her to speak.

She stewed in her chair for a minute, pissed off that she couldn't think of anything cutting to say. In the end she settled for 'Whatever' and wished she had simply kept her mouth shut.

He nodded and stalked away.

She exhaled.

Only once he had gone did she let herself tremble. She wanted to be sick.

The worst was that, even when she'd lowered her head to listen at his chest then pressed her lips to his, even then Finn hadn't seen fit to tell her about this.

The butterfly she had fed earlier flittered back to her table and fanned its wings there. It took off again and circled in the air until, with a sharp slap, she knocked it down. It flapped about on its side on the floor. She stood, carefully lifted her chair and brought one of its legs down hard, screwing the bug into the ground. She spat out the taste of her honey drink, and made her way back towards Prospect Street.

11

THE GORGEOUS
PALACES

Bad weather ran wild through Thunderstown overnight, rattling latches and tapping on windowpanes. Elsa slept fitfully, woken every so often by the noises of the wind.

Come dawn, she was too tired to be angry. When she had gone to bed she had felt as if she were lying down in her own fury, sinking into it and tucking it up around her. She had been angry at Finn, angry at Daniel for telling her about Betty and the lightning, angry at herself for letting her defences down, angry with the world for always adding one more complication.

But in the morning she felt neither anger nor anything else. While she slept her heart had curled up into a ball.

She was not one of those people Daniel had accused her of being. She *did* believe that a person should learn from the lessons of others. All she had done was refuse to let him see it, because she didn't want to offer him the satisfaction.

She remembered visiting her dad's storm-chasing friend Luca in hospital. His wife Ana-Maria had been there too, sitting wordlessly at his bedside and picking at the stems of the flowers Elsa's dad had bought her. Her father had been just a stone's throw from Luca when the lightning bolt hit, and he was acutely aware that it could have been him, not Luca, lying in the hospital bed. Ana-Maria had clearly been thinking just that, and wishing it too.

The lighting that had taken the sight from Luca's right eye had left a sickle-shaped burn that ran from his eyebrow to his jaw. Likewise it had removed the pupil and the iris from the eyeball, leaving only a startlingly pink globe which the doctors had covered with a bandage.

It had been the kind of strike every storm-chaser feared. The one against which no precautions could be taken. Dry lightning. That meant a bolt from the blue or, more technically, a bolt from a storm some ten miles away and perhaps even out of sight, which could fork in an instant across the distance. The sky above Luca's car had been clear and summery, for they were some miles yet from the storm they were chasing, which here was but a grey fringe for the horizon. He had sat on the bonnet, humming along to his stereo, while Elsa's dad took a leak among nearby bushes.

Had she been offered the choice, Ana-Maria would have accepted Luca's partial blindness as a lucky escape; compared to the real damage, his blown-out eye was inconsequential.

The doctors explained that no human mind was built to withstand such electricity, and that the lightning had scrambled the natural circuitry of Luca's brain like a power surge frying a computer chip. Dreams, memories and learned behaviours had all been carried out of place on the currents, and had settled in new configurations. They warned that, when he came to, Luca might not be Luca any more. He might be a new man, born again with no grip on his reality. Dreams might have turned to memories and memories to dreams forgotten upon waking. All Ana-Maria could do was wait and pray. Even she might have become just a dream figure to him, an image fading from the waking day.

Yes, Elsa was well aware of the perils of lightning.

The overnight rain had made all the difference to Thunderstown's convoluted streets, making the cobbles in Tallow Row shine like a haul of fresh oysters. She did not mind the drizzle as she walked, nor that her jeans stuck to her thighs and her hair turned slowly bedraggled with the water.

Avoiding the pull of Saint Erasmus, she headed instead for Old Colp. Her route took her west through Tinacre Square, where a charm-seller stood all alone amid the drizzle, her red hair dark and damp against her neck. From Tinacre Square a quiet passageway led towards Feave Street, a shortcut where the raindrops landed lightly on the walls.

At the end of the passage, before the next began, lay a modest courtyard enclosed by the windowless backs of town houses. It was brighter than the passageway and smelled of new rain on slate. The drizzle consolidated into heavy drops, each a vertical flicker through the air.

Something landed on her hand. She looked down expecting rain but saw instead a bug, which she swatted instinctively. She made contact, but when she drew her hand away there was no squashed insect on her knuckles. There was only water. Another bug droned through the rainy air, and she realized that the walls were thick with them. They were the size and shape of ladybirds, but had dull grey shells without markings. They dotted the bricks and mortar like drops of mercury.

She froze. Something here was amiss. Her stomach had clenched because of it, but her mind took a moment to work out what was wrong. Then she realized that she had left wet footprints across the courtyard floor, which was bone dry, despite the falling rain.

A transformation was happening at knee-height. She watched a raindrop break there prematurely, shattering against the thin air. Then the shape of its suspended splash became that of spread insect wings, and then the wings flickered into life and the raindrop flew upwards. Through the wing-blur appeared a bug's minuscule antennae and dangling legs. It whizzed away to join its fellows on the courtyard walls.

With timid steps she approached the nearest wall, where she held her breath and leaned in close to inspect one of the bugs. Its body was like murky water, and similarly translucent. Through it she could see the grit of the bricks. Likewise she could find her own reflection, warped across the insect's concave back.

She reached out to touch it. It came off the wall and welled into a raindrop on her skin. Its little legs, hairs-breadth eyes and crystalline shell all vanished, and it became only a wavering drop on the tip of her finger. She laughed with wonder. Then straight away she was unnerved, and stepped back sharply.

'Finn,' she said aloud. He had invited her into the world of these insects and the world of his own strange body, and on the threshold she had faltered because he had not been straight with her about its dangers. She wanted to enter, dearly she did, but she couldn't ignore the memory of Ana-Maria's face as she sat at Luca's bedside.

She hurried on towards Old Colp.

The rain ceased as she climbed, leaving the sky smeared with so many clouds of so many shapes and shades that it looked like a painter's palette. On the lower slopes, a wind blew cotton tufts out of the grass. She paused as they floated around her, half-expecting them to transform into insects or birds, but they were just seeds wrapped in fluff. Further up the mountain she came to a gurgling little brook, its surface glimmering with crescents of sunlight that, for an astonished moment, she believed were carp swimming in the water. They were just reflections, but she had to splash her arm through the brook to be sure of it. She felt as if all appearances here were but masks, and nothing could be trusted.

When she reached the bothy, a cloud shadow swept across her and she shivered, although she could not tell whether it was from fright or excitement or simply the cold of the shade it cast. A wind hummed against the rocky bluff the cottage backed against, coaxing deep, eerie music out of the stone.

She knocked fast on the door and folded her arms. 'Hi,' she said when Finn answered.

'You look tired.'

'So do you.'

'I didn't sleep well,' he said.

'Me neither.'

He wore a jersey of black wool, frayed and unravelling at the cuffs. He looked just as troubled as her. 'Daniel told me he'd spoken to you.'

She took a deep breath. 'And is it true? What he had to say?'

'Yes. I promise you I never meant to do it. Until that moment I didn't even know I had lightning inside of me.'

'I *know* it was an accident. That doesn't matter. What's difficult is … why didn't you warn me?'

'I … I tried to tell you I was dangerous.'

'But you didn't say how.'

'I didn't want you to hate me.'

'I *wouldn't have*. But I might have been more cautious about putting my ear to your chest! Or about kissing you. Now I don't even know whether I can trust you. What if I'd found out in the same way your mother did?'

Another cloud shadow fell across them. In its shade his skin looked foggy grey. 'It wouldn't be like that,' he said. 'Lightning isn't predictable.'

'Is that supposed to reassure me? Is there anything else you've kept from me? Anybody else you've hurt?' She didn't want to make him suffer, but she had to have this out with him.

He hung his head. The cloud shadow lifted, but the soft sunlight that followed could not brighten him and he remained overcast.

'I've only ever hurt one person, and that was my mother, whom I loved very much. But there have been other moments of lightning. In the months after she left, when I missed her so badly, it kept taking me by surprise. It would come out of me while I ate, or walked in the mountains, or even while I slept. Each time it felt like my spine had been ripped out, but each time it earthed in the ground. I made sure it could never hurt anyone again, by hiding away up here. I should have told you, Elsa, I should have and I can't believe I didn't. But somehow you made it impossible.'

'You're saying it's *my fault*?'

'No. I was going to say something else.' He bit his lip and looked away up the mountain.

'Well? Whatever it was, you'd better say it now.'

'I didn't tell you because you made me feel like my hair was standing on end, even though I don't have a single hair on my body.'

She was taken aback. She glanced around at the slate and the brown mountain grass, anywhere but at Finn.

'You …' She struggled for the words. Eventually she found some of her old resolve, but was not sure she liked the hard way it made her feel when she said, 'You still haven't answered my question. Is there anything else you've kept from me?'

He closed his eyes. 'Yes,' he said in a faint voice. 'There's something else.'

'Then now's the time to tell me.'

'I can't. Not here. I'd have to show you.'

'Where?'

'Further up the mountain. You'd have to come with me.'

She hesitated. 'Is it far?'

'Not far.'

Given what she had learned, she knew it was unsafe to be near him, although to her frustration she still wanted to see whatever it was he had to show her. As so often seemed the case in her life, what made sense and what she wanted were opposed. She nodded briskly and they set off, over slopes of whisky-hued soil, banks of black pebbles and spry grass. She hated that the silence between them, which previously she had so treasured, had turned so quickly into a gulf. On their way uphill he sprang tensely over the new mud and slicked thickets while she stumbled here and there, her feet slipping in the soil or tripping over roots that seemed to have been washed free of the earth. Then at last they reached the entrance to a tunnel, as tall as her. It looked like an old entryway to one of Thunderstown's mines, over which the timber boarding had cracked apart long ago. From its dark mouth she felt a changed air blowing against her cheeks, as if she were standing in front of an open freezer. He led the way inside and immediately something crunched under his foot: one shattered half of a miner's lantern, with a cobweb ball where a candle would once have burned.

'My torch is inside,' said Finn. 'I usually go down there without it. I can feel the way from the air currents. So to start with it will be dark for you.'

'What's in there? What if I hit my head on something? What if there are pits or sudden drops?'

'There aren't. And the ceiling is high. You'll have to trust me, although I suppose that will be harder for you now.'

She looked back at the blue sky framed by the lip of the tunnel mouth. 'Go slowly. I'll say if it gets too much.'

Further in, the smell of grass and heather that clung to Old Colp's slopes gave way to lungfuls of cold, mineral air. They quickly reached the edge of vision, where it became too black for even mosses and moulds to sprout on the walls. Here there was only smooth, blasted rock. A few steps further and the tunnel turned a corner into utter darkness. Each pace became harder than the last, for no sooner had she imagined an impending underground cliff than she had convinced herself that she was about to plunge over it. She came to a halt. 'Finn,' she said, and a long echo repeated off the F.

'Here.' He sounded only an arm's length away.

She wanted to reach out for him, but she battled back that desire. She would rather show anger than fear. 'Finn, what the hell is going on? I can't see a thing in here!' A powder of rock dust showered on to her face and tongue.

'Shh!' he hissed. 'Don't shout! Shouting,' he whispered, 'could bring the mountain down on us.'

Elsa bunched her fists. 'What can be so important that we have to go to all this effort to reach it? Can't I just wait here while you fetch it for me?'

'No. It can't be moved. You have to see it to understand. I can guide you, if you like. But to do that you'd have to take my hand.'

'I'll be fine, thank you. Carry on.'

It took great effort to follow him as slowly as she did. Her legs objected with every straining muscle. If he found it difficult to progress at such a nervy speed he said nothing. He was as silent as he was invisible.

Then a light burst on like a supernova. Elsa slapped her hands to her eyes and shrieked, thinking *lightning*. Rock dust shook in the lit-up air, but there was no thunderbolt. It was only the glow of a hand torch and she relaxed her guard, although after the total darkness it pained her retinas.

'We're here,' he said.

She blinked and blinked until eventually she saw the expanses of a cavern around them, and Finn offering her the torch by the handle. She snatched it and held it tight. Her eyes slowly accustomed to the underground and the reluctant colours locked in the rock walls. Stalactites broke the high cave roof into countless archways and winked, milky pink and orange, in the torch beam. From the ground, stalagmites pushed up to meet them, and in places the two had met and fused into palatial columns. In one instance, a frail stalactite hung like a photo of a lightning bolt, while out of the ground its nubby counterpart rose, its pearly head stopping only a millimetre beneath. She had once read an article about stalactites, and she knew it could be a century before they at last fused.

She swung the beam around the cavern. The far wall stretched upwards in a gradual curve. The flinty rock face shimmered green and peach like the skin of a trout.

Finn pointed in that direction, where in the dark a body of water oozed. 'Shine the torch over there.'

The light hit the water's surface and diffracted up the wall on the far side.

'Shine it higher.'

Beyond the water, the rock was coloured with seams of mineral. 'Higher still.'

Elsa raised the light and it revealed a cave painting.

It was a pattern of shapes painted in dark and sanguinary substances. All the cave paintings she had ever seen in books depicted bison, hounds, huntsmen or mammoths, but this was a painting of broken triangles and abstract nothings. She tried to imagine Palaeolithic painters reaching at full stretch to daub pigment on the stone. If this water had flowed here then, they would surely have risked their lives to do so.

She ventured as close as she could without losing her balance and pitching into the arc of the water. The torch trembled in her hand, making the cave painting appear to dance. Then she swung the light away and shone it at Finn, who screwed up his eyes and raised a hand to shield his face.

She lowered the light a fraction. The painting was not a pattern but a sequence. It progressed from left to right like the frames of a cinema reel. 'It's a story,' she declared. 'Each of these shapes follows on from the last.'

As far as she could tell, the story in the cave painting went something like: Once upon a time, there were cottony shapes, indistinct things with indefinable boundaries. Then, for reasons unknown, the shapes became definite. They morphed from smudges into triangles. None of the triangles were perfect: one had cracks running down it; one had a corner so smoothed away that it was now almost a half-circle; one had a dent taken out of its top.

'This one,' she said, focusing the torch and wishing she could keep her voice as steady as its clean line of light, 'is the Devil's Diadem. This one is Old Colp.'

Finn stared into the tar-black water. 'Yes, and there's more. Shine it higher.'

She did so eagerly, and discovered a painted ceiling. All the animals of prehistory were there, horses and hounds and horned goats. Yet no beast was complete. Part of each dissolved into the stone. A rearing horse had hindquarters that vanished into a craggy overhang. The forepaw of a dog stretched out and became a stalactite.

In the corner of the ceiling were the humans. They too broke down in places into blank nothingness and shadows. And some – these had been painted curled up, or bowed in despair – had white lines flying out of their hearts.

'Who are these people?' she asked. 'What does this mean?'

'I don't know for certain.'

Again she turned the torch on him. 'What do you mean, you don't know? I asked if there were any more secrets and you led me here.'

'I brought you here because I thought the paintings might help you understand.'

'Understand *what*?'

'Me. That maybe I'm not so unusual.'

She stepped away, confused. Part of her wanted to shine the

torchlight into his every pore. Part of her thought she had already risked enough.

Then she heard a faint noise like the leftover tremble after a cymbal is struck. 'Finn? What was that?'

'It was me,' he said. 'It's the thunder I have for a heartbeat, the same sound you listened to when we caught the canaries in the woods. It's just that, in these caves, it's quiet enough to hear it without putting an ear to my chest.'

Elsa felt suddenly claustrophobic. When the thunder whispered out of Finn again, it felt as though all of the weight of the mountain was about to crash down on her. She gripped the torch tightly, and flashed the light back towards the tunnel they had come from. Stalagmites and stalactites swung shadows through the beam.

'I can't stay here, Finn.'

'Elsa, please … is there no way we can get past this?'

'It's like you said – I just don't know. For now I need some space.' She shrugged and struck out towards the lightest part of what was before her, trusting the hard rock of the tunnel wall to lead out of the cave.

Behind her the thunder sounded louder, slow and melancholy, like a lament. She took a few more faltering steps, then could not help but turn to shine the torch back.

'Elsa, a week or so after I struck my mother, she tried to tell me that she still loved me. She stood before me one sunny afternoon, and I could see her lips trying to form the words. But she had become so frightened of me that she couldn't get them out. That was the worst thing I have ever seen, and I would never risk seeing it again. Soon after that she left Thunderstown. But when you placed your ear to my chest, I felt like we were safe. I felt like we were too attuned for there to be lightning.'

His body was as still as the stalactites, but he was crying. The beam of light glittered. The air had filled with diamond dust, icy particles dancing in and out of the light. Each of Finn's tears, as it emerged from the duct, crystallized at once into a glittering speck that flew forth. The tears swirled and shimmered in the space between Elsa and Finn, and some caught the light like prisms, filling the cold cave air with rainbow colours.

Elsa stood, enchanted, in the tunnel. She wanted to stride back to Finn and melt through his wintry sorrow with the heat of a kiss. But she had always known not to toy with lightning. She turned back through an excruciating half-circle, then left him behind her in the darkness.

12

GUNSHOT

At the humid close of the afternoon, Daniel walked Mole into Thunderstown. The old dog waddled slowly, pausing every few minutes to regain her wheezing breath, her good eye shut tight and her blind one fixed on the middle distance. In this stop-start fashion they made their way under the cold shadow of the Church of Saint Erasmus and eventually to the door of the Thunderstown Miners' Club. It stood in the mouth of Widdershin Road, where the leaning eaves kept it in constant shade. These days its concave door was hard to budge, and the wood strained when Daniel held it open for Mole to enter.

Inside, an old lamp hung its broken bulb over an unstaffed desk. Through a door lay the common room, which would smell forever of the generations of pipe smoke that had turned its wallpaper yellow. Bolted to its walls were pickaxes and rusty hand drills, and black-and-white photos of stiffly posed workmen or of the mines themselves, dark squares charred into the rock face.

Now that there were no miners left in Thunderstown, their club had a ragtag bunch of patrons: tradesmen and clerks and gossiping men like Sidney Moses, Hamel Rhys and Abe Cosser, who sometimes met in the common room to play chequers or sip broth and who always wore their rain caps, even indoors. Daniel never attended such gatherings, although he was counted among the club's members. The head man of the Fossiter family (although none had ever been miners) had always been given a seat at the club.

A ring of hand-me-down armchairs stood in the common room, and Mole curled up at the foot of one of these and tucked her nose into the crook of her foreleg. Daniel watched her for a minute, thinking how pitiful she was, to have changed from a huntress as lethal as a bullet to a stiff sleeper like a taxidermist's masterpiece.

He crossed to a smaller adjoining room, where shafts of light slanted down from high windows and bookshelves spanned the walls. He ran his forefinger over the spines of the tomes there. These were Thunderstown's family trees, most of which had finished branching decades ago, or else had been left incomplete by the present generation. Only the ten-volume sequence marked *Fossiter* remained dust-free, and it was the final book in this collection that Daniel now selected and took down from the shelf.

The binding still showed the stretched scars of the goat whose skin it had come from, as did the leather clasp he now popped open. The yellowed pages were all unnumbered and scrawled with handwritten notes. Connections forked down and interconnected from the top of each page to the bottom. Cousins had married second cousins; widows had been passed on to unmarried brothers. The name Daniel itself was repeated over and over: there had been a time when it occurred once in every generation. Now it was the only remnant of that grand family, a reverse Adam who would leave the final pages blank.

He returned to the common room and took a seat. Mole whimpered in her sleep, which he was glad to hear since it reassured him that she was still alive. He mimicked her stillness, sitting with his fists on the arms of the chair and the family tree open on his lap.

The names of his forefathers had all been written in the same scratchy script, in the same ink turned brown by age. His father had completed the final page at the time of Daniel's birth, drawing a straight line down from his own name to that of his son. When Daniel had discovered it he had not known whether to hate or pity the old man, for as far as this family tree recorded it, Daniel had originated out of the body of the Reverend Fossiter himself. To rectify this untruth, he had borrowed one of Sally Nairn's antique writing pens and a pot of ink that was like a jarful of tropical ocean, then returned to the family tree to slowly scratch his mother's name and the line that bound her to him. Only when he had finished writing did he wonder whether he had made a mistake. He had written Maryam Fossiter, because she was his mother and he had come from her and he was Fossiter in every cell of his body. But she had not been a Fossiter. She had not even married his father, let alone taken his name, and that had been his father's pretext for driving her away. 'It's as the Lord told us,' he had said. 'Those who are not with us are against us.'

Daniel closed his eyes and let his memories of her take centre stage. He could not picture her face (he had not been able to in decades), only her black hair dangling down to her waist. He could picture her forearms and hands and hips because he had been so small when she left that those had been the parts of her he saw the most of. He knew he had been in pain when she left Thunderstown, but it was a different kind of pain to the one that came when Betty went away. He had been too young to understand it. It had been an ocean on which he had drifted.

In his memory his mother hummed and leafed absent-mindedly through his father's theology books, chuckling now and then as if all those essays by all those learned men were but the amusing mistakes of little children. His father watched her, incensed by her unbelief but silent nevertheless. That was one of only a handful of memories, which Daniel tended to as diligently in his thinkings as he did to these family trees.

He had, however, one stranger memory of her, one which did not comfort him but rather left him cold. In it, she sat in a rocking chair, on the porch of the vicarage. He – a little older than a toddler – had been digging about in the garden and had returned to the house to show her something he had unearthed. To his dismay he'd seen two wild dogs sitting with her, their muzzles resting on her lap. Their eyes were half-closed while she stroked their heads. He'd shouted, and ran towards her, screaming and waving his arms, and the dogs had sprung up and fled into the mountains.

He harrumphed. He sometimes wished that that particular memory of his mother would recede into the past, and not present itself every time he recalled the happier ones. He got up and returned the family tree to the shelf.

Once, long ago, he had brought Betty to the Miners' Club to show her his mother's name here, along with all those hundreds from his father's side. Back then, old Mr Nairn had cooked in the club kitchen every Sunday afternoon. Mr Nairn had been a man who found vegetarianism a hard thing to comprehend, and Daniel had known that his sloppy potato patties and brown cabbage would be fried in the gloopy white fat of a swine. Although that risked turning Betty's stomach, he'd needed to bring her here to help her understand who he was and from what stock he'd come, and she had seen that and accompanied him with good grace. So many hours of so many Fossiter lives had been idled away in this common room that he could almost see the ghosts of his forebears holding forth in the armchairs that still bore the imprints of their bodies. He had brought Betty here not to taste Mr Nairn's cooking, but to introduce her to the impressions made in the furniture. He had felt so proud to have her at his side. He had always been a big man – even as a child he had towered over his classmates – but with Betty beside him he had felt weightless, as if he were floating a foot off the ground.

There was a gunshot. He blinked and for a moment did not know what year of his life he was living in. Mole had heard it too and was struggling to her feet, her ears straining and her bad eye weeping. It had come from out in the street, and Daniel headed straight for the exit from the club, Mole puffing along behind him.

They went a little further down Widdershin Road, where a junction led into tree-lined Foremans Avenue, and from there onwards to Drum Head. Thirty yards along this avenue lived Sidney Moses, who now stood outside his house with his rifle in his hands. He did not notice Daniel when he approached, for he was too fascinated by the goat that was sitting in the shade of one of the avenue's trees. Fragments of bark and lichen were stuck to its panting tongue, and a bullet wound in its neck was flushing blood into its beard. It knelt reposefully, as if dying were a state as ordinary as basking in an afternoon's hot sun.

'You fool!' yelled Daniel, snatching the rifle from Sidney's hands. Sidney offered no resistance. Daniel readied the gun, steadied his aim against the anger rushing up from inside of him, and shot the goat between the eyes. Mole barked painfully as the shot rang out. The goat's horned head dropped down to the pavement.

The gunshot brought Sidney to his senses, and he looked at his rifle in Daniel's hands as if he did not remember how it had got there. 'Mr Fossiter, I …'

'What were you thinking?'

'I shot a goat. It had been eating the trees.'

'But you didn't shoot to kill.'

'No, I—'

'I know full well that you can fire a rifle, Mr Moses, and I declare that you did not shoot to kill!'

Sidney lifted his rain cap to wipe a line of sweat from his forehead. 'Of course I shot to kill!' He puffed out his cheeks. 'I damned well shouldn't have been forced to! This town employs a culler to keep these vermin from its streets. Have you seen him today, Mr Fossiter? He's a big man with a beard – hard to miss. He would have been useful here earlier, while this beast was munching its way along the trees of Foremans Avenue!'

'I was in the Miners' Club. You know I'm often there. You could've at least *tried* to find me.'

Sidney stole another glance at the goat, and there was that same grim fascination. He licked his lips. 'We never know where we can find you, Mr Fossiter, because you do not tell us where you are going to be.'

'Yes you do, Sidney, you all do – you know I am going to be culling the goats.'

'In the Thunderstown Miners' Club? I don't believe there are many goats in there, except for the heads of some your great-grandfather shot. And I see you have even brought that terrifying bloodhound with you!'

As if on cue, Mole sneezed and shook her head.

'I don't need a dog to catch goats.'

'And just as well – that sorry creature wouldn't say boo to a goose,' said Sidney, flourishing his arm towards the animal beneath the tree.

'Mr Moses. What do you plan to do, now, with your kill? Do you know how to skin the hide and chop the meat, or do you plan to leave it to fester here in Foremans Avenue?'

Sidney shrugged. 'I own plenty of shirts, coats and jerseys, Mr Fossiter. I have radiators in my house and I have a freezer full of chicken, lamb and fish from the market. So I need neither fleece, leather or goat mutton. What's more, I own a motor car and a trailer, with which I intend to drive this carcass out of town and dump it in the ample wilderness surrounding us, where I fully expect the crows to finish the job.'

Daniel was about to retort, but managed instead to bite his tongue. He knew full well he could not best Sidney at words. Mole sneezed again and shivered as it moved through her. Daniel stepped briskly past Sidney, grabbed the goat by the horns and made to drag it after him. 'Do not trouble yourself with your trailer and your motor car, Mr Moses. I will make leather out of it.'

He began to plod away towards his homestead, with Mole labouring behind.

'And then what?' called Sidney after him.

'I will return to my duties.'

'Must we be rivals, Mr Fossiter?'

Daniel stopped walking and turned back to him. 'I have no wish to oppose myself to anyone. You, on the other hand, seem to delight in it.'

Sidney spread his arms and looked hurt. 'You misunderstand me.' He put his hands in his pockets and sauntered closer.

'You would modernize,' said Daniel. 'You have talked about helicopters and satellite … satellite—'

'Satellite tracking,' said Sidney gently.

Daniel snorted. 'Have the goats changed in the last hundred years? Have the wild dogs begun to use helicopters? The methods of my family have always been sufficient. And always will be.'

Sidney sighed. 'We've talked about this. I don't want you forever catching goats and wild dogs. I want you to get to the root of the problem.'

Daniel scoffed. 'I would have to kill every goat within a hundred miles of Thunderstown to get to the root of the problem. I would need an army to do that.'

'I'm not talking about goats, as well you know.'

Daniel looked away shiftily down the length of the street. A wind blew and ruffled the fur of the goat he was pulling, puffing its dusty smell up into his nostrils.

'And I have told you before – Old Man Thunder's just a story. Come on, Mr Moses, there are so many tales here, why must you persist in believing this one? I'm telling you: not I, nor anyone else, will ever catch Old Man Thunder because *he does not exist* – he never did.'

Sidney smiled, but Daniel did not trust it. He was being tested, he knew, but on what subject he could not guess.

'People say they have seen him.'

'People say a lot of things. Words mean nothing, Mr Moses.'

Sidney studied him for a moment, then shrugged and licked his lips. 'Imagine for a moment that he does! Just pretend, just humour me. Let's say I did things my way, with all the new equipment I can lay my hands on, and I found him and brought him to you tomorrow. I dragged him down here to town and presented him to our culler for his judgement. What would you do?'

'You would need to prove he was Old Man Thunder.'

'And if I could? If he was stood here before you, riddled with weather, confessing *I am he*. Then what?'

Daniel snorted. 'Then nothing. This is idle speculation.'

'Would you do your duty then, Mr Fossiter? If the thing that eluded all of your forefathers was there for the taking?'

Daniel cleared his throat. 'Mr Moses, I am not sure what more I can say. I do not believe in Old Man Thunder. I have endeavoured to make that clear to you.'

'No, Mr Fossiter,' said Sidney sweetly, 'you have endeavoured to avoid the question. I do not think you could do it. The townsfolk are concerned, and think you have gone soft. That Munro woman, that one who came from overseas, she took something from you that you have struggled to get back. She left you confused and without ruthlessness, doting over your blind old dog.'

He bristled at the insult, and his shoulders squared and as they did so the fur of the goat bristled in the wind. 'Listen very carefully, Mr Moses. Were you to bring me Old Man Thunder, and were he to exist and be proven to be all that people say he is, I would slit his throat without hesitation. So that's said, and you can tell the townsfolk to forget their concerns. One more thing: Betty Munro took nothing from me, and gave me things that you could never understand. If I seem weak-willed to you, it is because I always was, not because of her.'

With that he headed for the homestead, and left Sidney Moses behind him.

13

OLD WIVES' TALES

After the ceremony they held for her father, Elsa stood in the crematorium garden, drawing in deep breaths of the whipping wind. The flowers were in full bloom in their beds, bobbing in the blustering air. Elsa wondered whether the owners of the crematorium had planted bird of paradise as a joke, since its orange petals looked like flames wavering in the wind. Then again, everything became symbolic after a death. She had argued with her mother about the shape and colour of the urn, until both of them, in tears, ceded that it didn't matter and chose the least ostentatious one. She had seen a sun dog the other night, a blue and orange half-halo shining to the right of the sun, and had believed it to be a sign from her father, even though she had no faith in an afterlife and knew that sun dogs were just refraction. Only when she could not decide what the sign meant did she give in to her rational mind, and her rational mind left her to sob the evening away.

The other mourners remained near the door to the crematorium, chatting and occasionally shooting a concerned glance in her direction. The sharp-tipped evergreens that overlooked the cemetery sowed their needles on the grass, scenting the air with their aroma of pine. She took a deep breath.

Her mother came up beside her and squeezed her hand, and

Elsa turned to her teary-eyed and said, 'Can I ask you a kinda awkward question?'

'Anything you want, Elsa.'

'Well … you're a religious person. What do you think happens to Dad now?'

Her mother didn't look Elsa in the eye, but squeezed her hand all the firmer between both of her own. The wind tore through the high branches. Green needles rained on the path. She wiped her eyes with her sleeve and said, 'The thing is … the thing is, Elsa, that your father didn't live a good life.'

The wind that had been hurrying through the pine trees paused. There was a heartbeat's silence. Then it flew on, whooping and howling.

Elsa tugged her hand away and shoved it as a fist into her coat pocket.

'You did ask,' her mother said in a small voice.

Elsa stamped away up the path. She didn't think about the direction she was taking and the path led to a dead end where wasps hummed above the crematorium's trash cans. Her anger changed to embarrassment. She had to turn back the way she'd come and pass her mother (who was now in tears) to get back to her car.

'This little car,' said Kenneth Olivier, slapping the vehicle's white bonnet fondly, 'was Michael's. It's small, but it's good enough to take you up the Devil's Diadem.'

Elsa was setting off to make good on her promise to Sister Dot at the nunnery. I am old here, Dot had said, and Elsa hoped that age could offer her some perspective. All night she had lain awake, thinking about the way she'd left Finn crying diamond dust in the heart of the mountain.

She climbed into the car and felt the seat beneath her depress comfortably. It must have been a long time since Michael had driven it, but it still smelled faintly of a young man's fragrance: allspice and moss and bonfire toffee. Kenneth sat down on the passenger seat beside her, ostensibly to demonstrate what buttons operated what, but she could tell from the heavy way his ribcage swelled with each intake of breath that he had got in to absorb just a little of his boy's scent.

'Kenneth,' she said, 'can I ask you a kinda awkward question?'

He folded his hands on his lap. 'Anything you like.'

'What, um, what do you think happens?'

He looked at her patiently. 'I'm sorry, Elsa, I'm not sure I follow you.'

She cleared her throat. 'Well … you're a religious person, aren't you?'

She waited in silence.

'Ah!' he declared suddenly. '*Ahh*, I think I understand.'

She stared at the car keys in her hand.

'I don't know,' he said.

She closed her eyes.

'Does that disappoint you?' he said.

'No … it's just … I thought … my mum's religious, too, and she told me …' She wished she had a bottle of water, because her tongue was so dry.

'Is this about your father?'

Elsa nodded.

'Well, let me tell you, I thought long and hard about this after Michael died. He didn't believe in anything, you see.'

'So … so … Does that mean you think he's …'

Kenneth began to chuckle, then tried to hide it and failed so spectacularly that his laughter escaped in great splutters. 'If you are trying to ask whether I believe my son is in *hell* simply because he was not a religious man when he died, then no!' He wheezed, and mopped his eyes with the sleeve of his jumper. 'No, Elsa, dear me, no. To believe in hell would be to compromise who I am.' *But*, if you were to ask me where else I think he might be, then my answer would depend on when you asked me. Sitting in his car right now, how can I believe he has simply vanished? I am surrounded by him. I can smell him here, for goodness' sake! Then again, ask me in the winter, when the rain is beating down on the windows, and nobody's ringing the telephone and nobody's at the door. Then I suppose I might say that a person stops existing when their body stops breathing.' He began to chuckle again. 'Am I allowed this kind of answer, Elsa? One in which Kenneth Olivier has no damned clue? Am I allowed to say I change my mind depending on how miserable I'm feeling?'

'No!' she said with a smile, wiping her eyes. 'You were meant to have an answer! Isn't that the whole point of believing in something?'

Then, quick as clicked fingers, he was serious again. 'I would love to have an answer. But what I believe is that I *can't* have one. Which is a good deal healthier than believing that I can, and then only accepting the worst answer I can think of.'

She rubbed her face. 'Sorry,' she said. 'I miss my dad, that's all. And I'm not good at being stoic like you are.'

'It takes time,' he said sagely, 'and a great many cricket matches. You do know you'll never stop missing him, right?'

They watched a leaf fall on to the windscreen. It was pink, with scarlet edges. There were no trees nearby; the leaf had been placed there delicately by the breeze.

'Right,' Elsa said.

Kenneth cleared his throat and jingled the car keys at her. 'You will need these. And you have the map there on the dashboard, although there is only one road.'

She nodded. 'Thank you.'

He got out of the car. 'Safe journey,' he said. He closed the door behind him and slapped the bonnet to wish her on her way.

The slopes of the Devil's Diadem were pitted and potholed. Streambeds scored the earth, long since abandoned by water and filled now only with briars and the bones of those unfortunate animals who had slipped into them and become trapped.

As she left Thunderstown it felt good to be driving again. She'd not driven often in New York, but back in Oklahoma she'd loved to race an old truck flat out over the long roads even when it made her mother freak out. Now, as she relaxed into the sensation, the command of wheels gave her a liberating buzz, like she'd had in that truck. Then she started driving up the mountain's steeper road and the winds came out to meet her. She had to slow right down, fearful that a gust might flip the car on its back, so powerfully did they howl at its chassis.

Driving higher and closer, the many peaks of the mountain seemed to her like the altars of a pantheon, summoning winds to the slopes below. She felt the gusts throwing themselves at the windscreen. Then one hit the boot and threw her forwards. The seatbelt jerked her shoulder and her teeth came together with an enamel crack.

She was glad, then, when she neared the base of one of those peaks and saw, in the shadow between it and the next, the dark cube of a solitary building. As she drove closer it gradually enlarged into a walled complex, containing a small tower on which a crucifix was mounted. The outer walls were pebble-coated stone and had eroded until none of their buttresses or edges were defined, so that the whole place had the crumbling appearance of a sandcastle. Even the crucifix had weathered. Wind wrapped around it like the tremor of a heatwave.

This was the nunnery of Saint Catherine, and there was no need for a car park, given the hard, blow-dried dirt on which it was built. Elsa parked on a patch of it, took a deep breath and stepped out of the car. At once the wind grabbed a handful of her hair and yanked her back towards Thunderstown. Shocked by its ferocity, she grabbed the car for balance. Dust rushed into her eyes and she had to turn her back on the nunnery to rub the grains away. The wind did everything it could to shove her off course as she approached a tall white door in the nunnery wall. It had a large brass handle and – she was surprised to see – a lucky horseshoe nailed into the wood. She twisted the handle and to her relief found the door to be unlocked. With the wind buffeting her she half-stepped, half-tumbled inside, where she had to grit her teeth and shove with all her might to close the door again. It slammed back into its frame and the wind roared and pounded against it.

She had entered a small antechamber, a kind of airlock against the elements. Straight ahead was another large door, which she supposed led into the convent's cloister. She tied back her hair, which had become weather-tangled, and bracing herself for another assault from the wind, she opened the door.

A deep lawn coloured the cloister a lush green. Delicate plants grew in various flowerbeds, with brown bees hovering above their still petals, patiently exploring them for nectar before returning to a hive box fixed to a wall. Some of the plants boasted orange flowers as big and wafer-thin as paper crowns, and stalks so slender she supposed a single breath could snap them. Yet all was motionless, without a breath of an air current. The wind still flared high above (looking up she saw the blue sky shimmering with its disturbance), but not a flutter blew down to this sanctum.

Then she noticed that all over the walls, numbering into their many hundreds, were charms such as the one that had hung from the sill of her bedroom that she had destroyed on her first night in Thunderstown. They were made from feathers, coins in pairs, scraps of fur and canine teeth. There were so many of them it was as if they, and not the mortar, propped up the nunnery.

In another wall stood a dovecot from which drifted the smell of bird droppings and down. Opposite this, above a turquoise double door and two stained-glass windows, stood the parapet of the chapel. She wandered across to it and heard high-pitched, wavering voices singing within. The nuns were finishing prayers. She turned around to look for somewhere to sit, and then noticed an elderly man sitting on the ground with his back against one wall and his hands folded over his knees. Although he was clean-shaven, one or two white hairs spiralled perfectly amiss on his olive-skinned face, wrinkles as dark and deep as his nostrils. His eyes were pearly white, without even a fleck of a pupil or an iris. A bee buzzed unnoticed across one of his ancient cheeks, examining one of those rogue white hairs as if it were the stamen of a flower.

At that moment an old lady emerged from the dovecot with a dove perched calmly on her shoulder. She wasn't a nun, but all the same was dressed entirely in grey. She walked in a doddery zigzag to the place where the old man sat, and joined him on the ground.

Elsa copied them by sitting down, choosing a spot of soft grass where she too could rest her shoulders against the sturdy stone of the courtyard wall.

She kept thinking about Finn. In her few minutes of sleep last night she had dreamed a nightmare in which she swept around and around a whirlpool as dark as her sleep. In the water with her were the bones of lost miners, all loose and mingling in the gyre. Through lap after lap she span, until in a final dizzying plunge she dropped into the whirlpool's dark heart.

The doors of the chapel opened, interrupting her thoughts, and the nuns filed out, chattering. Elsa sprung to her feet, worried she might not recognize Dot amongst the identical habits and diminutive bodies, but no sooner had she thought it than one of the nuns hooted and hobbled over to her: Dot, her face crinkling up with excitement. 'Ah!' she croaked, 'My young cloud-spotter!' She reached out and pinched Elsa's bare arm with her buckled fingertips.

'I hope I'm not disturbing you.'

'Not at all,' said Dot, eyes a-twinkle, 'In fact, I have been expecting you. This way!' She took hold of Elsa's hand and pulled her busily towards a door in the wall. Bees droned around them as they walked, and buzzed among the tall flowers and the elderly pair sitting on the bench.

'That man over there,' whispered Elsa, 'and that old lady with the dove on her shoulder – neither of them are nuns.'

'Well, obviously,' laughed Dot. 'William and Beatrice are two of our patients. We've several folk up here who medicine can't mend.'

'What's wrong with them?'

They had reached the door. It opened on to a cool, bare corridor, and only once they were inside and Dot had closed it behind them did she explain in a low voice, 'They were struck by lightning. It's a small wonder they survived, and in some ways you might say they did not. William lost his sight when the lightning struck him. But now he says he can see things that others cannot: angels and suchlike. As for Beatrice … she can no longer maintain a conversation, unless it is with the birds. She says she has forgotten English and learned to speak Doveish only.'

Elsa thought of the lightning that had hit Luca, and Betty, and her father.

'That's awful,' she said in an unintended whisper.

They proceeded along a plain corridor and up to the second floor. Here they entered Dot's own room, a cell simply decorated with a reed mat, a reed cross on the wall, a small window and an electric lamp. Dot reached happily under the bed and struggled to lift out a pile of huge, thick books, each the size and weight of an atlas. Elsa couldn't help but take a sharp, thrilled breath. These weren't atlases of the earth, but of the sky. Books like the one her dad had given her, which had been her pride and joy until she had hurled it out into the rain after him on the day he left. Her mother had thought that good riddance, but Elsa had done it not to be rid of him, but to try to show him how desperate she was for him to stay.

'I used to have one of these,' she said, staring sadly at the cloud atlases as Dot laid them out on the bed.

The nun smiled and laid her fingertips on the cover of the largest and oldest, which was leather-bound and Bible-thick. Stuck to its cover was a sepia photo of stacked storm clouds blocking off the sun's rays.

She opened it to the first page. The spine creaked like a hinge and set free the aroma of dried ink and paper. She turned the pages through more sepia shots: single puffy cumuli or mackerel skies. Then she came to a photograph of a giant cloud made from black mist. It was like a rook from a chess set, a black tower with blistering battlements. Lines of rain tethered it to the ground. At its heart it was so black that Elsa could see Dot's reflection in the page.

'A storm,' said Elsa.

'Cumulonimbus,' whispered Dot, and the word was like the hiss of snaking winds between grasses, or the dry creep of a thunder fly. Cumulonimbus, the storm cloud. Elsa had read the name so many times in books, lumped in with cirrus, altocumulus and the rest. Yet rolling over Dot's tongue the word sounded like it had when her dad had pronounced it. Like the name of an archangel.

'This one,' Dot said, tapping the picture, 'was larger than Mount Everest. He had as much energy charged up inside of him as in five of the bombs that blew up Hiroshima. The lightning in him burned ten times hotter than the surface of the sun. And all this is commonplace in Cumulonimbus.'

Elsa stared at the picture.

'There are some,' said Dot slowly, 'who see Cumulonimbus and think he is the power of God himself, or else of witches or devils, for surely something this powerful must come from more than water and dust.'

Elsa closed her eyes and saw her father in the visiting room, on the last of her visits to the jail, at the point when he'd taken to staring at the ceiling, convincing himself he could see clouds moving across it. When she had stood up to say goodbye for what would prove to be the final time, he had looked at her with a dumb grin and pronounced, 'It's raining, Elsa.' 'Dad,' she'd said, 'we're inside.' He'd pointed at her cheek and she'd touched it with a finger. She'd withdrawn her finger with a teardrop glinting on its tip. Then he'd turned again to the ceiling and whispered, 'See? Raining.'

Now Dot reached across and took her hand. 'Let me show you something else.'

She opened another, smaller atlas, and began to flick through its pages. When she found the one she wanted she laid it side by side with the sepia cumulonimbus. The page she had selected showed a frame full of fog. In the fog floated the dark silhouette of a figure, with inhumanly long limbs and a head made of shadows. Dot turned the page and there were more snapshots of the same phenomenon: a towering shade with black tapering arms and legs.

'This ...' said Elsa under her breath, 'I've seen pictures of this before.'

'It's a cloud spectre,' whispered Dot reverentially. 'A very rare thing. The first recorded sighting was in Brocken, in Germany. A shepherd on a mountain got lost in the fog and was trying to find his way out when he saw something that looked like this. Imagine it! One minute you're miles from anyone, the next there's a figure stalking you through the clouds. The shepherd was so haunted by the sight of it that for the rest of his life he only ventured out on fair weather days.'

'But it's a trick, isn't it? A trick of the light.'

'Yes, of course. His shadow projected on to the cloud. But do you know,' Dot's tone lowered, and her old eyes sharpened through the giant lenses of her glasses, and the atmosphere of the room seemed suddenly electric, as if before a storm, 'that Betty Munro once saw a Brocken spectre?'

Elsa felt her skin tingle. For a moment she could hear the wind outside walloping the masonry. 'I think I have heard bits of this story. Can you tell me anything about her?'

Dot's eyes crinkled up behind her glasses. 'Where to begin? The first time she came to visit me here, it was because she'd heard of an old folk-cure for childlessness. Climb a mountain in a storm and drink rainwater until you're sick from it. Yes, I told her I'd heard it said. Should she try it, she asked me, and did I think it would work?' Dot sat down slowly on the bed, amid the cloud atlases. 'I told her it might work and it might not, and it might do both at the same time in ways she couldn't predict.' She sighed. 'I should have been more to the point, but I underestimated how hard it was for her, knowing she couldn't have a baby. I gave up on that urge long ago, and I suppose I had forgotten how strongly it can call to you. Sometimes someone else's life can be the only thing that makes sense of your own.'

'She tried it, then?'

'Yes. She went up into the mountains, hoping for storms. There her hopelessness turned slowly into anguish, and her anguish made her scream at the sky, and stick her head underwater and yell into empty mountain lakes. *Anything,* she promised, to anybody above or below who could hear her. *Anything anybody asks. Just give me a child.*'

Perched on the edge of the bed, Dot looked like a storyteller poised around a hearth. Elsa sat down cross-legged on the hard floor.

'One day,' continued Dot, 'up in the mist on the mountain, what did Betty see but a figure! A silhouette standing in the fog. No doubt it was a trick, a Brocken spectre, her own lonely shadow projected on to the clouds. But to her, in that moment, it was someone who had heard her! The next day she came to see me again. She wanted me to explain what she had seen.'

'What did you tell her?' ventured Elsa.

Dot pointed to a glass of water on the window sill. Elsa got up and fetched it for her, and the old nun sipped from it and smacked her lips. 'What would you have told her?'

'I don't know. I guess I would have tried to show her it was just the weather.'

Dot frowned. 'Well, I would never do anything like *that*. No. It was something to believe in, was what I said.'

Elsa frowned. 'And that was enough for her?'

'That was enough. That kept her sneaking up to look for her spectre. I don't think Betty ever did see it again, but she imagined signs of it in every rock and landslide. Then, one day,' Dot lifted up the first cloud atlas, still showing the black tower of the storm, 'Cumulonimbus came to Thunderstown. Betty was convinced that he was the one she'd seen in the mists. She said she knew it in her belly. So she climbed Drum Head in the pouring rain and tried to drink the raindrops until nausea overcame her.'

'And? What happened?'

'Have you ever tried to catch rain in your mouth? Enough to make you sick?'

'No.'

'It's as near impossible as you'd imagine. And Betty never managed it. Maybe, if she had, the legend would have been proved true. But no. Instead, Betty was struck by lightning. Bang! A million volts of electricity, aimed right at her belly. And then the storm cleared and it was a fine evening.'

Dot put down the book, and closed it so the balmier skies of the cover hid the cumulonimbus within.

'What had happened to her?' asked Elsa.

Dot's eyes twinkled. 'This much you already know, Elsa. She had become pregnant. She told it to the search party when they found her sleeping peacefully on the mountain, though they thought she was raving. Pregnant! Only, it wasn't quite what she'd wanted. It wasn't her baby, just as it wasn't anybody else's baby. It was Cumulonimbus.'

Elsa was too lost in the story to notice at first that Dot had removed her glasses and plugged up her eyes with her bent palms. She joined her on the bed, placing a gentle hand on her shoulders. 'What's wrong, Dot? Why are you crying?'

Dot found a handkerchief from under the pillow and dabbed her eyes. Then she reinstated her spectacles and patted Elsa's knee. 'I'm sorry, it's just that I didn't want to stop her. She was so happy to have him that I couldn't bear to remind her *he's not yours*. Because she thought he was, you see? And I wasn't ever sure if it mattered.'

'No. I don't get it. Who else did he belong to?'

'Himself! He was Cumulonimbus. Elsa, in these mountains the weather can take many forms, but never a person, or so I always thought. A person would be too complicated. But that night, Cumulonimbus did it! He made himself into a speck of baby, even though it took all of his power to do so.'

'Wait … wait.'

Dot reached for her hand and squeezed it with all her small might. 'You have fallen in love with a storm cloud, my dear.'

'*Wait*! Nobody said anything about love.'

'Oh. Forgive me. I thought that was why you came up here.'

'I … I …' She swallowed. She had kissed him. She had touched her ear to his chest. She had chatted with him and he had been nervous and embarrassed and pleased to be with her. 'I …' she said.

Dot retained her grip on Elsa's hand. 'When Finn – Cumulonimbus – was sixteen, he struck his mother with a bolt of lightning. Daniel Fossiter brought Betty here to be treated, but I did not get to talk to Cumulonimbus, as I would have liked. I must confess, I am somewhat jealous of you for getting that chance. But you deserve it. And I think you do love him, don't you?'

'How could I *love* him? We only just met. I can't even work out how – if – I can I ever get close to him.'

Dot's eyes were half-closed. 'Put it this way: one of the terrifying things about my life is that it belongs to me. It has never been lived before, nor will it ever be again. Every second is a brand-new possession.'

'You're talking in riddles again.'

'And *you* still haven't answered my question.'

'What question?'

'Do you love him?'

'You can prove that love is just chemicals and electricity in the brain.'

'Of course you can, but that doesn't help you deal with it. Do you love him?'

'What if I can't answer?'

Dot shrugged. 'Be lost, Elsa. That is the best advice anyone can give you, and I get the feeling your father would have approved of it. And now be on your way.'

14

BIRTHDAYS

On the day when Finn had shown her the sunbeam birds, she had made a secret plan to throw him a birthday party. The idea had come to her when they'd returned to the bothy. He'd kicked off his shoes and left them in the doorway, where they'd looked so tatty and busted open that she'd wanted to bury them. She had sneaked a look at the inside heels and seen his shoe size in faded ink, then remembered he'd said he had not celebrated his birthday since his mother left Thunderstown. Her plan had formulated in that instant, then been forgotten amid the distractions of the subsequent days.

Now she stood outside a cobbler's workshop on Welcan Row, admiring the overstatement of its tradesman's sign, which read, *Bryn Cobbler: Cobbler*. She pushed open the door and took a deep sniff of the polished air. Whatever in the shop wasn't leather was fashioned from wood just as brown, and Bryn Cobbler himself was a tanned man in a buff shirt and hide apron. She'd envisaged buying Finn a pair of colourful sneakers such as she might choose for herself, but she quickly realized that was out of the question. From moccasins to boots, everything on sale was made from a leather as brown as caramel. 'It gives you lucky feet,' explained Bryn, 'and makes you tread as safely as the goats it's made from.'

She bought two pairs of shoes, since the prices were reasonable and she wasn't sure which would fit Finn better. Then she headed back to Prospect Street, where Kenneth had promised to help her with the second part of her plan.

Kenneth was chuckling with enthusiasm when she reached him. He had all of the ingredients lined up on the kitchen counter, and when the electric whisk purred too hard and threw mix all over the two of them he guffawed and she thought, *At least I have made his day, which is a good start.*

Then, when the cake came out of the oven, he provided her with the *pièce de résistance*: a set of fine, tall candles, each with a crisp new wick and a scarlet thread twisting through the white wax. She paused for a moment, staring at them.

'Everything all right, Elsa?'

'Yes. Yes. Perfect, thank you.'

She had been remembering a cake that her mum had once baked her: a sloppy chocolate mound with candles drowning in the icing. Nevertheless it had been delicious and she had been happy sitting at the table with her parents, eating and eating until their bellies could take no more and their chins and cheeks were sticky. Then, after they had cleaned themselves up, her Mum and Dad had given her a present in a long thin package. She had caught them glancing conspiratorially at each other as she unwrapped it: they knew they'd found her something perfect. It was a parasol, an artwork of stunning lace, with silky white clouds sewn into its canopy.

She helped Kenneth plug the candles into the cake, and was soon on her way.

En route to Old Colp, in a yard in Auger Lane made green by weeds uprising against the flagstones, a pair of old women had set up spinning wheels. They talked in a hushed pitch as they spun, only their consonants carrying over the click and whirr of their machines. Elsa slowed to watch them for an engrossed moment, and as she watched the spokes turn and the thread cycle through the wheels, she remembered the afternoon of that chocolate cake birthday, when they had gone to the hedgerow maze in which she had run off ahead, trying to find the centre on her own. She remembered trotting along one leafy route and hearing familiar voices from the path parallel to hers. The hedge grew too tight to see through, but she knew the voices were those of her parents, laughing and teasing each other about who knew best which turn to take. There was no question about it, they would not take different paths, and Elsa eavesdropped with pleasure until at last they headed along the one chosen by her mother, jibing each other as they went.

When she shook off that memory and left the women to their spinning, she was too distracted to remember where she was going and ended up back at Saint Erasmus. Still, she was pleased to find that her memory had left her resolute. If she were to be lost, she would be lost along with Finn.

The first thing Elsa noticed when Finn opened the bothy door were the blisters on his cheeks. Each was a cauterized pink and teardrop-sized, such as a case of frostbite might leave. His eyelids were red and lacerated around the ducts. He looked abject, but cheered up when he saw her. 'I didn't think I'd see you again.'

'Finn! What happened to you?'

'I'm okay,' he said. 'I suppose I just can't hide the things I feel.'

'Finn, I was angry at you.'

'You were within your rights to be.'

She plunged her face forwards and seized his lips with her own. She reached up her hands to hold his bald head. She realized when he whimpered that she was holding him as tightly as a treasure, almost biting to hold his lips between hers. She pulled back and loosened her grip.

He looked astonished. 'I thought—' he said, but she silenced him with a finger over his lips. With her other hand she traced lines between the sores on his cheeks. At her touch they gave up little whispers of steam that followed her fingers.

They kissed again, and once more she couldn't help but cling hard to him, locking her arms around his back and shoulders. When they stopped he gave a bewildered gasp. She savoured his breath against her face, breathing it in. It smelled like dew at the crack of dawn. It made her lungs feel fresh and full of him. Then she noticed a diffuse glow across the side of his scalp. It was a fine haze of cloud picked out by the sunlight, and then it was gone in the blink of an eye.

'Finn ...'

'What's wrong?'

'There was... a kind of haze across your head. It's gone now.'

He rubbed his head cautiously.

It had been such a fine, ethereal substance that she could not find it frightening. 'Never mind,' she said, and kissed him again. Then she squeezed his hand and said, 'Happy birthday.'

'Um ... it's not my birthday.'

'It is now.' She opened the cake tin to show him. 'I just need a plate and a knife.'

In the bothy, all of the paper birds had gone, although the bin overflowed with white litter. In place of them Finn had been making paper people. With these he seemed to have been having difficulty, and had only managed a dozen.

He cleared his throat with embarrassment when she saw them, then hastily began to scoop them up to press them into the bin. She grabbed his arm to stop him, and took the damaged models from his hands to admire. Half of them were paper women and half paper men, and she knew without asking that they were meant to be the two of them.

'Yesterday I visited the convent on the Devil's Diadem.'

'That old place? What were you doing up there?'

She took a deep breath. 'Asking an old nun some questions. She made me realize that I'd treated you badly.'

'No, Elsa, you were right. I should have told you about what was inside of me.'

'But you were right too. I might have freaked out and we'd never have got to where we are now. And anyway, it's not *what's inside of you*, is it? It's what you are.'

He hung his head. 'Yes, I suppose so.'

'See, I think it's wrong to be upset by that. It's what makes you who you are, and it's the reason that I, you know …' She gulped. 'Like you. I mean … the reason why I more than like you.'

He blushed gratefully. 'I more than like you, too.'

'You know, Finn, I think we can work. I'll trust you as long as you trust yourself. Then you'll know, I reckon, and be able to warn me if things become too much.'

They kissed to broker the deal.

'And now,' she asked, 'have you got any matches?'

'Matches?'

'For your birthday candles.'

After she had pulled the curtains and brought the cake through with its tiny flames wavering in time with the tune of her happy birthday song, he blew them all out in one great big puff. She thought of the blowing cloud faces carved into the wardrobe in her room in Thunderstown, and about huffing out the sinking candles of that sloppy chocolate birthday cake, and about being blown loose from her old life and drifting into this one.

'There's a present, too. Two presents, actually, but they're both the same. I just hope one pair fits.'

The larger ones were just right for him. He walked around the bothy with a grin on his face, and the new leather creaked luxuriantly with each step. As he walked, she saw again a momentary gleaming brushstroke of cloud across the top of his head, such as she had seen after kissing him earlier, and then it was gone. She sat back and reckoned she would be happy just to watch him walk in circles, around and around forever.

15

PAPER BIRDS

On the morning of Betty's departure, Daniel had paid an unexpected visit to her house on Candle Street. It was a chill day, a premonition of autumn adrift in summer, and over the rooftops the sky was pressed white by clouds as fine as swan feathers.

He was surprised to discover her car parked on the curb, its boot open. Two bags had already been packed inside it, and now Betty hurried from the house carrying a third. She jumped when she saw him, then collected herself and put down the luggage.

She looked cold there in her threadbare jumper. Her blonde hair was a damp mess and her makeup had been applied in a hurry. 'Hello, Daniel,' she said. 'I was just on my way to see you.'

He looked suspiciously from Betty to her car. He disliked the distance a vehicle put between a person and the ground, which was a damned deal more than its foot or two of suspension. 'You've a lot of luggage for a trip across town.'

'Daniel, listen, I'm … going away for a bit.'

He frowned. 'Where to?'

'Just somewhere I can find some perspective.'

He panicked, although he didn't show it. He wanted to dismantle the car's engine and run his knife through its tyres. He licked his lips. 'Can I come with you?'

'I'm so sorry, Daniel. No, you can't come with me. Nobody can.

I need space. Everything that's happened … it's just too much.'

He had to look away for a moment, up the street towards Old Colp's ebony dome. 'What about Finn? Are you taking him?'

'No, and he doesn't know about this just yet. He's gone up into the mountains today.' She gestured to the open front door. 'Come in out of the cold for a minute.'

He had forgotten the temperature, but he followed her gratefully into the house. The rooms were the cleanest he had ever seen them. Everything had been put away, unless it had been packed into the final bag lying in the hall. The house was as tidy as a show home.

He held a hand to his forehead. All of a sudden his knees and ankles felt like nuts and bolts worked loose. 'Betty,' he managed to ask, 'how long are you going for?'

She shrugged.

Commit every detail of her to your memory, he thought to himself. He stared into her face, at the green hue of her irises, the diamond-shaped space where her lips parted.

'Daniel?'

The mole on the underside of her chin, the patterns of her earlobes, the drift of freckles over her narrow nose and the tops of her cheeks.

'Daniel.' She stepped forwards and wrapped her arms around him. She pressed the side of her face against his throat, her head fitting neatly between his beard and collarbone. His back was too broad for her arms to wrap tightly around it, so her hands held to the knobs of his shoulder blades. Her thighs touched his, her hips his, her breasts his ribcage. She was warm and skinny and smelled of fresh soap and water. He looked down into her hair and refused to blink, knowing there was no second worth losing, and no hope of committing this to memory in all its fullness.

'Betty.' Her name came out of him like the groan of a beast bleeding in a trap. 'Don't go.'

She stepped apart from him. Very carefully, he reached out to support himself against the wall.

'I have to. I'm sorry.'

He could barely feel his legs. His belly was in free fall. He knew if he were to let go of the wall he would collapse into a heap on the floorboards.

She emptied a smile at him. 'Please do something for me. While I'm gone.'

He managed to nod.

'Take care of Finn for me.'

He would do anything she asked.

'Okay, then,' she said.

She stepped up on tiptoes to kiss him, then backed away and picked up her final suitcase. 'All right,' she said. 'I think that's everything. Will you lock the house for me?'

He nodded.

Then, as if a leash she had been straining against had suddenly snapped, she sprang out of the door and down the path and quickly climbed into her car. He staggered out into the yard to watch her disappear along Candle Street. When the car turned out of sight he let himself drop. He hit the paving like a stack of stones. He stayed there for a long time, staring down the length of the road. Then at last he dragged himself back into the house and moved slowly through it, sitting on every chair, inhaling the air of every cupboard, pressing his face into Betty's pillow. Eventually he came to Finn's room and noticed on top of a pile of his things an envelope, crisp and newly sealed, with *Finn* written on it in Betty's beautiful handwriting. When he picked it up it weighed as much as all the jealousy and confusion that accompanied the discovery. Why had she left no envelope addressed to *Daniel*?

He slipped the letter into his shirt pocket, and when he returned to the Fossiter homestead, that was where it remained.

Take care of Finn for me.

He realized he did not know how he would do as she asked. He could keep a roof over the boy's head and keep him well stocked with groceries, but there was another duty implicit in Betty's request, one that required more than practical measures. How to shepherd the weather in the boy? He turned to the memories of his father and grandfather for guidance, but they were cowering away from him and telling him to do the thing the darkest part of his heart instructed, the thing he would not do because the love of his life had requested that he *take care of Finn for me.* He reflected that during his own formative years his father and grandfather had abandoned him to deal with the turmoil inside of himself alone. There had been times in his youth when his emotions had risen up from the depths of him as implacably as floodwater, and he had felt as if he were drowning. He had cast around for help then and found neither his father nor his grandfather present. All he could do was try to tread water until the flood receded.

He had ignored the damage those waters left in their wake. For just as a flood in a house leaves an aftermath of warped timbers and weakened foundations, he recognized there was a rotting and ruined layer inside of him too.

He knew by these criteria that he could not look after Finn, and within an hour of Betty's departure he had already failed in the task, when he told Finn the news and the boy asked, disbelieving, 'Did she not leave anything for me? Not even a note?'

'No,' he replied, 'not a thing.'

With those few words he had made it impossible to ever hand over Betty's letter. So he clung on to the envelope, and never told Finn of its existence. Eventually he become too fond of it to think of it as belonging to the boy in the first place. For that single specimen of her handwriting was the freshest piece of Betty he had left. To begin with he kept it tucked in his shirt pocket. For days and restless nights it remained there, on his person at all times like a locket. When finally he had to wash that shirt, that her fingers had brushed against and her chest had pressed to, he transferred the now crumpled letter to the pocket of his new shirt, and continued to carry it with him everywhere he went.

Eventually it had grown so dog-eared that the seal had started – tantalizingly – to peel open. This at last made it too much for him to carry around, so he locked it in his trunk with his father's Bible and his grandfather's violin and still did not tell Finn it existed.

Time passed. No call, no mail or message from Betty. And as the long months congested into the first half-year of her absence, the letter in his trunk took on a new significance. Secreted in its envelope were words of hers, words he had not heard before. Not only did he long for the sight of her handwriting, but he hoped that to read it would prompt the sound of her voice in his head. He began to want badly to unseal the letter and read it for himself. She would be disappointed in him, of course, and the threat of that guilt kept the letter locked up and safe.

Further months passed. Betty neither returned nor made the slightest contact. He tried fruitlessly to track her down. He sought out the telephone numbers of old friends and relatives, but they knew nothing of her whereabouts and were as anxious about her as he was. Still he resisted reading the letter, although as time slouched by his motives for doing so shifted. Now fear stayed his hand instead of guilt. Were he to read it, there would be nothing new of her left to experience. He did not know whether he could cope with that. So he kept the letter sealed, even though every so often he took it from the trunk for his fingers to play at its corners, teasing him of their own accord.

He began to dream about the lifeline of her handwriting, but he could no longer imagine her voice with clear diction. When he tried to replay things she had said she sounded suppressed, as if she were talking on the other side of a wall. He strode the mountains with his thoughts bent on the envelope in his trunk, hoping that to read her words might return her voice to him.

Back in the homestead he would sit turning the envelope between his fore and index fingers, hypnotizing himself with its revolutions, just as his grandfather had so often with a playing card. He would think about Betty's request – *take care of Finn for me* – and he would ask his thinking whether there was something he could give the boy to replace the stolen letter.

A year after Betty's departure his thinkings gave him the answer. He and Finn sat in garden chairs in the sunshine behind the bothy, with the rock walls of the bluff dashed golden and the sky full of blue, and he cleared his throat and said, 'I would like to teach you something that my mother taught me.'

His mother had shown him this thing not long before her own departure from Thunderstown. That departure had not been a shock like Betty's had been, although it had plagued him as sickeningly as an infection. He had always known she was going to leave. He had known it even when he learned to crawl, even when he learned to tug her little finger and call her Mama. More specifically, he had known it since he first watched his father berate her.

She did not leave without teaching him the trick which had delighted him since infancy: paper birds. She had kept their creation a closely guarded secret. He would find one waiting for him on his pillow at night, or tucked into his school bag, and he would immediately set upon it and take it apart, trying to understand how the folds built beak and wing. But he couldn't comprehend their designs, and his mother kept her silence. She seemed to possess innate understanding of the design of a bird, so that she could fold without instruction any species from a flat expanse of paper.

Then, in her final week in Thunderstown, when her bags were already packed, she had sat him down in front of her with a stack of crisp sheets and helped his fingers through the folds.

He did his best to teach Finn, well aware that his own blunt attempts retained little of the magic of his mother's. Still he tried his hardest, meticulous with concentration, poking his tongue out beneath his moustache. He held the result up to the sunlight. A paper dove with outstretched wings.

Finn took the model from Daniel's hands and turned it around and around in awe. He tugged at its wings as if there were a danger of wounding it.

'I thought you'd like it,' said Daniel, and offered Finn a sheet of paper. 'Could you tell how it was made?'

Finn nodded and hungrily set to work. If the boy made a mistake, Daniel would silently reach out and reposition his fingers, motioning them through the line a fold should take.

'Pretty good,' he whistled when Finn had finished. The boy's dove was easily as accomplished as his own, with a wonky wing its only imperfection. They looked at each other, and for a moment, were unguardedly amazed. Daniel marvelled that this skill had passed from his own self into Finn, just as once it had passed from his mother into him. He felt as if the three of them were layered together, as closely as the closed pages of a book.

Finn was eager to try again. Daniel sat back and observed, without interruption, the best dove so far take form. Finn laid it delicately between his first attempt and Daniel's, so that the three birds perched side by side. Then for a while they just stared at them, remembering the missing third member of their company, the one more perfect than the two that remained.

For a while after that, Finn would make Daniel a paper bird every time he paid a visit. Daniel would come to the bothy after church and find one waiting for him on the table. He kept them all, placing each carefully into his trunk beside his father's Bible and his grandfather's violin. Sometimes he would test their flight before storing them, and the birds would always soar true, and this would excite Mole into yapping and pouncing after them as if they were butterflies, at which they proved just as elusive and dinked at the last minute away from her biting jaws, and this in turn reminded him of Betty and Mole chasing one another around the lawn beside the homestead, which was like Betty dancing, which was like the marvellous night of Mr Nairn's one-hundredth birthday, when he and Betty had stamped and flicked their legs in time with each other until the last note sounded from the fiddles of the band.

Then one day Finn did not give him a bird when they met. They ate together at the bothy, and afterwards Daniel left. Only once he had reached the bottom of the mountain did he realize that his hands were empty. He did not comment, presuming the boy had forgotten. Likewise he left it unmentioned when the same happened after their next meeting. Reluctantly he supposed that Finn had grown tired of giving presents, and each time they parted thereafter he would look down at the creases of his palms and still be surprised to find himself wishing they held a paper bird.

A mile outside Thunderstown a gorge with grizzled rock walls severed the foothills of the Devil's Diadem. The gorge's base was a dark road of sharp stones, but its sides were as rugged as any canyon's and hewn with dangerously narrow tracks that only goats could tread. On inaccessible ledges eagles had built their eyries, but the eagles here were tatty-feathered birds and they flew without majesty. Above them, rough cirrus clouds hung in the sky, each like the scratched claw marks of some wild beast.

Elsa had followed Finn up here with her hand held in his, except for in one steep stretch of the trail where hands were needed to help climb. They made up for that moment's parting with a kiss, and as they kissed they pressed their bodies in a close embrace and Elsa delighted in the smoothness of Finn's shape.

She had carried a rug with her from Thunderstown, while he had brought a long cardboard tube, tucked under his arm. They were making their way along the top of the gorge, where the path squeezed between the sheer drop on their left and a screen of jutting boulders on their right. Elsa held on to their knobbly surfaces as she walked, feeling the height of the cliff as a tingle in the nerves of her toes. She was glad when they found a place to sit down, a U-shaped cleave among the boulders, sheltered on all sides bar the cliff's. A lizard who had been basking on the rock walls watched them for a moment, then begrudgingly vacated the spot, his legs peddling away over the tawny stone.

'This is the best place for it?'

Finn nodded enthusiastically and she threw down the rug. He opened his cardboard tube and sat down beside her on the fabric. The rocks enclosed their spot so dependably that when he took out and unrolled the sheets of paper they lay still on the floor.

'Time to teach you,' he said.

'I'm pretty bad at this kind of stuff. I can barely fold a letter into an envelope.'

'This is different.'

He folded a sheet in half, turned its corners into flaps, bent it in on itself again, and then she lost track. Folds, twists, turnings in on turnings, and then all of a sudden a paper dove, nestling in the palm of his hand.

'May I?' She took the dove and began to unfold it, trying to understand how it had been constructed. She could see that the angle of one fold allowed its wings to take shape, and that the halving of the paper defined its back, but beyond that the folds bent mystically into folds. When she had unfolded it entirely, only the creases were left. Nothing bird-like about it.

'Your turn,' he said.

'Honestly, Finn, I won't be able to.'

He began to instruct her. Even at dummy's pace she found it impossible to follow, but when she erred he led her hands back into position, setting right each finger as carefully as if it were the needle of a record player. His touch was cool, refreshing in the heat, and his instructions precise. He seemed to understand the workings of her hands as instinctively as he did the making of the bird.

She quickly gave up trying to comprehend what she was doing. Under his tutelage she simply took each stage as it came. At last the finished article lay upside down on the rug.

She laughed. 'It looks more like a scraggy old pigeon than a dove.'

He scratched his head. 'I don't understand what went wrong.'

'It's me, stupid.' She shrugged. 'Don't worry, I came to terms with my lack of creativity a long time ago. But I'm afraid I wouldn't back this thing to fly.'

He took it from her, opened it up and tinkered with its folds. Then he handed it back to her, beautified slightly. 'Try it.'

She tossed it into the gorge.

It dipped to begin with. She thought it was going to drop like a stone, but it swooped unexpectedly at the last, out along a flat trajectory then up in a half-circle against the yawning air. She grinned and threw his bird after hers. His soared instantly, catching the updrafts, wind making its paper wings flutter. The two birds drifted at different altitudes, his gliding gracefully, hers with a laboured bent, until with a croak an eagle flapped up from the gorge's depths to investigate. It chased Finn's bird, caught it and stabbed it hard with its beak. The paper buckled and lost its buoyancy. The broken dove dropped quickly into the shadows.

Elsa cackled and clapped her hands. 'Does that make mine the winner?'

He offered her another sheet, but she raised her hands.

'I'll quit while I'm ahead. I'm happy just to sit back and watch you. Do something complicated, something difficult.'

He squinted up at the eagle, pursed his lips, then began to fold swiftly until he had built an eagle of his own, with a hook in its beak and wings with saw-toothed edges. He threw it into the air and watched it ascend majestically. The first eagle, the blood-and-feather one who was still patrolling the thermals, shrieked as its paper counterpart whooshed past. It fled the scene and left Finn's bird circling.

Elsa gave him a round of applause. 'That's perfect! How did you do that? You're amazing, Finn!'

He blushed, and even though they had been kissing on the way up here she felt goofy for gushing that out in such awestruck tones. She was still unused to the openness that had so readily fallen into place between them. Her relationship with Peter had been a sort of cautious dance, a series of suggestions and cool flirtations. If what she had found with Finn was any kind of dance at all, it was the unconscious ballet of two sleeping lovers who wake throughout the night to find their limbs in new tangles.

'Well,' he said, 'I can't take the credit because I don't really think about it. It's just something I've had a knack for since I first tried it.'

She watched his eagle flutter and roll, and bank to the side through the hot air. 'I think it's wonderful.'

Finn stared out across the cleft of the gorge.

She shuffled conspicuously closer, so that their bodies were touching.

'Elsa,' he asked, 'did you ever lie on your back as a kid, and watch the clouds go by?'

'Yeah, of course. I loved doing that.'

'And did you ever get the feeling that that was the right way up to be? With your back against the planet, looking straight out at the universe?'

'I used to lie like that until I no longer felt like the sky was up. The sky was forwards, and up was whichever direction my head happened to be pointing in. That way the clouds were in front of me, on a level with me, and it felt like they could be reached. I used to love that. The world felt, I don't know, like it had always meant to be that way up. As if it had been knocked over, and to lie like that was to put it right again.'

'That,' he said, 'is exactly how I feel when I'm with you. You've put me the right way up. You've fixed me. For the first time since I was tiny I feel like I fit together.'

'Finn?'

'I don't have to choose between being a man and being the weather. You've helped me see that. I can be both at once.'

'Finn, hang on, there's something stuck to your cheek ...'

She reached across for what looked like a bit of cotton or fluff, but it broke apart at her touch. It was a wisp of cloud. She brushed it away and beneath it his skin was smooth. Then she saw another strand on the crown of his scalp, as white and curled as a pillow feather. She stroked her palm through it and it dispersed.

'What is it?' he asked, trying in vain to look up at his own head.

She left her hand caressing his cheek and temples. Another lock of mist emerged along the curve of his ear and masked the detail of the lobe. 'I don't know,' she said. 'It's like a tiny cloud.'

He touched his fingers to his head, confused. Another ribbon of cloud shimmered across his scalp, as bubbly a vapour as the gas that floats free of opened champagne. 'This has never happened before.'

She reached out for his hand as delicately as she might for a floating bubble. Cloud clung to his fingers where he had touched his head.

'What do you think we should do about it?' he asked worriedly.

A longer drift of cloud had appeared along the inside of his collar, and now another thickened out of a haze along his brow.

'Nothing,' she said. 'This isn't like storm cloud. This is like those clouds we used to watch as kids. You're still in one piece, aren't you?

Perhaps this is exactly what you were just talking about. Perhaps this is being a man and being the weather at the same time.'

It was not long before so much of the strange soft mist had emerged that it outlined his body. It kept coming, fuming gently out of his pores and reaching ethereally into the air. At its thickest it was white as snow, but its edge began to catch the light and the sun outlined it in yellow.

'You've got a silver lining,' she whispered, and kissed him.

While their lips moved the cloud grew, and filled their little boulder-backed enclave with mist. The gorge vanished, the sky vanished. It was just the two of them in a cottony world. Then he tensed and she stopped kissing him and backed off slightly. 'What's wrong?'

'Nothing.'

She knew there was something. The cloud had made him blurred, like an unfocused photograph, so it took her a moment to notice the bulge in his jeans.

For a moment everything was quiet. She heard his tiny groan of embarrassment. Then she roared with laughter that something so earthly had overcome him. 'Finn!' she exclaimed, and threw her arms around him. The mist shimmered. 'It's okay!'

'Then why are you laughing?'

She pushed him on to his back and the cloud swirled around them. She reached down lightly to touch him and he made a dumb contented noise.

'Are you okay with this?'

He nodded. She undid the popper at the top of his fly.

They undressed in a nervous flurry of clothes. At first he didn't know what to do. He just sat there naked and hazy with the sunlight diffusing through the vapour and framing him in a corona. They locked lips again and then she climbed on top of him. When his confidence grew she moved on to her back.

Then, as he lost himself in her, she gasped because the sunlight dropped a blanket of rainbow through the cloud. It settled over their two skins with a prismatic shudder and they were bound together in seven colours.

16

BROOK HORSE

On the stroke of midday, when the sun was directly overhead and its rays could find no route through the windows, the Church of Saint Erasmus was at its darkest, and a congregation of shadows occupied the pews and aisles. Here, in the murk, Daniel sometimes sat from mid-morning, enjoying the failing of the light. A private eclipse, with all the lonely silence of the church to share it with.

Today's gloom was just such an exquisite affair. He reclined in it as other men might in a hot bath. There was a darkness such as this inside of him too, which this one helped appease. It made him feel undone out of his skin, so that it was hard to tell where Daniel Fossiter ended and the world began. In this way he felt released, an uncorked genie floating for a few precious moments beyond his lamp.

He heard someone whisper his name. 'Daniel.'

Startled, he looked around him. The church was too dim to be sure, but all of the pews were empty and when he sprung to his feet and searched behind the pillars he found nobody hiding there.

'Daniel.' There it was again. 'Daniel Fossiter.'

He covered his ears with his hands to test whether the voice was inside his mind, but there were only the silent flowings of his thinkings, and no sooner did he let his hands drop to his sides than he heard it again, louder this time. 'Daniel Fossiter!'

'You fool, Daniel,' he scolded himself, as he realized it was not a whisper but a yell, coming from outside.

When he threw open the doors and screwed up his face against the sunlight, his name was shouted enthusiastically. Some fifteen townspeople were approaching the church steps. They had with them a pony, a bedraggled-looking thing that walked with a limp. Sidney Moses held a rope tied around its neck and by this he had evidently forced it to Saint Erasmus Square. 'Mr Fossiter!' he cried up the steps. 'Look what Abe Cosser found up on Drum Head. A brook horse!'

Sidney clapped Abe across the shoulders, knocking the scrawny shepherd two steps forwards, and urging, 'Tell him! Tell him, Abe! Tell Mr Fossiter what happened!'

'Well, sir,' mumbled Abe, 'it was like this. I was up on Drum Head, you see, to check how the sheep had done in that rain we had, and maybe to move them down a pasture, if they were up to their necks in boggy ground. And, well—'

Sidney clapped his hands. 'Cut to it, Abe!'

The pony snorted and flapped an ear at an interested fly. Daniel folded his arms.

'Well, sir, it was like this. Up there the rain must have been a damn sight heavier because the tarn at Gravel Point had filled up so much that she'd burst her banks and all the earth around her had turned to mush and puddles.' Sidney Moses cleared his throat as a warning, but Daniel raised a finger. 'Let him finish, Mr Moses. In your own time, Abe.'

Sidney rolled his eyes.

'*Well*, sir, what should I see stood dumbly in the mud but this brook horse? Since I meant to spend the better part of the day up there with the flock, I had some provisions on me. Nothing a brook horse likes more than a fishy sandwich, my old man used to say, and it just so happened I had, well ...' He waved a nibbled sardine sandwich through the air and the pony whinnied eagerly.

Daniel plodded down the steps. 'Why do you think it is a brook horse?'

'You've only got to look at its tail,' chipped in Sidney. He stepped right up alongside Daniel to demonstrate how he should do just that.

Daniel laid both hands on the pony's back and made a deep noise in the back of his throat. The pony puffed algae-smelling air from its nostrils and lowered its head as if it were in need of sleep. Daniel rubbed the coarse hair of its flank and moved along its side to examine its tail.

Instead of the long, swishing appendage common to other wild horses and hill ponies, this beast had a tapering stub, bald and calloused at its end. It did not look diseased, more likely that the pony had been born with it deformed in this way. At the very tip of the tail Daniel discovered three hard plates of skin, each the size and shape of a fingernail. He pondered these for a moment, the only noise that of a rook croaking as it settled on one of the church's eaves. The crowd's excitement was palpable, but they knew well enough to stay silent while Daniel conducted his examination.

He crouched down to inspect the back leg, for he had seen how lamely the pony had limped after Sidney Moses. This too did not look diseased or injured. Instead, its muscles were thin and its hoof was too small to support its share of weight. Around the ankle were a dozen more scaly callouses like those on the tip of its tail, and between these drooped a thin inch of transparent skin which Daniel ran lightly between his forefinger and thumb. It had a wrinkled, slimy texture that reminded him of the fin of a fish.

He sighed. He was feeling soft today. He could sense the bulk of the church behind him frowning like the ghost of the Reverend Fossiter. Just like his father, who had deserted his role as culler because he opposed what the crowd now expected from it, Daniel had no wish to execute this brook horse. A goat was one thing because a goat was full of greed, but this poor being would have shied away from Thunderstown had it not been led down here. Abe Cosser was a fool for capturing it and bringing it to a man as bloodthirsty as Sidney Moses.

'Be hard like an anvil,' his grandfather used to say, 'and then the hammer blows stop hurting.' Daniel looked from face to anxious face, until doing so returned him to the sorry brook horse. He wondered how many times his grandfathers had stood in this plaza surrounded by men with names like Cosser or Moses, and with them some deviant creature of the weather brought forth for Mr Fossiter's judgement. This thought gave him comfort. His own feelings meant little in the torrent of history. What he was about to do was in his very flesh and bones. It was the only way he knew.

Then he remembered out of nowhere his first encounter with Miss Beletti. In this square, against the walls of this church, he had broken the neck of a wild dog and she had confronted him afterwards, with her anger as brilliant as a sunrise.

'It is a brook horse,' he sighed, and every member of the crowd took a satisfied breath. 'But I have no knife. Mr Moses, hand me that rope leash. I will lead the devil back to my homestead and do right by it there.'

Sidney licked his lips. 'It's all right, Daniel. I didn't expect you to take your knife with you to church, so as luck would have it I stopped by my house and grabbed hold of mine.'

Without breaking eye contact, he reached down to his belt and retrieved a long steel blade with a plastic handle, which he offered to Daniel.

Betty, thought Daniel out of nowhere. How she had so hated this sort of thing. He took the knife and considered it with disgust. A good culling knife should have a handle of bone. It showed its purpose. A plastic handle was Sidney through and through, and Daniel longed to return it to him with the blade sheathed in his stomach.

He shook himself. His father; Betty; Elsa: none of them would agree with this. Only his hateful grandfather, who had once axed the head from a chicken just to laugh at its body racing around the yard. So why did it trouble him what a contemptible man like Sidney Moses thought? Again he scanned the earnest faces of the crowd, asking himself who he cared for among these people. There was Hamel Rhys, a pervert and a snake. There was Bryn Cobbler, a drunken shoemaker. There was Sally Nairn, whom he did care for, who had helped him once choose the right flowers to present to Betty, but who now would not meet his eye. She was as subscribed to this as the rest of them. All of them had come here for a killing, for a sacrifice to their own good fortunes.

'Mr Fossiter,' prompted Sidney, 'we are waiting.'

It's in your bones, whispered the voice of his DNA, it *is* your bones. Without it you would have no shape.

'I fear,' said Sidney, sideways to the crowd, 'that Mr Fossiter is not himself.'

Daniel wanted to return to the church's dark. There, in the shadows where everything was without limit, he could cope better with the mess of his thinkings.

'I fear that Mr Fossiter has not been himself in a very long time. Not since Betty Munro took the heart out of him.'

Daniel patted the pony's grey neck, scratched its mane, felt the warmth of its throat. 'You have made a very big show, of late,' he said, turning back to Sidney, 'of being the one who tells me who I am and who I am not.'

Sidney looked affronted. 'Well, it's as I've always said. Everybody must be accountable. Nobody is bigger than the town.'

'Except you, Mr Moses, isn't that right? You with your fingers soft from paperwork and your lips gone crooked from too much politicking.'

Sidney bristled. '*Mr* Fossiter!' His eyes goggled and his chin retracted into his jowls. He looked as ridiculous as a turkey. 'All I have ever asked of you is that you be more ambitious in the way you conduct your business. That you help us find Old Man Thunder!'

At that name the crowd murmured their assent.

'What if conducting my business has taught me when and where it is needed? I have no desire to kill this animal.'

Sidney was flabbergasted. He spread his hands theatrically. 'Since when has desire come into anything? You are employed to carry out a duty! If your *desires* have so confused you of your purpose, perhaps it is time for somebody else to take the lead. We will never catch Old Man Thunder if we dither over cases such as this.'

One or two more impressionable townsfolk drew in a sharp breath at this flagrant opposition to their culler. Several pairs of pleading eyes fixed on Daniel, and he fancied that they carried no more love for Sidney than he did. They wanted him to break whatever spell had enchanted him and turn the knife on the brook horse.

He looked down at the blade and tested it with the side of his thumb. To Sidney's credit it was sharp enough to draw a trace of blood. He gripped the handle hard.

'Who on earth is going to take that lead, Sidney? Who knows the ways of the mountains like I do? You? You would trip over your own pot belly and fall to your death on the Merrow Wold. If you think that all there is to culling is taking potshots at goats while you lean on your garden fence, then you are greatly mistaken.' He snorted and tossed the knife at Sidney's feet, where the steel clattered against the paving. 'I will not kill this brook horse. Abe, lead it back up to the place where you found it, and set it free.'

With that he turned and began to plod away towards his homestead. He tried to carry himself steadily, but the thrill of what he had just done made him want to dance. Dance a jig, like he and Betty had danced at Mr Nairn's one-hundredth birthday party. Waltz and whirl, because he had disobeyed not only Sidney, but all of them, back through history.

Then he heard a brief whinny and a horrible pop followed by a tearing noise.

He turned in time to see Sidney pull the knife from the brook horse's jugular.

If they had judged wrongly and it were a true pony, Sidney and the crowd might have been kicked and thrown about as the animal struggled against death, but it was a brook horse so it only collapsed to its knees. From the wound in its neck, water frothed where blood should have flowed, spattering on to the paving and Sidney's polished shoes.

The frame of the animal sagged and its back rippled. It flopped on to its side, still gushing water. The crowd retreated a few paces as the last of the liquid bubbled out of its throat. Its hide wrinkled and drooped into the puddle it had made. There was a smell of stale water and sediment, for where one might have expected bones and muscles to have filled the brook horse's skin there was only dirty flood water, seeping outwards from a shrivelled coat.

Sidney was doing all he could to hold on to the knife with trembling hands. His shirt was soaked and stuck to his skin, showing his pink belly through the cotton. Some of the crowd had covered their mouths with their hands, but others were staring angrily at Daniel. Sally Nairn looked betrayed. Abe Cosser looked like a kicked dog. Others regarded the man holding the plastic-handled knife with a newfound respect.

'Th-that,' declared Sidney before clearing his throat and trying again, 'that is what we'll do to Old Man Thunder.'

Daniel stared at the hide in the puddle. The crowd whispered to each other, and then someone said, 'Hear hear,' albeit cautiously. Daniel felt as if he had woken from a blissful dream to find himself in the dock of a courtroom.

'Let's not get carried away,' said Sidney, regaining confidence enough to raise one commanding finger. 'Mr Fossiter evidently needs rest. He needs time off. Should, after that, he decide to honour the wishes of his employers and return to work, well, then I'm sure we shall be very glad to consider it.'

Somebody at the back of the crowd hit a few claps of applause. Somebody else crossed themselves and stared at Daniel as if he had been unmasked as a witch. Daniel looked at the dead brook horse and the last liquid flowing out of it and searched himself for the feeling of a minute earlier. Where before he had felt free and liberated, now he only felt lost.

When he arrived, shaken and pensive, back at the homestead, Mole was dead beneath the table. He crouched and rubbed her back, but there was no warmth in her. He lifted her and carried her outside and laid her gently on the grass. Thirty yards from the homestead a lifeless, slanting tree made a circle of shade over a row of small gravestones. He found his shovel and plodded over to this tiny cemetery, reading the names of all of the hounds who had been buried there. Flint, Hunter, Sharpeye, the list went on in this fashion. Then Esme and Prosper, his father's housedogs. Then the patch of green grass he had been keeping watered and soft so it would be ready to dig on this day.

He looked back over his shoulder at the small black shape lying by the homestead. 'Get up,' he urged, beneath his breath, and tried with all his might to will it into happening. The grass shifted in the breeze. A speckling of cloud blew across the sky. He put his shovel down. 'Don't worry, Mole, I won't make you rest with these.'

He went to the workshop and collected his axe. Then he returned to the dead cemetery tree and began to chop at the parched lower branches. When he had severed a good many, he split them into lengths and carried them in armfuls to a good flat place to pile them.

Once he had got the fire going around Mole, he crouched at a distance with his sleeve across his mouth and nose. The black fumes came up from the flames, dancing and leaping. A plaited column of smoke rose high into the air. He thought about the days when Mole and Betty had chased each other across this very spot, and rolled in it laughing and barking, and he wished he could go back, and fall about with them in the green grass.

17

KITE

A dragging day of work followed, in which she filed the photocopies she had made on her prior shifts there. At lunchtime she overheard her supervisor Lily gossiping about her with another girl who worked in the offices. Lily was recounting what Elsa had said on her first day at work, about coming to Thunderstown *to find out what I wanted life to be*. At this both Lily and the other girl giggled snidely. 'She thinks this is another world,' sniffed Lily. 'And she left New York for it. Can you believe it? New York!'

She spent the day with the click of the hole punch, the snow of its emptied paper circles, the snap of the ring binder opening and closing. In the evening she ate, with Kenneth, a coal pot stew he'd cooked with so many chillies that, after her final mouthful, she slumped exhausted in her chair and could think of nothing but an early night. Her bedroom was hot and she slept without sheets. In the small hours she woke from the heat and pushed both the windows open. It did little to lower the temperature, but it brought in a dry air that smelled of heather blossom.

Just before dawn she woke to a thump above her. She propped herself up on her elbows and listened. Another thump, then another, as if something were moving on the roof of the house. A tickling breeze came in through the open windows. The sky was a navy blue, with a pale fuzz building along the outline of Drum Head.

Then, rushing through the window and welling in the dead end of her room, came a wind. Her hair fluttered and a book she had left on the bedside table opened its cover and flicked its pages. A paper goose that Finn had made her took off from the shelf where she'd decided to display it. The wardrobe door – which she had left ajar – swung open.

Suddenly, something more than blown air came in through the window. She shrieked and huddled backwards against the headboard. A pour of grey fur had landed in the shadows at the foot of her bed. It looked up at her with navy eyes and its ears pricked up. She bunched her fists against her mouth, too petrified to call for help.

The dog lost interest in her almost at once and lowered its nose to the floorboards. It sniffed along the wood until it came to the opened wardrobe. Placing its forepaws on the base, it ducked its head inside and snuffled around among her things.

When it backtracked out of the wardrobe it had the presents her mother had given her held lightly between its teeth. They were, of course, still wrapped in their sparkling red paper, but even though she had left them unopened her heart lurched at the idea that the dog might steal or damage them. It carried them across the floor and pounced up on to the window sill.

She threw herself out of bed, yelling, 'Wait!'

The dog seemed unfazed by the three-storey drop. It tensed its grey haunches and bent its knees, as if preparing to leap.

She reached out her arms. 'Give those back! Please!'

It wagged its tail. The fur thudded against the window frame. 'Please.'

It crouched. It was going to jump.

She lunged forwards to seize the packages, but at the last minute it dropped them gamely into her reaching hands. As she cuddled them to her chest, the dog flickered its tongue out across its nose and stepped casually out of the window. When she looked out after it, it was nowhere to be seen. There was only a weathervane turning south.

She closed the window and collapsed on to the bed, still cradling the presents. She did not know whether to laugh or cry or just sag with relief. Nor did her diaphragm, which made her hiccup with a mix of gratitude and fright.

After a minute she wiped her eyes on her t-shirt and placed the presents side by side on the mattress. Both were flat and square, but one was rigid where the other flexed. She realized she loved the scarlet glitter of the wrapping paper her mother had chosen, and when she slid her finger under the tape of the first present she did so with the utmost care.

When she saw what was beneath she had to look away and wait for the beaded tears to drop from her eyelash. She heard the wind hum back past the window.

It was her favourite record. Nina Simone's *Live at Town Hall*. She must have been five years old when she stole it from her dad's record collection and determined to carry it with her everywhere she went. 'Just think what good taste you have,' her dad remarked once, but she had taken it because it was his favourite too. She had loved other records since, records that had arrested her with an incisive lyric or a melody that cut straight to the heart, but it was for this LP that her affections endured. She'd grown up on its songs, turned back to them in times of need. Just the other day, in fact, she'd been missing this record, when all along it lay wrapped in her room. It was the only possession of her father's that her mother had not thrown out with the man himself, and it had been Elsa's soundtrack to becoming a young woman, her soundtrack to leaving Oklahoma. On her first nights in New York she had played it as loud as her cheap record player could bear. Played as the walls rattled when the subway passed, or when she sat in the window frame as she had had the habit of doing back then.

In the weeks before she'd left New York for Thunderstown, she had sold off or scrapped all of her possessions. Only a handful of them survived the clear-out, and these she had delivered to her mum's house in Norman, to be stowed there in her attic. Her mother must have found the record among those items, and recalled at once its importance to her daughter. With no means of playing it now, she held the record in her hands and stared at the photo on the cover, which showed Simone from a distance and from behind, on a stage in the spotlight, absorbed in her piano. Elsa thought of her mother, all alone in her living room in Norman.

There was no need for a record player: the songs struck up of their own accord in her head, made her mouth hum them and her tongue sing their lyrics on the edge of her breath. She remembered splashing about in puddles when she was younger, trying to recreate the moody chords of Simone's version of 'Fine and Mellow' by whistling through a cardboard tube. She remembered discovering with a thrill that the plinking notes of the piano sounded like falling rain, and Simone's voice like the breathy cooing of the wind itself.

Likewise she had listened to that song on the day of her dad's release from jail, when she had played it on the car stereo as she drove excitedly to meet him, taking with her his old plastic raincoat. He'd loved that watertight coat, which was as yellow as a fisherman's, because, as he liked to point out, 'Fishermen and weather-watchers are like family. Spending all of their time staring into water. Hoping for a sight of something.' She'd hoped it would bring back some of his old cheer. In her final few visits he'd been a total wreck, and all he could talk about was weather. 'The lightning doesn't strike,' he'd repeated on each occasion. 'It's a connection made in secret by the earth and the storm. Only when it's made does it catch fire, hotter than the surface of the sun.'

'Yeah,' she'd said. 'Yeah, you told me about that before.'

Then he had lied to her about the time of his release and when she enquired at the gate she discovered to her horror that he had left the jail four hours earlier and was long gone on his way into the prairie. She had held his plastic coat in her arms, sitting in disbelief in her car outside the prison gates, a copy of this album playing on loop on the stereo.

She put the record down on the bed and dried her eyes again. Just as those songs could still disturb the air, should the needle take its slow spiralling journey towards the centre of the vinyl, memories of her father could still stir up such intense feelings in her that she could barely breathe. She looked at the phone in the corner of her room and wished there was a number she could call which would lead to his voice breathing down the line. She wanted badly to tell him about Finn and what she had found in him. But there were billions of combinations of digits you could punch into a telephone and not one single string of them could connect her to her father.

She put the record aside.

When she tried to unwrap the second gift, her hands were trembling and she had to put it down again. She considered for a moment picking up the handset and miming the act of dialling her dad's old number. Then she could pretend he had answered and let him know all the things that she felt. There was so much to tell him that she would not know where to start. Perhaps she would start by telling him that ... Perhaps she would ...

She fanned her face because the blood had rushed to her head and tears were threatening once more.

She would tell him that he was a bastard. He should have been there on that day when she – the only one who still cared – arrived at the jail with his beloved yellow raincoat and Nina Simone playing on the stereo and money saved up to help him get back on his feet. Instead he had vanished, found himself a tornado to die in, left everything *unfinished*.

He had made her feel as if he loved storms more than he loved his daughter.

She grabbed a handkerchief and blew her nose. Then, with bleary eyes that meant she tore the paper, she opened the second present.

It was a kite.

A diamond-shaped kite made from quartz-white fabric. The tail, bunched up in polythene, was tied with silver bows. As she took it from the packet the tail fell to its full length with the grace of a waterfall. Her chest tightened and her shoulders bunched forwards. She picked up the phone and this time she did not mime but punched in the numbers. The clicks and crackles of receivers connecting across continents. Then the ringing tone that itself reminded her so much of her mother.

'Hello? Who is this?' Her mother sounded shattered, and only then did Elsa realize that it would be the middle of the night in America.

She had no idea what to say. She pressed the handset tight against her ear and cheek.

'Who's there? Do you know what time it is?'

'Mum ...'

'Elsa! Oh my God!'

'Hello, Mum.'

'*Elsa!*'

'Um, thank you, Mum, for my presents.'

If her mother was cross with her for not calling, or upset that she had only just now opened her gifts, her voice didn't show it. 'You liked them? Elsa, I can't believe it's you! Have you flown the kite yet?'

'No, I ... I'm going to fly it today. With someone I met here.'

'I'm so pleased, Elsa. I've got the receipt if it's no good. But I guess you're a long way from the store ...'

'Yeah. Yeah, I probably am.'

Silence – apart from the rummaging static of a few thousand miles of crossed air and leapfrogged oceans – but she had learned from Finn that an unfilled silence could be worth more than a hurried word.

'And the record?' her mother asked. 'It still plays okay?'

'I don't have a record player, but that doesn't matter.'

'Ah. It was ... I know it's funny to give you something that's already yours but, you know ... Oh, Elsa, I can't believe it's you.'

Elsa looked down at the telephone cord twisted round her fingers. It wasn't already hers, it was and had always been her dad's. Her mum used to infuriate her with such mistakes, but not today. 'It's perfect, Mum. I mean, it's a massive surprise because it was ... because it was ...'

'Because it was your father's?'

'Yes.'

She could hear the breath passing over her mother's lips. She wondered whether, if she could but listen hard enough, she might hear the clock ticking on the wall above her mum's phone, or the Oklahoman wind blowing through the avenues of Norman.

Mum blew her nose. 'Sorry, Elsa, it's just so marvellous to hear your voice. I wonder, did I ever tell you what my favourite line on that album was?'

'I didn't think you cared for it, Mum.'

'"*Like a leaf clings to a tree, oh my darling cling to me. Don't you know you're life itself ...*"' She cleared her throat. Elsa knew it was hard for her mother to talk about her emotions, even if it was in quotation marks. 'Your father,' she continued, 'played that to me on the night we got engaged, after we got back from the beach where he proposed to me. Do you want to know what he told me after that?'

Elsa bit her lip and nodded silently. Her mother waited for a moment and continued. 'He said human beings were like a wind blowing. He said that sometimes we're loud and sometimes we're a whisper, sometimes we're warm and sometimes we're frighteningly cold. But however we blow, we blow onwards, and leave no sign of us behind.'

'Mum,' Elsa gulped, 'I think I fell in love.'

She yelped with excitement. 'What? Love? I never thought I'd hear you say that!'

'Well, I – he – changed my mind.'

'Who *is* he?'

'His name is ...' she hesitated. She was tempted to say Cumulo-nimbus. 'His name is Finn.'

'And what does he do?'

'He, er, he makes me happy.'

'Good. Good. He sounds very mysterious. Although he'd have to be, to cut through all your opposition to falling in love.'

'Well, you know, you and Dad never really made the best case for it, Mum.'

Her mum didn't reply at once, and Elsa cringed and wished she hadn't said that. It was so easy to slip back into the old ways of talking.

'I loved your father very much, to begin with, but with all his storm-chasing he might as well have had another woman on the go. You won't believe it, but when I was pregnant with you, I was the more whimsical, the one who did things on the spur of the moment.'

'I know. I never even thanked you for all those practical things you did.'

'Don't be silly, dear, of course you did.'

'That's kind of you, but I know I didn't.'

'You don't need to say something to mean it.'

'All the same ... thank you.'

Her mum blew her nose again, an explosion of snorts and gasped breath, distorted by the long-distance connection into something truly horrific.

'So,' said Elsa when they had both recovered, 'are you not going to ask me where I've gone?'

'I'm not allowed to, am I?'

'Oh, Mum, I'm so sorry. I just ... I needed ...'

'I know. You don't have to explain.'

'Well, you can call me whenever you like.' And she gave her mother her telephone number and address and she told her about Thunderstown and Kenneth Olivier and each of the mountains and again, eventually, about Finn, although on that subject there was very little more she could say.

By the time Elsa's phone call had finished, the sun was up and the winds were blowing above the mountains, chasing a bunch of white clouds through the high fields of the sky. She pulled on her sneakers and left the house, the kite rustling under her arm.

As soon as Finn opened the bothy door, she sprung on him and wrapped her arms around him. She leaned her head against his neck and heard the small swallowing noises of his throat and beneath that his breath, the expansion and contraction of his chest. Surprised, he returned her embrace. Their bodies fitted together like separated continents.

After a while she took a step backwards so she could look at him. 'I've got something for us,' she said, and handed him the kite.

He took it out of its packet, the bows shimmering as he shook out the tail. He ran his hand over its glittering surface.

'I want us to fly it together,' she said.

'But I don't know how to fly a kite.'

'I'll teach you.'

A wind came rushing down the mountain, throwing up leaves and dust and humming through the bothy's walls.

'It's the perfect day for it,' she said.

He leaned forwards and kissed her. 'Come on, then.'

Old Colp's higher reaches inclined gently, giving way to meadows of dark tufty grass and dried-out ferns curled up into orbs. Finn led Elsa to one such place, an expanse dotted with poppies that had – for the time being at least – dodged the attentions of the goats. Their scarlet heads bobbed in the sweeping wind, and the meadow grass keeled left and right in its currents.

'It's easy,' Elsa said, when they were standing side by side and the wind was eagerly flapping her hair. 'We each take one end of it, and I hold the guide strings. Then we run. As fast as we can, and when I shout to let go we throw the kite into the air. Got it?'

He nodded, concentrating, and took his side of the kite. She looked at him, laughed at how seriously he was taking it, then shouted, 'Run!'

And off they shot, over the springy grass with the wind racing along with them and surging up their backs. The fabric of the kite crackled like a firework about to go off. They ran at breakneck speed – she hadn't run this fast in years – and then she yelled, 'Throw!' and they launched the kite into the air. It took off with a hungry crackle and ripped upwards on the currents. They skidded to a halt, and Elsa turned to guide its flight with the strings, although all she really needed to do was to anchor it. It looped high above them in a dazzle, the sunlight making the colour glitter in its fabric.

'How do you control it?' he puffed.

'Like this,' she said, demonstrating. 'It's easy, especially in this wind. Here, have a go.'

He took the guide handles from her as cautiously as if they were eggshells, but he quickly grew in confidence. He tugged experimentally at one handle and the kite dinked to the side. He grinned and made it reverse the other way. He had mastered it in no time, just as he had mastered the art of folding paper birds. Now he made it dance a figure of eight, now zigzag across the deep sky. Its tail coursed in its wake.

Elsa watched Finn's face. It would not be possible for his grin to be any larger. 'I wonder if ...' he mused as he experimented with the strings. 'Watch this!'

He made the kite move at a blur through an arc and another arc, so that it traced an E in the sky. After that it shot vertically in a straight line, then shimmied back down on itself. Finally it zipped through a circle, signing off with a dash.

'You wrote my name!'

He nodded happily, and offered her the strings. 'Your turn.'

She got through a loosely defined F, then sent the kite crashing down to the ground where its fabric ruffled indignantly, caught in the grass. They picked it up together and dusted it off.

'Try again?' he asked.

'Damn right!'

She began to run. Finn chased along beside her and the kite crackled between them, already straining to ride the wind. They raced across the flowery earth and she was about to shout, 'Now!' when she tripped and flew forwards, losing her grip. The sheer surprise of it made him trip too. He yelped and clutched in vain at the kite's tail as he fell along with her on to the grass. They rolled on to their backs just in time to watch the kite shoot free, wriggling away like a snake swimming through water.

Elsa laughed.

'You aren't cross that it's gone?'

'No. It was fun while it lasted.'

He nodded.

She moved across to lay her head down on his chest. There was a noise in there of distant thunder. She lay against him, looking up at the kite until it diminished into a white dot, a star in the daytime.

'We should go too,' he said.

'What? We only just got up here.'

He became serious. 'No. I mean, you and I should go away. We should have an adventure together.'

She stared outwards at the great blue atmosphere and wondered how far their kite had flown. There was infinity beyond that cerulean expanse. 'Where would we go?'

'I don't know. That's the exciting thing about it.'

'I've only just started my job. I might not be able to book the holiday.'

'Elsa, that's not what I meant. I meant we should leave Thunderstown.'

'Oh. Wow. That's a big step.'

'Yes. That's the whole point of it.'

'Finn, I've only just got here. It was only this morning that I told my mum where I'd gone.'

'You don't have to lose touch with her again; I'm not suggesting that. But think how exciting it would be to pick a horizon and head off for it.'

What if, she wondered, Thunderstown had never been her destination, but only the starting post for an important journey that was to come? She tested herself to see if she had grown too attached to leave. She had not fled New York in search of a change of bricks and mortar. She had left it in search of a different life. Kenneth would be disappointed, and she realized just how much it would hurt to leave him; but they could always stay in touch.

The wind gushed above them, playing the air like a saw. She remembered the dog that had intruded into her room that morning and taken the kite in its teeth. Already now that kite was far away, lost over undiscovered country.

'Deal,' she said.

'What? Are you serious?'

She yanked his arm so that he followed and lay across her, looking down at her with only an inch of air between them. 'Deadly. But for the moment let's just stay here.'

He grinned. Then, once again, that champagne-cloud began to show around the outline of his head, catching the light and giving him a silver lining. A gaseous halo, this time stretched and snatched at by the wind. She stroked her hand up over the bald dome of his head and the cloud parted at the motion.

'This is your happiness,' she whispered, 'and I am so glad that I helped you to discover it.'

18

THE LETTER FROM BETTY

In the morning Daniel trekked up Drum Head, to check the traps he had set there. He could taste moisture on the air – a change of weather was due. The sky was rugged with altocumulus, apart from in the north where the pointed peaks of the Devil's Diadem had torn strips out of the clouds. Above him, the sun looked perched on the peak of the mountain, as if it were considering turning back down the far slopes. Below, in Thunderstown, somebody was having a bonfire: a thin helix of smoke drifted up from somewhere in the vicinity of Corris Street.

He huffed, and turned his back on the town. He was still hurting from his treatment at the hands of Sidney Moses and his followers. He should have done his duty and killed that brook horse, not indulged a weak-hearted mood that must have made him seem like a silly, bleating little lamb.

He came to a part of the mountain where bristling spears of slate jutted out of the earth. To progress uphill he had to wind his way between them – the slate spears were as regular as trees in a tight forest. This was a good place to kill goats, for the routes between the stones were narrow and could be laid with traps until the place was like a minefield. He trod carefully, watching the pebbly ground to ensure he didn't fall victim to one of his own concealed devices. 'Hah!' he cried, the noise ricocheting between the trunks of rock, Sidney Moses would not last five minutes up here. He would no doubt chop his own hands off when he tried to prime his first trap. Likewise, Hamel Rhys would be done for within moments, and Sally Nairn too, and even a man such as Abe Cosser, who knew something of the mountains, wouldn't survive.

The first and second traps he came upon were empty, but in the third he found a young nanny who had died overnight in a vice of steel. He unhinged the metal jaws and slumped her body against a rock, where it would make quick crow fodder. He reset the trap, winching back the lever that helped open wide the jaws and lock them in their deadly circle, then he stood for a while with his hands in his pockets, looking at the saw-toothed metal.

If you judged it rationally then of course it was futile. Even his grandfather had admitted that. One man with a rifle and a collection of snares could never hope to keep in check the population of an entire species. What mattered was the trying. A culler's real work was not done up on the mountains but in the perception of the townsfolk, where it affirmed that somebody was out there in the wild, keeping Thunderstown safe.

With a snort he crouched down and picked up a chunk of slate. He tossed it up and down a few times, then hurled it as hard as he could at the trap. With a crack and a clang the rock hit the pressure plate and the jaws slammed closed. He picked his way along the winding paths until he came upon his next trap, and this too he disarmed, and so on up the mountain until, come late afternoon, he had neutralized them all.

When he got back to the homestead in the afternoon, he washed in cold water, sieving handfuls of cool fluid over his hair and face. Then he regarded himself in the mirror for a time, droplets occasionally falling from his beard. He tried to count all of the new wrinkles and grey hairs that Betty would not recognize if she ever came back, but there were too many.

When he had dried himself he plodded down to the kitchen, tore a hunk of bread and sliced tomatoes across it. He took this through to the main hall and living space of the homestead. Stout wooden columns propped up the ceiling, and in a wall at the far end an impressive fireplace (lit as rarely as Daniel felt the cold) was surrounded by soft chairs that he never lounged in. The walls of the hall were crammed with portraits of Fossiters past, each sporting the same furrowed eyebrows and clipped black beard that Daniel wore. Previous generations had raised large families in this place, but there were no pictures of children or their mothers on these walls. His ancestors had had little time for either.

He sat at the sturdy wooden table at which the Fossiters had eaten for centuries. He picked at the food, but no sooner had he sat down to eat it than he lost his appetite.

He had always known that he was of two minds. His first was the slow-paced, sombre mind that the townsfolk recognized as Daniel Fossiter's. This mind was the one he used to think and plan and reason, but with his other mind he could not manipulate or second-guess. It surged in the depths of himself, just as an ocean surges beneath the boat bobbing on its surface. It had its own thinkings, to which he was not privy, but which sometimes, looking down, he would glimpse for a second like the shape of a whale moving underwater. At other times it rocked him with such intense waves of feeling that all he could do was cling to some solid and rational thought until it stilled. It always did, eventually, or at least it always had done until now.

He got up and crossed to his trunk, gently lifting the wooden lid. Inside were the paper birds Finn used to make him, which he parted carefully so as not to dent their wings. Beneath them lay his father's Bible and his grandfather's violin and, tucked between those, the letter Betty had written long ago for Finn.

He returned to the table and placed the letter squarely on its surface, making sure it lined up perpendicular to the edges of the table. He wondered whether he could wait any more.

He summoned his most treasured memories of her. A birthday of his on which, as with all prior birthdays, he had let the occasion go unacknowledged. He remembered that he had returned to the homestead after an afternoon's labour to find it springing all over with flowers. A cake on the table, a russet-coloured sponge with fruit pieces as dark as ink blots. Betty, its baker, waiting for him in the doorway, wearing a silly pointed party hat and holding something wrapped in bright paper that was a present for him.

Another memory, this time in the dead of night, when he heard a noise at his bedroom window. He sat up startled in bed, fists raised like a boxer's. There Betty was, scrambling in through the open window in a dress pale as the moonlight. It made marble sculpture from her bare shoulders, but instead of sitting gobsmacked and admiring her, he protested that there was a front door downstairs designed for entering the premises. She cut back that life was better like this, if you let yourself be carried on it.

He needed her wise words now more than ever, so he started to pick at the seal of the envelope. Then he paused and thought that to open it with his thick fingers would be like opening a jewellery box with a battering ram. He rushed to the sideboard and found the thin silver letter opener of his father's. This he sliced precisely through the space between the sealed gum and the corner of the envelope.

He raised the paper to his face and pressed his nose against the seal. It did not smell of Betty, as he had hoped, so he tried to imagine her favourite perfume. He found that he could not.

No matter. The words were what would count. After eight

patient years he would at last receive some sentiment of hers. The sheer shape of her handwriting would be enough.

He opened the envelope. He had speculated, fantasized, dreamed about this moment so many times that to begin with he could hardly look.

Inside were two sheets of paper which he unfolded. He stared into the grid of her handwriting and at first didn't let himself read the words. He savoured instead the moment, absorbed the arrangement of her sentences, treated them like a dance he could imagine her hand and her pen fox-trotting through. Then he wiped his face on his sleeve and began to read.

Finn,

There have been so many different versions of this letter. I have spent all day trying to write it. And if there's only one thing you take from these words, it should be this: I have not left you. Please don't think it even for a minute.

Things have changed in these last few months and I need room to set my thoughts in order. You should know, though, that I don't blame you for the burns I received from the lightning. It wasn't your fault, and nor is it your fault that I'm going away for a bit.

I've always known that you had lightning in you, and I've always accepted it. Daniel warned me again and again that you might be dangerous, but I couldn't make him see that perhaps each of us is a danger, if we don't know what's inside of us. Now you understand about it too, and I feel like I should have given you some warning long ago. At your last birthday I tried to explain it. Sixteen years old seemed like a fitting time to tell you, but I could not find the words. Do you remember your birthday picnic on Drum Head, when I sat in silence and you asked me what was wrong? I was trying to tell you then. Trying to tell you that you were a thundercloud once, but that I love you just the same.

And yet, I am frightened. I'm writing this and not speaking it because I could never say such a thing in person.

How can I explain this fear? It's like this … The greatest joy of parenthood is passing things on. It's what I always dreamed about doing – giving away all the things I thought were good in my own life and holding back all the bad. And I have wondered whether all we ever are is this: a filter of the good and the bad, trying to work out which is which, which we should withhold and which we should pass on. So before I digress and restart this letter for the hundredth time, here's the start of the point I'm trying to make: I loved Daniel Fossiter for a little while. He was so absorbed in his fears, but sometimes I could prize them open and let out a part of him that was like a little boy, able to lose itself in life again, and that was the thing I loved. Yet all along, at the same time, he was trying to pass something on to me. Those fears he had grown up with and surrounded himself with, he wanted me to feel them too. They were, ultimately, all fears of things unexplainable. Fears of things like you, Finn.

When the lightning came out of you he said it was proof. That there was something terribly wrong with you and that it needed righting. I said it only proved you were a miracle. Then a kind of zeal came over him and it made me sick to look him in the eye. He was so eager for us all to be doomed. And then I went to you, and as I have said I held nothing against you because of what happened, but no sooner did I see you than my body froze up with fear.

I grew up in a rational world, Finn. A place far, far away from here. I am used to reason: if I know I am not frightened of you, then it follows that I am not frightened. But my body doesn't think in the same way. I had worked everything through in my mind, and I intended for nothing to be different between us. Then I saw you for the first time after you struck me, and you looked so small and sheepish, and I was nearly paralyzed by fear. I am so, so sorry for how that must have made you feel.

I ran back to Daniel after that. At last I understood him, for it was his fear that I now had inside of me. It had been passed on, just as he always hoped to pass it on by persuasion. No sooner did I understand him than I did not love him any more, and I realized I needed to be away from him and from Thunderstown.

You are my salvation: a child when before I could have none. But now I feel like I am suffocating whenever Daniel is near. It's like his words are smoke in the air. I flinch every time he opens his mouth. So I am going away, and by the time you read this I will have left Thunderstown. I have asked him to look after you. Please do your best to look after him in return. He is shrill with fear, and he does not know the first thing about it.

Don't worry, I will be back soon, I just need to breathe some fresh air and be in the company of strangers. You're perhaps too young to feel the need for such a change, but I've learned that sometimes the things we don't understand are the things that compel us most profoundly, and we have to decide whether to suffocate them or let them carry us. There's no middle way.

One more thing to say: you are a man. Now that you know what's inside of you, you've grown up. You couldn't be a child again even if you wanted to be. And the bleak and wonderful thing about growing up is that you have to work everything out on your own. You will do a fine job, I am sure, and before long we will be together again.

Your loving mother,
Betty

For a time Daniel did not move. The second hand on the old clock made its slow struggle around the face, and only after it had turned a full circuit did he give a great bellow and batter his fists against his knees. He tore at his beard. She could not mean these things she had written. She could never have been so affected by the things he had felt about Finn.

'Because I was wrong, Betty!' he wailed. 'Wrong!'

Had he – with his constant haranguing – *had he* been the one who had changed her thinkings and strangled her feelings for him out of her? Man, his father had said, is cursed to love. To feel it as powerfully as he does. Man, his grandfather had said with a grin, dreamed up love because he was weak-willed, for a lover is a man who lets his guard down, and after that the killing blow comes in.

'Except,' he growled in reply to the voices of his ancestors, 'you don't say what is to be *done* about it.' It seemed ridiculous to sit and speculate, when love was a thing that grabbed you by the guts and not the head and you did not know how to ride it out. He did not give a damn about whether love was a weakness or a curse, since trying not to fall in love was as doomed to failure as trying to murder yourself only by holding your breath. If the whole of Drum Head had been torn out of the earth and placed down on his chest, it would not have weighed as much as did the realization that he had put his own wretched fear into Betty, even though he had loved her with every atom of his body.

Worse still, she had intended to leave only briefly. At times during these last eight years he had hoped that when she'd said as much, on the day that she'd left Thunderstown, she had lied to him. If it were a lie and a lack of caring it was possible to imagine her forging a new life in a new landscape, and although that was painful at least it meant she was alive to live it. What if, by accident or design, she had taken that journey from which there was no possible return?

From the walls of their homestead the Fossiter portraits watched in silence. 'Damn you,' he growled at them, including himself among their countenances. 'Damn you all.'

He could not bear to be in their company so he charged outside, into the climbing sunlight of the morning. In the yard he paused and bit hard on his tongue. He wondered what he might have done for her or said, had he known what he did now.

He blundered across to the workshop. In here hung the corpse of the last goat he had hung, beheaded and drip-dried now of the blood that had filled it. He unknotted the cords that kept it dangling from its hooves and thumped it on to his butchering table, a wood-topped counter stained by the blood of generations of goats, spilled by generations of Fossiters. Its surface was notched like a prison wall by the tally blows of their cleavers.

He had often wondered what differentiated the goats' burly, braying existences from a man's. A goat lived its life like every goat in every generation before it. It chewed on anything it could, polished its horns against tree bark, moulted in the autumn, rutted in the spring. All this it did with dull stony eyes and a placid expression, as if its life were a routine played out a million times, a chore lived with duty and not wonder.

But a man ... a man had a fire, a spark in his eye. His life seemed to him an exquisite flame, and he would tend it greedily. What was that fire, wondered Daniel, and where did it come from?

'Betty!' he gasped without planning to do so, croaking up at the ceiling.

And why did he address the ceiling? Because he thought God lay up there? God in the heavens? God in the workshop's loft? The goats did not croak at the sky when they died their slow deaths with their legs bent in metal jaws. All that was up in the sky was water and dust on the wind, and then a nothingness beyond human imagination, so everlasting that it could not even be measured in light years. He closed his eyes and pictured God the Father seated on His throne, and God the Father had a serious brow, a long nose and a black beard. God the Father was a Fossiter.

He took up his flaying knife and returned to the carcass on the butchering table. Parting the dirty hair around the goat's crotch, he worked the knife into its groin and cut out an exit for the slop of its innards, which he dragged out in his fist and plopped into a bowl. Then he set to work with the knife, drawing with its blade the practised patterns of cuts and slices that gave him a grip on the animal's skin. With tugs and pulls he undressed the body of its coat, as easy as if it had been a cardigan on a human being.

He rubbed salt into the newly removed goat skin and hung it up to cure. He chose another cleaver and chopped briskly through the meat and bones, separating out the body into joints and chops. Then he could go on no more.

He twisted around and flung the cleaver through the air. It whistled as it flew, then slammed into the woodwork of the door frame. He kicked over the bleed trough so that its liquid mix of innards and viscera sprayed out across the workshop wall. His hands were shaking and he screwed up his eyes and yelled into the darkness of his thinkings. After yanking free the cleaver he headed back into the homestead. The first thing to hand was his father's bookshelf, which he broke from the wall with one powerful blow, so that all of the books fell in a mess to the floor. He dropped after them on to his knees and one by one slammed the cleaver through their covers until the floor was snowy with paper. Then he sprung up and swung the cleaver at his grandfather's favourite armchair, hacking through the arm and ripping open the cushions until he spluttered on the dust and the feathers flying forth. He kicked over the table, and butted his head against a painting of his great-great-grandfather so that the canvas smashed in. He slashed and scored his way along the wall of portraits, until he came to his old trunk in the corner. Greedily he threw it back open – and then stopped.

The paper birds turned his rage into a ceremonial fury.

He lifted from the trunk his grandfather's violin and his father's weighty Bible. He righted the table and placed both objects on it, the instrument on top of the book. He regarded them for a moment, then raised the cleaver over his head with both hands and slammed it down with all of his might. It carved cleanly through the violin, sending frayed strings thrumming to both sides. It split the Bible in half like an apple and wedged into the wood of the table.

He crashed back on to his rump and sat there panting. After some time had passed he began to realize the wreck he had made of the homestead. Filled with sudden doubt and superstition, he reached out and touched the nearer half of the violin. To his surprise he saw that there was a folded piece of card taped inside it. His grandfather must have secreted it there by sticking it into the bole of the instrument. Daniel removed it and unfolded it cautiously.

A photograph of his mother and father.

His mother, Maryam. It was the first time he had seen her since he was seven years old.

He gasped at the sight of her. 'Look at you!' he said, pawing at her. He had always considered his looks to be yet one more product of the Fossiter lineage, but he marvelled to see that he also looked like her. She had his severe brow and dark eyes, and hair as black as his, although hers was long enough to reach down to her elbows. And there was something in her eyes he could not quite place, a cold kind of knowledge. She looked as if she were withholding some immense secret. 'Look at you,' he whispered, tracing her outline with his finger.

Her gauzy dress was tailored from a translucent cloth, and at the moment the photograph had been taken a wind had puffed and the dress had billowed and flapped out along with her long black locks and she looked half woman and half mist. For a while he didn't blink, in case this image of her would prove as fleeting as the ones in his dreams and vanish under other memories. Eventually his eyes were swimming and he had to refresh them, but to his delight the photo remained when they reopened. He slid on to the floorboards and lay on his back, gripping the photograph tight. He felt cut off from the man he had been yesterday, even from the man he had been one hour ago. Cut off and stranded, lost in a chill dark. He began to shiver. It was a hot day and the sunlight flaring in through the homestead's windows lit him directly. Even so he felt icy cold.

Then he realized that he could see his breath hanging in the air.

He got up and retreated on all fours, but his next exhalation, and the next too, hung where he had breathed it. A trilogy of sparkling clouds, as if the warm air of the homestead were freezing. Terrified, he dared not breathe further. He clasped his hands over his mouth until he turned red-faced and his veins began to throb in his neck and forehead. Still the clouds of breath hung there glittering, until reluctantly he gasped and his heart fluttered with relief because his next breath was invisible again.

The three clouds dispersed gradually in the air. He puffed out several times, just to be sure. Nothing. He pinched his cheeks, wiped his palms across his shirt to remove the cold sweat that had formed on them, then pressed a hand to his chest and felt for his heartbeat. To his relief it did not boom with thunder, but with the powerful pump of ventricles.

He did not know what to make of what had just happened, so he turned again to the photograph of his parents. He collected the cleaver with which he had destroyed his house, and carefully scored a line between the couple. His father he left amid the destruction of the homestead. His mother he regarded for a long minute, then slipped into his shirt pocket, to walk out with her into what promised to become a fine summer evening.

He stood for a long while in the yard, leaning on the fence, staring upwards at the azure heavens and feeling as groundless as the clouds that passed above.

When he looked down he was surprised to see a man approaching from the west. He moved with such zip that it took Daniel a moment to realize it was Finn. Even when he reached the homestead, Daniel did not know what to say.

Eventually Finn said, 'You look different.'

Daniel looked down at his hands, dried in places with blood from his earlier butchery, and stuck here and there with bits of debris from the chaos he had made of the hall. He cleared his throat. 'I feel different.'

'We need to talk. Can I … I mean, are you going to invite me in?'

Daniel nodded sideways at the front door. 'Lead the way.'

Finn took a few steps inside, then stopped to gape at the damage. 'Daniel … what have you done?'

Daniel rubbed his beard. 'I don't know why I did it, but I think … it was the right thing to do.'

Finn approached the ruined portraits. The top half of one sitter's face remained in the frame, but a sweep of the cleaver had slit the canvas beneath the nose and the bottom half of the painting had flapped away. 'This was your grandfather!'

'Yes.' He stood beside Finn to look into the oil of the old man's eyes.

'You … you have nothing but respect for your grandfather.'

Daniel reached up and tore out the top half of the canvas, which he discarded on the floor.

Finn was astonished. 'Daniel, what's happened?'

'The past,' he said, sweeping an arm through the air to indicate the entire contents of the room, 'became the past. And you,' he raised a commanding finger, which to his dismay Finn flinched from, 'are owed a thousand apologies.'

'What for?'

'I let my fear get the better of me.'

'Daniel, this is all … really unexpected. And … and …' He smiled nervously. 'If it will make you feel better, then apology accepted.'

If only, thought Daniel, *the two of us could start anew from here.* He relished, for a moment, the way the destruction had made the two of them unguarded, then he turned away from Finn and with a sigh took the letter from Betty off the table. 'Here. It was meant for you. Back on the day she left us. I hoarded it because … I loved your mother deeply. I know I had the wrong ways of showing it, I … I do not acknowledge your acceptance of my apology. Not until you have read this letter, when I suspect you shall be glad of the chance to retract it.'

Finn received the two sheets as if they were halves of a treasure map.

When he had finished reading he folded the letter but continued to stare at its ageing paper. Daniel steadied his ankles and locked his knees, as if bracing to be crashed into by a great wave. *At least,* he thought, *I deserve this.* He wrung his fingers, and waited.

Finn threw his arms around him and embraced him. He squeezed his shoulders tightly, while Daniel could do nothing but gawp.

'All my life,' said Finn, stepping away, 'you have seemed so invincible. When I was a child you were terrifying. I thought I might wake one night with your hands around my throat.'

Daniel looked down and screwed up his eyes. 'Is there anything I can do to make amends?'

'I think you have done it. And if there's anything I should know it's this: people can change, just like the clouds. I forgive you.'

'I do not deserve it.'

'If you didn't deserve it, I wouldn't need to forgive you.'

'I will be better to you, Finn, I swear. For the rest of my days.'

Finn looked away. ' I thought coming here would be difficult, but not because of this. It was because I've got something to tell you and now I don't know how, but… I'm leaving, Daniel. I'm leaving Thunderstown.'

Daniel stared at him blankly, expecting a punchline. When none came he swallowed and asked, 'Is that the truth?'

'Yes. Elsa and I, we're going away. Together. It feels like we're meant to.'

Daniel righted a chair he had thrown over in his earlier fury, and slumped into it with his hands between his knees. 'I had hoped for the chance to make amends to you.'

'Yes. I can see.'

'Where will you go?'

'Somewhere. Anywhere. Not having a destination is sort of the whole point.'

For a moment he pictured Finn wracked with lightning in some busy street of the bustling world, and he opened his mouth to forewarn him, but then stopped himself to let the fear go. To his delight he was able to do so. Unanchored, it drifted away from him.

'You must do as you see fit,' he said, 'although still there are practicalities. There are things you will need.'

Finn shrugged. 'We'll muddle through.'

'I had hoped to make up for lost time.'

Finn puffed out his cheeks. 'I never thought we would have a conversation like this.'

Daniel got up and paced over to his trunk, untouched amid the debris. 'As you know, I have never been a spendthrift.' He removed from the trunk a clasped wooden box. 'So I have saved up some money, as well as the sums that I inherited from my father and grandfather.'

He popped open the box and inside were squeezed wads of bank notes, tied together by string.

'Take these with you, and all practicality is dealt with.'

'Daniel, it's too much; you might need it.'

He held up a hand. 'On the contrary it is too little. Besides, I like the thought that my forefathers' savings will be turned to the purposes of romance. It will be a kind of revenge for me.'

Finn sighed and accepted the box. 'We'll come and see you before we leave.'

'I would be grateful for that. I will try to get the place in better shape before then. I have some mess to clear up, and a bonfire to make.'

Finn laughed, hesitated, then hugged Daniel again. Daniel could not remember ever having being clasped with such affection.

'Finn,' he said when they stepped apart, 'there's something caught on your ear.'

Finn reached up and retracted his hand with a scrap of mist looped round his fingers. More of it formed out of the side of his head, blowing in clumps as light as blossom.

'This keeps happening,' he said. 'I think it means I'm happy.'

Daniel pointed to himself. 'Because of what we just said?'

He nodded. Daniel's mouth opened and closed, but since it seemed their earlier words had been such marvellous things, he chose not to risk muddying them with any more.

'For now,' said Finn, 'I'd best be on my way. Elsa is telling Kenneth Olivier that we're leaving, and then we're going to meet each other in the square. We're going to take a goodbye tour of Thunderstown.'

Daniel walked out with him and stood in the road. He waved to him as he walked off towards town, and marvelled at the faint haze of happiness that glimmered in Finn's wake.

19

THINGS SPIRAL

Elsa took a deep breath. 'I'm leaving Thunderstown.'

They were in Kenneth's front yard, where she had found him sitting in a polo shirt of many clashing colours, and rereading one of his well-thumbed almanacs. At her news he slumped back with a puff. 'Oh,' he said, and looked lost for words.

The day had reached an in-between hour, neither afternoon nor evening. The sun was still trying to shine, but so many pinched rows of cloud were moving from west to east that the sky looked like an upside-down sea, and the sun some great sunken orb glowing underwater.

Kenneth looked up for inspiration. 'Well,' he said eventually, 'can I ask why?'

'I met someone.'

Kenneth was too genial to let his disappointment hold back a smile, or to prevent that smile from turning to a chuckle. 'I might have known! A Thunderstown man?'

'Kind of. His name is Finn. Finn Munro.'

Kenneth frowned. 'Hmm, I can't put a face to that name.'

'That's because he, er, well …' She wanted to tell him the truth, and reckoned he had been good enough to her to deserve it. She cleared her throat. 'This is going to sound strange,' she began, and then told him everything in a hurry, every detail of all that had happened: the way she'd first caught Finn dissolving into cloud;

the sneaked visits to the bothy and the way he'd shown her air in his veins instead of blood; their trip into the cave and the paintings there; the reasons Dot had given for Finn's strange body; the way, now that he was happy, he became prone to a hazy lining. When she'd finished talking she was breathless, and waited for him to announce his disbelief.

'I have to confess, Elsa, I knew some of this already.' He looked embarrassed. 'When we made the cake it was obvious that it was for someone special. But also, well, little old nuns are such fiendish gossips. Dot said you might need my support, but I don't think you need much help from anyone except this Finn. It sounds like – if I may be so bold – you have begun to know your own heart. I think perhaps that that's what you came to Thunderstown hoping to do.' He stood up and held wide his arms. 'So,' he said, 'congratulations! I wish you all the very best.'

They hugged, then he stepped back with his hands still on her shoulders. 'And you will take Michael's car with you.'

'What? No, Kenneth. I couldn't.'

'Yes. How else will you get out of Thunderstown? Don't worry, it's not a selfless gift. I hope it will remind you to send me a postcard now and then.'

She grinned. 'Before long you'll be wishing you hadn't asked that. I'll send you heaps of them. And I'll call. I want to stay in touch. It might sound corny, but you really saved my neck when you let me stay here. I wouldn't have gotten anywhere without you.'

He bowed. 'You're too kind, Elsa. Will I get to meet this strange lucky cloud of yours, before the two of you depart?'

'Oh, of course. I'd like to see his face when he tries your chilli coal pot! Not even lightning burns like that stuff! But for now I'd better go and meet him. We're going to kiss goodbye to these old streets. I've become quite attached to them while I've been here.'

Kenneth remained on his feet to watch her walk away, and she wished somehow that she could take him with her, even though of course it was out of the question and he would never come. Before she turned down Welcan Row she looked back over her shoulder and saw him still standing there. He looked older than she had thought him, even with his shirt like a fruit salad.

She waved, then set off down the road towards Saint Erasmus, although she knew she could walk in any direction and be pulled there. She would miss these circling streets and decaying buildings when she left them, but she supposed that she and Finn were already being called elsewhere by another secret gravity.

Finn was waiting for her in the shade of the church. He looked smaller, down here in the town, and he kept shifting from foot to foot, as if the presence of so many bricks unsettled him.

'The walls can't bite you,' she said as she drew close.

'It's not that.'

Elsa embraced Finn, pressing her forehead against the underside of his jaw while he held her for a quiet moment. While they stood there, a haze again emerged from him, beginning as a white band like a cloud tiara, then spilling out across his skin until it was a patina of mist. Above them a wind moved, and whistled under the church's arches.

'I went to see Daniel,' he said, while she stroked her hand across his cheek, 'and he was ... so nice to me.'

Elsa could barely even picture it. 'You sure he'd not been drinking?'

'No ... he was in a strange mood. He'd smashed up his house, for one thing. But I genuinely think that he meant it – the kindness, I mean. Do you know, I think this is the first time in my life that he's said a kind word to me?'

'I can believe it.'

Finn looked thoughtful. The sun was too low now to turn his haze into a silver lining, but it flushed it nevertheless with the faintest rose hue, which found out the dimples and fluctuations in the cloud. Then Finn told her about the letter from his mother and the money Daniel had offered them, and while he talked a handful of leaves blew in a circle around their feet and then skittered onwards across the square.

'I reckon you deserve all that,' she said when he'd finished.

'It certainly wasn't what I went there expecting. It left me feeling so full of energy. I was here early, because I walked so fast from Daniel's house. When I stepped out of his door I felt like everything was new. If he could change so drastically, anything might be possible. It's hard to explain.'

'You don't need to,' Elsa said. 'You're growing into yourself. You're getting used to whatever, whoever, you are. You're getting used to being Finn.'

She stroked her hand across his forehead and fragments of cloud broke around her fingers. It suited him, this faint second skin of vapour. She was about to kiss him again when she realized they were being watched. A stern woman in a shawl stood midway across the square, then scuttled away when she realized she'd been spotted, breaking into a trot as soon as she reached the entrance to Feave Street.

'Shall we take our farewell tour?' suggested Elsa.

'Let's,' Finn said, and they joined hands.

When they were a little way down Feave Street, somebody behind them shouted her name. She looked over her shoulder and saw the woman who had been watching them, along with a small bunch of townsfolk whom she must have alerted. One of them called her name like a summons, and a shiver rippled through her.

'Ignore them,' she said, 'and just keep walking.'

This was a narrow street of three-storey terraces, each with an overhanging roof like a frown. Elsa had never much liked this road, whose paving dipped and bumped so that she couldn't tell what was supposed to be flat and what was supposed to be uneven. In the distance, the Devil's Diadem and the crinkled cloud cover did nothing to help, forming a hatched backdrop of lined rock and atmosphere.

Finn looked back. 'There's nine or ten people following us. Are they friends of yours?'

'I have no idea who they are. Finn, I have a bad feeling about this. Can we just skip our tour and go back to your bothy?'

'Elsa, I don't think we need to be frightened of them.'

The small crowd was still out of earshot, but she whispered nevertheless. 'You have a coat of cloud, Finn, all over your skin. *They're* the ones who will be frightened.'

'Well, if they say anything, perhaps I can persuade them that there's nothing to be scared of.'

Elsa sighed. She looked up at the rooftops, where the weathervanes were all pointing away towards Old Colp. 'I don't know, Finn. Call me crazy, but can we just get out of here?'

She heard her name called again.

'They want to speak to you.'

'I don't care what they want.'

'Okay,' he said, and they cut back on themselves down Auger Lane.

Before they reached the next junction a man stepped out in front of them, his hands tucked in his pockets. He wore the same rain cap and coat as most men of the town, but still she recognized him from his plump neck and intrigued eyes.

'Just thought I'd head you off here,' said Sidney Moses, 'to ask you a question or two.'

Elsa glanced across at Finn. He did not appear at all troubled, even though – she bit her lip – cloud still hung against his skin like dusty cobwebs.

'We've got places to be,' she said.

The small band of townsfolk caught up with them, one or two of them out of breath from the speed at which they'd followed.

She didn't like how grave they looked, nor how they all hung back from taking the final few paces towards Finn, glancing instead to Sidney for guidance.

'Haven't you all got something better to be doing?' she asked.

Sidney licked his lips but didn't answer at once. A pair of magpies took off from further down the street and flew overhead, arguing in rasps as they went.

'The thing is,' said Sidney carefully, 'that Sally Nairn just saw something.'

'That's him, Sidney,' said the stern-faced woman in the shawl.

'Sally said she saw a kind of fog around this boyfriend of yours. And lo and behold ...' He gazed with a mixture of disgust and fascination at the delicate vapour that smudged the air around Finn.

Finn folded his arms. 'I have a name, you know, which you can address me by if you can be polite enough to ask for it.'

Sidney turned his attention to Finn. 'When Miss Beletti arrived in Thunderstown, it wasn't long before we all knew her face. Yet I don't recognize yours, lest it's from a story I once heard. When did you arrive?'

'I've always been here.'

Elsa winced. 'Finn, this guy just wants trouble ...'

'It's okay, Elsa. They're just confused by what they're seeing.'

Sidney nodded. 'What are we seeing, exactly?'

'I have a storm inside of me.'

The crowd wrung their hands and whispered to each other. Sidney looked as if he had unearthed buried treasure. 'Do you admit to it, just like that?'

'I am not ashamed of it any more. And I'm sick of hiding up a mountain. I'm as safe to be around as any of you.'

Sidney puffed himself up. 'You are very brazen, to come down here and say such things, after all that you have done to us.'

'This is ridiculous,' said Elsa, rolling her eyes. 'He hasn't done anything.'

Sidney didn't take his gaze off Finn. 'We know who you are.'

She tugged at Finn's hand. 'Come on, Finn. Let's get going.'

'You are Old Man Thunder.'

She bristled. 'Don't be so stupid. You know nothing about Finn. How could you possibly suggest that?'

Sidney glared at her. 'Just because Kenneth Olivier says you're welcome in Thunderstown, it doesn't mean that you are. *He* isn't much welcome here either.'

One or two of the crowd looked doubtful at that, but they didn't protest. Elsa's stomach knotted when she saw how quickly their obedience overcame their doubts. She became acutely aware of how greatly they outnumbered her and Finn. Again she tugged at Finn's arm. He didn't budge.

'Daniel told me about you, Mr Moses,' he said. 'But I thought he'd made you out to be worse than you actually are.'

While they had been talking, the strands of cloud clinging to Finn's bald head had thickened. Now they were as opaque as ash. Sidney watched them with grim interest, and turned to the crowd. 'Look at him! Look at his skin. What do you see?' One of the townsfolk whimpered, '*Weather!*' and they all started burbling like frightened hens.

Elsa remembered the fear on these same faces on her first day in Thunderstown, when Daniel killed a wild dog. A cold anticipation locked the joints of her elbows and knees. 'Finn, please,' she said, wishing she could spirit them both away like a magician.

'Prove it,' said Sidney.

'Prove what?'

'Prove that you're real.'

'What do you mean? Of course I'm real.'

'You would say that. But we don't think you are. We think you're a storm, pretending to be a man.'

Deny it, Elsa thought, *even though there's cloud all over you.*

'I'm not pretending. I am a storm, and a man as well. But I'm not Old Man Thunder.'

Sidney gaped at the crowd with theatrical disbelief. 'Do my ears deceive me? First he looks like a storm masquerading as a man. Then we give him a chance to deny it, and instead he pleads guilty!'

The crowd had bunched up shoulder to shoulder. Abe Cosser's left leg was jittering, his old boot rapping off the stone road.

'Come on, Finn,' said Elsa, tugging at his arm.

He resisted. 'No, Elsa. We can make them understand. What proof do you want from me, Mr Moses?'

Sidney reached down to his belt and unclipped the knife that was attached there. He offered it, still sheathed, to Finn, saying, 'They say Old Man Thunder can't bleed.'

Finn didn't take the knife. 'I'm not going to cut myself open for you. Don't be ridiculous.'

But as he spoke a wind blew down the street and tried to steal away the cloud clinging to his skin, stretching it out for a moment like silver tresses, then scattering it across the air. In the crowd, a terrified Abe Cosser commenced the Lord's Prayer.

'Does it always have to be the case,' asked Finn, and there was a rumbling edge on his voice that didn't come from his vocal cords, 'that people find devils in the things they don't understand? Believe me, I've been frightened by myself too, but doesn't that make me all the more able to explain it to you? I used to think I was a kind of monster, but all it took was a little kindness to realize – ' he squeezed Elsa's hand in recognition ' – that I'm just like any of you.'

For a moment Elsa was proud enough of him to forget her anxiety, but when she turned triumphantly to Sidney he had spread out his arms to address the townsfolk and she could see where this was headed and it was as if her heart had dropped out of her.

'He admits to it!'

'He didn't admit to anything,' said Elsa, but her voice sounded reedy.

'He *admits*,' declared Sidney with steely composure, 'and that's all we need to know.'

The crowd looked like a satisfied jury.

'He didn't admit,' objected Elsa, 'because there's nothing to admit to.' She wished they had just kept on walking. Even if the crowd had besieged them in the bothy they could have at least locked them out. She remembered suddenly a fight on the sidewalk a few years back, some alcohol-fuelled altercation between a stranger, who had said something about her, and Peter, who had drunkenly tried to stand up to him. 'Let's go, Finn. All he wants is a fight.'

Finn was about to say something more, but she pulled his arm so hard that he got the message, nodded and turned away. Together they walked down the street, but no pace was fast enough for her. She felt like she was trapped in a flinch. All of her clothes felt too small.

'Don't look back,' she whispered.

They walked fast along Auger Lane then turned off into Candle Street, which led uphill towards Old Colp's reclusive slopes. A scruffy cat, who had been sleeping on a yard wall, fixed its yellow eyes on Finn and hissed. The crowd trailed them and she hoped like hell that, when the going got steep on the mountain slopes, they would lose interest. Above Old Colp the clouds appeared to be clearing. The sun flung late light through the gap, and all of Thunderstown's shadows lengthened.

Suddenly Finn lurched forwards and clutched the back of his head. Elsa heard something rattle off the flagstones. It was a nugget of slate. Finn crouched, blinking hard with pain, one hand held to his crown. She could hear the air hissing out where the slate had cut him. At first she couldn't move because a panic filled her up as if with needles. Then she exclaimed 'Finn!' and grabbed hold of him. 'Are you okay?'

He nodded groggily. Wild-eyed, she spun around to confront the townsfolk, but Sidney Moses looked as surprised as her. Somebody else had thrown it.

Finn had still not stood upright, and now there was a deeper noise behind the hiss from his cut, a noise like a distant train passing. Layers of dark, heavy gas opened out of the cut like the petals of a flower. The cat who had hissed at them sprang down from its wall and fled as fast as its four legs could carry it.

Elsa railed at the townspeople. 'You should be ashamed of yourselves!'

They all ignored her, enraptured by the dusky cloud growing out of Finn's gashed scalp. It grew fat and puffy, a gaseous tumour expanding by the second.

Elsa crouched beside him, supporting his shoulder and whispering his name. He was staring, dazed, at the floor, with his face beaded by drops of clear water. Every now and then one of them welled big enough to fall and splash against the road. The cloud kept swelling, now the size of his head, now twice the size. Then it skewed and distended, and broke open across his back so that he was crouched under a fleecy heap. Elsa tried to think of what to do, but her heartbeat was a din in her ears. All she could think was to squeeze his arm and whisper his name. Beneath the cloud his shirt had become damp.

The townsfolk edged closer, until she snapped at them, 'Get away from him!' and all bar Sidney Moses took a step back.

'Elsa ...' whispered Finn, and when he spoke a patter of rainwater dribbled over his lips. She whimpered to see it, and clung to him tighter.

'Finn? How badly are you hurt? Do you think you can stand? Here, I'll help you.' She steadied herself to support his big frame and helped him, although she was a very shaky prop, back to his feet. The cloud spilled to either side as he stood, so that he was framed in an oval of fog. It kept coming from him, pouring out grey filaments so that he looked like a smouldering effigy.

'Who ...' he began, and more water dribbled over his chin and fell in a sheet to the road, 'threw ...' He swooned for a second and she had to throw her whole weight against him to help him regain his balance. At the same time the cloud mushroomed and a shadowy cap rose out of its highest point. A raindrop formed and plinked off the flagstones. Her own clothes were becoming speckled by them. Her breathing had become sharp, each inhalation like a slap to her lungs.

'Who did this?' Elsa hissed at the crowd. 'Show yourself.'

Heads turned to quiz one another, and then the crowd parted and left little Abe Cosser isolated, clutching another pebble of slate in his shaking fist.

'You ...' said Finn, then spat out water again, 'don't need to be frightened. The weather is just like you.'

Abe looked from Finn to Elsa to Sidney to his peers, but all seemed to have cut him loose. He looked down at the slate in his hand. 'Lord have mercy,' he muttered, and threw the stone at Finn.

Elsa shrieked when it struck Finn in the jaw and his head snapped sideways with a gargle. She had to catch him again, grabbing hold of him and leaning into him to help him steady his balance. She wished she was bigger and stronger: she had never felt so slight in all her life. He pawed at the cut the stone had made, which immediately began to fizz with gas. His jawline became bandaged with it, a second outpouring that pushed the cloud to new heights. In no time at all its dense cap had bulged some ten feet into the air, while to the left and right it unfurled like a wingspan. A chill trickle condensed on the back of her neck and raced down beneath her collar.

'Finn,' she gasped, holding him up, 'do you think you can walk? Do you think we can get out of here? I'll help you, Finn.'

She threw one of his arms over her shoulders, but she did not have the strength to pull him along with her. She looked back through the cloud that was now swirling tightly around them, and saw Abe Cosser still stranded from his fellows, trembling and clutching one more stone.

'Please, Mr Cosser,' she cried, 'please stop this!'

Abe looked at her with rabbit-in-the-headlights eyes but, before he could respond, Sidney Moses stepped up beside him and put a hand on his shoulder. 'You're a good man, Abe. Whereas this is not even a man at all.'

'Please,' Elsa implored them, '*please* leave us alone! We're going away! We're going anyway! You don't need to do this!'

Sidney shrugged. 'This does not concern you, nor your plans. This is saving our town from the weather. Best to step away from it now, Miss Beletti. It's a cloud that has duped you into thinking it's a man, but as you can see its disguise is easily removed.'

'He's *both*!' Elsa tried to get Finn to take a groggy step towards Old Colp. She did her best to guide him, but with each plod she feared they'd both tip over.

'Step away from him, Miss Beletti.'

She ignored him. It was going to be difficult to get Finn up the mountain in this state, but once they reached the bothy she would look after him and not leave his side until he had recovered. Now the cloud had become too large to see its extremities: it had filled the street from eave to eave and shut out the sky. She squeezed Finn's hand, and much to her relief, he said, 'Thank you, Elsa,' amid a patter of drooled water.

Abe Cosser threw the stone.

It scuffed off the top of Finn's head and clattered away somewhere against the wall. Finn went down, pawing at his scalp, and an instant spout of soot-black cloud gushed up into the greyer stuff that fogged the road. Elsa shrieked and knelt beside him, but the cloud wrapped them up too opaquely for her to even see her outstretched hands. People were shouting and someone grabbed her beneath the shoulders and she was dragged across the rough paving screeching and thrashing. She kicked someone but it made no difference. She could see nothing in the fog, save for gloomy outlines closing in on Finn.

But he lit up.

For a split second, lines of white fire branched through his body. It was as if his entire nervous system had turned to light. She heard Sidney screech and smelled burned meat. Then the light fizzed away into the stone and the flagstones reeked of coal and the townspeople erupted into shrieks and yells. Elsa was dropped roughly on to the floor, and she heard people fleeing in every direction, and somebody mewling like a baby while they hoisted him away.

When she stood, she was too frightened to straighten her spine. Nor could she close her mouth, since her lips were seized back in a grimace.

She staggered through the fog with her arms out in front of her, and nearly tripped over Finn when she found him lying on the road. He was on his back with his arms and legs outstretched. His eyes were open but unblinking.

'Finn!'

She grabbed his hand and clenched it between hers. His fingers felt more brittle and thinner than she remembered them being.

'What did they do to you, Finn?'

Still the cloud thickened, and now it steamed so dense that even when she bent her face down to touch his it made a veil between them. She held on tightly to his hand, but it felt light now like something he had made from paper. Through such fog it was impossible to tell how badly they had hurt him in those last moments, so all she could do was throw her other arm across him and cling to his torso. 'Hold on,' she whispered, not knowing what else to say. 'Please hold on.'

Yet the issuing cloud did not hold on. It became a blindfold. She clung to him as he became fragile and frail. His chest seemed to shrink and harden. She pushed her lips against his, hoping that to kiss him might save him, but his head felt skeletal in the murk and his lips were like the wrinkled skin of a deflating balloon. She kissed them regardless, and they were limp and rubbery between hers. She heard something barking above her, and something howling in the sky. His soaked shirt sagged over his accentuating ribs. His fingers, when she groped for them in the fog, were as thin and cold as icicles. Then for a moment she thought she felt warmth return to them and she yelped with joy, but it was just her own fingers, for his had melted away . She clawed around to try to find them again, but they had vanished and her fingernails scraped on the stone of the street. His ribcage sank and was flat. Panic filled her. She chased her lips after his, but they only kissed wet stone where his head should have been, and she was lying face down in the thickest fog of her life, with only Finn's soaked and emptied clothes between her and the cracked surface of the road.

She lay on the floor, convulsing with sobs. The cloud fumed around her until, eventually, it began to rise into the air. The rain knocked on her back, but she did not move. It pulsed across the road and rang off the walls. After a while she found the strength to roll over and feel the water scattering her face and making her clothes weigh heavy.

The cloud had lifted off the ground and formed a charcoal ceiling for the street. Because she did not know what else she could do, she groped around her until she had bundled up Finn's empty shirt, drenched jeans, underwear and the new shoes she had bought him for his impromptu birthday.

She lay there until his cloud heaved itself off the rooftops and took to the air, rising with unstoppable buoyancy. As it lifted, the sun slipped in beneath it and she remembered that it still had not set. For a minute the light turned the rain shafts to harp strings, then was put out again by the expanding cloud.

It kept ascending until it shuddered with a light of its own and gave a shout of thunder so human that she sat up and cried out to him. He did not reply, but the rain redoubled and hissed as it hit the stone.

A second sheet of lightning floodlit the street and for a moment made every drenched surface shine white. Elsa found herself praying to whatever remnant of her mother's God she still believed in, asking to have this all turned around, but still the rain fell in harder blows until an opening salvo of hail rattled off the masonry and nipped at her skin. She let it sting her. She had no desire to take shelter. If she wanted to go anywhere it was up, to follow Finn into the air.

The street was deserted now. Elsa pictured the townsfolk locking themselves indoors, terrified of what they had unleashed. She hated them and hoped Finn's storm would break down their doors and smash their lives apart.

The cloud kept growing. It was a slow black vortex coiling around itself. It swelled up like a lung inhaling. A line of lightning throbbed across it like a brilliant white artery and she could feel the electricity accumulating in the earth in response, attracted from the deep places by the magnetism of the storm.

Her eyes widened. She stood up and covered her mouth with her hands. She'd had an idea, so dangerous it might just work.

She set off at a run, racing down Candle Street with rain and hail exploding around her and lightning testing its range across the blackened sky. When she swerved into Auger Lane, a forked bolt jagged into life and whipped down to blast apart a chimney. She skidded to a halt in time to dodge the avalanche of broken bricks, then skipped over them and pelted onwards until she reached Saint Erasmus Square. There the storm cloud floated like an ark above the town. Around it the last of the evening light ducked away, and then there was only the cumulonimbus.

The entire plaza fizzled with jumping raindrops. The gutters gurgled as they tried to drain the deepening water. Behind the rain the church was a defeated giant, its dark dominance laid low by the storm. With an ear-splitting crash, lightning slammed into the church's belfry. The strike rang a warped echo out of each and every windowpane in the square. Then, in its aftermath, all seemed to fall silent and a residual tremor tingled underfoot. Elsa swallowed. That was where she was going, up there where the church bell resonated with a brassy hum.

She splashed across the square and up the church steps, heaved open the door, bundled through it and shoved it closed behind her.

Being in the church was like being inside a drum. The storm's noises boomed between the pillars and made her ears pop. The panicked pigeons in the rafters threw themselves about, flying into each other or the stone walls. One lay dead where it had collided with the pulpit. With her hands over her ears, and leaving a trail of wet footprints along the aisle, she made her way to the door that accessed the belfry. It opened on to a spiral staircase leading upwards into darkness. Up she went, her soaked sneakers slapping against the steps, round and round until the dim light from below could reach her no longer and everywhere was pitch black. The weather howling against the stone compelled her on, until she was dizzied and felt as if she were ascending a tornado.

Just when she thought her legs would take her no further she realized she could see the stairs. Light had stirred into the darkness. She could see moisture shining off the stone walls, and then – so alien after the countless steps that she had to press her body against the rough surface to be sure of it – a door.

The moment she lifted the latch, the wind flung it open for her. She staggered out on to the balcony and was nearly bowled over by it. It screamed as it flew around her, and Finn's storm heaved with thunder in reply. The sky was as black and unstable as a lake of boiling tar.

Pressing herself against the wall for support, she edged her way along a narrow balcony. Beside her in the belfry the great Thunderstown bell vibrated with a bass tone. She looked down and saw the streets and houses made miniature, the weathervanes twitching and spinning like whirligigs, and the plaza bulging with water. She looked up and saw only roiling darkness.

'Finn,' she whispered. Raising her voice would be pointless, even if she had the breath left after her rushed climb. 'Finn, can you hear me?' She felt her way further along the wall until she found what she had come up here for: the lightning conductor. She gripped it as tight as her freezing hands would allow.

'Lightning doesn't *strike*,' her dad had told her for the umpteenth time, on the last day she had seen him alive. She had looked down at her fingers in her lap and felt empty that their relationship had descended into this single repeated conversation. 'The earth and the storm make a connection, Elsa, and the lightning is that connection on fire.'

She felt the earth's deep electricity filling up the church below her, just as the floodwater filled the streets. It flushed up from ancient rocks and secret subterranean caverns, from the gyro of the great globe itself, up into the foundations and the vaults, rising through the stone walls, surging up the church's pillars, playing over buttresses and arches, adding its whine to the bell's hum. It filled every cell of her body. Billions of particles of the earth's electricity channelled into her, a mountain of energy of which she was the peak. Her jaw fell heavily open. Her mouth tasted full of lead.

'Finn,' she managed to croak. She couldn't move. She could sense the energy rising out from the top of her head, lifting her hair with it, reaching up for the storm. She closed her eyes and imagined Finn's face was only an inch away from hers.

A pillar of white. Everything in freeze-frame. Raindrops suspended like perfect pearls. And everything getting whiter and whiter until it was all so searing and bright that it was as if her eyes had been replaced with stars. She heard a scream from somewhere. She guessed it was her own.

The lightning didn't strike. It set their connection on fire.

20

AS DREAMS ARE
MADE ON

Elsa came to. She thought she had opened her eyes because she could see lights twinkling in their hundreds. After a moment she realized she wasn't blinking. The lights were inside her head and her eyelids were closed.

Somebody said something. Her body felt like a bottle bobbing on an ocean. She drifted back into unconsciousness.

She came to again, slower this time. She was lying on a firm but comfortable mattress. There were no lights, only the blotched darkness of her closed eyelids. With great effort, she opened them. Looking at anything felt like staring into the sun, so she quickly shut them again.

Somebody spoke, but the words were just fuzz in her ears. She tried once more to open her eyes and found the bright world a fraction more bearable. She could make out surfaces, although they all seemed aglow. A shape loomed over her. 'Try to focus, Elsa.'

Slowly the shape took on colours, hundreds of them dancing a scintillating jig. Her eyes rolled out of concert with each other.

'Elsa, it's okay.'

She took a deep breath. The colours kaleidoscoped across her

vision. She choked her need to cry out. At last the colours settled
into rows of diamonds, each a different shade and each sickeningly
vivid. Together they made a pattern.

One of Kenneth Olivier's jumpers.

She shielded her eyes.

'Elsa!' Kenneth cried out with relief. 'Thank God! How are you
feeling?'

She nodded and looked away, at anything but his clothing. This
strange bare room she was lying in had grey stone walls, a grey
stone floor and a grey stone ceiling, although her blurry vision
added green hues to everything she saw, as if the room were lit
by gaslight.

'Where am I?' Her words tasted bitter.

'Drink some water.'

She sipped from the glass he offered her, unable to look at him.
The water felt like molten metal in her throat.

'You're in the nunnery of Saint Catherine. It's where we take all
people who are struck by lightning.'

Of course, she remembered it now. She had been on the belfry
with the wind tearing at her clothes and the rain crackling in her
ears. She had looked up at the pitch black underside of the storm
and whispered Finn's name.

The lightning strike had lasted under a second, but she had
experienced it as if in slow motion. It started with the air constricting,
pressing bluntly at her jugular and the pulses in her wrists. Then
her hair had lifted as if she were underwater. She had stood very
straight, her spine like a taut rope, and felt the connection her
dad had described so many times. A line of electrified air that had
joined her to Finn's storm. She'd stared upwards, awaiting the
bolt, but it had not come down from the cloud. It had begun in
her, her vision blazing with more light than it felt possible for her
eyeballs to contain. Then white fire had ascended in time with

her whisper. 'Finn.'

For a moment she'd felt so interconnected with him that it was as if they were inside each other's minds. Her thoughts had boiled with things he remembered and things he felt, carried on the lightning to the root of her imagination, so that they became as lucid as scenes of her own life flashing before her eyes. Betty turning out the light after kissing him goodnight; a canary materializing out of sunlight on to his cupped palms; a mouse creeping over the doorstep of the bothy; a broken vase; a winter's day when icicles hung as long as swords; Daniel demonstrating how to fold paper birds; Betty laying out cakes and sandwiches for a picnic; starting a campfire by rubbing two logs together and feeling immeasurably pleased at the first fizzling spark; the shockwave of lightning that had flicked Betty away from him; the self-hatred that followed; and at last *her*, on the day when he first saw her outside the ruined windmill.

Then, like a fire stamped out, all of it had been over and gone and she had tipped backwards into darkness.

Kenneth tried to stop her from sitting up. He needn't have worried because a pain in her ribcage nailed her back to the mattress. She grunted as she hit the pillow.

'Elsa, please go slowly. You need rest.'

'Kenneth …' She tried to wet her dry lips, but her tongue was like a pebble. 'He's up there! I saw him … in the lightning!'

She tried to sit up again, but hot tears of pain rolled from her eyes. She wheezed and screwed up the bed sheet in her fists. 'What's wrong with me?'

'Nothing a good rest won't heal, but all of your muscles seized up when the lightning struck. It will be a while before you can get out of bed.'

She shook her head. 'That's no good. I have to get back to him.' Again she tried to sit up and again her muscles mutinied. She flopped back in stiff pain.

'You can't go anywhere,' lulled Kenneth. 'You simply need to rest.'

She began to sob, and her strained muscles doubled her hurt. She had connected with Finn, but she did not know what it meant to have done so. Even if, as it had seemed in the lightning strike, he was up there somehow, disembodied in the chaos of the storm, how could she reach him if she were stuck in this bed?

Although the cell walls were built from thick stone, she thought she could hear a hushed rumble beyond. 'Is he still there, Kenneth?' she sniffed. 'Please look out of the window for me.'

The cell had a window that overlooked Thunderstown. With some reservation, Kenneth got up and peered out of it. After a moment he came back to her bedside. 'It's a strange thing. Up here the night is so calm, but down there the storm is still raging, yes.'

She gasped with relief. She grabbed Kenneth's hand and squeezed it fearfully. 'How long do you think he can last for?'

'Elsa, what do you mean?'

'How much longer do you think he can rain for?'

'I … I don't know what to say, Elsa. I think you should save your energy. It's a terrible thing to lose a person. Preserve your strength.'

An appeal of thunder penetrated the cell. She could feel it in the springs of the mattress beneath her.

'Don't say I've lost him. How could you say I've lost him when you've seen for yourself he's still up in the sky?'

He sighed. 'I don't know, Elsa. I just don't know.'

When once again she tried to sit up she could barely even budge an inch. The bed felt like a coffin and she grunted in frustration.

'Elsa, Elsa,' soothed Kenneth. 'Rest. Things are going to be tough for you. You need to look after yourself. You can't leave this bed until tomorrow.'

Stuck like this, any hope that she'd woken with deserted her. Back came the powerlessness that she'd felt in Candle Street, and a red-hot hatred for Sidney Moses and Abe Cosser, and a sense that love – in which she had banked her trust – had betrayed her.

Her dad, too, had let her down. His old story about the lightning's path to connection – she had been sure that would be her rescue. But what good did it do to connect with Finn for only a fraction of a second? All it did was demonstrate how helpless she was.

'Elsa,' Kenneth mopped her mouth with a handkerchief, 'you are very unwell. Perhaps you should go back to sleep.'

'How can I sleep when he's right there? When the next time I wake he might have rained himself away?'

'Just know that you are among friends and we will do all we can. Dot will be back soon. And Daniel, I expect.'

'Daniel?'

'Yes. He was here for a while after he brought you in. He waited by your bedside and fussed about you and argued with the nuns over what was best for you. Then, when you almost came to earlier, he panicked. He said he'd be the last person you'd want to see, and headed off to hide in the chapel. As for me, I'm just glad he found you. If he hadn't thought to check the church was secured against the storm … I dread to think what would have happened.'

Eventually Elsa managed to drink some more water, but that used up all her energy. After that Kenneth wished her well and said he should go and fetch Dot, who would want to check in on her now she was awake. He hesitated, then kissed her, father-like, on the forehead. He nodded after doing this, embarrassed but satisfied, and shuffled out of the room.

She exhaled, taking in the stony shade of her surroundings. Her eyes were still hypersensitive from the lightning, making her bed seem to stretch forever, a nightmare of perspective headed for her distant feet. A moth flew in silence around the ceiling, and she wished she could share in its fluttering freedom. There was a chair and a low bedside table, but there was not so much as a vase of flowers or a Bible occupying it. The room was as bereft of distractions as she was of ways to get to Finn.

The door opened and somebody cleared their throat to request entry.

'Come in.'

Not Dot but Daniel, who stopped just inside the doorway and bobbed there in an agitated manner that she wasn't used to seeing in him. 'Elsa, it is good to see you awake. Um … I'll go away again if you would prefer.'

'No, it's okay.' Anything to take her mind off itself. 'I'm just surprised to see you. Kenneth said you were holed up in the chapel.'

He looked unkempt, as if he had slept there, but he sat down urgently at her side and bent his bearded head close to hers. 'Elsa, I … I have come to apologize. I have been a fool beyond reckoning. I never should have tried to get in the way of you and Finn. I hope there is something, someday, that I can do to make it up to you.'

She sighed. His interferences seemed like years ago now. 'Unless you can turn clouds back into men, I doubt there's anything you can do.'

He ran his hands back through his hair. 'I will see to Sidney Moses.'

She grimaced. 'I don't want to know. I can't bear to think about him.'

He nodded, and bunched his fists together between his knees. After he had heard what the townsfolk had done, he had been full of the need for justice. He had considered taking his rifle to the Moses residence, but he had been needed elsewhere. He knew, from bitter experience, what unfulfilled love could do to a life, and he longed somehow to save Elsa from the agony of it.

'Is it true,' she asked, 'that you apologized to Finn?'

'Yes. Although now my promise is as good as broken. I would have made it mean something with deeds, but I never got the chance.'

'Do you … do you think he's gone, then? Kenneth was talking as if he had.'

'I don't know. There is a storm above Thunderstown, so in a sense he is still there. Elsa … what possessed you to go up to the belfry?'

She told him about her dad's lightning mantra, and how on its advice she had climbed the church tower. Daniel listened gloomily, and after she had finished he could see no more hope than her.

He chewed his lip. 'Elsa, you know I have never been good at letting things go. Heaven knows I have spent my whole life clinging on to things that I should have left behind me. Only lately have I learned that sometimes you have to let the past leave you. You cannot return to it, and if you cling to it life marches on without you.'

She covered her eyes. 'It's just that … when the lightning struck me, I saw him there. I can't give up on him after that. But I don't know what I can do now.'

'You misunderstand me. I meant to say that I will not let go of him, even if every last raindrop falls out of the sky. Even if every last trace of him evaporates and the sun shines through. They will say I am mad, no doubt, and that this particular madness of mine has held me back my whole life. But that will only make me well practised.'

'Thank you. That means something to me.' Elsa stared up at the ceiling. She took a deep breath and it made a dry rasping noise like the call of a crow. Daniel steepled his big blunt fingers and pressed them to his forehead, tapping them against his brow while he thought. Far past the nunnery walls, the thunder moaned once more, but now the noise just made her hurt. There would have been a time when she would have enjoyed the hard light enforced on the world by the death of a thundercloud, when the sun knocked down the storm wall and bored a rainbow through air it had turned violet. Now she dreaded that spectacle more than anything else.

'What do you think will happen to him,' she whispered, 'after the last of the rain falls?'

He frowned. 'I hope it will not come to that.'

'But if it does?' She found she could not imagine, even though she wished she could, any alternative. She would lie here prone in a nun's cell while the man she had fallen in love with poured himself apart in the sky.

'There is some medicine if you wish for it,' he said, picking up a packet of pills left by the nuns. She took two of them with a grunt, but had to keep swallowing to drag them down her aching throat.

The moth that had been looping on the ceiling settled. It spread its wings and stilled. She followed its example, finally letting the pillow support her heavy head, finally closing her eyes and surrendering to the fact that all she could do was listen. She awaited each distant murmur of Finn's storm, each faint hiss of the lightning. How tired she was. Or perhaps that was because of the pills. She fought sleep because she needed to be awake to rescue Finn, although she did not know how she was going to do it. She closed her eyes. She thought she could hear an ocean. She thought she was flying high above a whirlpool. She had drifted off to sleep.

Daniel ran his hands through his hair and stood up. He moved to the cell's window and stared at the world without. Up on the Devil's Diadem the sky was bare and the land calm. Finn's cloud over Thunderstown was the only one in the sky, but it was grey and massive like a fifth mountain. The sun had already set beyond Old Colp, but a red sheen still coloured the western sky and bloodied the upper reaches of the storm.

When his father died, his grandfather had expressed no remorse, no softening of the enmity he had felt for his son. But when his grandfather's favourite hunting dog had died that same year, then his grandfather had wept into his glass of beer. That night he'd burst into Daniel's bedroom long past midnight, turned on the light and crashed down reeking of alcohol on to the bed beside his grandson. 'It feels as if, wherever he has gone, he has taken every other one of my ribs with him,' he'd said before passing out. At about three or four in the morning, having not slept a wink, Daniel could no longer resist the temptation to feel in the dark for his grandfather's ancient ribcage, to run his forefinger over the bones. All the ribs could be accounted for, and Daniel had stayed confused and wide awake until the sun took the night away.

He left the cell window and paced to the door, then back to the window, then so on back and forth over the stone floor. Now at last he understood what the old man had meant. If that sensation had been inflicted on his grandfather by the death of something as simple as a damned mutt, how much greater was Daniel's own hurt at the loss of Finn, this sudden feeling of multiple cavities in his torso, and the accompanying feeling that his legs and arms and even his skull had been cleaved in two, and the greater halves stolen away from him?

He became aware of the sound of his own breathing. Worrying that he might disturb Elsa's sleep, he slipped out of the door and walked the cold corridors of the nunnery.

He was as familiar with this place as he was with the vaults and aisles of the Church of Saint Erasmus. When he was a child his father used to bring him up here, even though he was more often than not a strain on his father's priestly duties. While the Reverend Fossiter conducted longwinded meetings with the abbess, Daniel had sulked in the courtyard or played hide-and-seek with himself in the cloister. On other occasions he had run madly through the laps of the corridors, or along the route of the chapel's prayer labyrinth, which was a pattern of concentrically circling red tiles embedded before the altar. Once, his father had caught him whirling along that path and right away forced him to lean over a pew while he struck him with the back of his hand. Then he made him walk in contemplation along the red line of the tiles, until he reached the centre and promptly burst into tears.

The nunnery's cloister, when Daniel emerged into it, was deserted. Overhead the first stars were peeking through. There was no wind: that was all down in Thunderstown, playing in Finn's storm.

He crossed to the chapel, which was just as empty. Inside, the only movement came from a flickering bay of prayer candles burning in an alcove. With no light in the sky to shine through them, the designs on the stained-glass windows were hard to make out, but he had been here enough times to have memorized their depictions. They showed fearful saints on their knees, praying to their god in the clouds for miracles and signs.

He slumped down on the back pew, throat dry, head sore with sorrow. He pushed aside the Bible and the prayer book on the shelf in front of him. He kicked away the cushion used for kneeling.

'I would have become something gentler,' he whispered through clenched teeth. 'I would have been like a father to Finn.'

He wiped his eyes and tried to focus. 'What might be done?' he muttered. What might be done? His thinkings drew back with no solutions.

The chapel door squeezed open.

Kenneth Olivier slipped inside, letting the evening air of the cloister into the waxy murk of the chapel. He closed the door softly, then stood in the aisle with his hands in his pockets, alongside Daniel's pew but not facing it, looking instead at the tidy altar and its cream-coloured cloth, embroidered with a cross.

'I don't know about you,' he said after a while, 'but I'm terrified for her.'

Daniel's eyes swivelled up to look at Kenneth. The two of them had shared the space of the Church of Saint Erasmus on more occasions than Daniel cared to remember, but aside from Sunday pleasantries they rarely talked. Their last meaningful exchange had been on that awful day when Kenneth's son went missing in the mountains.

'Are you aware,' asked Daniel gruffly, 'that this is entirely my fault?'

Kenneth shrugged. 'You say that, but I think it's mine. All of it.'

Daniel frowned. 'No. How could you possibly think that?'

'How could *you*?'

Daniel opened his mouth to respond, but Kenneth stopped him with a raised finger. He opened a bag he had with him and displayed, as tenderly as if they were eggs in a nest, two cans of beer.

'You and I have not really talked for a long while,' he said.

Daniel motioned to the altar, to the prayer labyrinth painted on the tiles before it, to the statue of Saint Catherine raising her face to the heavens, to Christ nailed to the cross on the far wall.

'Not here, of course,' said Kenneth, and took hold of the door handle. 'But will you join me?'

With a laboured puff, Daniel put his hands on his knees, stuck out his elbows and eased himself to his feet. 'After you,' he said, and the two of them left the chapel.

Kenneth led the way through the short antechamber that exited the nunnery. Beyond the main door the slopes of the Devil's Diadem skidded all the way down to Thunderstown, whose rooftops were nigh on invisible beneath the darkness of the rain. From this distance Finn's cloud looked like some jellyfish of the ocean, its downpour like graceful tentacles stroking the buildings beneath. The last of the coloured sunset had faded, and a ring of stars encircled the storm.

The rocks and sparse slopes of the mountains were all deathly still, and when a shudder of lightning branched across the cloud they lit up and looked as fragile and white as porcelain. The thunder sounded moments later, a rush of sound that could be felt as well as heard.

The two men rested their backs against the nunnery wall while

Kenneth cracked the ring pulls of the beers and handed one to Daniel. He proceeded to drink his while Daniel stared through the opening of the can into the dark liquid within.

'It's my fault,' said Kenneth after a sip, 'because I should have done more to warn her. I had so many chances to tell her about the ways of this town, but I never did. I thought she might laugh at me, I suppose, and I let that stop me. I let her come to this town with only me for a guide, and yet I never warned her of its true character.'

Daniel raised his eyebrows and drank deeply from the beer. 'It's not your fault. I am responsible for this. I should have stopped Sidney Moses.'

'You couldn't have done. You weren't there.'

'Precisely.'

Kenneth sighed. 'We could argue about it forever.'

There was a short silence.

'It's been a while now,' he said, 'since Michael went away.'

'Yes.'

'Did I ever tell you how grateful I was to you for everything you did?'

'Yes,' said Daniel. 'You gave me a bottle.'

He remembered the rum Kenneth had presented to him, sweet and stinging at once, like eating honeycomb along with the bees that had made it. He had shared it with Betty and they had underestimated its potency and dozed off flopped against each other.

Yet he also remembered the reason for the gift, the diving and diving into and into the tarn in which Michael was last seen. Scouring the gloom of the water for any trace of him and finding nothing. Diving again and again until long after every other rescuer had abandoned the cause, surfacing and submerging until he lost track of what was water and what was air. Only when, because of his confusion, he inhaled liquid did he stop, and only then because his body failed him. His lungs had spasmed and forced him to lie down in defeat on the banks.

'I wish,' said Kenneth, 'I could have drowned instead.' He paused to control his emotions. 'Today I realized I've come to thinking, completely without meaning to, of Elsa a little like I thought of Michael. Having her around, hearing her footsteps going up and down the stairs, catching a noise of her singing in the shower, her coming and going all hours. Just having a younger soul around the house.'

Daniel nodded.

'Now, seeing her lying in that bed, so unwell …' He shivered. 'It's terrible.'

'She will be all right. She's healthy enough to pull through.'

'Yes, of course, when you put it like that. But that's the other thing, isn't it? She's lost someone. That doesn't heal like the body does. Now she will be like you and I. Heartbroken.'

Silence.

Kenneth, stood up, shaking his empty can. 'I had better get back inside and check on her.'

Daniel nodded and watched him go. He finished his beer, then dropped his can to the ground and screwed it medallion-flat with his boot. Maybe it was the alcohol, of which he drank so little these days, or maybe it was something Kenneth had said. Either way, he could feel some deep part of his brain carrying on with the thinkings to which his forethoughts were not privy. When he tried to focus on them they eluded him, but he sensed them all the same, as if they were the preparatory movements behind a stage curtain, before it lifts for a play. He waited impatiently for that performance to begin, then when it did not he trudged back to the chapel.

Inside, he let the door swing shut behind him with a judder, while he stood in the aisle with his rain cap rolled up tightly in his fist. While he had been talking with Kenneth, many of the prayer candles on their frail metal table had burned out. He approached them and counted fifteen exhausted rings of tallow: fifteen secret woes that had called for their burning. He dropped some coins in the collection box and replaced each candle, mesmerized by the tiny flames that duplicated on to each wick they touched. When all were alight he turned from the bay and walked into the sanctuary, not to pray at the altar but to stand on the prayer labyrinth that was marked out like a mosaic on the floor.

In his memory it was an expansive crimson spiral, but here in his present it was a faint pattern like the age rings of a tree stump. It took only a few of his big paces to circle into its centre. There he remained for a while with his eyes closed, hoping for a revelation. He wished he had a mind like his father's, which could work through any disaster with ice-cold rationality.

Only when more of the candles began to wink out did he move again. He might have been standing there for hours, but his mind had made no progress. All he could think was that he had lost Finn and that he did not know what could be done about it. He hung his head and plodded towards the chapel door, pausing with his fingers on the handle and hoping that some final inspiration would strike. Then he exited into the cloister, where the distant hum of Finn's storm was at odds with the balmy night and the glinting constellations. Starlight found the metal and enamel in the countless charms hanging from the walls.

He pulled his handkerchief – his great-grandfather's and embroidered D.F. – from his pocket and blew his nose. He had meant what he'd said to Kenneth. All of this was his fault, or at least the fault of his family, for whom he was responsible. If they had been different men they might have guided the town to peace with the weather. What might have happened if they had followed the example of his mother? She had not plied the teeth from the corpses of wild dogs to string up with paired coins and tatty feathers in the hope of driving them away. No, she had petted them and stroked them and they had growled pleasurably in her company.

He reached into his pocket for the photograph he had found of her. He admired it. Her hair was black like a dream, her dress a frost's silver. Then abruptly he remembered how his breath had crystallized in the air when he found this picture. He tucked it back into his pocket, screwing up his eyes and drumming his fists against his temples in the hope of shaking out a way to save Finn. None came, so he returned via the shadowy corridors to the cell in which Elsa slept.

Elsa found his presence reassuring when she woke next. At first he did not say anything to her, did not even nod. She preferred it that he didn't. They kept each other company, saying little. Theirs was a shared seriousness that did not require any mask of small talk and gesture. Every so often Daniel asked her something about Finn he said he hadn't understood, then would listen rapt to her answer, then fall back into frowning, contemplative silence.

'Did Finn ever tell you,' he asked eventually, 'about my mother?'

'I don't believe he did.'

'Maryam. I have a photograph of her.'

She took it when he offered it. Maryam's eyes and brow were just like Daniel's, serious and severe. But there was also something lighter than Daniel in her looks. Or perhaps that was just an impression made by the wind blowing through her dress.

Elsa held it back out to him. He did not take it.

'I would appreciate it if you kept this likeness of her.'

'Daniel, I can't ...'

'I insist.'

She sighed. She could not find the strength to argue. 'I'll only accept it if you do something for me.'

'What's that?'

'Take me to the window. I want to see the storm. In case it's my last chance. I don't want him to rain away without having seen him one last time.'

He was hesitant. 'You're not supposed to leave the bed.'

'If you say no, you're having this photo back.'

He reached his arms under her shoulders and lifted her as gently as he could, but gravity tore at her muscles and she screeched through gritted teeth. At the window he propped her down on her feet and she leaned against him, one of his arms supporting her shoulders and the other her waist.

'Can you see?'

She nodded, giddy with pain.

Finn's storm was spread out over Thunderstown. He looked so still from this distance – apart from when lightning turned all his black billows white – but she knew up close there would be so much *life*. There would be arteries of arctic cold, pumping fist-sized hailstones around his body of cloud. A heart of water, keeping him alive.

A jagged white line danced across him. Then came a flutter of short flashes and a jolt of lightning the noise of which reached them two seconds later. She savoured the reverberations it made in her bones, even though they twanged at her muscles. She longed for the next stroke of thunder, so that she could feel him again.

Meanwhile, Daniel watched the lightning earth in the town and marvelled at Elsa's bravery. She had charged up to the belfry to try to reach Finn, with no thought for her own fragility. Again the storm flashed bright, and for a moment a line of light coursed out and branched down fifty paths. The sound came seconds later, a bass rumble that washed over them while they stood pressed together.

'What possessed you,' he whispered with marvel, 'to climb up there and be struck by lightning?'

She laughed bitterly. 'I told you. It was that thing my dad used to say. I remembered it and for some reason hoped it might save Finn. He used to say, over and over again, that the lightning is a connection, not a one-way strike. So I thought that maybe I could use it to connect again with Finn.'

He was about to respond, but then he shut his mouth with a *clack* and his whole body tensed. She noticed the hairs on his forearms rising.

'What's wrong, Daniel?'

For a silent minute he stared out at the storm, and she could have sworn he did not blink in all that time. Then he turned to her with a mad look in his eyes and whispered, 'It's going to be all right.'

'Daniel … I can't believe that. Now it's you who needs some rest. I'm not sure if it will ever be all right. I came to before and I thought I could get him back somehow. But now I can't see a way. All I know is that I'm going to fall apart when the last of his rain falls. Is that what you mean when you say it's going to be all right?'

She broke down again into tears, sobs that were like blows punched into her breastbone.

Daniel stared bluntly back at her.

'See? See?' she gasped, 'It's no good you saying it will be *all right!*' She wiped the tears from her cheeks but instantly they were replaced by fresh ones.

He helped her back to the bed. She let herself be carried, the pain now feeling like a natural extension of the emotions inside her. She had done all she could. She lay back on the mattress and he tucked her up like an invalid, which she supposed she was.

'You know,' she sniffed, 'when you hear people say that life is short, that you should live every last second to the full. Well, it's too hard. *Hard*, when trusting someone can let them hurt you, when you don't really know your own mind, when the things you want turn out to be the things you never wanted, when you can't connect with friends and family, when there are groceries to buy and dishes to be done, and photocopying and filing and timetables and diaries and *distractions.'*

He reached down and she felt him lift her chin, with the exact same gesture her dad used to use to raise her head and restore her confidence when she was a little girl.

And then he did something she had never seen him do before. Not once, she realized, in all her time in Thunderstown.

He smiled.

He had the largest, heartiest smile she had ever seen. His teeth were strong and white and the lines of his face that were usually so set in contemplation or a frown fell away, and new lines appeared that accentuated the depth of his beaming, heartening smile.

He has gone mad, she thought, to think he has found something to smile about.

And then he let go of her hand, and the smile dropped from his face like snow slipping off a branch. He became earnest again. He met for a long moment her eyes, then nodded and left the room.

And although she did not know it then, she would never see Daniel Fossiter again.

21

WERE ALL SPIRITS, AND ARE MELTED INTO AIR

Daniel Fossiter stood on the Devil's Diadem in the windless night, with his back to the walls of the nunnery and Finn's storm still pouring over Thunderstown below.

The night had become too dark to distinguish the cumulonimbus from the black sky surrounding it. Only when a blade of lightning stabbed down at a chimney or at Saint Erasmus's belfry was its shape revealed: a citadel of fumes with towers as high as any of the mountain peaks. Sometimes the lightning revealed steep ramparts of cloud, with battlements reflecting the light as coldly as stone.

This was not the first storm he had watched from the nunnery's vantage point. He remembered being up here with his father once, as a child, not long after his mother left, watching a storm drift away into the east. It had been a red flotilla in the sunset, and Daniel had looked from it to his father and seen – for the only time in his life – the old man on the edge of tears. 'Just watch it go, son,' his father had whispered, 'and don't blink. Don't forget one beautiful second of it.'

Daniel heard his name spoken and turned around. Dot had come out to find him. When she spoke, her voice seemed able to anticipate the lulls in the storm's noises and to dart between them. 'It's getting late. Do you want to come inside for something to eat?'

He shook his head. A blue-white flicker of lightning sputtered inside the storm.

Dot regarded him for a moment: his coat buttoned up to his beard and his broad-brimmed hat wedged on his head. 'You look as if you are going somewhere.'

He shrugged. 'I believe I am. Although I am not sure where.'

Thunder passed over them like the beating of wings. Dot waited for it to boom into the distance, then asked, 'Would you like us to keep some food out for you?'

'There's no need. I hope I do not come back.'

She stayed quiet, digesting what he'd just said. 'I think,' she said eventually, 'I understand you. Are you sure you know what you're doing?'

In his childhood memories of this place, she was just as ancient as she was today. He could remember first encountering her, back when he was three or four feet tall. Then to his young eyes her age had seemed preposterous and grotesque, barely even human.

'No,' he said, 'but someone has to try it, and it should not be Elsa.'

'Perhaps I can give you something to take with you?'

He laughed. 'What more do I need, other than my own two legs?'

'How about a story? When your father used to come up here, when he'd spend long hours in conversations with the abbess ... well, sometimes I was present for those discussions.'

'Forgive me, Sister, but I'm not sure that stories of my father are what I need to hear right now.'

Dot ignored him. 'Mostly we talked shop, but on one occasion the Reverend Fossiter wanted to confide in us.'

'Confide what?'

Dot drew a deep breath. 'That your mother, when she left Thunderstown, didn't go to Paris or Delhi or Beijing, or anywhere like that. She went somewhere both nearer and further away. She went back to the place she had come from.' She placed a buckled hand on his arm. 'Upwards, Daniel. But you had guessed that already, hadn't you?'

He nodded mutely.

'Your father said he had fallen in love with a witch. That was what he wanted to confide in us. *A monster of the air*, he called her. He said that he had thought her to be an angel to begin with, but that after a time she had convinced him she was of the devil, because of the way she would defend the weather.'

Daniel clenched his fists, rueing his father's superstitions.

'Of course,' Dot continued, 'she was neither devil nor angel. She was utterly ordinary. There are three thousand of her kind present on the earth in any given moment.'

Daniel waited for this to sink in, but he discovered that his thinkings had already prepared him for it. It was as if they had known this secret all along. 'If that were true,' he scratched his head, 'shouldn't I be like them too? I assure you that when I am cut I bleed blood, not air. Only once have I ever – only a day ago, in fact – seen anything like weather come from inside of myself.'

Dot smiled sadly, her face folding up under her wrinkles. 'Perhaps some of us don't see it as often as we might. Perhaps that means we have lost touch. Or perhaps those of us who do see it need to be better at holding ourselves together.'

'What about me? Do you think I am enough like them? To do what I have to do now?'

'I don't know. I suppose it depends on whether Finn is still there to be saved. I suppose if you believe he is, it may be possible.' She patted his arm lightly. 'I think that is all I can offer you. I wish you well, Mr Fossiter, wherever you are going.'

And with that she pushed him gently in the small of the back.

He set off like a racer at the starting gunshot. When he was some distance down the slope a wind arrived to spur him on, and when on a ridge top he looked back over his shoulder at the now distant nunnery, the wind smeared his black hair across his eyes so that he could not see and be tempted to turn back.

He raced downhill, towards Thunderstown, but only when he reached its outskirts did he truly appreciate the severity of the storm. The town hid behind a curtain of rain, and he had to hold his arms up in front of his face to make his way through it. The sky smashed open again and again with lightning. Torrential rain hammered the pavements, smashing off the flagstones like sparks off an anvil. It stung his eyes and soaked his clothing, bringing with it hailstones hard enough to chip the paint from doors. He shielded his eyes as he got his bearings, then toiled in the direction of Saint Erasmus Square.

In Welcan Row, old mine shafts were overflowing. Rotten ropes, mushed mosses and scrap metal emerged and were carried away on a stream of filthy liquid that slicked the street. In Corris Street he splashed through shin-deep water, then headed south through Bradawl Alley, where the cobbles had turned to islands. In each street the floodwater was deeper than the last, but he sloshed onwards with his boots soaked through and squelching.

In Foremans Avenue, trees rattled and creaked as the storm shook them. With a noise like a record distorting, one cracked down the length of its trunk. The road beneath it popped open and roots sprang out, then the nearer half of the tree crashed down with a bending squeal and a shiver of leaves. He looked up as he passed the Moses residence, and was satisfied to see floodwater frothing under the front door, and one window blasted out of its frame by lightning. He hurried on. He had to get to the Church of Saint Erasmus.

Rain pinged off car bonnets, twanged off the pavements, flicked him with hard ice as he struggled, grabbing now and then a lamp post for support, to the end of Widdershin Road and at last into the wide church square. He could barely see a stone's throw in front of him, let alone up to the spire. Rain scratched out all visibility. The plaza was awash, gurgling with scummy white eddies.

He had to wade the final few metres before he reached the high ground of the church's steps. There he looked back for a moment across the square. Liquid rushed in from every street, bearing debris and caked scum, churning in the pattern of a whirlpool around the church. Watching it made him dizzy, as if not just the water but the entire town were turning in that gyre.

He battled into the church and slammed the doors behind him, then paused to collect his breath. How still the air was in here. The roof rang with the strikes of so many raindrops that their echoes combined into a single throbbing note. It was so dark that he was forced to squint his way along the aisle by memory, picturing the place as he had known it through the years. His memory added the details: his father at the pulpit, with his face bunched in devoted prayer; his grandfather slouched bored or tipsy in a back pew; Betty, watching him with a look he still believed had been a fond one, on that single time when he had tried to give a reading from the book of his namesake and his tongue had sunk into silence at the lectern. 'I, Daniel,' he had read, 'was troubled in spirit, and the visions that passed through my mind disturbed me.'

He walked slowly towards the altar. He paused at the front pew where he himself had sat every Sunday for years. He stroked the cold wood, removed his soaked leather hat, and laid it on the seat. Then he crossed to the side door and climbed the spiral staircase to the belfry. The stairwell was full of the din of falling water.

When he emerged on to the belfry he at once felt the electricity humming in the stones beneath him, hissing in the tumbling rain. The masonry zinged with energy. And there was the storm in an indigo expanse.

This high up, he felt almost intimately close to the thunder. He was convinced that if he reached for the cloud – which he did now, raising himself on his tiptoes – he would be able to stroke his fingers through it. He touched nothing and retracted his hand, feeling foolish, but the sky had seemed too small for such a monstrous cloud. It puzzled him that something so enormous could not be grasped. Hail rattled on the belfry like thrown dice, and stung the skin of his upturned face. Rain made the old stone sizzle. A sheet of lightning flashed. In the half-second that it lasted for, that which had seemed limitless became clarified. If time could have paused in that moment, he thought he would be able to take in every detail of the thundercloud, for every wisp and fold of steam became defined in a photojournalist's black and white. When, in the next instant, the world plunged back into darkness, he felt as blind inside as out. He wiped the rain from his eyes and groped around for the lightning rod. His hands were shaking when he seized hold of it. The sense of purpose that had driven him up here had been lost to the darkness like words to spilled ink. He was afraid, he realized. He had never been more afraid.

There was a white light.

And then there was nothing.

22

THE LOVER OF THUNDER

Come morning the storm had died out. It would be a fine day of sunshine, with a pleasant south-westerly breeze tempering the heat.

In Thunderstown, men and women stood dumbfounded in their doorways, staring at the cyan sky reflected in the floodwater. Otherwise they used buckets and tubs to bail out their houses, shaking their heads and cursing Old Man Thunder. Canaries alighted on the weathervanes, or were yellow blurs chasing each other between the chimneys.

On the belfry of the Church of Saint Erasmus, a body lay face down on the stone. It was a man's body, burly and black-bearded. The sunshine had dried off its flesh and hair, but had not yet evaporated the puddle in which it had lain since the storm faded. Every so often the body would give a meek cough or a judder of its shoulder blades, then lapse into another hour of stillness. Now, finally, it groaned and tried to prop itself up. It raised itself an inch before it flopped back into the puddle. It lay there for a little while more, occasionally dribbling up a mouthful of water. Then, finally, with a moan, it rolled on to its back. Sometime later it pulled itself up and sat against the wall. Fluid drooled from its mouth and nostrils.

It tilted its head to drain water from its ears. It rubbed its eyes. After a while more it managed to stand up, as shakily as a newborn calf. When it got the better of its balance it squinted around at the bright rooftops and the dazzling sunshine on the windowpanes of the town. It looked down at itself and sneezed. It rubbed its bearded face.

It stopped very still.

It rubbed its face some more, plying its cheeks and groping at its neck.

'Uhh …' it murmured, then shook its head. 'I … huhh …' It felt again across its cheeks. It twisted its fingers through its drenched black locks.

'I have hair,' it said.

But when it tugged on it, clumps came out on its fingers. It looked at the black scraps in its hands, then tugged experimentally at a part of its beard. This came loose too, pulled free as easily as moss off a stone.

It got down on its knees and leaned over the puddle to view its dim reflection. It reached out a tentative, pointing finger for the face it saw there, then jumped in alarm when the reflection broke into circles.

It kept pulling at its hair. It scruffed it up with both hands and it came free everywhere. It splashed water over its scalp and washed away the last of it until its head was totally bald. It did the same thing to its beard, spitting and slurping when it got a clump of it on its tongue. It rubbed its head, exploring its smooth jaw and crown. Now that the puddle had settled, it inspected its reflection for a second time. It had missed something. Its eyebrows, which rubbed free as easily as chalk off a blackboard.

'Who am I?' it asked of the water. It waited for an answer and when none came it screwed up its eyes and rubbed its head and looked vulnerable and confused.

It got up and staggered to the door. It tripped and nearly tumbled several times as it made its way down the spiral staircase. In the empty church below it paused, because on a pew lay an object it recognized, although it could not tell from where. It picked it up and punched it into shape, then plied for a moment the brim, which was still damp from the storm.

After a minute it remembered. Daniel Fossiter's rain cap. All that had happened came crashing back.

It had begun with a dream of falling, but instead of sleep's darkness everything had been white-hot. Falling for a long time, head over heels, long past the point when the rush of plummeting jerks the dreamer awake. Down and down it had fallen, with a sickening sense of its own weight, until heaviness itself had been the thing to slow its fall. Heaviness had become a kind of gravity, and it had no longer felt as if it were falling but compacting into a nucleus. Eventually it had simply hung, paralyzed by its own solidity. And then it had not been hanging but lying, and it was a prone man on a church belfry.

After a while, the man folded the hat and tucked it into the pocket of his trousers. At one point, during his sensation of falling, he'd sensed another presence, travelling in the opposite direction.

'I will miss you,' he said.

When Elsa woke to the sunlit morning and its postcard-blue sky, she pulled the sheet up over her head. She lay in the narrow bed in the nunnery cell, with the smell of pollen drifting in through the window, and she longed for rain to replace the honeyed burblings of songbirds. She had already cried until her tear ducts were dried out, and she knew she would cry again once they were rehydrated.

She slept the first half of the day away. Daniel was nowhere to be seen. She missed him and began to think he had given up on her. Probably he was holed away in depression in his homestead.

In the afternoon she was able to leave the bed for the first time. Her muscles tightened with each step and she managed only a single lap of the room before she collapsed back on to the mattress.

Sleep gave no relief. She dreamed of rain pouring from the heavens.

When she woke next it was evening. Through the high window of the cell she could see stars emerging, so she turned on the bedside lamp. She didn't want stars. She wanted black skies venting water.

All she had to distract her was a cloud atlas borrowed from Dot. The old nun had warned against it, but reluctantly loaned it to her when Elsa insisted. Now she wished she'd taken Dot's advice, for the moment she opened it and saw the black prow of a cumulonimbus she felt strangled, and threw the book across the room.

She rested her head on the pillow and stared at the ceiling, thinking of her dad, and how ceilings had to be very sturdy things to survive all of the prayers and pleas directed at them.

The moth who had become her cellmate was still up there with its brown wings flattened across the plaster. Now that the bedside lamp was aglow it came alive, dropped from its resting place and zoomed around the aura of the light. When it started throwing itself against the lampshade, it cast elastic shadows across the ceiling and she thought of Finn's mobiles, which would be circling abandoned in his bothy, and she wished she had the paper goose he had made her, or even the paper skyscraper. She had to turn the lamp off and suffer the stars, just to stop the moth from reminding her of them.

A breeze passed by the window.

She sat bolt upright and was rewarded with jarring pains in both sides. This time, however, she had strength to bear them. The wind passed again, with a noise like a tuneless note from a flute, and then died away. She waited impatiently for it to come back, listening to the moth's clicking wings in the interval. When the wind returned it sounded as if it were panting, then faded away into the distance.

When she got out of bed her legs stiffened with pain and she walked as if on stilts to the window. The stars and a sliver of moon made the mountainside light, but at the bottom of the slopes it was as if Thunderstown had vanished, for Finn's storm had cut the power to the streets and they were lost in the gloom.

This time she saw the wind before she heard it. It was patrolling along the length of the nunnery wall, pausing here and there to sniff the mortar before trotting on with its silver tail wagging behind it. She knocked on the window and it looked up at the noise.

'Hey,' she said.

It yapped at her, once, then sprang away as if she had thrown a stick. When it came running back it barked more aggressively, as if it were frustrated that she hadn't followed.

At that she felt as if the lethargy in her bones had run off into the night. She dressed in impatient silence, pulled on her sneakers and her jacket, then slipped out of the door, turning the handle and gripping it on the other side before closing it gently, so that the mechanism lowered silently into the latch and did not cause a sound. She did not want to be stopped by a well-meaning nun.

She padded along the corridor, down the stairs and out into the cloister. The moon was only a crescent, but still it seemed especially bright, glazing the stone walls white.

It was impossible to open the big cloister doors without their beams clunking, but their sounds did not seem to disturb anyone and she swiftly closed them behind her. She was in the antechamber that kept the weather at bay, and only the outer door remained between her and the mountainside. She paused there, wondering whether this was such a good idea. She was in no fit state to wander off on the Devil's Diadem at night.

No sooner had she doubted herself than the wind thumped against the door. Another blustered past, and then another, and then one that whined and one that howled and she listened with her hands around the door handle as the noises built into a great, hollow, gale-force roar. A charm hammered into the wall beside her began to jingle on its hook, until it worked itself loose and smashed against the antechamber floor.

She took a deep breath and opened the door.

Outside, the world lay motionless. She'd thought she'd be immediately overwhelmed by the in-rushing winds, but the air hung still and delicate. More stars than she had ever seen shimmered in the blue night. Together with the moon they paled the dusty mountainside, making boulders into alabaster and the grass into etched silver. And, all down the slope before her, they shone on the fur of at least a hundred wild dogs.

The beasts stood or sat on their haunches as far as the eye could see. Their alert poses made them look more like sculpted statues than flesh and blood creatures. They watched her expectantly. The moon reflected as a white arc in each canine eye.

She waited, unsure of what they required from her. Then, as one, they turned their heads and gazed down the slope.

She had to take a few steps forwards to see what they saw.

A man, toiling up the uneven path to the nunnery.

He had not yet seen her, for all his focus was on his struggle with the steep ascent. Her heartbeat trebled when the moonlight told her he was bald and big-framed, but she would not believe her eyes, since it was impossible for him to be the one she wanted.

Her feet believed them. She stumbled down the slope towards him.

He looked up. He seemed different. Details had altered. He had worry lines on his forehead and crow's feet around his eyes. His physique had become more precise and more world-worn. Yet who else, she thought as she stumbled over the last few paces and halted an arm's reach from him, could have irises that looked like hurricanes? She would recognize him even if half a century had passed between them. He was like a cherished soldier coming home from a long war.

He smiled at her. She threw her arms around him so hard he lost his balance and they fell with an *oof* to the dusty ground.

They were laughing. She was poking his face and pulling at his cheek to confirm it was real. He was grinning. He was nuzzling his face close to hers.

The winds took off in unison and yipped beneath the gleaming stars.

She gave him her lips. They kissed.

And she was in love with the thunder.

ACKNOWLEDGEMENTS

Thank you to Susan Armstrong for her constant encouragement and her commitment to this novel, to Sarah Castleton, Margaret Stead and Clare Hey for their editorial contributions, and to the Desmond Elliott Charitable Trust.